WHERE THE HEART FESTERS

THE BLOOD OF EITH, BOOK THREE

GILLIAN GRANT

DEDICATION

For Heather, who inspired a whole race of giant spiders with one hilarious session. And for Taylor, who didn't believe I would write him in as a giant, man-eating spider. Jokes on you Moses, he's now a major character.

FOREWORD AND TRIGGER
WARNINGS:

This is something new for me, and not something I realized I needed until talking over the book with some friends as I was writing it. I knew going into book three that it would test me. Whether it was my mental state while I wrote it, or Evren's, or both, this was by far the hardest one to write. I say this after finishing the first draft of the fourth book, which flowed really well. *Where the Heart Festers* was just a tough nut to crack for everything I wanted to do in it, and while I'm proud of how it came out, I'm exceedingly glad that it's done.

I always meant this book to be a mental and moral struggle for Evren, as well as a physical one when it came to the mystery of her magic. While I feel like I delivered on that, it is in my mind some of the darkest things I've written so far. Due to the nature of Evren's powers (spilling her blood making her stronger) and her physical state in this book (terminally ill), a lot of Evren's thoughts and actions veer towards self-harm. This is something I've stayed away from in previous books, but couldn't in this one due to the nature of the plot, although I kept it to a minimum. This is the primary reason I'm doing this trigger warning, although a list of the rest are below, because I would prefer to be warned of these ahead of time instead of reading it as a surprise.

• Alcoholism, blood, bones, child abuse (mentioned), mother dying in childbirth (mentioned), death, depression, emesis (vomiting), emotional abuse, fire, gore, hallucinations, pedophilia (mentioned), racism, self-harm, spiders, terminal illness.

PRONUNCIATION GUIDE

People and Creatures:
- Sahar Al Fazil: Sa-**har** Al **Fuh**-zil
- Nerezza Quill: Ner-ehz-uh
- Drystan: **Drih**-stan
- Eirunn: **Ai**-roon
- Keres: Keh-**ruhs**
- Mortova: **Mor**-tow-vuh
- Ikedree: **Ike**-dree
- Evren: Eh-v-r-eh-n
- Gyda: **Gee**-da
- Sorin: Sor-en
- Abraxas: Uh-**brak**-suhs
- Arke: ar-**kuh**
- Solri: Soul-**ree**
- Viggo: **Vee**-go

Places and Countries:
- Etherak: Eh-ther-ahk
- Vernes: **Ver**-nes
- Terevas: Ter-eh-vahs
- Boreal Sea: **Baw**-ree-uhl

- Melkarth: Mell-karth
- Gratey: Grah-**tay**
- Orenlion: **Ore**-ren-lee-on

Things:
- Xirstine: Zir-stine

Terms:
- krevas: kruh-**vas** - a dwarven term for dishonored one, coward or traitor
- levenya: lev-en-**ya** - elven word for family, clan, or group
- foya: **foy**-ah - Ikedree term for father

The Banished Faith:

Once a nearly universally worshipped religion, the Banished Faith is now solely clung to by those in Etherak and few others. Once, the Divines were able to give their closest worshippers great power, and their absence has left the once powerful kingdom of Etherak crippled.

- The Banished Divines:
  - Haphion, God of Light and Flame
  - Nutvian, Goddess of Ice and Order
  - Vuhione, Goddess of Honor and Justice
  - Holtia, Goddess of Love and Healing
  - Emion, God of Music and Dance
  - Mandros, God of Knowledge
  - Elos, God of Change and Freedom
  - Eitrix, Goddess of Industry and Money
  - Roania, Goddess of Nature
  - Zelmis, Goddess of Darkness and Chaos
  - Nomien, God of Wrath and Fire
  - Mituna, Goddess of Tempests and Seas
  - Vyone, God of Death
  - Nuris, Goddess of Illness and Envy

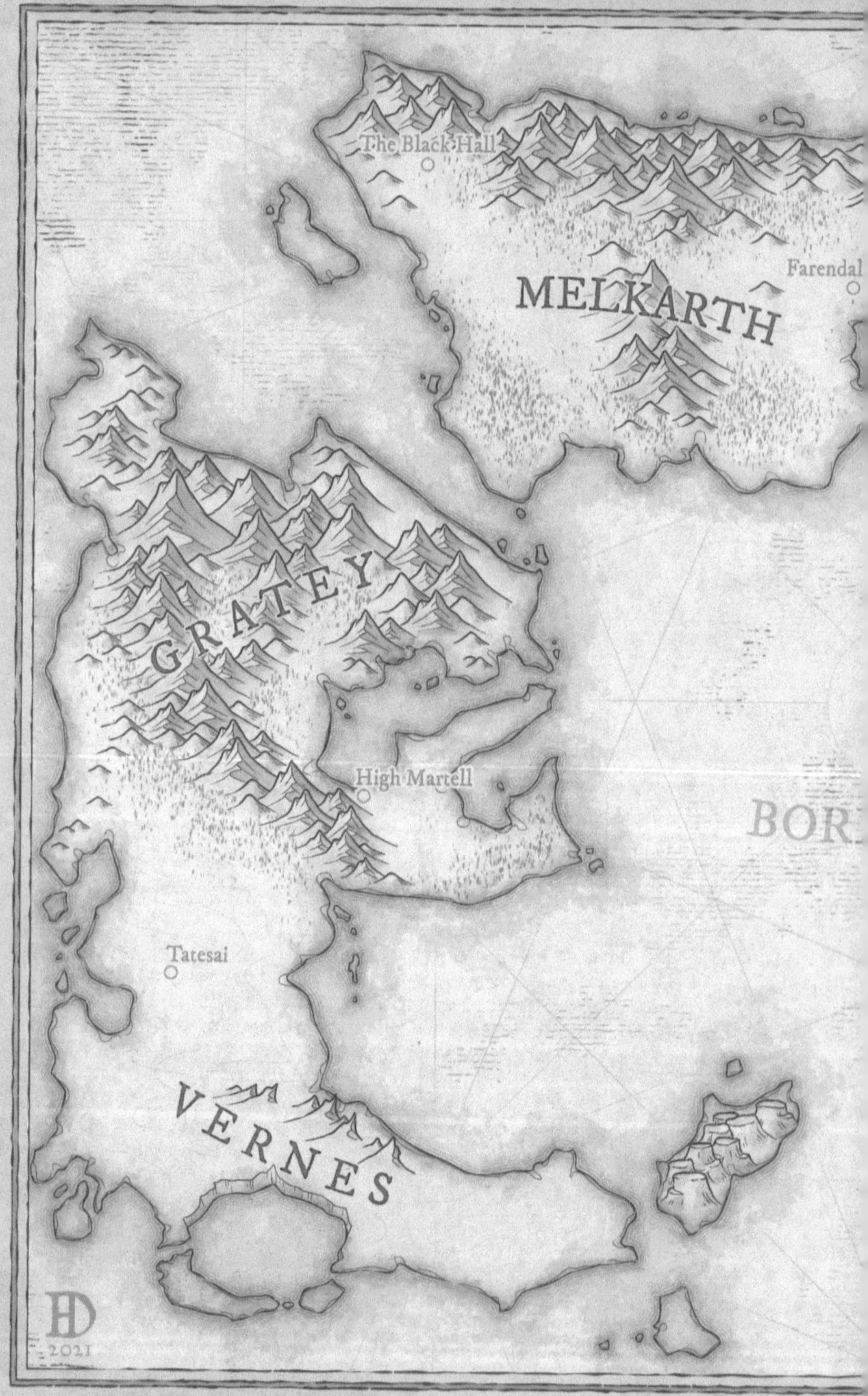

The Black Hall
MELKARTH
Farendal
GRATEY
High Martell
BOR
Tatesai
VERNES
HD
2021

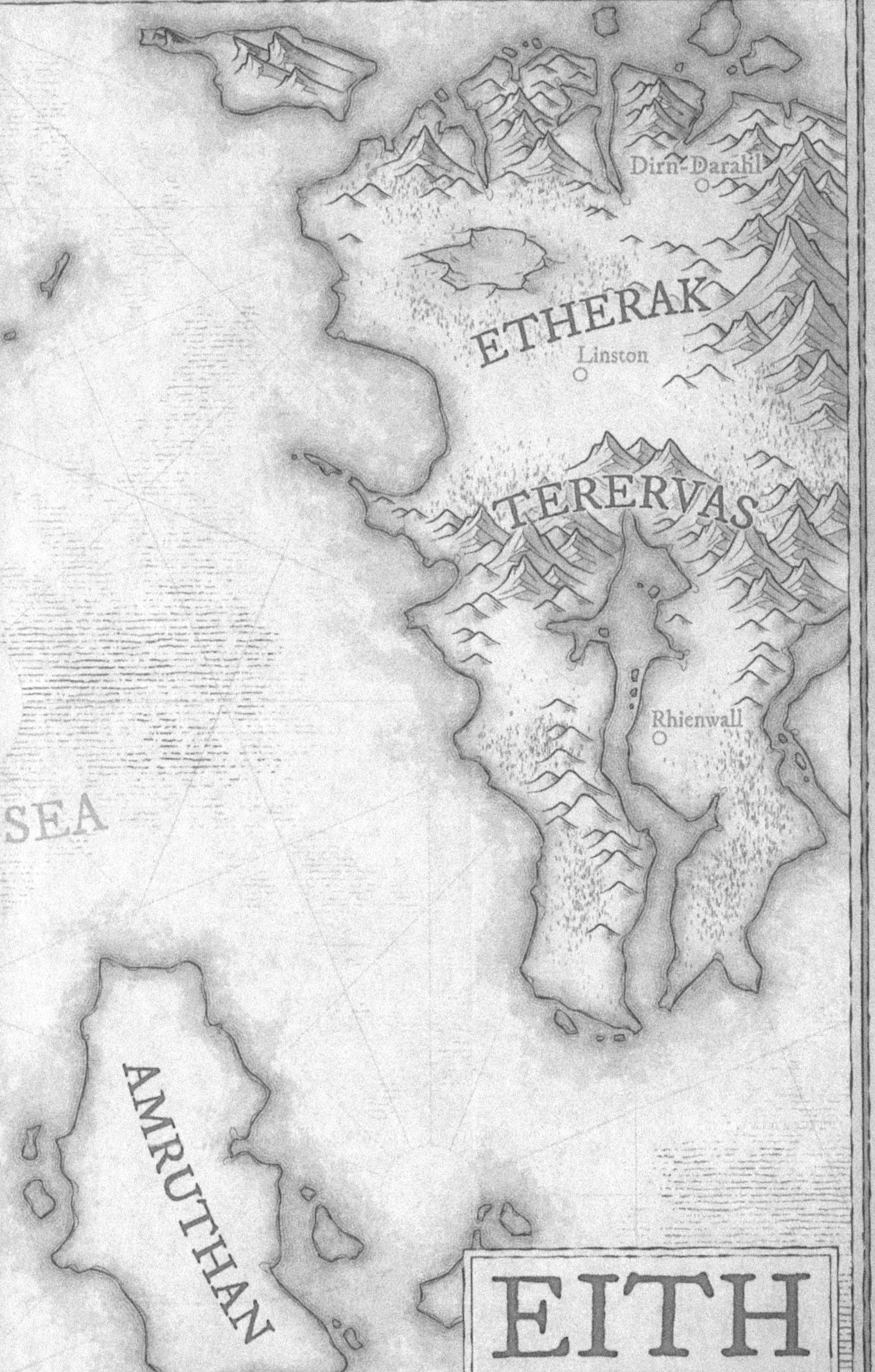

Dirn-Darahl
ETHERAK
Linston
TERERVAS
Rhienwall
SEA
AMRUTHAN
EITH

1

The ghost only came by moonlight, and only to Evren.

At least, she assumed it was a ghost. Either that or she truly was going mad, which wouldn't be that much of a leap for her. Not now.

She didn't like how it looked. The way it glided instead of walked, the way it shimmered and spun like moving mists in the pale light of the moon and barely tried to take the form of a person, irritated her. As if it was trying to remind her, gently, that she couldn't do anything rash to it.

On the nights where it said things that stoked the ever-growing fire of rage in her chest, its etherealness made her scratch red welts into her arms. She always stopped herself before she could bleed, but her skin caked under her fingernails was a poor substitute for what she wanted to do to the ghost. Those were dreadful nights. She never spoke back on them.

There were never any good nights. Just ones where the ghost's words weren't so barbed and cruel, and where her fingers stayed steadily on her thighs without the urge to hurt. Those nights, she didn't mind it with her. At least she wasn't alone.

Tonight was one of those nights. Bright moonlight filtered in through the tavern window, pooling in silver streams over the two beds. One, the farthest from the window, was empty and cold. The dwarf that had slept in it still hadn't come up for bed. It was well past midnight. In the other bed, Evren sat curled up next to the window. She rested her forehead against the cool glass, shivering at the reprieve it gave her fever-heated body. She didn't look away from the view of the sprawling village outside, but she felt the ghost when it appeared.

"It's too close." She murmured. To the ghost, the glass, and the dark smudge of forest beyond.

The ghost was quiet for a while before it whispered, "It's a large forest. Orenlion isn't as close as you think."

Evren pursed her lips. The voice always threw her off at first. Deep and soothing, even when it spoke harshly. She never could bring herself to hate it.

"We'll leave soon," she said.

"Will they let you?" it asked.

Always with the obvious fears. It seemed able to pick out what she dreaded most and say that aloud. Evren shivered again.

"They'll leave if I ask."

The floorboards didn't creak to show it was moving. The air just got a little damper and cooler, as if she was passing through a soft patch of morning fog. It was by her bed now.

"They brought you here, even when you protested," it said. "They think being near will convince you to go back."

"It won't."

"Why?"

Evren shook her head. Under her nightshirt, she could feel the massive scar on her chest throbbing. If she had a heartbeat, she would guess it was in time with that. But the hole where her heart should be was just that, a hole. The strange throbbing only made the dull fever she'd had for weeks now more prominent.

Outside her window, the village of Angel's Fall stood stocky and proud against the night. The last piece of Etherak before the towering trees of the Deep Wood swallowed the ground. She couldn't see the stars unless she craned her neck up. The black of the Wood blocked them out and left nothing but a shadowed wall at the edge of the forest.

"I can't go back," Evren said. "I'm not like them. Orenlion isn't home. If I go back, I'll never leave."

"And if it could save your life?"

"Whatever took my heart isn't the kind to give it back," she said. "I won't find it again."

"How can you be so sure?"

She scowled, and irritation bubbled in her empty chest. "I'd rather die out here among people I care about than trapped in there for the rest of my days."

"What if your friends won't let you? They won't watch you die."

"They'll be fine."

"I won't watch you wither away."

Finally, she turned away from the window. Her head throbbed as she rounded on the ghost. The absence of cool glass made her feel stuffy immediately.

He looked as he always did. Long white hair, elegantly braided away from his face. His dark grey skin was softer now that he was a specter. His moth-wing robes fluttered in an invisible breeze. The ghost looked like the Viggo she remembered, the one she left behind in Serevadia and sealed the tunnels over. He hadn't wanted to leave his home, but it still felt like she'd killed him. Even more damning to see him like this. She'd cried the first night. Now she just narrowed her eyes at him.

"You don't get a say," she said hotly.

He frowned at her, like he always did when she bit her words at him. That was more often now, the sicker she got.

"I know that," he said gently. "I'm merely trying to help you."

"Then you're not playing your role as Viggo very well, spirit," she said. "Viggo only helped when it suited him."

"You still don't believe it's me," he said flatly.

"It's not."

"I've explained this—"

"And I'm done listening," she snapped. "Either you're a spirit taunting me with whatever form you think is easier, or I've lost my mind and I'm arguing with myself."

"You haven't lost your mind. Not yet."

It wasn't a threat, but the harsh truth of the words settled over her like a sticky blanket anyway. She rolled her shoulders, now constantly sore, and tried to think a little clearer. Anger normally helped. If not that, then pain. But she was too tired to be truly angry at the ghost tonight. And if Sol found her with any fresh marks, she'd be furious.

Instead, Evren put her head in her hands and tried to massage the ache from her temples. Her hair, now past her shoulders and long enough to irritate, fell around her like a waterfall. It blocked Viggo from view.

"Whatever you are," she said. "I'm too tired to argue. With you, or anyone else. I just want to rest."

"No, you don't."

She laughed darkly. "Sure feels like I do."

"You don't remember, Evren," the ghost said. "What took your heart?"

As always, a blank wall of nothing greeted her when she tried to remember. Nothing but a few splintered memories of traveling in the leaf-dappled sunlight, and then darkness. The memory that Ainthe had clawed up was painful; a nightmare she hoped wasn't real. The claws in her chest felt real, though. The storm, the screams and blood in her throat, too. But where that ended was more black.

"It doesn't matter," she said.

"Liar. You never could resist a good puzzle."

She snapped her head up, an argument already forming on her dry lips. But it was gone. The room was still and shadowed, and she was alone.

She took a shaky breath and let her heavy eyelids close as she slipped underneath the blankets again. It was mostly for show. Whenever the ghost suddenly left, it usually meant she wouldn't be by herself for long. And, just as she predicted, soft footfalls crept outside the door. The latch clicked up and the hinges barely made a sound as Sol slipped quietly into the room and shut the door behind her.

She was always quiet and careful, but even more so in the past few weeks. Evren could smell the ale and smoke on her from the table the Wandering Sol's preferred right by the fireplace. She felt, more than heard, Sol's hesitation at the edge of her bed.

But Evren forced herself to breathe deeply, and slowly. She tried to let her eyebrows relax, so she looked more like she was sleeping fitfully. She couldn't tell if it worked or not, but Sol's soft sigh filled the room as she traded her clothes for her night-shirt and slipped into her bed. It took all of five minutes before the dwarf was snoring, her earthly worries forgotten in the blackness of sleep.

Evren didn't sleep. She rolled over, her face to the moonlight and the dark wall of trees looming in her vision. She was closer to home than she had been in over a year. Why did the dread in her stomach feel so heavy when Orenlion was all she could think about while she was in Serevadia and the Reino Terminan? Hadn't she been dreaming of the woods and warm breezes to lessen the blows of the harsh adventures she'd been on? Shouldn't she want to at least try to fix herself?

That weighted dread dragged her down. She wondered, dimly, if Gyda had felt the same way on the edge of Enrial Wilds. Closer to home than ever, and the darkness she'd left. Gyda had faced it and come out whole.

Evren had a feeling that if she went into the Deep Wood again, she wouldn't come back at all.

~

By day, it was easy to see where Angel's Fall got its name. Anyone not familiar with the village would think someone named it after a beautiful waterfall tumbling from the sweeping river it sat beside. But the Glasgus River was very gentle and wide. The land it carved though would dip into a few rapids the farther west it ran, but next to Angel's Fall, and coming from the Deep Wood, it was calm enough to swim in during warmer months.

No, the village got its name from the small, but impressive crater it was built around. It was old and weathered, but the imprint of a large humanoid in the rock hadn't been erased by time. There were debates on what made the crater. Of course, the popular theory was a fallen angel, if one believed in them. Unlike devils, who made themselves known and were frighteningly real, angels were even harder to imagine than gods.

"You think someone did it?" Sorin asked, peeking over the side to glimpse the imprint of the body below.

"What?" Evren asked.

"That." He gestured to the imprint. "They could've carved it into the rock."

Beside him, Sol shook her head. Her blond hair gleamed in the bright spring sunlight, and hung down to her shoulders. She played with it idly. "I don't think so. It looks old."

"Well, the crater is old," he argued. "Some crusty priest could've done it when he first found it."

"But why?"

"I dunno. Why do priests do anything?"

"The mayor said the crater has been here for thousands of years," Sol said. "If you believe Etherak's history, then humans weren't around yet."

Sorin frowned. "Why does the priest have to be human?"

"Because only a human would go through the trouble of taking an already mysterious crater and adding an angel to it," Evren said with a small smile.

The Vasa snorted. "We wouldn't. At least, no Vasa human would."

"Would a Vasa know what to do with a rock if he had it?" Sol joked.

He threw his hands up in the air. "You know what? Forget it. I feel attacked. I shouldn't have dragged you two out here. All I wanted was to do some *normal* sightseeing like a *normal* person before something inevitably crawls out of the ground and demands we answer its riddles three or get destroyed."

"That's specific." Evren raised an eyebrow.

"I had a weird dream last night." He waved her off. "A giant made of cheese said if I didn't answer its riddles, he'd make me into his next block of rariso."

Sol balked. "His what?"

"The cheese!" he said. "You know, it's really pale. Red veins. The good kind has holes in it."

"Why would there be a cheese giant?" Sol asked. "That makes no sense."

Sorin pointed to himself. "It's my dream."

"Did you win the riddles?" Evren asked.

He scowled. "They weren't riddles! They were stupid philo-sophical questions. The ones that have no right or wrong answer, but you'll end up pissing someone off, regardless. Somehow, they also centered cheese."

"Well," she breathed. "That explains your breakfast."

The three turned away from the crater and walked back into town. Angel's Fall was like any other Etherakian village. Most of the buildings were small, brown houses with thatched roofs divided by dirt roads and plenty of mud. It was bigger than most, though. There weren't many hunters who routinely made trips into the Deep Wood, but those who did found great game. That, the crater, and the Glasgus River giving an easy ride west towards the coast made Angel's Fall a bustling tourist spot.

The smell of wood smoke and cooking meat permeated the

air. The laughing of children overshadowed the sound of the river flowing in its bed. Barking dogs chased after treats while hunters shouted back and forth at each other. It was almost picturesque.

With the river curving around the village on one side, the crater on the other, the towering forest of the Deep Wood to the north, and rolling hills of green to the south, there was an unrivaled sense of beauty and peace in the village. Like all things Etherak, it held a wild edge. Something barely civilized clinging to a land that refused to be tamed, even after centuries of cities, villages, and roads. The people were the same way. Their tongues were as sharp as their blades, and smiles were warm but guarded. Living on the edge of the Deep Wood, far from any other city, meant danger. From beasts, monsters, or ravaging storms.

And yet, they thrived. Evren had respected it the first time she set foot in Angel's Fall, when she'd left Orenlion. That respect hadn't waned.

"Any word from Sahar?" Sorin asked casually, as if the question itself wasn't enough to send spikes of anxiety through all of them.

Sol shook her head. "Nothing much. Her last letter said she's back home in Rhienwall. She visited where Nerezza said she grew up, and the people running the orphanage didn't know who she was talking about."

Evren grimaced. That wasn't new information, but it at least confirmed another one of Nerezza's lies. Sahar had gone south to Terevas, determined to find something there to help find her old friend and last remaining member of her adventuring party. The letters she sent were all the same; uncovered lies and no new leads.

It should've been easy to track Nerezza. A mage with that much power, especially if she was using it, would be noticeable. But long after Evren and her party had left the Reino Terminan, it was like all traces of her had vanished.

"Do you think she went back to Serevadia?" Sol asked as she stepped around a pack of hunting dogs.

Evren gave them each a passing scratch behind their floppy ears. "I don't think so. We still don't know how she got away from her kidnappers. Why join the Ashen Bond? Why didn't she go back immediately? She has a plan; we just need to figure it out."

"No chance it's easy and right in front of our faces, right?" Sorin chuckled. "With our luck, she's all the way in Melkarth. Wouldn't it be nice if she was hiding out in the Deep Wood, huh? What a perfect place to hide. With all those . . . trees."

A soft hiss escaped Sol's lips, but the damage was done. Evren stopped in the middle of the road, her back purposefully facing the towering wall of trees. She didn't want to glare at Sorin, but a familiar hot prickle of anger was heating her already sweating body. Sorin had the good decency to look ashamed and shuffled his boots in the mud.

"I take that as a no?" he offered.

Evren took a cooling breath. The morning air, while quickly warming, was still damp with last night's mists. "We've been over this, Sorin."

"Have we, though?" he asked. "I feel like every time we get started, you cut us off."

"We need to focus on finding Nerezza," Evren said. "And nothing points to her being in the Deep Wood."

"What we need to focus on is you," he argued, and some iron leaked into his words. "You're our best chance at finding her."

"What do you think I'm doing?" she snapped.

"For starters? Suffering."

Evren pursed her lips together. The villagers gave them a wide berth, but she could see them eyeing her as they walked past. Arguing in the middle of the street was not one of her finer decisions. Between her and Sorin, Sol was fiddling with her hair again, and the stark worry etched across her face was clear for all to see. She flinched at Sorin's words but didn't dispute them.

Sorin took a step closer, and Evren was all at once hit with a wave of déjà vu. In an icy tavern at the edge of an eternal night, they'd stood like this. Only the roles had been reversed. Sorin grappling with his mortality and suffocating fear, and her trying to comfort him. How had things changed so drastically? He was far from fixed. Evren still saw a darkness in his honey eyes that hadn't been there before Heliodar plunged a dagger into his chest. There were still dark bags under his eyes, and his smiles weren't quite the same.

But now he was feeling strong enough to force her into an argument she was sick of having.

"You look terrible, Evvie," he said gently. "And I know you don't feel well, either."

"I'm fine."

"No." He shook his head. "You're not. Why don't you want to fix this?" Sorin pointed at her chest. Her shirt hid the scar on her chest, but seemed to burn hot against the fabric when he mentioned it.

"It's not that simple, Sorin," she said hollowly. "I can't even remember how I lost it. Going into the Wood now would have us wandering aimlessly for years."

"Trollshit," Sol finally spoke. "You can track anything, and you know those woods."

Evren shook her head. "It's a waste of time. We're focusing on Nerezza."

"We came here to focus on you," Sol said. "The entire party did."

Evren's eyes throbbed, and she struggled not to rub the pain away. "We came here to resupply before heading down to Terevas. Passing through the Vanguard Mountains won't be easy. Sahar is waiting for us."

"You've been repeating that so often lately it's losing all meaning," Sorin said.

Something in Evren finally snapped, and she whirled on him. "What happens to me is nothing compared to what Nerezza can do if we don't find her. Am I in the best health? No. But I can still fight. I can still get you to Sahar and from there we can find Nerezza before she does any actual harm. Or have you forgotten what Gail did?"

Sorin's eyes flickered over to Sol, who was forcibly ignoring both of them now. He looked back at Evren. "I haven't." he muttered. "But Nerezza isn't Gail."

"No." Evren stepped back. "She's more powerful than him now. She still has Keres's soul, and Gail's, on top of the dozens we didn't save in time. That kind of power broke Gail. What can it do to an already powerful mage?"

Sorin shook his head again. "But Gail was isolated. He lost his entire crew, his family, and was starving and desperate before he turned to Keres. Nerezza—"

"Lost her party," Evren finished. "She watched Vox die for her. She knew Drystan was dead before we went into the Cairn. And she's been isolated ever since they took her from Serevadia."

"But she had Sahar!" he argued.

"Exactly," Evren said. "She'll go back to her eventually, fractured mind or not. Which is why we need to be there when she does instead of wasting time *here*." She waved her hand around at Angel's Fall, taking in the villagers, huts, dogs, and the sweeping river in one gesture. "Please, Sorin. Let the Deep Wood go. For me."

He looked like he would argue. Knowing him, he could go on until the sun set and the stars wheeled overhead. But Sol gave him a knowing look and gave a soft shake of her head. He sighed, his shoulders drooping.

"All right," he said. "You win this one."

It didn't feel like a victory. Not when he looked at her with barely disguised worry, and Sol had already started walking away. But she took it anyway and followed the dwarf further into the village.

There was a part of her, not so easily buried, that knew they were right. She'd pushed herself too far during the Long Night, dipped into magic she didn't understand, and she was paying the price. The fever and the constant headaches she'd dealt with once they left the mountains were irritating but manageable. But how long before she *couldn't* manage them? She only felt herself when she was in a fight. The sudden crisp clarity had her blood singing and all her pains forgotten. But afterwards she crashed, hard. And she was getting worse.

She spared an upward glance at the Deep Wood. The leaves aching to brush the sky, the trunks supporting the twisting branches thousands of years old. No tree in the Deep Wood had been cut, ever. They rose and fell as time allowed. And there was a time Evren knew them like her own mind. Even when Orenlion felt more like a prison than a home, they'd always been there to offer solace when she snuck away.

So, why did the mere sight of them now send a spike of fear through her?

She tore her gaze away from the shadowed forest as they came closer to the village's biggest tavern. *The Gilded Feather* was an impressive three stories tall, and sturdy as all things Etherakian made. Springtime meant another season of hunting, which meant it was packed with hunters, both noble and peasant. The other three taverns were as well. It was only by Sol's charm they could get enough rooms for the party to stay.

Already the smell of baking bread and bacon was in the air, getting heavier the closer they got. Evren's stomach rumbled with hunger, and she inwardly winced. She'd forgotten to eat breakfast, again. She'd have to sneak a plate before her friends noticed.

"Sounds like a party in there," Sorin commented.

Evren frowned and drew her thoughts away from breakfast. As she did, she picked up on the sound of raised voices, the cracking of wood and the breaking of glass.

"That sounds like a fight," she corrected. "Who—"

The nearby window shattered in a spray of sparkling glass. The trio barely staggered out of the way as a man tumbled through the broken window. He collapsed on the ground, groaning and holding his bleeding nose.

"Oh, look!" Sorin said cheerfully. "How much gold do you wanna bet that Gyda's made some new friends?"

2

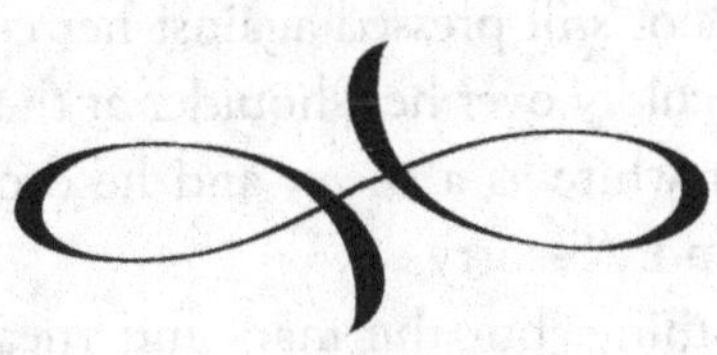

Bursting into *The Gilded Feather*, Evren noticed three things all at once.

One, half the tavern's patrons were taking part in the brawl. They had knocked tables over, smashed chairs, and broken bottles. Someone had spilled a whole tray of breakfast over one unfortunate human who was taking his time picking the eggs out of his hair.

Two, a bard in the corner was dodging flying plates and food while playing a jaunty tune on his flute

Three, Abraxas and Gyda were in the very thick of the fighting.

Gyda towered over everyone in the room. Most wisely went for Abraxas instead, but the elf was still a force to be reckoned with, even without his armor and sword. He ducked out of the way of a clumsy punch and jammed his elbow into the man's stomach so fast he was a blur. The man fell to the ground, wheezing for breath, and Abraxas jumped over his prone form to the next opponent.

The next man, a stern looking older human, was bleeding from a cut on his elbow. His hair was plastered with wood splinters, and the table behind him looked like it was well past any hasty repairs. He dodged Abraxas's blow, the elf's fist glancing off his forearm. With a roar, he ran at Abraxas and, before the elf could twist out of the way, caught him by the waist and sent them both tumbling behind the bar.

A shriller battle cry came from across the room as a younger human ran up behind Gyda and smashed a chair across her back. The wood broke on her like a wave against a rock, and she barely flinched. Boot still pressed against her current opponent's chest, she looked coldly over her shoulder at the boy.

His face went white as a sheet, and he dropped the broken chair leg in his hand. "S-sorry . . ."

Gyda said nothing, but the man underneath her boot spat and twisted her leg. She stumbled, not quite falling but losing her center of balance. He clawed up to his knees and fumbled around until he found an intact bottle on the ground. He swung wildly, his arm stopping inches from her head as she gripped his wrist in a bone cracking vise. She grabbed the bottle from his limp fingers and smashed it over his own head.

As he crumbled to the ground, she dropped him and turned to the next fighters.

"Shouldn't we help?" Sol asked and ducked under a piece of flying breakfast. "They look like they're all going after Gyda and Abraxas."

"I love a good tavern brawl!" Sorin had already shed his jacket and rolled up his sleeves. Before either of them could say otherwise, he dove into the fray and was lost in the fight.

"Where's Arke?" Evren asked. They'd left the goblin in the tavern to sleep late. But she couldn't see him in the chaos. When Sol didn't answer, she turned to find the dwarf climbing behind the bar where Abraxas had disappeared.

Evren sighed, closing her eyes. Her head throbbed in time with the flute's tune. She felt someone crash into the table next to her with a cry of outrage.

"I'm going to pay for this later," she said before tying her hair back and marching into the thick of the fight.

She stepped over the bodies of men and women who hadn't gotten back up. A scarred woman launched herself at Evren like a furious bull. She easily sidestepped and sent the woman careening into the next table.

The young man who'd hit Gyda with a chair stayed rooted to the spot where she'd left him. Evren came up and put a light hand on his shoulder.

"Hey, what's going—"

He whirled around in a panic, and his fist slammed right into her nose.

Evren stumbled back a step as white sparks of pain danced in her eyes. But with that pain, her fever and throbbing head faded to obscurity. She tasted blood as it dribbled down her lips. When she opened her eyes, everything looked clearer. The air filled her lungs and excitement rippled through her body. She dabbed the blood with her fingers and gave it a curious look. The crimson was dark enough to be black on her fingertips. She looked up at him.

"Oh, shit on a stick!" he cursed, his blue eyes wide and terrified. The eyes of someone who was in way over his head.

Evren took him by his shoulder and, without saying a word, shoved him away from the fighting. He yelped and didn't fight her.

The woman she'd dodged earlier was picking herself back up. She helped another fallen human onto his feet. They looked between her and Gyda, and the choice was clear. After all, who'd go after a woman seven feet tall with biceps thicker than their heads, when they could go after the sickly looking half-elf instead?

Evren picked up the fallen chair leg and flipped it experimentally in her hand. Barely giving the two of them a second glance, she beckoned them forward with a finger.

She didn't know who had started the fight, or why, but she would not stand for people beating up her friends.

They went after her at the same time. The woman swung

high, and Evren ducked out of her way. She slapped the flat of the chair leg against her back and sent her stumbling away. She then kicked the other human making a run for her legs. Her boot just clipped his ear, and he spun around with a quick recovery. His fist went for her face, and she swung her chair leg like a cudgel. His fingers audibly cracked under the heavy blow and he cried out. This time when she kicked him, her boot landed solidly and sent him groaning to the ground.

Evren's chest was light and she smiled. Fighting always felt good. She turned to see how Gyda was faring just as a powerful set of arms wrapped around her neck and yanked her to the ground.

She slammed into the woman behind her, putting all her weight into the fall to knock the wind out of her. But as strong as she felt, she didn't have the bulk to back that move up. The woman below her barely grunted.

They grappled for a while before the woman flipped them over. Evren's cheek pressed firmly against the gritty, ale-soaked floor and her arm twisted behind her back. Her bones ached at the unfamiliar position, and her opponent straddled her back with strong thighs. Evren struggled to get out of her grip. Her other arm arched back, but her elbow was slow and lazy enough to deflect and pinned down next to her.

"The little mutt defending a war criminal?" The woman's breath was hot against her ear. "How cute."

"Let me go and you'll see how cute I can be," Evren spat.

Before either of them could respond, the door slammed open again. Bright sunlight flooded into the room, and a lone elven figure stood silhouetted against the light. He took a step inside.

"ENOUGH!"

The order rang out over the tavern, cutting through the fighting. All the fighters immediately froze, except for Gyda, who didn't bother to stop her punch mid-swing and sent a man careening to the floor. The woman pinning Evren down cursed under her breath and her grip loosened. The flute trailed off its last note pitifully, and the tavern fell into an awkward silence.

Evren wiggled free and threw the woman off her. She ignored her, pulling herself onto her feet and standing at attention.

The tavern was silent enough to hear a pin drop. The elven figure stepped further into the chaos, stepping over broken tables and holding his hand out to help up a fallen human. A soldier, Evren noted, far too late. All the fighters were wearing simple, but well-made clothes. No armor, but all uniform in dark greys and blacks.

The elf was different. He didn't wear a uniform, but well-cut traveling clothes. The kind that were obviously expensive and cost a small fortune, but any noble would think was discreet. He had flawless olive skin, and thickset brows over storm grey eyes. His black hair was chopped short and neatly combed. The sword at his hip looked far too shiny to be used often.

"What happened?" he asked, after he'd taken in the view.

"Your Highness." The woman that had pinned Evren bowed low. "It was a simple brawl in your honor."

Your Highness.

Evren groaned and her head thunked against the floor as she laid back down. They were thoroughly fucked.

"Highness?" Sorin's voice came from under a pile of limbs, and he poked his head out with an eager smile. "No way! You're royalty? And you've got shitty guards like this?"

The woman scowled at him. "Hold your tongue! That's the future King of Etherak you speak to."

The future King of Etherak held his hand up to silence her. "Lieutenant, practice some kindness and explain what happened here."

She drew herself up taller, her hands clasped behind her back. "The men and I were awaiting your return, Your Highness, when Lorel found a known war criminal among us."

"And did they start the fight?"

Gyda shoved past a few soldiers too stiff to stop her, her face hard and stormy. "No. The first blow belonged to your soldiers."

The future King raised an eyebrow at her, a healthy dose of unease flickering across his eyes. "I see . . . Lieutenant, is this true?"

The lieutenant pressed her lips into a firm line and looked straight ahead. "We were defending Etherak's honor."

"Is that what tavern brawls are called now?" Evren wheezed from the floor.

The elf gave her a passing glance before returning to his soldiers. "Where is this supposed war criminal, then?"

Behind the bar, Abraxas emerged with Sol. His hair had been torn from its binding and glimmered with broken pieces of glass. But none of the men he'd fought rose with him.

"That would be me, Your Highness." He bowed low. "Forgive me, the fighting got out of hand. But your soldiers held their own quite well."

The elf's eyes widened by a fraction. "Abraxas Kain, is it?"

"Indeed. I'm surprised you remember. You were just a boy when I last saw you."

"My uncle speaks of you often." The elf smiled, and his demeanor changed from that of a stern leader to a young prince. "I couldn't forget."

He swept his gaze back over the room, pausing on the rest of the Wandering Sol's. With every member, he looked more and more giddy. He finally stopped on Evren, and she had the sudden urge to bow despite being prone on the floor.

"And you must be the Wandering Sols, yes?" he asked, and she nodded. "Marvelous!"

He fished out a large sack of gold and put it on the bar. At the sound of clinking coins, the tavern owner emerged from his hiding place, his face flushed and jowls trembling.

"For your troubles." The prince nodded to the tavern. "That should be enough to cover repairs, and my soldiers will clean up the mess left behind."

"Th-thank you, Your Highness." The portly man stuttered and took the gold with wide eyes. "This is most generous."

"Nonsense! We destroyed your good tavern. I'll see it fixed. Lieutenant, you'll oversee that. Make sure we give any men needing healing attention. The rest will stay behind and clear out the damages."

She scowled but hid it behind a stiff bow. "Yes, Your Highness."

Evren hadn't left the floor yet. She heard the clicking of claws against the wood as Arke came up to squat beside her head. His sharp-toothed grin was full of bacon pieces as he looked down at her. "Good mornin'!"

She groaned and wiped her bloody nose. "Where the hells have you been?"

"Placin' bets. Won thirty gold off Gyda."

"Wonderful," she muttered and pushed herself up into a sitting position. As she did, Gyda was there with a helping hand. Evren murmured her thanks and let her pull her to her feet.

"Now!" The prince turned back to them. "I'd like a word with the other half of this fight. Might we take this privately?"

Evren looked at her party. They all shrugged, one by one. She turned to the prince, knowing before she even said the words what the answer was.

"Do we have a choice?"

They did not, in fact, have a choice.

After a flurry of introductions, cleaning up, and confusion—mostly on the tavern owner's end—the Wandering Sol's found themselves in a private room on the second floor with the crown prince, Barrion Rhys.

They weren't truly alone, of course. Two of his guards were stationed at the door, and Evren was sure of more waiting out in the hallway. But the prince was smiling and sipping his ale.

The room was a little dingy. Heavy maroon curtains blanketed the walls to add a little soundproofing, and the window was covered as well. The lantern in the middle of the round table was bright, however, and gave the room a cozy, smokey feel.

Evren dabbed the remaining blood from her sore nose. It wasn't broken, but still stung. With the adrenaline wearing off, she could feel her headache coming back. She slouched a little in her seat, not quite ready to nurse her own ale like Sorin was.

"So," Barrion tapped his fingers against his mug, "shall I apologize again for my men's rude behavior?"

Gyda grunted and shifted in her seat beside Evren. "Your apologies mean nothing when your soldiers don't share them."

Barrion waved her off. "Nonsense! They just didn't know who you were."

"I believe the problem was that they did," Abraxas said. His knuckles were bloody and split, but he'd made no move to clean himself up.

Beside him, Sol tucked her frayed hair behind her ears. "What was that about? What war criminal were they talking about?"

Abraxas looked at her calmly, as if it was obvious. "Me."

Sorin barked out laughter that was too loud. "That's ridiculous! A war criminal? Abraxas? Obviously not." When silence followed his words, he frowned. "Well, don't everyone agree with me all at once."

Barrion lost a little of his friendly smile, his eyes darkening as if he was recalling a particularly painful memory. "There's no one in Eith that was not touched by my late father's conquests. The knights under his command did unspeakable things, and many detest them. None more so than Etherak's own people, who view the loss of our Divines as their fault."

Evren looked at Abraxas. His face was calm, almost serene, but his shoulders were still laced tight, as if he was waiting for another fight. Or fighting one internally.

"Maybe your people should be angrier at the man who gave the orders," Evren said sharply, "instead of the ones who carried them out."

Barrion smiled ruefully. "If only it were that simple. My father has been tried, and mercifully executed for his crimes against Eith. But my people suffer, and where they suffer, they seek someone to blame."

Sorin snorted. "Well, that's fucking stupid."

Abraxas raised his hand. "It's all right, Sorin, I'm used to it."

Evren squirmed in her seat, finally reaching for her ale. It tasted bland on her tongue, and as she drank, she couldn't help but think of all the times she'd argued with Abraxas about the same problem. What King Eldridge had done to Eith was unspeakably wrong, and the way Abraxas told it, he followed those orders willingly. There was a part of her that resented him for that, for not seeing the wrong he'd done until it was too late. The man she knew was better than that. A little cold perhaps, and stubborn, but good.

There were things he never bent on, like the situation with the dead spirit Keres. He and Keres would never get along. A spirit from Vernes forced to flee their home because of the war Abraxas and his fellow knights had brought to their shores. Abraxas, however much he'd changed, still couldn't see the undead as anything but evil. He'd been furious at Evren for letting Keres go with Sahar after they left the White Cairn. But that fury had faded over time. And so had Evren's own resentment.

Evren and Abraxas were very different people, but that didn't make them any less friends.

She might not believe in his Divines or understand his faith, but she hadn't been alive during his time. She didn't see what he saw. In the end, what he'd done in Vernes was in the past. The man who'd followed severe orders, thinking it was divine justice, was not the same one who made bad jokes just to get her to smile and take care of herself.

Arke seemed oblivious to the tension at the table. He counted out his coins, slapping Sorin's hand away any time the Vasa tried to fidget with his careful stacks of gold. He didn't look up as he said, "So, what's the private meetin' about?"

Barrion put his mug away and folded his hands on the table. In the lantern's flickering light, he looked far older than he should've. Evren wondered if Abraxas saw a shadow of Eldridge in the young prince.

"I'm on a bit of a mission," Barrion started. "Etherak, as you know, has never fully recovered from my father's costly campaigns."

"Nor the amount of gold paid to those he wronged, I'll bet," Sorin muttered into his cup.

Barrion nodded in agreement. "And we have few allies. While my uncle will never admit it, we need help, and badly. I mean to find some."

"Surely Terevas is still friendly," Sol prodded. "They took their independence quietly, and legally. No bad blood."

"That's true." The prince nodded. "But the Terevasan crown can only give so much. And by continuing to be a trade partner with us, they risk alienating kingdoms like Gratey and Vernes. They're pulling away, bit by bit, and it's costing us."

"So?" Gyda asked.

Evren winced and tried to soften the blow. "What do you plan to do about it?"

He was tapping his mug again. "An alliance. A new one, as a matter of fact. Etherak's few allies can't give anymore. Melkarth is shaky anyway, and my uncle prefers to leave them alone. Dirn-Darahl is still building up their new government, as I hear, and is in no financial situation to help."

Evren's stomach sank. The aftertaste of the ale tasted like ash on her tongue. "You mean to strike a deal with Orenlion."

He nodded slowly. "And there you see my problem."

Gyda frowned. "What problem? Are they not willing to trade?"

Barrion winced. "Less that, and more that they are difficult to find."

"And they're unwilling to trade," Evren said softly.

"As you probably know, Orenlion resides in the Deep Wood, not too far outside this room." Barrion said. "They dubbed the city 'The Moving City,' for no one will ever return to the spot they first saw it and find it again. The elves there are extremely private and hidden from the rest of the world. Not to mention that a forest as old as the Deep Wood is brimming with more monsters than one can prepare for."

"And what does this have to do with us?" Arke asked, as if he hadn't already guessed.

Barrion blinked at him, looking confused as he glanced

around the table. "Well, I thought it would be obvious. I need your help finding the city and surviving the Wood."

He dug in his pocket and pulled out a crisp piece of parchment bearing the seal of the Collective and some familiar handwriting. As he did, Evren closed her eyes and leaned back into the chair.

"I reached out to the Collective, and Professor Elend Vaughn recommended your services. Extraordinarily, he said you'd be here waiting for me. I assumed he sent word ahead of the job."

"He did not," rumbled Gyda.

Evren heard the paper being passed around. Arke hissed at it, and it took only a few moments after that for the smell of ink-heavy smoke to fill the air.

"Uh, I take it you and the professor aren't on good terms?"

"We ain't his biggest fans."

"But he spoke very highly of your skills."

"Lady Al Fazil has a very tight hold on his balls," Gyda said, to which Sol started choking on her ale.

"Be that as it may . . ." Barrion hesitated. "Your party is the only one with a member familiar enough with the Deep Wood to guide us."

And there it was.

Evren sighed. Already, the fever was creeping back into her bones and dragging a heavy weariness with it. If she kept her eyes closed for much longer, she was going to fall asleep at the table.

She forced her eyes open, unsurprised to find everyone looking at her. Evren ignored everyone except Barrion. There was no ignoring the desperation in his eyes.

"I'm sorry, Your Highness," she said, and watched his face fall. "But we have an important quest of our own. We take to Terevas, and we can't delay."

Barrion sat back in his chair, looking like he was lost for words and staring at the ashes of Elend's letter. Evren expected Sorin to argue, or even Sol, but it was Abraxas who spoke up.

"Evren . . ." he said gently. "We don't know that she's in Terevas."

"She will be."

"There's no need to rush when we can still do good here in Etherak."

"You know there is," Evren bit out at him. "For Gail, at the very least."

Abraxas didn't back down. "And for someone closer to home?"

Barrion might've thought the question was about him, or even Abraxas himself. But Evren, and everyone else at the table, knew better. She tried not to let the irritation show. She didn't want to snap at Abraxas the way she did Sorin, and especially not in front of his prince, so she settled for digging her nails into her palm.

"We've discussed this. We don't need to go to Orenlion."

Sorin cleared his throat, looking into his empty cup as if there were a hidden message in the dregs. "Yes, but now we have a reason."

She glared over at him. "Sorin."

"I'm just saying . . ."

Barrion started to get up out of his chair. "Should I leave this for you all to discuss alone . . . ?"

"No," Evren said.

"Yes," Abraxas said in unison.

"There's no point." Evren pushed her chair back and stood up. "We don't have time for another quest, especially one through the Deep Wood."

"You know it," Barrion said flatly. "The forest, I mean."

"Yes," she said stiffly.

"So, you know the dangers."

"I know some," she corrected. "And you want Orenlion. The city only shows itself to those that are worthy, and I promise you, that isn't me. I can map out what I remember and give you a list of things to avoid, plants to stay away from, and creatures to watch out for. But, beyond that, I'm afraid I can't help you."

Before Barrion, or anyone else, could protest, Evren pulled back the heavy curtain, unlatched the door, and walked out of the stuffy room.

She marched through the hallway and down the stairs, keenly aware of the burning in the back of her throat reminding her of how unreasonable she was being. What was wrong with her? Everything her party was saying was true. Even if there wasn't anything wrong with her, turning down Barrion's offer was stupid. To let the only heir to Etherak's throne lose himself in the Deep Wood was as good as shooting him with an arrow; it was just a slower death.

The floor of the tavern was nearly spotless as she quickly picked across it. Only a few pieces of glass crunched under her boot. She didn't see the owner trying to wave her over, or the remaining soldiers watching her as she left. She was sweating again as she opened the door and walked outside.

The spring breeze cooled the sweat beading on her skin. She rolled her sleeves up anyway, rounding the corner of *The Gilded Feather* to find the back of the tavern blissfully free of people. And, more importantly, it kept the Deep Wood out of her view.

Evren slumped against the wall and took another lungful of clean air. Her breathing had gotten faster without her realizing. She closed her eyes, willing herself to breathe deeper and slower. The creeping dizziness faded before it could sink its claws into her head. All at once, she felt weak again.

She got winded from marching downstairs and out a door. Sure, she was still chewing on the conversation upstairs, but that shouldn't have been enough to wind her. None of it should have. How was she going to do anything if she was this weak?

Evren let out her breath, slowly this time, so she could feel every inch of air leak from her lips. She needed to last until they found Nerezza. The mage was the only other person Evren knew that had similar magic. She used it in ways Evren couldn't understand, so maybe she knew a way to fix Evren herself. Perhaps fix the hole where her heart should be.

Nerezza had said blood magic was only achieved through sacrifice. The mage had woven Evren a convincing web of lies about a little girl who was born with that magic. A little girl who bled and made the flames flicker and was always sickly.

Evren knew better now. It was another lie to make her seem more approachable, or trustworthy. Nerezza cut off her hand for blood magic, and that was a willing sacrifice. But all of Evren's memories about losing her heart didn't feel voluntary.

It wasn't given; it was taken. And she didn't know how to get it back.

Nerezza was her only chance. She was the only person in all of Eith who knew about blood magic and was willing to experiment. And, somehow, she didn't suffer the same way Evren did.

"A heart's a little more vital than a hand," she murmured to herself. It was a miracle she'd survived this long. And she had no idea how she was still breathing without a beating heart to drive her on.

The spring breeze picked up again, carrying the scent of pine from the forest, and a hint of leather and sword polish. If frost could have a scent, Gyda would carry it as well. The ice never truly left her.

Evren opened her eyes.

Gyda was standing a few feet away, a sickening look of concern on the warrior's face. She'd traded her thick hide armor for something cooler. The new armor focused on just a leather cuirass fitted well to her body and left her arms bare. Her pants were made of a thinner material as well, but her boots were the same sturdy and worn set she'd had since they met. Gyda's tolerance for cold was supernatural, but she couldn't stand the heat.

"Well?" Gyda asked.

"Well, what?"

"I'm waiting for you to explain your outburst."

Evren scowled and looked down at her boots instead of

Gyda. It was easier to think that way. "I meant what I said. We don't have time."

"We'll make time."

"Oh, sure, let me just pull an extra month or so out of my ass. I'm sure whatever Nerezza has planned can wait."

Gyda's shadow suddenly fell across Evren, and the air felt a little chillier than it had moments before. Despite herself, Evren looked up. Gyda towered over her an extra two feet, so she was always looking up at the part giant. That didn't make it any easier to meet her eyes.

"We'll make time," Gyda said, every word carrying the weight of mountains.

Evren swallowed, her mouth suddenly dry. "Why do you care about the prince?"

"I don't. I care about you."

"I'm—"

"You're being irrational." Gyda cut her off. "Reckless with your life. I do not understand how you can fight so hard for others, but refuse to stand for yourself."

"This isn't about me," Evren snapped, which was impressive considering that the wall behind her was the only thing keeping her from swaying in the breeze like a particularly sickly blade of grass.

Gyda took another step towards her. A small one, but it was enough for Evren's spine to straighten and press further against the wood. The warrior put her hand on the wall, leaning close enough for her breath to fan against Evren's face.

"It is now," Gyda said. Her eyes held a steely determination that made Evren shiver. If she didn't know Gyda better, her words would've sounded like a threat.

"You won't let this go, will you?" Evren's voice sounded fragile in comparison.

Gyda shook her head. "Why are you afraid?"

Evren scoffed. "I'm not afraid."

"Then why fight so hard to not go home?"

Evren shut her mouth, wanting for all the world to melt into the wood and disappear from her friend's discerning gaze. But there was no escape short of wiggling away from Gyda and taking off down the street. Even she wasn't that far gone to consider running. Besides, Gyda would catch her when she inevitably collapsed a few roads down, anyway.

The lump in Evren's throat grew, and it took her a few tries to swallow it down. She couldn't tell if her cheeks were burning from the fever, or embarrassment, or from Gyda being so close.

"I ran away from a lot," she finally said. "Going back . . . I don't know if I'll be able to leave again." Her words were as soft and fragile as fog in the early morning. At first, she didn't think Gyda heard her until the warrior took a step back and let her arm fall to her side.

"What happened in Orenlion, Evren?" she asked gently.

Evren shrugged, feeling useless and hot with shame. She couldn't quite look at Gyda. "I don't know. It's like I told Arke when we first left Direwall. I don't remember how I lost my heart. I can't remember anything beyond running away from my wedding and then finding myself in Angel's Fall. If you'd asked me back in Dirn-Darahl why I left, I would've said I ran away from my wedding and that was that."

Finally, Evren looked up at Gyda, meeting her glacier eyes. There was no judgment there, no pity. Just a longing to understand.

Evren's hand went to her chest, where the scar burned under her shirt. "But I didn't have this before the wedding. And I don't remember how I got it."

"Missing memories." Gyda nodded slowly.

"Could it be magic?"

She shrugged one of her muscular shoulders. "Maybe. But it's not uncommon for warriors to forget something traumatic. The pain the memories bring is as bad as the pain of healing, perhaps worse. You could be ignoring what happened to you, in favor of protecting yourself."

"But I've tried to remember," Evren protested.

"Then we take it to the source. We go back to the beginning and retrace your steps."

A flash of feverish heat fired through Evren's bones. The ache behind her eyes spiked, and she felt heavy enough to sink to the ground. She shook off the feeling, urging away the sudden wave of weakness and the panic that brought it on.

"What if it's worse?" she asked, sounding winded. "What if we can't fix me?"

"We will."

"But if we don't—"

"Evren." Gyda cut her off again, this time with no harshness. It was enough to calm her quickening breaths. "You followed me into what should have been my death. You defended my people. You found me and brought me back to myself. You had your soul ripped out to attempt to save the boy behind it all. Evren, you risked everything for me. Let me try to do the same for you."

Hot tears pricked the corners of Evren's eyes, and she didn't know what brought them on. Gyda's words, her own pain, or perhaps the sudden surety that she might not have to suffer anymore.

"No matter what happens," Evren said. "Whether or not we fix my heart, I might not be able to come back."

"You will."

"We don't always have a choice."

"Then we'll make one," she said confidently. "We'll find a way. We always do."

4

Evren waited until sunset for the cloaked figure to appear. She waited for the shadows to grow thick and dark enough to hold a person, for the trees to swallow the sun's golden rays. She waited because, while she'd told Gyda she'd go to the Deep Wood, she wanted to make sure she was making the right decision.

The mysterious figure that had shown up both times before she embarked on a dangerous adventure always seemed to know more than she could comprehend. It knew about Serevadia, hidden from the world for centuries, forgotten. Gail had been missing for decades, locked in icy isolation, and it still warned Evren of the boy and his aurora. It had warned her, saved her life, thrust her into danger, but had never revealed itself.

Keres had cautioned her about such a creature. Something as powerful and all-knowing as it appeared to be would be a force to be reckoned with, if angered. And, for some unfathomable reason, it was attached to her. She intended to find out why.

But maybe there was another reason she stood breathless in the twilight.

Maybe she waited because if the figure showed up, she'd know if she made the right or wrong choice. She could force it to tell her what waited in the Deep Wood, or to give her some clue on how to make it back out. Maybe it would tell her that Terevas was really the right way to go, and she'd have a stronger reason to pull her party out of Prince Barrion's quest.

But as twilight grew to night, Evren knew it wasn't coming. And perhaps that was an answer in itself. If the figure didn't want her to go into the Deep Wood, it would've intervened and told her, right? Surely something so invested in her actions wouldn't abandon her now.

Unless, of course, it had accepted her death and moved on to someone else.

Evren forced that thought out of her head as she made her way back to *The Gilded Feather.* Inside was warm and glowing with golden candlelight. The kitchen's meal of choice tonight was a mystery to Evren's nose, but her mouth watered regardless. Despite that, the tavern's main floor was still mostly empty, save for a few regulars who didn't care to find a different tavern, no matter the coin they were offered. Barrion's soldiers had been told not to bother them, and it pleasantly surprised Evren to see the tavern clear of any black and grey uniforms.

This time, when the tavern owner caught her eye, she actually nodded in response. She met him at the bar as he pushed her a steaming plate of rice, sliced marinated beef, some vegetables she didn't recognize, and a piece of crusty bread and butter.

"Anthin' to drink for ya?" he asked, wiping his hands on his apron.

She opened her mouth, just as Abraxas came up behind her and answered.

"Just water for her, thank you."

The owner's warm smile fell, but he nodded quickly and scampered back behind the bar.

Evren turned to scowl at Abraxas. "Just water?"

He nodded. "No ale until you're healthy again."

"Oh joy, I've taken an involuntary vow of sobriety."

It wasn't long before she had her glass of chilled water and Abraxas was ushering her up the stairs.

"I'm glad Gyda convinced you to see reason," he whispered.

Evren huffed as she climbed the stairs. "She would've dragged me into the Wood kicking and screaming if I'd said no."

"You can't tell her no. You never have been able to."

"She makes it hard, I'll admit."

"Regardless," he helped her up the last stair and held her elbow as she caught her breath, "I still think this is a good idea."

Evren wheezed. "It's a terrible idea. Orenlion won't ally with Etherak."

"That's not our problem. Our job is getting the prince to Orenlion and back. What we do in between is help you."

Evren cut him a look as her breathing slowed. He didn't fool her. "You'll fight for his cause, Abraxas. Don't lie to yourself."

His eyebrows furrowed, as if he was trying to pick apart which of his thoughts were true and which comforted her. When he finally spoke, his words were soft and slow, as if he were sounding them out for the first time. "I have given a lot to Etherak. Sorin would say too much."

"He'd be right."

"Perhaps." Abraxas's eyes found the door to their private dining room, where Barrion and the others would be waiting. "But he's going to be an excellent King, should he live to see that day. I'd like to help him, if I can."

She bumped his shoulder with her own, sloshing water over her hand. "And this has nothing to do with trying to redeem yourself?"

He smiled ruefully. "I am far past redemption, and Barrion couldn't give it to me if he wanted to. I will help him, but I will help you first. Come, they're waiting for us."

Before she could mull over his promise, he was pushing her through the door and past the curtains. Their conversation was forgotten.

The gathering night made the candlelit room more cozy than

stuffy. Everyone was seated where she'd left them earlier, although the whole day had passed and Evren knew Sorin and Arke had gone out to see the crater again. Hells only knew where Sol had snuck off to, or if she and Barrion had spent the whole day chatting in the room. She settled down beside Gyda again, noting that everyone else had almost finished their dinner plates.

"Sorry to keep you waiting." She tried to smile.

Barrion waved her off with a soft hand. "No apologies necessary. Lady Solri said you were waiting for someone? I wasn't aware there was a seventh member of your party."

"There isn't." Evren said. "They're more like . . . council, I guess. They give insight."

Sol looked at her expectantly. "Anything?"

Evren shook her head.

Sorin scraped up the last bit of his rice with the crust of his bread. "Honestly, is that a bad thing? I take it as a good sign. Seeing as every time it pops up we have to deal with terrors that no gold can pay off."

Barrion looked puzzled, but every one of the Sols ignored him. After the White Cairn, Evren took Solri's advice and opened up more about the strange figure. Before then she'd been vague, embarrassed, and half-believing she'd dreamt it up. But after Sol saw it, it was more real than ever. And no one in the party liked the idea of a mysterious figure watching their every move.

"All right . . ." Barrion took their silence as an end to the strange conversation. He turned back to Evren hopefully. "I heard you've reconsidered. I'm in your debt if that's true."

Evren tapped her fork against the metal plate before answering. When she started to, Abraxas pointed to her plate. She rolled her eyes but forced down a few bites before swallowing and turning back to Barrion.

"I have," she said hesitantly. "But you should know that the issues I mentioned before haven't changed."

"Which ones?" the prince asked.

Fair enough.

"The Wood itself," she explained.

"Ah." He nodded. "I take it that even with your help, this won't be easy."

"It'll either be extremely easy, or extremely painful. I see no reason to sugarcoat this." She picked apart her bread. The crust crackled under her fingers. "Orenlion itself will be hard to find. My warning that the city might not reveal itself to me still stands. I didn't leave on good terms."

Gyda put her elbows on the table and leaned forward to stare Barrion down. "Which is another problem."

Evren nodded to her. "I have no wish to return to the city, but I do have business in the Wood itself. Once the trail becomes clear, you'll be able to find your way there and we will leave you before you reach Orenlion."

Barrion frowned. "Truly? I do not mean to pry, but what would cause such a rift between you and your people?"

Evren wanted to laugh, but she forced herself to eat her bread instead of playing with it. Once she'd washed that down, she knew she could say anything to Barrion, and he'd take it as the truth and move on. That kind of trusting nature was admirable. It would also fuck him over in Orenlion.

"An arranged marriage." She smiled thinly. "Let's just say I pissed off everyone but my future husband by leaving."

"I see . . ." He steepled his fingers and turned her words over in his mind. He started nodding to himself and humming as if he was exchanging words in an imaginary conversation with himself. Then he folded his hands and smiled at her. "I understand completely. Although you would have my protection if you followed me into Orenlion."

"That's kind, Your Highness, but my presence there will do more harm than good."

"Very well then. To Orenlion and then we part ways. Can I count on your escort back?"

"Assuming we survive the trip in, getting out will be easy." Evren shrugged. "It's about the unexpected, and so long as you know what to expect, the way out is as simple as following a map to Angel's Fall."

Arke chuckled lowly. "Ain't like them damn Fey-infested woods in Terevas. You go in? You don't come out."

"Because of the Fey?" Barrion asked.

"Nah. Mostly the trees. They get pissy and eat ya."

The prince visibly paled. "Ah, well, that's enlightening. No carnivorous trees where we're going, I assume?"

Evren shook her head. "No, but there's plenty more that will kill you. The Deep Wood is old; older than Etherak. Getting lost is easy, but that's true anywhere. A forest that big and ancient, you'll have to deal with a lot of predators. I gave your people a detailed list of what to expect."

"And what should I expect?"

Evren chewed on her beef for a little while before answering. "The biggest threat will be your common pack hunters. Worgs, wolves, and the like. They're smarter than the ones you've dealt with, though. Smart enough to ambush hunters. You might come across the occasional wyvern; in which case you should hope it's an adult and not a juvenile."

"Why?"

"The young ones hunt in packs until they're old enough to realize the others are a challenge. Then they'll eat each other."

"Ah . . ." Barrion took a long drink of his ale.

Evren wasn't stopping, no matter how uncomfortable he was. He needed to be aware, and she didn't care if it scared him. "There are rumors of a dragon in the Wood. She hasn't been seen in a few hundred years, and Orenlion's best scholars are sure she's dead. But it's best to be prepared. She wasn't known for being friendly. The Archdruids of the Wood are powerful, but reclusive and not aggressive unless you threaten their protected territories. Occasionally, smaller trees and shrubbery can come to life and try to kidnap you. They won't eat you, but the witches that also live in the forest might. There are also the spiders."

This time, it was Sol that looked sick. "Spiders?"

Sorin looked at Evren. "I take it these aren't the tiny ones Arke finds and eats, huh?"

"No." Evren shoved her plate aside, and the goblin grabbed it with gravy-slathered fingers. "The spiders in the Wood can get about as big as a horse, although I knew a few hunters that swore they saw them bigger."

"Are the giant spiders friendly?" Sol asked hopefully.

"The spiders have been the only threat to Orenlion's existence for as long as the history books have been written. They're aggressive, to say the least."

"Oh . . ."

Barrion ruffled his hair as if he was trying to shake out his own fear. "Will they be a problem?"

Absolutely.

Only then did Evren think about sugarcoating the truth. Not for Barrion, but for Sol and her friends. The Weavers were terrifying and seemed to have a deep-seated hatred for any other vaguely elven-shaped thing. As a child, she was brought up with horror stories of them crawling into her room at night if she left the window open and taking her to their nest to eat alive. Elves were taught young how to defend themselves from giant spiders and watch for signs that they were walking into their territory. It seemed to go far deeper than a mere predator fighting for food, because even wyverns knew to leave large hunting parties alone. A giant spider would go out of their way to hurt an elf, even if it was suicide.

And, of course, they were terrifying to look at.

"There's a good chance," she admitted. "But I know the signs of their hunting grounds and where they prefer to nest. I should be able to keep us away from them, but that's no guarantee that they won't attack us. They're wild and savage. My elders used to say that they had more rage than a dragon."

"Such rage is usually earned," Barrion said.

"Maybe. But as far as I've read, they've always been like this. Territorial, spiteful, and dangerous. But not unbeatable."

"Very well. I trust you to lead us safely, Lady Evren."

She held her hand up. "Just Evren, please."

He nodded. "Anything else?"

"It's important to remember that this isn't a normal forest. It isn't just big, it's ancient. Not even Orenlion has all of it mapped. It remains the wildest piece of land on this continent. While there won't be any Fey trickery, there's plenty of other things that can kill or harm you. And it's . . . strange."

This time it was Arke who looked up from her old plate and spoke. "Yeah? What 'bout it?"

"For one, it'll be hotter in the Wood. The trees give off a lot of heat. It's nice in the winter but gets hotter than normal around this time of year. Sorry Gyda."

Beside her, the warrior was already scowling. "Everything in the south is hot. This is ridiculous."

Sorin laughed. "You can walk out in the snow nude as the day you were born, but can't stand to be warm?"

"No."

He shook his head, tsking softly. "Someone is going to be cranky the whole trip."

Evren smiled, despite the worry tugging at her chest. She knew the Deep Wood was dangerous because she'd grown up learning how to survive and best those dangers. But listing them out, even just the ones she remembered off the top of her head, was reminding her of how dangerous it could be.

But she wasn't going in blind like Serevadia. And the very air itself couldn't kill like in Direwall. She could deal with monsters.

Evren turned back to Barrion. "We'll need some supplies before we go in. Enough for at least a month's travel."

"Of course, you will have whatever you need."

She blinked at him, confused. "What? No, I meant to just give us some time to get the supplies."

He fixed her with a stare that was either entirely too boyish or bordering on kingly; she couldn't decide which. "Evren, please, this is my quest and you are all my guides. Give me a list of what you need, and what you recommend for my people, and you will have it in the morn."

Arguing felt useless. One look at Abraxas and she knew it was. So, she agreed and quickly scribbled down all the supplies she needed for her party, and his people, as well as recommendations to make their uniforms more comfortable in the forest. He took it and folded it twice before tucking it into his sleeve.

"As I said," he grinned, "by the morn. I will see you all at breakfast."

With a flourish, the prince was gone, and the Wandering Sols sat alone at the table to mull over their sudden and very imminent quest.

"You know," Sorin's voice was a little higher than normal. "I was a lot more excited about this trip before Evren started lecturing us like my old quartermaster."

"What did you in?" Arke rasped. "The spiders?"

"No, she lost me at the shrubs that serve witches."

Abraxas smiled. "Truly? I thought it was the wyverns."

"Those too! Do you know how ridiculous I'll be praying every night for a full-grown wyvern instead of one still in need of a trip to the brothel?"

Gyda laughed and took a long swig of her ale. She finished it and wiped her mouth with her hand. The tankard thudded against the table. "I want to see the dragon."

"The fuck you do!" Sorin squeaked. "That's death, Gyda. Straight ass death. You wouldn't last twenty seconds!"

"I give myself a few minutes in the fight. It would be a glorious death."

Sol was still pale at the far end of the table, nursing her ale and looking as scared as Evren had ever seen her before. "There are spiders, *giant spiders*, and you're worried about a dragon?"

Sorin guffawed. "And you aren't?"

"Gyda will distract it enough for us to get away." Sol jerked her thumb over to the warrior, who was looking more and more thrilled at the idea of facing 'straight ass' death. "The spiders will do us in."

Abraxas patted her shoulder. "Evren won't lead us into a nest, don't worry."

For the first time since she'd come to terms with dying, Evren found herself truly smiling. Not just to trick her friends into thinking she was all right, or to put on a show in front of strangers. But genuinely, warmly, smiling.

"I'm sorry," she said as the table grew quiet. "For being a pain in the ass this whole time."

"Oh, you're always a pain in the ass, Evvie," Sorin said with a grin. "But the apology is nice."

Arke cackled. "Yeah, you didn't think we were gonna let you keep gettin' away with it, huh?"

She sighed. "I suppose not."

Sol leaned over the table towards her. "And don't think for a second you're not still paying for it the entire trip."

Evren froze. "Oh no . . ."

Abraxas's shit-eating grin was a scary mirror image of Sorin's. "That's right, cooking duty."

"No!" she groaned, putting her head in her hands as her friends laughed.

"Every night," Gyda added.

"Until your debt for being a dick is paid in full," Sorin announced proudly, like he was a judge at her trial.

"I'm going to poison all of you," she mumbled into her hands.

"Maybe," she heard Gyda smile, and then felt her warm hand on her back. "But it is a small price to pay for curing you."

The cheerful tone didn't diminish entirely but ebbed away until something like warm contentment settled over the table.

"We've got your back, Evvie," Sorin said.

"I know," Evren said, and smiled in her hands.

5

Barrion had spared no expense with the supplies and was prompt with his delivery. Rations, potions, extra rope, lanterns, enchanted ink and paper for Arke, arrows for Evren. The list went on. And Evren knew from experience that none of it was cheap.

As promised, it arrived the following morn, and they began preparations to leave. In the cool hours of the dawn, Evren tried to quell her restless nerves as she finished putting on her armor. The laces fumbled in her fingers as she tied the bracers down. Already her skin was itching under the armor, like she'd put it on while it was crawling with ants. She wanted the familiar comfort that came with the weight of her armor and found nothing but memories instead.

Her fingers traced the stitching, new and old. The pale blue of the giant door on her right gauntlet, and Alkimos curled on her left pauldron in lavender. On her right pauldron, the sea serpent Mortova mirrored the giant worm. Right below him, a thick band of simple grey circled her bicep. It still hurt to look at, and Evren forced her hand away before she became lost in the memories of the Ashen Bond.

Vox's serene smile before they ripped his heart out. Drystan's pale, dead eyes as Sahar wept.

Evren sucked in a lungful of air and put them out of her mind. It was only slightly comforting to know that Drystan would chastise her for being so sentimental about his death.

A knock came at the door, and Sol peeked her head through the gap. "Ready?"

The dwarf hadn't been able to sleep all night. Either from fear or excitement, Evren couldn't tell. She'd been up and dressed before the dawn and somehow made her sleek black leathers elegant. Her hair had been braided back from her face, a few golden wisps hanging in front of her ears.

"Your hair looks good," Evren said, instead of answering her.

Sol beamed. "Truly?" Her hand went to her braid, smoothing nonexistent fly-aways. "I haven't been able to do anything with my hair for so long. Ever since . . . well, you know."

Evren nodded as Sol's good mood evaporated slightly. Among her people, long hair was a symbol of wealth, noble position, and honor. She'd lost all of that, and her hair, when she'd been framed for conspiring against the King. Evren was glad to see her let it grow. Hopefully, the dwarf had accepted that what she'd done in Dirn-Darahl did not make her any less worthy of her family's honor.

"Do you want me to braid yours?" Sol asked, breaking both of their thoughts on Dirn-Darahl.

"Maybe next time," Evren said with a smile. But the idea of a stiff braid pulling at her throbbing skull didn't sound appealing in the least. She loosely tied it up and off her neck, buckled her quiver onto her back, and took up her bow.

The light wood was well worn. It was smooth in some places but notched and scared in others. Evren hadn't been gentle with it through her adventures, but it showed no signs of cracking. Strong and enduring like the tree that made it. It was going home too.

Evren gripped it tight. "I'm ready. Let's go."

Outside, Angel's Fall was still heavy with sleep and curling mists that glowed golden in the approaching dawn. The air was damp and sweet. There was a strange calmness about it, as if time had slowed to a restful pause to watch them gather at the edge of the Deep Wood.

The shadows of the trees were close enough to cool the spring morning to a shuddering chill. The trunks swelled far past the size of any normal tree and would've taken five or more people to encircle them. Evren knew they only got bigger the further they went in. She tried to see just the awesome beauty in them as she craned her neck up to look up at the towering canopy. Instead, it felt like a hundred looming, disappointed parents watching her slink back home, sick with shame.

Evren looked away.

Barrion had chosen a dozen of his people to follow him to Orenlion. The other dozen were to wait for his return in the village. The soldiers looked naked with their sleeves and armor doctored. Evren recognized the scarred lieutenant among them, as well as the young soldier who had punched her. He avoided her eyes as they came up.

The rest of the Wandering Sols waited at the forest edge. Arke had forgone his cloak, while Sorin stuck stubbornly to his sea-weathered coat. Gyda's great sword gleamed in the early morning light. The new rune on the hilt made the air hum with arcane energy. Abraxas looked every bit himself in his blackened plate armor.

"You're going to bake in that," Sorin told him as they approached.

Abraxas gave him a flat stare. "Sorin, I used this same armor in the desert for many years just fine."

"You sure?" He raised an eyebrow. "Maybe that heat made you all dark and grumpy."

"Among other things," was all the elf said in reply.

"It'll get stuffy, but it shouldn't be enough to burn," Evren said. "Abraxas will be fine."

Sorin scoffed. "We'll see. I give it two days."

Arke grunted from the ground. "Five. He's stubborn."

Abraxas narrowed his eyes. "If I make it to seven, will you leave me alone?"

"No," the duo said in unison.

Gyda nudged Evren gently and jerked her head across the way. She turned to see Barrion striding towards them, his own fine clothes altered to be more comfortable, and his hand resting on the hilt of his sword.

"We're ready when you are." He nodded to Evren. "My people are prepared for whatever monsters lie in wait."

But not for the snakes that you want to ally with, Evren thought bitterly. She nodded anyway.

"Just stay close to us. Follow what I say and do, and don't wander off." She looked at him meaningfully and was a little pleased when he squirmed under her gaze. "If I tell you to run, you need to do so immediately. No hesitation, no questions asked. Got it?"

"Evren, I can defend myself," he said as gently as possible, as if not to upset or offend her.

"Maybe," she admitted. "But steel won't always be able to save you. We can."

Barrion looked over them all, a resigned mask falling over his handsome features before he nodded again. "Of course. I will follow your word from here on out."

It took only a few waves of his hand before Barrion had his dozen soldiers around the Wandering Sols. Many of them eyed Abraxas with barely disguised disgust. Others jumped whenever Gyda moved. None of them had forgotten about the tavern brawl. Hopefully, none of them were stupid enough to start anything like it again.

"I'll tell you as I told your prince." Evren raised her voice, so it rang loud and clear. "My party and I are your guides. If we tell you to turn back, circle around, or force you onto a fresh path, there is a reason for that. Never wander off on your own. Teams of three, at the very least. The Wood isn't always kind to visitors. So, be smart, be quick, and listen to your instincts. If we do that, we'll all make it out."

There was nothing incredibly strong or inspiring about the little speech. When she stopped, she felt out of breath and struggled not to let it show. The soldiers nodded, but most weren't good enough to mask their unease. Why wouldn't they be worried about Evren leading them? She knew she looked sickly; like she couldn't make a hard day of hiking.

Barrion turned back to his people with a kind, dazzling smile. The kind that people instantly warmed to and trusted. He looked at all of them like they were his personal friends. Evren watched them smile back.

"We do this for Etherak," he reminded them. "For the people back home, and the land we've fought to live on. When they write about this moment in the history books, this moment that feels small compared to everything else in the past, they'll write about how it was the beginning of a new chapter for our kingdom. No more food shortages, no more of our people sleeping on the streets. With this alliance, we will bring hope back to our land and make history in the process. And all of you will help me do it."

A hearty chorus of cheers rose in the air. An impressive volume, considering the small group. Barrion stood in the middle of it, beaming like the rising sun.

"He knows how to work a crowd," Sorin muttered.

"He does." Abraxas nodded. "Jealous?"

"Considering the last time I rallied an army I got stabbed in the heart? No. Let prince charming do his thing."

The moment they quieted down; Barrion's soldiers lined up behind the Sols. Barrion himself stood just beside Evren. She could feel the excitement pouring off of him in waves as he stared down the tree line. She wished she shared it.

"Let us make history, shall we?" he said, with that same charming grin.

Evren nodded and took a step towards the ancient forest. With each step, she forced another. One after the other, until the shade turned to green-tinged shadows, and they plunged into the trees.

Let us survive, she found herself praying.

~

THE DEEP WOOD swallowed them whole, sound, souls and all. The wide tree trunks closed like teeth in a massive maw around them and Angel's Fall disappeared entirely. It took only twenty minutes of walking to feel like the village built around the strange crater had never existed.

Leaves, dead and leeching green, blanketed the forest floor. It was wide, and almost cathedral like in its emptiness. The trees towered above everything. Their branches twisted far above their heads, blocking out the sky and making a roof of tangled limbs and shining leaves. The roots mirrored the branches, twisting the carpet of damp, fragrant soil into little nooks and caves around the bases of the tree trunks. There was little in the way of under-growth, but Evren could pick out the creeping vines slithering like parasitic snakes on the trees. Clumps of vibrant mushrooms grew in the moist corners the roots held.

There was a moment, however briefly, that Evren felt like she'd never left. Like she was still a little girl clutching her training bow and darting behind the trees to hide from her father. The Deep Wood hadn't changed. The air, the foliage, the soft humming heat all felt the same. Only the leaves were differ-ent; bright green when she'd left them golden and red.

Her boots made a little sound against the blanket of leaves. The childish part of her wished they crunched instead. She remembered how achingly beautiful autumn was, how the fall of red and orange from so high looked like a rain of fire-colored petals. Autumn left the branches bare. But the dazzling rain of red and gold leaves made Evren want to lay back on the ground and wait for it to come again.

"Don't look too bad." One soldier sniffed behind her. "Don't even need a trail with how far apart these trees are. I can see a hundred feet in every direction."

"And what do you see?" Evren asked without turning around.

The soldier paused for a moment before answering. "Trees, milady?"

"It's Evren," she corrected him. "And that's the problem. Look behind you, behind your friends. Tell me again what you see."

She heard Arke snickering as the soldier did, and a few others followed his action.

"The same, mi—" he caught himself, and coughed. "The same."

"It's easy to get lost here. Everything looks the same, unless you know what to look for." She wasn't looking behind her when she waved him over. A couple of others trailed behind him as she strayed a little farther from her chosen path, close to one tree.

It radiated a warmth, like a massive candle. Not hot enough to burn, but easily noticeable. Already she could smell the sweat from a few of the Etherakian soldiers. Men and women who were used to cold winters and mild, wet summers. Nothing like a constant heat.

She knelt down next to one root, easily as thick as a man. Out of the corner of her eye, she noticed Barrion had joined them and was watching with boyish interest. The rest of the Sols stayed with the remaining soldiers and waited for them.

Evren ran her hand along the top of the root, feeling the bark warm her fingertips. "What do you see when you look at this?"

The soldier, a middle-aged human with a flat nose, frowned

at the root. For a moment, she thought he'd say something obvious. *That's a root, milady. A big one.* Instead, he leaned closer.

"Looks like scuffing," he said. "But it's black. Like it's burned?"

He looked at her for confirmation, and she nodded. "The animals know their way through the Wood. They leave trails. Some you don't want to follow, like this one. This was made by a baby wyvern, who was probably dropped out of his nest to learn how to fly. But there are tracks leading north showing he walked it off."

"So, there's a nest nearby?" Barrion asked.

"Yes." She pointed above them. "It's quiet though. They're out flying and hunting, or else I would've heard them."

"So, this is the wrong way to go," a female soldier said. "How do we know the right way?"

Evren stood up and dusted the soil off her pants. "It's a lot of elimination. We can't go north because the wyvern's territory is north. But even if you didn't know that, you could still find the path forward."

Evren moved past them, pointing to the ground she'd been leading them on. "You see leaves and roots. I see a fresh trail used by many animals, all normal prey for the wyverns that have adapted to avoid them."

"So . . ." the soldier said slowly. "Follow the animals that won't kill you?"

She winced. That was far too simple. Three of the creatures that used this trail could kill a full-grown man. One could do it by simply sneezing venomous mucus, not out of malice, but because it was startled.

"It's not that easy, but yes. Everything here can kill you; you just need to find the greater threats, eliminate their routes, and follow the lesser ones carefully."

"It can't just be elimination," the lieutenant retorted from the primary group. "These nests and trails are all random."

"Are they?" Evren asked. "Or do they unconsciously follow a

pattern set down through the ages, leaving a path for the worthy to follow?"

"It can't be the same," she said. "Wild animals change. They pick up nests, move somewhere else. They migrate and change hunting patterns depending on prey. You can't tell me that every wyvern ever has stayed in that tree."

"I could, and you'd accept it because I'm the only one here who knows these woods," Evren said. "But you're not wrong. Patterns shift and change. The only thing that remains is instinct, and right now you are lacking while the rest of the Wood has it in spades."

Evren stepped away from the wyvern's tree and led everyone back to the group. Gyda waited at the front with a small, almost prideful smile that didn't let up as they started walking again.

"What?" Evren asked.

"You enjoy this," she said.

Evren scowled and wanted to contradict her. But the truth was, she did. The Deep Wood was comfortable. She knew what to expect from it. The smell of moist earth in her nose, the sweet taste of sap on the tip of her tongue, the chattering of far-off animals. No matter the dangers it held, or the city in its folded branches, it felt a little like coming home.

But that was always how the Deep Wood had been to her. It called to her when she was cooped up in her house in Orenlion, when she was deep beneath the earth in Serevadia, and in the white death of the mountain blizzard.

It was also where something had stolen her heart. She could not relax. She would not, until she was face to face with the creature who did it.

~

THE DAY of hiking and avoiding the worst the forest offered put a visible strain on Evren. She was slow to move before the sun had reached its peak. Her wheezing was audible after their first break, and only got worse every mile they traveled. Barrion was kind, and offered her his water, medicine, or even to take up leading, even though he had no earthly idea of which way to go. He stopped offering after the fifth attempt. Or perhaps because Evren seemed to cut their path into circles.

There were no straightforward trails. They weaved and winded between the trees. Sometimes she told them to go in single file, and never utter a peep. Sometimes she backtracked. Near the end of the day, everyone was exhausted and sweaty. Exhaustion dragged at their bones, made even worse by the feeling that they weren't truly going anywhere.

The forest didn't seem to change. She knew that and was used to it. But she could see the frustration in the soldiers' eyes. Even her friends looked weary and often glared at the trees. But their eyes lightened when they saw her leading. Their trust was all that kept her moving.

They set up camp before the sun went down. The dwindling rays of sunset turned the shadows of the trees into grasping monsters. The echoes of bugs filled the air. Evren showed them how to make a small fire and keep it from catching any of the surrounding foliage on fire. Before long, the sun had set, the tents were up, and she had cooked her first apology meal over the fire.

They spared Barrion and his soldiers. Her party had to endure what she made from their limited rations.

"You know . . ." Sorin picked at his bowl. "I didn't think you could make rice porridge any blander. But you did!"

Evren blinked at him over the fire. "I used salt."

"I know I packed more spices than that."

"That's all I know how to use!" she protested.

Sol elbowed Sorin. "Don't be rude. She could let you starve."

"Fine!" He shoveled more food in his mouth. Complain as he may, he winked at Evren. She smiled a little in return.

Evren ate her food, which, she could admit, was plain and chewy. But it kept her from thinking about her aching body, and she wolfed it down. Maybe she could hunt tomorrow and use some of Sorin's Vasa spices. She might have time to fish, depending on if they crossed the river or not. It was hard to tell where in the Wood she had led them. The only comforting part was that location didn't really matter when it came to finding Orenlion. The city could appear tomorrow, or a few weeks from now.

They gave their bowls to Abraxas, who volunteered to clean them for the night.

"So . . ." he said, settling back down with his rag and water. "All in favor of Evren's punishment ending?"

"She's suffered enough." Arke snickered.

Evren threw a handful of leaves at him and laughed for the rest of the night.

~

HER TENT WAS DARK, and the hour was well past midnight when something forced her eyes open. Evren stifled a groan, rubbing the grit that had already begun to gather in the corners of her eyes as she sat up. She wanted to go back to sleep, but she wasn't sure what had woken her, other than her instincts, and they were rarely wrong.

Her body thrummed with the fever, echoing the heat of the tree roots they'd camped next to. She pushed away the discomfort and forced herself to listen. The sounds of the forest were all normal, coupled with the crackling fire and snoring people. She waited one minute, then five, and then seven before huffing.

Nothing sounded different. She knew that Gyda and Sol had taken watch with a couple of Barrion's soldiers. The rotation meant they'd be changing soon. She had no reason to be up yet since her friends wanted her to sleep off her illness as much as possible.

But she couldn't shake the feeling that something was wrong, and it pulled her from her bedroll and out of the tent with her bow and arrows in hand.

The fire was a dim glow of embers against the black blanket of night. There was little difference between the trees and the shadows in between, and Evren picked her way forward carefully. Across the camp she could hear murmurs of conversation, but no one on watch seemed to notice her. No one seemed out of place either. She put her back to the fire and forced her eyes to adjust without the memory of the flames obscuring her.

She blinked until, slowly, the forest floor in front of her became a little clearer. Black on grey, instead of black on black. And a figure was moving away from camp, deeper into the forest. They were stumbling over roots, cursing quietly but driven forward.

No forest creature would bumble around like that. She rubbed some life back into her face and started after them.

It wasn't easy for Evren to navigate the floor, either. With little light, there was just a thick blanket of darkness at her feet. But the roots gave off heat as well. Heat enough for her to feel before they tripped her. In the dark, she followed the chill, and was gaining on the figure.

It took no time at all to recognize the broad shoulders and short stature of Barrion's lieutenant. And the woman was determined to get farther from camp. The closer Evren got, the more she saw how frantic she was. How desperate.

Evren's blood went cold under her feverish skin.

"Lieutenant?" she called ahead of her. Her voice echoed roughly through the forest. She winced, imagining every predator in a mile radius turning towards her.

The lieutenant didn't answer her. She didn't stop either. Instead, she picked up her pace.

Evren bit back a loud curse and shouldered her bow. Her hands in front of her, she felt heat moments before her palms met rough bark. She launched herself over the root that was hip height and broke into a jog.

"Lieutenant!" she hissed between her teeth.

If the woman heard her catching up, she didn't let on. Evren was resigned to a full run until she saw her stop in her tracks. She barely stopped in time, so she didn't run her over.

Her head throbbed, her muscles burned, and if it was daylight, she knew her vision would be blurred to the point of uselessness. But she struggled to calm her breathing and grabbed the soldier's shoulder. The other woman didn't even fight her as she swung her around.

"What the hells are you doing?" she hissed at the woman. She tried not to lean on her, but her body was swaying, anyway.

Evren watched the lieutenant's face shake from side to side. She looked back the way she'd been heading, the whites of her eyes gleaming. "I don't understand. I thought I saw . . ." she snapped her mouth shut and looked towards Evren. "Someone was watching us. I saw them!"

Evren shushed her harshly and squeezed her shoulder to get the point across. Not a peep came out of the other woman while Evren waited to hear any stalking predators. When she heard none, she sighed in relief.

"Most likely, yes."

She shuddered, her eyes darting back to the trees. "And you're just fine with that?"

The truth was quite the opposite. Evren was terrified of someone or something watching them as they slept. But it would do no good to chase after it, or feed it fear.

"There are many curious things in the Wood. Often, they're content to watch and leave so long as you are." Evren shook the lieutenant's shoulder until the woman looked back at her. "Don't go wandering off, especially at dark. Not everything here is malicious, but plenty is."

A shaking breath left the woman's body. "I fucking hate this place," she murmured. "Nowhere is safe."

"It will be," Evren said.

"How?" She didn't seem to believe her.

"When you stop feeding it fear." Evren turned her back towards camp. The orange glow of the fire flickered on the trees; a lot farther than she thought they'd gone. "Come on, I'll walk you back."

As they trudged through the roots and fallen limbs, the silence was tense between them. Evren's own ragged breathing barely broke it, and the lieutenant's boots snagged on every root and branch. Evren tried not to show how badly her jog affected her, but she knew the other woman was judging in silence. Until the lieutenant finally sighed and looked over at her in the dark.

"My name isn't lieutenant," she said.

"I don't know your name." Evren coughed through her words. Her lungs loosened their vice grip and let more air in.

Another heavy pause, and then, "Mira Kester."

"Evren Hanali." Evren smiled, even though she was sure Mira wouldn't return it or even see it.

"Thanks for saving my ass," Mira said. "But let's leave it at that."

"Considering you broke a table with my back, it's only fair you pay me back."

The fire caught Mira's startled eyes. "What do you want?"

Such distrust, Evren thought. *The Wood will snap her in half if she stays like this.*

"Follow me up front tomorrow," she said. "I'll teach you what I know."

"Why?" She sounded almost offended at the offer.

"So you can relax," Evren spelled out. "The Wood preys on the most obvious. Its animals will feed on your fear."

"And the only way to stop being afraid is to learn." Mira pursed her lips. They got to the edge of camp and the firelight caught her scars. "Fine. One day, unless you're not bullshitting us. Then every day."

"Whatever it takes."

Mira nodded and didn't say another word as she crept back to her tent. Evren watched her go and waited until she was sure

Mira wouldn't sneak back out again. Then, as she was turning to go back to her own tent, she stopped.

Her skin prickled, like she was being watched. Her mind immediately went to Keres, even though she knew they were down in Terevas with Sahar. She turned around, back to the darkness she'd walked so easily through before.

There, by the edge of camp and just in the shadows, was a cloaked figure. Nothing about this one was like the one that Evren had seen before. This one had no light inside its hood. She saw claws on its long fingers. She watched it for as long as it watched her, before it turned away and disappeared into the Wood.

6

___

"**W**hat in Haphion's glorious knickers is that?"

Mira's rough voice grated on Evren's ears. She winced, but ignored the older woman. Three days of traveling with her at the helm beside Evren made it a little easier to endure her ever evolving string of curses.

Instead, Evren turned her attention back to the thing that definitely did not belong in anyone's knickers, glorious or not. The tip of her arrow picked up the delicate string of silk from its fallen spot next to the tree. In the leaf-dappled sunlight, it shone silver. It was old, barely a sliver of a web that would've been more massive. But as a light breeze lifted it into the air, the sticky material clung stubbornly to the shaft of the arrow. Evren frowned as she picked it off. The sticky silk on her fingers made her shiver.

"Nest nearby?" Abraxas asked lowly, so none of the soldiers would overhear and panic. Mira was the only one who heard him, and she narrowed her hazel eyes at him.

Evren stood up and put her arrow back into her quiver. "Maybe."

Mira snorted. "Maybe? What's that supposed to mean?"

"It means the silk is old," she told her. "Maybe a year. It's hard to tell. But it's only a piece, not the full thing."

"Could something have gotten out of the web and dragged that piece here?" Abraxas asked hopefully. Pieces of onyx-colored hair stuck to his brow, slick with sweat. He still refused to take off his armor.

Evren hesitated. She wanted to say yes and agree with him. But her instincts told her no. Even wyverns were victims of the webs, all their burning venom couldn't get them free. The silk was as strong as iron and didn't readily let go of its victims. But Evren saw no other signs of a nest.

"Maybe," she murmured, to which Mira groaned at but didn't argue. She turned to the lieutenant. "What does your gut tell you?"

Mira folded her bare arms. A unity band was tattooed around her biceps, the dark ink stark against her pale, flushed skin. "You're asking me what I think?"

"I haven't been dragging you with me these past few days for the conversation."

She huffed and looked down at the abandoned silk. Her eyes darkened. "This is one sign the spiders might be nearby."

"Yes."

Mira's eyes combed through the surrounding forest. She was looking for more glittering strands of silk, maybe even a telltale darkening of the wood Evren had told her to look out for. The spiders left the forest darker and colder in their territory. When she found none, she started chewing her lip.

"Don't see anything else ahead. But say we avoid this?"

Evren shrugged her aching shoulders. "We backtrack. Cut through some worg territory instead."

Mira sucked on her teeth. "Don't like worgs."

"You'll like the spiders even less."

"Fair enough." She shrugged. "Play it safe and deal with the worgs. Or risk it and go through what might not be bug territory. What's your plan?"

Evren's current plan was to find the nearest stream and dunk herself in the water. Her skin felt like she was on fire. But she breathed through it and rolled her shoulders back. "I'm leaning towards risking it. If there is a nest, we see the signs and turn back before they catch on to us."

"But you're not sure." Mira pressed.

Evren shook her head. "No."

Abraxas stepped between the two women as if to stop an argument. They were two days past that, but Mira recoiled a few steps from him. Her nose wrinkled, as if he stank of something worse than dirty divine knickers.

"Let's leave it up to the prince, then," he said. "This doesn't seem like a deadly decision."

"It could be," Evren pointed out, but he was already waving Barrion over.

The heat was as kind to Barrion as it had been to the rest of his soldiers. Which was to say, not kind at all. His dark hair was perpetually damp, and his thick shirt clung to his sweat-soaked skin at all hours of the day. But his smile was serene as he approached, as if he wasn't at all uncomfortable. Evren wasn't even sure she knew what comfort felt like anymore, let alone pretend she felt it.

"How do our odds fare at these crossroads?" he asked lightly.

Mira grunted but stood up straighter in his presence. "We found a piece of a web."

His red cheeks paled visibly, but his tone remained the same. "Ah, I see."

"It's old, according to Evren." Abraxas bowed his head slightly. "Only a piece that might've snagged on an escaped meal."

"Or it could be the leftovers of a remodeled nest." Barrion raised his eyebrows at Evren in a question. She nodded.

"Could be," She agreed. "But the trees ahead don't show any signs of more."

"So, what are our options?" he asked.

Mira scuffed her boots against the tree root nearly as tall as she was, as if the silk were there and clinging to her. "We could go back and take on the worgs to play it safe."

Barrion frowned. "You said the worgs would be aggressive."

Evren shrugged. "Worgs are always aggressive, but they're simple. Far easier to deal with than the spiders. Their territory wouldn't be as large, either."

Barrion rubbed his eyes. "And the other option is taking our chances with the path ahead."

Evren and Mira exchanged looks. "Yes."

Mira added a "Your Highness" at the end of her confirmation.

"The choice is yours, Your Highness," Abraxas said. "Whatever path you choose could be dangerous, but you have good men and women at your side. And the Wandering Sols have sworn to get you through this alive, no matter the enemy."

Barrion looked less and less sure as he stared at the silk on the ground. No doubt he was imagining all the horrible things Evren had told him, made worse by his fear. And the pressure of leading his people through it all. He caught Evren's eyes for a moment, soft storm-grey against feverish black, before he nodded and stepped back.

"We'll circle back. Worgs we can deal with and maybe get some fresh meat. I'd rather not chance the spiders."

Mira gave him a curt nod. "I'll spread the word." And then she marched off to the rest of her people.

Abraxas grasped Evren's shoulder. "It's the safe choice."

"It is." she agreed. But her eyes lingered on the silk, anyway. It was eerily beautiful, but fear crawled up her throat. A fear that had been ingrained in her since birth, which only ebbed as she turned her back on the silk.

Somehow, a dragon felt easier to face than a Weaver.

~

TRAINING MIRA TURNED out to be one of the better ideas Evren had had in months. Three hours deep into worg territory, the Wandering Sols were sent to scout ahead. If they could avoid the pack completely, all the better. If not, both Mira and Evren agreed the Sols would be the best fit to fight off the beasts.

Mira would lead Barrion and her people behind Evren. A simple task, since Evren made sure to clearly mark her trail. Once they were past danger, they'd meet back up again. Agonizingly cautious, but necessary when dealing with the sole heir of a massive kingdom.

Evren kept a quick but stumbling pace forward, her eyes swimming with green-tinged sunlight and her fingers tight around her bow. She was so focused on looking for stalking worgs she didn't even notice Gyda coming up beside her until the warrior spoke.

"Distract me."

Evren startled, not bothering to cover up the fact that Gyda had surprised her. When Evren looked up at her, she found Gyda scowling like a storm cloud taken form, and was pouring almost enough sweat to imitate one. Her scarf was dark and damp around her hair. Her scabbard slid back and forth along sweat-slick skin, and she fumbled with the strap to ease the discomfort.

"What?" Evren asked numbly as she tore her eyes away from Gyda.

"Distract me," she growled. "I can't breathe in this heat. Thinking about it makes it worse."

Evren felt a twinge of regret. This was far from the icy cold Gyda had grown up in. Even Evren was hot, so she couldn't imagine how the warrior felt, trapped under her sword and scabbard, with the still hot air pressing against her skin and not letting up.

"What do you want?"

Gyda grunted and shook her fists out. "Tell me about the dragon."

Evren smiled. It was always the dragon with her. "Orenlion called her the Storm of the Wood, because of the destruction she caused."

"I like the 'the' in the front. Like a living weapon."

"Well, she was." Evren marked a tree in passing, making sure it was eye height for Mira. "No one knows why she was bent on destroying the Wood. Madness, revenge, entertainment; your guess has as much weight as the best historian. All we know is that she nearly destroyed the Wood, to the point that the Archdruids were willing to intervene."

"Did they?"

"Not in time. The story goes the Storm held Orenlion hostage, furious that the elves were allowed to flourish in the same forest the Archdruids banned from her. Armies were sent to slay her, and none returned. Elite warriors, clever hunters, and powerful mages were all made champions, and all fell to the dragon. It seemed like none could stand against her and win."

Gyda wiped her brow. Evren could see a bit of the tension leaking out of her bare shoulders. "Who killed her then?"

"We don't know."

Gyda shot her an irritated look. "What do you mean?"

"I mean that the final warrior was a stranger. Not of Orenlion. Apparently, the haze of smoke and ash made it difficult to see who it was. All the historians saw was a lone warrior standing against the Storm, sword in one hand and dagger in the other. When the smoke cleared and the Archdruids rebuilt the forest, there was nothing remaining of the Storm or the warrior."

The two walked in silence for a bit, the rest of their friends trailing behind. Gyda seemed to chew on the story, her scowl more thoughtful than agitated now.

"That's a shit way to end the story," she finally grumbled.

Evren choked out a laugh. "That's the only end I know. How would you have it?"

"The warrior emerges victorious, of course. The dragon's

head in hand, plenty of fresh scars to remember the fight. And no dagger. That's a ridiculous way to fight a dragon."

"You've never fought any," Evren pointed out. "How would you know?"

"It's a ridiculous way to fight anything."

Before she'd even realized it, Evren's smile was sticking. Her cheeks were getting sore already, but it felt good. A soft breeze rustled the leaves overhead and Gyda's eyes partially closed in bliss. The cooler air was easier to breathe, even for Evren, and she let herself relax.

The only sounds were birds overhead, the chittering of small animals in the trees, Gyda's heavy breathing—soft and comforting—and a few feet away Sol and Abraxas muttering lowly to each other, with Arke butting in now and then with his own loud opinion.

Sorin was the loudest of them, even when he wasn't really talking. He was huffing and grumbling under his breath from all the way in the back. She heard him kick a pile of leaves, and then dig his heels into the ground to stop.

"Aw . . ." he said. "Aren't you cute?"

Great, Evren thought. *He's going to try and adopt another squirrel.*

"Such a cute widdle thing." Sorin's baby voice got ridiculously high pitched. "Are you hungry? Did your momma leave you alone?"

"Sorin," Evren called without stopping. "Leave it alone."

"But it's a baby!"

"Don't care."

"He's all alone. Look! he's shivering. C'mere little guy, I'll keep you warm. Such a fuzzy little puppy. You're so cute."

Evren turned around just as Gyda mumbled a curse. Together, they rounded a trunk to see just what Sorin had fallen in love with.

He was on the ground, sitting with a pile of dark fur in his lap. The puppy had a long snout he'd grow into and pointed ears, just flopping down at the tips. Tall, muscular shoulders, and large floppy paws. His black tongue lolled happily from his maw as Sorin cooed at him.

"Sorin," Evren said slowly. "Put it down."

Sorin waved the worg puppy's paw at her. "Come on, Evvie. Can you really let that face go hungry?"

"A worg puppy has an entire pack to feed it."

Sorin froze the worg's paw mid-wave. The pup was small but getting up into his adolescence. His face was far too close to Sorin's for her liking. Likely, the only reason he hadn't gnawed Sorin's thumb off was because he knew Sorin was offering food. Evren could see the hip bones protruding under his dense fur. Sorin had promised it food. It was waiting.

"Sorin!" Evren snapped. "Let him go."

He nodded and scooped the pup out of his lap. It curled its lip into a snarl, but did nothing else as he put it down and hurriedly got to his feet. The pup snapped at his boots, and he yelped, skittering away.

"What's wrong with him?" Sorin asked.

"You promised him food and then denied him."

"He understood me?"

"The ones born in this Wood do." Evren cocked her head, watching as the young worg raised his hackles and made himself look bigger. He growled at Arke, who didn't pay him any mind. Sol and Abraxas were waiting on Evren's word. "He's starving. And small. He should be bigger than this by spring." He only came up to Evren's knee, even puffed up.

"Why would his pack neglect him?" Gyda asked.

"They wouldn't." The answer was simple. Worgs were many things, but above all, they were dutiful parents. They would feed him first and they would never let him wander alone.

Evren's mouth felt as dry as the air in Vernes. She couldn't swallow enough to make her voice sound normal. "Something killed the pack. We need to leave."

Everyone nodded, not commenting on her cracked voice,

and started to move out. But Sorin stayed rooted to the spot, staring at the worg pup.

"We can't leave him." He insisted. "He'll die without us."

Evren winced. "Sorin, he has to stay."

"Why?"

"He doesn't belong with us. He's wild."

"I can take care of him," Sorin insisted. "Evren, come on. You can't leave a starving animal to die. Not one so young."

She shook her head. "We don't have time for this. We need to leave now."

"Then we leave *with* the pup."

"No, he's going to—"

Gyda drawing her blade shut them both up. The air around the great sword sizzled and shimmered with magical energy. Evren didn't have time to wonder why the blade was out. Gyda was shoving her closer to Sol, Abraxas and Arke.

The Sols huddled together. Abraxas drew his own blade and pulled Sorin away from the pup and to them. He barely protested. But the pup turned towards the tree line, teeth bared and long brown hair raised up sharply along his spine. He let out a growl, as fierce as a starved puppy could force, towards the seemingly empty trees.

And the trees growled back.

Evren nocked an arrow as the pup ran whimpering to Sorin and settled between his legs. She watched the trees, and her blood turned sluggish as dark, hunched forms on four legs melted from behind the tree trunks. They were massive by worg standards. Large enough to give Gyda pause. Evren wasn't surprised; a big forest meant bigger than normal predators, and these she was used to. But there was something different about these worgs. The way their fur hung off of them at odd angles, the way their eyes were glazed white as if they were blind, and their muzzles were stained with grey-tinged saliva. Tendrils of white wormed their way from under their matted fur into the air.

"I think we found his pack," Abraxas said. "Perhaps we give him back?"

"He's terrified of them!" Sorin hissed.

"So am I," Sol flashed her daggers in the sunlight. She turned around and elbowed Evren. "More behind us. Is this normal behavior?"

Evren floundered. Her head felt heavy and fuzzy, and all her thoughts weren't enough. All she could smell in the air was decay. It made her stomach roil.

"No," she finally gasped. "Something's wrong with them."

An illness? A parasite? The white tendrils weren't something she was familiar with. If so, why wasn't the pup affected? There wasn't time for questions. The worgs were pressing closer.

"Aim for the eyes!" was all Evren had time to say before the worgs attacked.

They leapt simultaneously, coordinated beyond the measure she knew they were capable of. Evren shot an arrow clean through the eyes of one with rotting teeth. The arrow's shaft dug deep into the skull. The worg stumbled and fell flat on the ground.

Beside her, Gyda's blade cut the head clean off a leaping worg. Cool, congealed blood rained over Evren. She dodged out of the way of the falling body.

Arke's magic floated in glowing runes around him. His clawed fist, coated in the ash of his spent spell paper, punched up. A wave of air hit them like a wall, but Evren and her friends stayed on their feet. Arke's wind knocked the worgs back. One slammed into a tree, and its skull cracked against the bark.

The air was a flurry of leaves and blood as Sol and Abraxas leapt to guard Arke's back. Sol darted underneath gaping maws and blood-matted paws to carve open bellies. Abraxas took off limbs and planted himself between the predators and the goblin.

Sorin's thin blade was like a flash of lightning as he lashed out at any that came near him and the pup. He cut the tendons to one worg, and it fell at his feet. Before he could finish it, the puppy let out a fierce howl and started tearing at the exposed neck of the worg.

The swirl of leaves caught Evren's eye as she shot down another beast. She and Gyda were back-to-back and inching ever closer to Arke and Sorin. Arke was casting another spell, the wind around them tearing at her hair. Evren's next shot went wide as the windstorm snatched the arrow.

She panted and squinted against the leaves and wind. Sorin had nearly fallen with the pup running between his legs and had three worgs pressing him back. Sol was covered in blood and barely dodging snapping jaws. Abraxas's shield was dented with the bite of a worg, its head still impaled by his sword.

Arke burned two more sheets of paper. "This one's gonna hurt!" he barked. The warning was clear; find cover.

She couldn't make it to the trees, not with so many of the pack still standing. Evren figured dead weight was better than nothing, and Gyda thought the same.

"Go!" she roared.

Evren ducked under one of Gyda's swings. The first worg she'd taken down laid a few feet away, the arrow still deep in his skull. The leaves tore at her feet and hair, and she slid on the blood-soaked ground behind the worg's dead body. It smelled thick with rot, and she gagged.

The next blast of air was sharp enough to leave Evren's ears ringing and push her dead worg a foot back by sheer force. She barely kept herself from being pinned down by the dead weight.

Panting, she pushed herself back up. The sounds of fighting were dull in her ears, but not gone. Her eyes fixed on the arrow in the worg's skull. Still good from what she could tell. She reached out for it, her fingers curling around the fletching and yanking it out.

The worg's jaws suddenly snapped around her arm. She bit back a scream as copper flooded her mouth and tried to pull away. But all that did was tear its teeth through her flesh and grind against her bones. She didn't even have time to savor the sudden clarity pain gave her before the previously dead worg pinned her to the ground.

One of its eyeballs was dangling out of its socket, useless, with the gaping wound tunneling all the way to its brain.

It should be dead. I'm so fucked.

The heavy paws on her chest cracked her bones, and Evren sucked in gasping breaths against the sparks of pain. It hadn't let go of her arm, and the wound was stinging with the foulness in its mouth. The used arrow slipped from her bloody fingers, and she caught it with her other hand. Then she shoved it through its neck.

All it did was growl around her arm in response, its one good eye seething with the hatred that was earned, not born.

And then, as if startled and scolded, it jumped off her. She cried out, its lock on her arm carrying her into a sitting position until it dropped that too. She clutched her bleeding arm and watched as all the worgs suddenly stopped fighting. Their eyes looked at nothing, but their ears folded back in fear. Even the ones Evren knew to be dead got up. The ones who cracked their skulls and spines against the trees got up on wobbly legs. Intestines and inner organs fell from the worgs Sol had disemboweled. Even Gyda's beheaded beasts started getting up and wandering back to the trees they came from.

Evren's eyes followed them as they stared to leave, as if called away. Her eyes found a cloaked figure. Claws for hands stretched out, grasping vines tangled between pale fingers and into the tattered cloak. In the light of day, she could see moss and mushrooms growing on its shoulders. The strange white tendrils curled like a mantle and left little puffs of spores in the sun. The hood was too deep to see their face, but Evren knew they were looking at her. Her blood felt cold against her skin.

One by one, the worgs melted into the Wood. The figure lingered and then stepped back. The tree swallowed it whole and then the Wood was empty and quiet as a graveyard.

7

The small creek they rested at was picturesque. Any other time, the sound of rushing water would relax them. The light breeze smelling of damp earth and sun-warmed rocks would put them at ease. But the cold water served only to wash the blood and spores from their bodies. Sorin had the unfortunate luck of landing inside one of the worgs during the fight and was now completely naked and submerged in the creek, trying to coax the worg pup in with him.

The worg didn't move from his warm rock on the bank and watched Sorin with unblinking black eyes. His jaw was damp from where Sorin had thoroughly rinsed it of bad blood.

The rest of the Sols were littered down the bank. They'd all checked themselves for signs of the same strange mushrooms that had infected the worgs, and found none. Abraxas was cleaning his armor and cupping cool water on the nape of his neck. Sol looked ready to dive into the water herself. Her blond hair was red with dried blood. Gyda found some relief from the heat by rolling her trousers up and dipping her bare feet into the water. The smiles shared between them all were stiff, as they always were after a battle where they weren't sure if they won or not.

No one had talked about the figure in the trees yet.

One of Evren's bracers was ruined. The strips of leather had been sticking to her bloody flesh and peeling them off took time. She tossed the gauntlet aside and ripped off the rest of her shredded sleeve. It felt good to free her skin a little, but the relief was nothing compared to the gaping wound on her forearm. She took the time to rinse it in the stream, watching the water run red and then brown before clear again. She shivered as she found pieces of already growing mushrooms in the wound and dug them out one by one. The pain was jarring but refreshing. She was shaking by the time she was done. It wasn't her worst wound, but it would leave a mass of scar tissue on her arm.

"Another scar," she murmured and shook her arm out of the water. The blood crept back through the gashes, but slower and sluggish now.

"Adds to your charm," Arke said and handed her a roll of gauze.

She slowly wrapped the ripped flesh up with Arke's help. Once it was tied and secured, she could see the red starting to stain the bandages. He handed her a glistening red potion, and she drank it all without tasting it. The warm itch of her flesh knitting back together barely registered in her mind. The cracked ribs at least popped when they healed. When she looked up, she caught Gyda watching her, and flashed the empty bottle to put her worries at ease. The warrior looked away.

"I don't have any charm, Arke."

Before Arke could say anything, a large splash rained water on them. Sorin cried out as Sol broke the surface of the water, laughing.

"Naked dwarf! There's a naked dwarf in my stream!"

Sol cupped some water in her hands and threw it at his face. "Says the naked human in *my* stream."

Abraxas looked at them with tired eyes. "Children, behave or you'll see a worse sight."

Sorin snorted. "Don't be so hard on yourself. Your ass might be lacking, but I'm sure the rest of you is fine."

"I meant Arke."

Arke cackled. "Ain't no one want to see me naked!"

"As your best friend, I'm inclined to believe you, buddy." Sorin shook water from his dreads. He turned to Sol. "Keep your grubby little hands on that side of the creek, yeah?"

"Jalaa's sweet arse, I am! Calm down. You're not my type, anyway."

"Excuse you! I am everyone's type."

Evren smiled a ghost smile at their bickering. She dipped her ripped sleeve into the water and cooled her neck, sighing softly. "It's good to see them like this again."

Arke grunted in response. "Didn't think he'd smile again."

"I didn't think he'd *genuinely* smile again. Or Sol. You saw she's grown out her hair?"

He nodded. "Yeah. Finally lettin' that wound heal, it seems. Not that I understand dwarves and their honor shit."

She gave him a long look. "She killed her King, Arke. I can imagine that goes against everything she believes in."

"Everything she used to believe in." He held up one claw to correct her. "I don't understand much 'bout her, but I understand why. She saw an old ass who couldn't lead, standin' next to the bitch that ruined her life. He let that happen. She did her people a favor."

"She can't go home because of it," Evren said softly. "She doesn't feel worthy. And I know she misses her life there, her home. She's the only one of us that wants to go back, I think."

"Yeah." Arke cut her a glare. "Gettin' you here almost had me prayin' like Abraxas. Which is dumber than shit, because we talked 'bout this. You takin' advice and fuckin' usin' it."

Evren started rubbing her temple with her good arm. "Are you still angry with me about that?"

"Damn straight I am. You ain't stupid, but you've been actin' it lately. And not just stupid, but different. A few months ago, you wouldn't have hesitated to help that pup. Today, you told Sorin to leave it behind."

Evren spared a glance at the worg pup. The sunlight made his softer puppy fur stand out from the brown, courser adult fur he was growing out. His mane was still fuzzy and grey. After Sorin had fed him, he'd stuck by their side. He probably would stay with them, seeing how his pack had ended up.

"It would've been the smart choice normally," Evren said. "The pack would've followed us if he took the pup."

"But he was starvin'." Arke jabbed a finger at her. "And it was Sorin, not you, who wanted to feed 'em. You see how that's different, right?"

Evren let out a heavy sigh and closed her eyes. She stuck to her decision, even if everyone else ignored it. She didn't feel guilty. But she heard Gail's voice in her head.

You need your heart back. Before you die. Or before you do heartless things.

"I'm getting worse," she murmured.

"No shit," Arke replied.

Evren opened her eyes, blinking back the tears that came with the bright sun reflecting from the water. She drew her knees up and rested her chin on them. "I saw that figure with the worgs before."

The tapping of Arke's nails on the stones was rhythmic and soothing. "Mhmm. When?"

"A few nights ago. Lieutenant Kester was following it out of camp in the middle of the night. I walked her back, but it was watching us."

"Sure it's the same one?"

She nodded.

He sighed. "Could be what got your heart. You talked 'bout witches before, and that sounds like their kind of shit. Think this is one?"

She shrugged helplessly. "I thought so at first. But I've never seen one take over a worg pack like that. And the way they all just got up again . . ."

"Kinda reminds me of Direwall." He grunted. "Ain't the same magic. Don't even feel like magic. But yeah, I gotcha."

The sun was past its peak. The water glittered like diamonds as Sorin and Sol splashed each other and laughed. Abraxas watched on, the worg pup pacing between him and Gyda. He smiled easily, and it made him look younger in the golden light. Like someone who wasn't carrying the weight of a thousand innocent souls on his shoulders. And Gyda, despite her tight smile and grip on her sword, looked beautiful with the water casting blue reflections on her face. A strand of her dark red hair fell from her scarf and brushed her jawline softly in the calm breeze.

And yet, it felt like Evren was seeing it through a frosted window. The sunlight didn't feel good on her. The water wasn't as refreshing, nor the air as sweet. This golden memory didn't feel like hers to be a part of.

"I think that figure is the one behind your shit," Arke said. "Or knows somethin' if it's been watchin' us."

"Maybe," she said. It was a good theory. A solid one. She should feel something about it, right? Desperation, excitement, maybe even anger? She felt nothing at all.

"I ain't gonna let you die," he mumbled, so no one could hear him.

And Evren smiled. Back in Direwall, those words had felt like hope. Now it just felt like the beginning of a very long goodbye.

～

THE SUN WAS TURNING the Wood orange when Evren realized she was going to have to go find Barrion's group. They'd left an obvious trail just in case, marking trees and digging ruts into the dirt. But after spending the afternoon by the creek waiting and seeing no sign of them, Evren was starting to worry.

Had the worgs gotten to them? The figure who seemed to command them? Had Mira gotten lost? Or had something worse happened?

Whatever the threat or reason, the party took no time getting ready. Sorin's and Sol's clothes were still damp from being washed. Evren had taken both sleeves off her shirt completely and just left her cuirass on. Everyone else looked like the battle hadn't changed them.

"We'll spread out and cover more ground." Evren said. "You might lose sight of each other, but you'll be in hearing range, especially to me and Arke. Whistle or call out often."

Sorin raised his hand. "So, possibly an idiotic question, but . . . what happens if we don't find them?"

"We will," Evren said, with more confidence than she felt.

"We shouldn't have split up," Abraxas said.

"It was a solid plan." Sol patted his elbow. "They shouldn't have gotten lost. But we'll find them."

They spread out, only a tree or two apart, but enough to make Evren feel like she was alone. The orange rays of light dipped into inky shadows as she took the trail forward. Up roots, down little valleys between trees. After five minutes, she whistled and got a chorus of whistled in return. And one howl of imitation. They passed the battlefield reeking of blood and rot. Evren put markers on all the trees just in case. But with every whistle check in, her hope was dying. There was no sign of Barrion, Mira, and their rest of their team. They weren't that far behind them. They couldn't have gotten that lost.

Another halfhearted whistle as the sun crept closer to the horizon. Another five responses. How long before Evren called it quits for the night, claiming they'd pick up the search in the morning, when she knew deep down that their lost charges wouldn't last the night if they were in trouble?

She gave herself five more check ins before she'd make that call.

Her arm was sore and throbbing as she climbed up another root. Cool, damp air tickled her exposed skin. It did not surprise her to find the ghost waiting for her up top. She didn't give it a passing glance as she slid back down.

Her boots thudded on the forest floor, and she whistled again. All five whistles back. She walked on; the ghost clinging to her side.

"It's a bit early for you, isn't it?" she asked irritably.

It gave her one of Viggo's trademark smiles. "It's been a while since we talked. You're never alone."

"You never want the others to see you." She shook her head and kicked some leaves up. "That's very trustworthy of you."

"You're trying to live. I'm proud."

She bit back a frown. "I'm doing it for my friends."

"Maybe start acting like it, then."

She cut him a glare out of the side of her eye. "Can you not right now? I'm a little busy."

If a ghost could wrinkle his nose in disgust, he did it well. It looked a lot like Viggo when he did. "You won't find them, Evren."

"Well, if I'm supposed to be acting more like myself, giving up really isn't in the cards, is it?"

"You're optimistic, not a fool. At least you used to be."

"I was fool enough to trust you," she retorted and whistled again.

Five more whistles back.

He was silent for a while. Evren crossed another mass of roots before looking at him. The hurt in his eyes was plain as day.

"Don't tell me I hurt your feelings," she said. "You're the one who lied to me."

"Hiding certain truths isn't lying, Evren," he said coldly. "I did it with no intentions of malice."

"And in the end, it still fucked me and my friends over."

"I remember saving you after that."

"Letting us go," she corrected. "Because you didn't have a choice. That doesn't seem to have worked out for you very well."

Another tense silence. Another whistle check in. Another five answers. Light was fading fast.

"Why are you here?" Evren finally asked. "I take it it's not to pester me."

"No," he finally said. "I'm here to help heal you. There is an Elder artifact in the Wood that might save you."

"There are ruins. No artifacts."

"The texts I studied before I . . ." he cleared his throat. "The texts I found state otherwise. A crown of stars, like the one the Horizon Walker wore. I believe that each Elder artifact has a piece of their soul. She was a healer and creator. That crown could be the key to saving your life."

She looked at him again. He had gone past his stumble and was watching her with cool interest. Something had happened to him while she was away. Something she should rage at the very thought of. That she felt numb didn't sit well with her at all.

"I think I would know if something that powerful was in the forest," she said flatly.

He snorted. "You never paid attention to the ruins as a child. You said so yourself. Is it that hard to believe me?"

She stopped walking and turned on him to say *Yes, in fact it is. Because you lie as easily as you bat your eyelashes. Because you think it's for the greater good, but your good will always differ from mine.* But instead, she stopped and slowly shut her mouth before the words could slip out.

Viggo lied, yes. But he lied for Serevadia and for the Convocation. He'd lost the latter when he let her go. And if he was here now, it seemed Serevadia had turned against him. He'd never lied to her about the Elders.

"Go on," she breathed. She didn't answer his question.

Irritation flickered across his misty face, but he nodded

anyway. "There are many ruins in the Wood. The one with the crown has a hidden passage. There will be trials to get to it; it seems only the worthy are capable of taking the power."

"But how do I find the ruins?" she asked.

"It only says they'll be revealed in the light of the swollen moon and the fall of silver. There is nothing aside from that."

Evren let out a hiss of frustration behind her clenched teeth. She shook her hair free of its tie and took her frustration out on the strands. "I can't just leave Barrion to find 'the fall of silver.'"

"You don't truly care about his quest."

"No, but I gave him my word," she snapped. "Him, and a dozen others are depending on me."

He frowned at her as if she were a child throwing a fit over something trivial. "You'll die if you keep searching for them instead of helping yourself."

Evren knew that's what the old her would've done. The one who still seemed to have a piece of her heart left before it died for good. She wondered when it died. Direwall? Lostwater? Maybe all the way back in Serevadia with Viggo. It should worry her more that she didn't care as much.

"I'll think about it," she told him. The sun had set for good now, and twilight was nearly as bad as pure night. She turned back to him for confirmation, but there wasn't a wisp of mist in the humid air left. Gone before she could say goodbye properly. That seemed like Viggo.

Evren shook her head free of thoughts of him and continued forward. She'd lost track of time talking to him. She'd have to find the rest of the party and set up camp before it got too dark.

She turned from her straight path forward and went left instead. She'd bump into someone, eventually. As she walked, she hugged close to the trees and used their warmth to guide her further. She hummed a little to herself, out of habit more than need. As she rounded her third tree, cool steel met her neck, and she froze.

The glowing blue of the giant runes cut Gyda's face into a beautiful, if not a terrifying, picture. But Evren scowled anyway.

She lifted the blade away from her neck with a gentle finger. "If you keep doing that with your sword, I'm going to start liking it," she said.

Gyda blinked slowly before lowering her sword. "You didn't check in."

"I thought I found something."

"And?"

Evren just shook her head. "No. Nothing. Abraxas will be furious, but we can't search in the dark. We should fall back and set up camp. Pick the search up in the morning."

Gyda's face twisted in a grimace. The idea of pulling Abraxas from the search was enough to sour anyone's mood, but the heavy lifting would fall on her; literally. "Fine. Let's find the others."

They turned together. Sol should be the one next to them. But as they went, a twig snapped behind them.

Evren's bow was drawn and Gyda's blade was ready before a bloody figure burst around the next tree. He stopped short when he saw them. His tear-stained cheeks caught the light from Gyda's runes and wisps of silver clung to his clothes.

"Oh, thank the Divines!" he cried and stumbled closer. "You found me. Please, you must help me."

Evren squinted in the low light. It took her longer than she'd like to figure out who he was. Beneath the blood and silvery strands was Chayne, the young human who'd made her bleed in the tavern brawl.

Gyda's sword lowered immediately, and she held her arm out to him. "Chayne, what happened? Where's Barrion?"

The silver caught Evren's eye again. Fresh silk that wouldn't wash off his clothes for months.

"Spiders," he choked out. "They ambushed us. They took everyone."

Evren remembered being small enough to squeeze through the banisters of her stairway when her father first warned her about the spiders. She knew about them before then, of course. But it was different when he spoke with fear in his eyes rather than cool indifference.

He'd held up a piece of silk, so light in the soft air she thought it weighed nothing at all. It glittered in the lantern light. She thought it was the most beautiful thing in the world.

"Peace, little Ren." He held the silk out of reach of her chubby, grasping fingers. "This is not a toy."

She'd pouted then, but sat cross-legged on the woven mat at his feet. She didn't notice when she was young how often he came home smelling of blood and death, and she never saw how heavy his eyes were when he looked at her.

"Has Master Yikao taught you of the Weavers?"

She nodded, her eyes still fixed on the silk. It reminded her of the gowns the noble ladies wore. They always looked so graceful, like moonlight skipping across ripples on a cool pond. She wanted to be just like them.

Her father twisted the silk around his fingers. Then she could see the sticky residue clinging to his skin, pulling it up as if to tear it from his bones. He let it sit there, curled next to his wedding band. "The Weavers have a hatred in their souls that sticks there like an infected wound. They are not animals, little Ren. They are not like the wyverns or wolves of the Wood who kill to survive. They are not like our Khama and their steeds, who protect us. The Weavers are intelligent, unique, and, above all, they are ruthless."

He looked her in the eyes then, and suddenly the silk didn't exist. Just her father, weary and cold, but perhaps trying to tell her without words too many things for her naïve eyes to understand.

"Remember that, Evren," he said softly. "Remember that they aren't beasts."

She nodded again. Because that's what he wanted, and she wouldn't forget if he wanted her to remember. No doubt they'd have this lesson again, and she could try to make him smile by reciting every word back. But she was still young, and the night was dark, and she hadn't seen him all day. She lifted her arms up to him, hopeful for an embrace she'd missed even if he didn't smell like himself. She watched him hesitate, and his fingers spreading a little. But the evening breeze swept through the round, open windows. The glass wind chime tinkled merrily and made Evren smile.

But her father's face fell. He looked back at the wind chime for a long while. Long enough for Evren's arms to ache. Then he turned back to her and tapped her chin lightly.

"Hurry to bed, little Ren. The morning will be here soon."

And then he'd left. And Evren had climbed into bed, chilled despite the trees, with the sound of wind chimes in her ears.

The tinkling of wind chimes rang in her ears even as she shook them off. In the present, the evening was ominous. It was hot, not cold. And it held a danger she'd never faced before.

Sol sat with Chayne on the forest floor next to their lantern. It wasn't nearly as comforting as a fire, but the light helped calm down the human. He was past the point of sobbing and was letting Sol treat his wounds. Cuts and gashes from his fall from the web. He was lucky he didn't break a bone when he cut himself free

"He got lucky," Evren whispered to the rest of her party, soft enough so Chayne wouldn't hear. "Cutting through is nearly impossible. They must've left his cocoon unfinished."

Abraxas winced. "Does that happen often?"

"No. They probably thought he was too weak to do anything. Fighters like Mira won't be so lucky."

Sorin was cradling the pup in his arms. The worg didn't look the least bit phased by the worried attitude of everyone in the party, but Sorin was practically radiating fear. "So, what do we do?"

Evren kept her mouth shut before she could say *nothing*, because she knew that wouldn't sit well with anyone. But every good instinct left in her told her to leave Barrion and his soldiers to their fate. She didn't want her party to end up the same way. But Abraxas caught her eye anyway, and if she hadn't known him better, she would've taken a few steps away from him in that moment. The look in his eyes was enough to make her forget he was a healer as well as a knight.

"You want to leave them," he growled.

One by one, the rest of the Sols looked at Evren with varying levels of disappointment and anger. A flash of her own anger warmed her already tight chest as she ground her teeth.

"It's not as simple as walking in there and cutting them down," she said. "We won't make it back out."

"Spiders are a lot more manageable than undead," he shot at her. "And you had no problems going into the White Cairn.'

"That was different," she insisted.

"Because it was Gyda and Sol?" he asked. "Or because there was no chance of walking away like there is now?"

Gyda shoved her way between the two of them. Evren hadn't realized how close Abraxas was getting. The part giant pushed them both back, gently but firmly. Her eyes were cold and unreadable. "That's enough from both of you."

Abraxas didn't bother to cut Gyda a glare, but he wrenched his shoulder from her hand. Her jaw tightened slightly, but she ignored him and turned to Evren.

"We are not leaving them."

Great.

"We'll be outnumbered," Evren argued.

"We normally are."

"Their nests are massive," she said, exasperated. "Unnavigable to anyone but them. Everything will be against us. The terrain, the enemies, the lack of light. There's no version of this that gets a happy ending."

"And there is no version where we turn tail and run like cowards," Gyda said.

"It's not cowardly," she shot back. "Barrion and his people probably won't even be alive by the time we get there."

"Then we should leave now and save as many as we can."

Evren once again found her hands tearing through her hair. Her jaw was tight and ached from clenching it so tightly. She was seething, and she hated it. She hated that they couldn't see what she saw. They hadn't grown up with the Weavers. They had no idea the destruction and death the weavers could cause. Couldn't they see she was trying to protect them? Why couldn't they just fucking listen to her instead of arguing?

"Evren." Arke's sharp voice drew her gaze down.

"What?" she snapped.

He narrowed his yellow eyes a bit and crossed his arms. "Remember what we talked about? This ain't you, kid."

All at once, the fire in her chest went out. She felt like that little girl again, waiting for an embrace she knew wouldn't come. Her sigh was hollow as it left her lips and her shoulders sagged. No matter how much Arke was right, she was still angry.

And afraid.

"Fine," she bit out. "We'll have to leave now."

Murmurs of hesitant approval filled the air. Sorin, who'd been watching with wide eyes that almost looked fearful, took a step forward. He held his hand out to put on her shoulder. That would've been comforting once. Not now. She flinched out of the way and ignored the flash of hurt in his eyes.

She didn't want that hurt. She didn't want the pity in Arke's eyes, or the disappointment in Gyda's. She just wanted it all to end.

Evren turned on her heel and marched back to Sol and Chayne. The human was trying to pry the silk from his skin. Tears were glittering in his eyes with every failed tug. Sol's smile faltered when she saw Evren, but it didn't disappear entirely.

"He's doing better," she said, so Evren didn't have to ask. "He wants to lead us to the nest."

Evren knelt next to him. She doubted he'd be able to find his way back through the shock in his body and the fallen night in the Wood.

"Tell me what happened," she said.

Chayne flinched and stopped prying at the silk. He swallowed nervously. "We heard fighting, about midday. Lieutenant Kester thought you might be in trouble, so she picked up the pace."

Evren nodded. "And then?"

He shivered. "It got dark. Not like this, but like a storm cloud passed in front of the sun. I got the feeling . . . well, if you've been watched before, you never forget how it feels. I tried to get up front to tell Prince Barrion. But something . . ." he choked up and started clawing at the silk again. "It was all over me. I couldn't even scream to warn anyone. I didn't know what it was. I couldn't see anything. The silk was everywhere, and I-I couldn't move. I was awake, but I couldn't scream or fight."

"It's a paralyzing toxin," Evren said. "Not deadly. It keeps prey from fighting too hard."

Chayne looked like he was going to be sick. He started tugging harder at the silk on his forearm, enough to pull at the fresh wounds Sol had just bandaged. The dwarf put her hands on top of his and he stopped, still shaking.

"Go on," Sol said gently.

Chayne nodded. He looked up at Evren. "When I could move again, all I saw was white. I heard voices, but they weren't human. I panicked and I-I almost lost my dagger. It took me hours, but I managed to cut free. And before I fell, I saw them . . ."

"The spiders," Evren said.

"You said we weren't in their territory," he whispered.

"We aren't."

"But they were there!" he insisted. "They grabbed us all and strung us up. We were so high in the trees, but the webs were everywhere, even on the ground."

"You said you saw them," Evren said. "Did they see you?"

"N-no."

"How did you escape?"

"I think . . ." he took a deep breath and brushed away his tears. "I think Lieutenant Kester was fighting them. I thought I heard her voice. They didn't pay attention to me, so I ran." He blinked teary eyes up at her, and behind her. The rest of her party had gathered to hear the story. "I ran to find all of you, so you could save them. You are going to, right?"

"Of course we are," Sol said immediately. She looked at Evren. "Right?"

"Yes," Evren said, and stood up. "But we need to leave now. If you want to help, you can, but it won't be an easy fight."

She expected Chayne to whimper, or maybe shiver again. But he set his jaw and stood up with her. "I'm with you, milady. All of you. If you can get my friends back, I'll owe you everything."

"Don't get too hasty, kid," Arke said. "We ain't started yet."

Behind her, Abraxas's voice was as cool and sharp as steel. "Evren, what should we expect?"

She turned to face them and fidgeted with her own bandage

to keep from looking him in the eye. "Elves in Orenlion call them Weavers. As far as I know, they've never named themselves. But they're not beasts—they're smart. It sounds like they planned this ambush."

"They're that smart?" Sol asked as she came up beside her. "As in, they left that trail of silk to make us go into worg territory?"

Evren pursed her lips. "Maybe."

"And then waited until we were split up and dealing with the worgs to take an easier target." Abraxas shook his head. "Smart enough to cover their tracks, too. If they know you're gone, Chayne, they might be expecting us."

"Or they've sent parties looking for him," Evren said. "They don't like their prey getting away."

Chayne let out a strangled little noise from his mouth but couldn't manage much more than that. Sorin started laughing nervously, and his grip on the pup was looking more and more like he was grasping a lifeline.

"Brilliant." He laughed. "First exploding lizards, then cave mermaids, then a giant worm, and of course, the sea serpent and the army of undead. What's a few dozen spiders?"

"Hundred," Evren corrected.

"What?" he squeaked.

"A few hundred. They nest large." She watched all their faces fall. Sol looked like she was on the verge of passing out herself. Evren shouldered her bow. "You said we handled worse, didn't you? So, let's go."

~

THE TREES WERE monoliths in the dark. Once again, Evren felt like a small child under the gaze of disappointed parents. Better the trees than her friends, though. The light of the lanterns and the two remaining Luminstones from Gyda and Sorin pushed the grasping shadows back enough to walk comfortably. The bubble of light seemed to act like a wall between them and the rest of the Wood. Eyes watched from between the trees, glowing against their lanterns. Vines shrank back from them as they passed.

They were not safe. But light gave the illusion that they were.

Chayne stumbled ahead, next to Evren as they lead the party further into the dark. Every little noise made him jump. His brow was pale and slick with sweat, and he gripped the hilt of his dagger tight enough to break it.

But he was surprising Evren. He had a soldier's resolve, despite his youthful face. He marched through his fear every time she expected him to turn and run. It shouldn't have surprised her, but it did.

"How long have you been a soldier?"

Chayne jumped at the sound of her voice, then covered his chest as if to calm his beating heart down. "Only six months, milady. But I trained for two years before I joined."

"Six months and you're protecting the crown prince on a dangerous quest?"

He smiled sheepishly. "I know. Doesn't seem right, does it? But His Highness wanted the most loyal of us. He chose me because he trusts me. I plan on repaying that trust."

Evren nodded, although she didn't really understand. She liked Barrion enough, sure. But she'd found no one of royal or noble blood to be worthy of her loyalty. Time and time again, they used her or betrayed her. Sol was the only exception, but she wasn't even a noble anymore. Heliodar, Mal, and Viggo had all used her. And then there were the snakes in Orenlion. There was only one worth trusting there.

Chayne slowed down in the wide space between two trees and stopped. Evren did too, watching his face as flickers of doubt slowly became overwhelmed with recognition. He pointed right. "It's this way."

"Are you sure?"

He nodded and kicked at a pile of leaves. Glimmers of silk gleamed in the lantern light. "I'm sure."

He marched forward again, and Evren followed, the Wandering Sols trailing behind. Chayne's trail was easy to follow. He'd disturbed a lot of the forest in his mad dash. His boot prints were stark in the mud, piles of leaves were scattered and disturbed. Bits of silk that had clung more stubbornly to the trees than his clothes acted like ghostly flags, waving them forward.

"I have a sister, you know," Chayne said, after a while of silence. "She's only seventeen. Wants to move to Terevas."

"Why?"

He shrugged. "It's pretty there, she says. Warmer. They say that in the big cities, they don't need magic to warm their water. They've got metal contraptions to do it for them. It's supposed to be a better place to live. Safer too."

She noted another scrap of silk fluttering in the breeze. "Is that what you want?"

Beside her, he shrugged. "All I want to do is get out of here alive with Prince Barrion in one piece. That's all I can ask for. Maybe after I'll take her to Terevas. If I make it out."

A part of Evren wanted to reassure him. Sugar-sweet lies wouldn't make either of them feel better, but it seemed like something she would have done before. Something to reassure him. It would help her take the weight of his words and perhaps shoulder them easier. He has a young sister; he has dreams and a whole life ahead of him. She had to get him back to her.

But in the end, nothing came out of her mouth, and they walked forward in silence.

When the silk stopped looking like torn scraps and more like webbing, Evren gestured everyone to get their weapons ready. If it had been daylight, she could've seen the dark stains on the wood of the trees. But the bark looked dull and black in the night. The webbing became denser, and the air smelled acidic. It tasted bitter on her tongue. The further she went, the more the forest seemed to draw in around her. The trees seemed closer, like they were leaning in. Swaths of webbing started appearing above their heads. The lanterns were put out, and the Lumin-stones were dimmed to where they could barely see ahead of them.

"Don't step on the webbing." Evren whispered over her shoulder.

It was coating the ground, too. Every step forward was slow and shaky. Each boot placed was deliberate. She wasn't afraid of getting stuck, but of alerting the whole nest of Weavers.

She couldn't see them, but she could smell them. The rank stench of their venom hung thickly in the air. She heard chit-tering mandibles above her, and odd hissing from every direction.

The fear curling in her belly was enough for Evren to want to turn and run. That fear had been hammered into her since she was a child.

Don't leave your window open, or the Weavers will steal you in the night for a snack.

Evren stepped around a fallen cocoon. She thought it could've been Chayne's, but the skeletal hand peeking out told her otherwise.

Never wander alone in the Wood, or the Weavers will take you away.

She couldn't see trees anymore, only white webbing and glit-tering silk. She gripped Chayne's arm to stop him as a large shadow skittered across the web above them. They all held their breaths until the web stopped bouncing from the weight.

Never go hunting for Weavers, or else you'll be hunted in return.

They came to a crossroads. Hollows of silk-carved corridors through the webs. There weren't any bare patches of ground anymore. They'd have to climb the rest of the way, and pray, if they were making a habit of praying.

Don't look a Weaver in the eyes, or you won't come back the same. If you come back at all.

Evren tried not to grip her bow too tight. She didn't want the white-hot fear shaking her to her very bones. She didn't want the hairs on the back of her neck to prickle like something was crawling there. Evren looked back, counting the heads of her party. Sol, who was clinging to Abraxas's leg. Sorin, who had put the worg in his bag and was muttering something to himself with wide eyes, taking everything in. Arke, who was sitting on Gyda's shoulder with his spellbook ready and a grim look on his face.

She couldn't even see the forest now. They were deep inside the nest.

Evren swallowed nervously and turned back to Chayne. He'd closed his eyes and was muttering a prayer under his breath. She'd heard Abraxas say it more than once, but never with this amount of desperation.

She gripped his arm and his eyes flashed open. "Which way?" she mouthed quietly.

He gulped and looked at the four branching tunnels one by one. When he looked back at her, his eyes swam with new tears.

"It's okay," she whispered and forced a smile. *Be like the old Evren,* she told herself. *Make him feel like everything will be fine.* "We have your back. Just show us which way. We have seen no torn webbing from your fall yet, so which tunnel did you come from?"

"I'm so sorry." He shook his head and pulled away from her hand. His foot hit the webbing, and she hissed in alarm. But he just kept shaking his head as more tears fell. "They promised me they'd let my friends live if I brought you. They swore. I had to do it."

Cold realization crashed over her hot fear. She whirled around, a scream on her lips. But when she turned, she was met with a sharp pain in her stomach. The creeping warmth of paralyzing venom swam in her veins. She didn't see her friends. She saw black, and a blur of stripes and long legs. The acid stench was right on top of her. How did she not notice?

Warm numbness spread like a wave over her body. Her breaths came out in tiny gasps; she couldn't even scream. Evren's legs failed her first. She couldn't stop herself from falling. And then warm, long legs were cradling her. Sharp hairs pricked her skin. The stinger left her body with a wet, sucking sound.

"*Little elf blood!*" the weaver chittered in her ear. "*Right on time.*"

And then the nightmare began.

9

———

Evren woke up choking.

She didn't remember passing out. Only the suffocating fear as something dragged her away and encased
her in silk.

She gasped for air, coughing, trying to keep her food down
as strings of silk fell into her mouth and tickled the back of her
throat. She gagged and tried to pull the strings away. But she
couldn't move her hands. Or anything. Tiny pricks of pain
danced around her skin, as if she was being stabbed by hundreds
of tiny needles over and over.

All she could see was white.

The silk in her mouth was slippery, not tacky. But she was
still choking on it and couldn't get it free. So she swallowed,
squeezing her eyes shut as the silk slithered down her throat an
inch at a time. She gagged once, and it all nearly came up. But
she forced it down, all of it, until her mouth was finally clear.

Her gasp of air sounded more like a sob as she sucked in one
lungful, and then another. The surrounding cocoon was new,
still wet and slimy, but strong as any chain. Her stomach rioted
at the memory of her eating some. It took all her willpower not
to throw everything back up.

Her chest was heaving uncontrollably. More wisps of silk were fluttering near her mouth, but she spat them back out before they got too deep. It wasn't until she tasted salt that she realized she was crying.

The tears ran like rivers down her cheeks and throat. She could do nothing but lay her head against her cocoon and let them fall. She wept until her skull ached, until her chest spiked with familiar pain and her eyes drained dry.

She was dead, or close to it. She'd grown up hearing horror stories about the pain of dying as a weaver's meal. How their venom liquefied their victims from the inside out while they were still alive. How long before she was a husk bled dry for a monster's meal? How long before Sol, or Gyda, or the rest of her friends joined her? Or had they already suffered that death and she was the last one standing?

She shivered, although the cocoon was quite warm. What happened to them was her fault. She may be changed. She may truly act heartless at this point like Gail warned, but she knew, above all things, that if she'd been smarter and waited for the sun to rise, she could've seen the Weaver's trap coming. If she'd watched Chayne, she would've seen the regret in his eyes sooner. She should've known he couldn't escape without the weavers letting him.

She should've seen it coming. Just like she should've seen Heliodar's blade before it was plunged into Sorin's heart, or Nerezza's simple disguise that made her look like a normal elf rather than a Serevadian. Evren should've seen it all, and if she had, it would've spared the people she loved so much pain.

The sharp tingling on her skin was fading. It started leaving her fingers and toes first, drawing back throughout her body to where she'd been stabbed. The wound there puckered and ached. She could feel the steady trickle of venom and blood running down her pants.

For what she guessed was almost an hour, she strained against the cocoon. She prodded for weak spots, tried to kick holes in it, and shook it so much she was sure it would knock loose from the rest of the web and plummet to the ground.

It didn't.

The best she managed was to get the webbing an inch away from her face, instead of plastered right on it. Her face stung and smarted from peeling it off. She was sure she was covered in red welts, or that she'd ripped her skin off entirely. But it made breathing a little easier.

She wiggled her fingers precious inches. She thought, or hoped, that she still had her weapons on her. Maybe she could saw free if she got one of her knives or an arrow. But she found her sheaths bare, and her bow and quiver absent from her back.

"Fuck!" she screamed.

Evren inhaled more air into her aching lungs and another wad of silk landed in her mouth. She kept her throat closed and spit it out, cursing. It landed right in front of her with a wad of her saliva. And then it started to melt.

Evren frowned and squinted. It was hard to see anything. She still wasn't sure if it was day or night. But the silk was . . . dissolving? No, that wasn't the right word. Changing for sure, but it was still there. It was just losing some of its structure.

And maybe some of its strength.

An idea formed in Evren's mind. A terrible, disgusting idea that she would likely never recover from if she survived. It made her gag just thinking about it. But her survival was optional, her friends' was not.

"This dies with me," she chanted. "Assuming it doesn't just kill me."

And then she gathered as much saliva as she could and spat. It was slow going. Her mouth dried up with every wad of spit she sent out, and she had to wait before she did it again. She tried to cover a wide area, but her head couldn't move too far. Her face was wet and sticky. But this was the simple part.

She had a good face-sized area of saliva-soaked silk in front of her. It looked different, too. More rubbery than stringy. Then she took a few breaths to steel her nerves, hummed a little tune, and chewed.

The first bite missed several times. Her teeth couldn't quite catch on anything and slipped past her damaged silk over and over. When she pressed her face against it and her teeth finally snagged something, she clamped down and tore at it.

It felt like trying to rip apart wet wool, and her teeth ached. But one chunk pulled free, and she spat it out and went for another. Over and over, she bit and tore and chewed. Eventually, even spitting the chunks back out took more time than she had. She swallowed them and didn't linger on just how terrible that was. The wet silk wasn't sticky. It wouldn't strangle her from the inside out.

It took maybe an hour to get through one layer, and her jaw was aching by the time she went for another. Soon she lost track of how much she'd eaten. Eventually, she saw light, and the air was cooler and far less stifling. She tore a chunk out and swallowed with difficultly, and then she could see again.

Evren sobbed in relief. The hole wasn't large; it was barely big enough for her head. But the fresh air smelled amazing. It looked like early dawn, and everything was grey. White webs spread as far as she could see, anchoring on to twisting limbs. She didn't see any spiders. She still had some time.

It took another hour for her to widen the hole, and thirty more minutes to wiggle her hands free. The wads of silk she'd spat out were working on soaking and weakening the rest. She felt a thrill of triumph as her fingers grasped the sides of her cocoon's hole and pulled.

Weakened or not, it was still strong. Ripping it open with her bare hands sent her vision sparking with black spots. But, one by one, her limbs came free. One arm, and then another. And then she was tearing frantically at the remaining silk to free her legs.

All at once, she was free.

She slid out of the cocoon and onto a bouncy layer of thick

webbing. It was the only thing that kept her from a neck-snapping plummet to the forest floor. Pieces of silk hung off her in foot-long strands. Her arms shook, and she couldn't push herself onto her feet. She could barely keep herself on her knees.

Evren was sobbing, and then her stomach finally revolted against her and she was vomiting everything up. Silk, bile, food, all of it left her body it a massive, cleaning heave. The wound in her stomach ached sharply with every heave. She spat until her mouth was clean and her body was spent. And then, on shaky arms and legs, she forced herself to stand up.

She stumbled away from where the silk was weakening at her feet. This webbing was different. Sturdy and thick, but not sticky. It coated the tree limbs that stretched like thick black veins under the white silk. What little sunlight came from above filtered through dense leaves and even more webs. She could see no end to it, and even though it was the only thing keeping her from falling, she wished she could tear it all down

Her weak knees wobbled underneath her, and she wiped her mouth with the back of her hand.

Survive first, destroy later.

The web underneath her feet bobbed with every step. She wasn't sure where to go, other than away from her broken cocoon before a Weaver found it and raised the alarm. She had to find her friends and get out before they noticed, or there'd be no leaving at all.

Evren cradled her stomach as she crept forward. It throbbed in time with her pounding head. The silk trailed behind her like an ominous veil. Her legs faltered until they hit something solid, a tree branch. Something solid and unmoving made the weakness in her knees even more apparent, but she pushed that worry to the back of her mind as she found the trunk of the tree. Wide, black, and sticky with warmth underneath the swaths of silk, her fingers dug into the rough bark as she circled around. One step at a time as the fear crept up her throat like tendrils of swallowed silk. One foot in front of the other as she took in another side to the nest, and then stopped.

If she had a heart, it would've plummeted. It went on, stretching deeper than she could've imagined into the forest. Evren saw gaps in the web, tunnels leading down and swathed in dark shadows. She shivered, imagining eight spindly legs appearing from the darkness to discover her at any moment. She turned away.

More cocoons. Her breath caught in her hollow chest.

There, the webbing was framed on the trees in a way that made it look like a wide hallway. Not a tunnel for skittering, but a corridor to walk and browse for one's next meal. The cocoons dangled in neat, orderly lines along the walls. Evren turned her back on the dark tunnels and headed towards the corridor.

There were no more tree limbs to walk on, and her feet sank an inch with every step on the silken floor. She neared the first cocoon, gently turning it to face her. It wasn't empty, but it was light. She heard bones rattling inside and staggered away to the next one.

She found the second, and then the next three to be in similar states. A part of her wanted to take the time to take the bones out. Were they elves from Orenlion? Hunters that strayed too far from their normal paths? Maybe they were old bodies, or fresh soldiers from Barrion's that had been recently eaten. She refused to believe they were anyone she called friend.

Evren tugged at another cocoon and was met with the empty eyes of a skull staring straight through her. The thrill of fear ebbed away as something landed at her feet with a dull thud. She gingerly bent over to pick it up, and the curved steel of the dagger glimmered in the light like a beacon of hope.

It was a simple blade, but the hilt was anything but. The metal was in the shape of a snarling wyvern, and the wings made to cradle the wielder's hand and protect it. An expensive blade that, while useful, was a gift. A common gift among Orenlion's elite, the Khama.

Evren turned back to the cocoon, and the skeleton laying half out of the torn shell. The armor was worn and dusty, but the individual strips of metal that were stitched together to protect but also be flexible, was incredibly recognizable. It was like a punch in her gut, seeing armor that she should've worn. That her father had worn when he left Orenlion for good.

"*Com ineeharas, bra then,*" she murmured to the corpse. "Peace find you, brother."

The words felt foreign and false on her tongue. It had been too long since she'd spoken her father's language, and longer still since she'd done it of her own free will. She didn't know this elf. They wouldn't have taken her blessing if they'd been alive, of that she was sure. But she had their dagger, and with it, a better chance of surviving.

Or, at least going down with a fight.

Evren turned away from the elf and went back to searching the corridor. The more she walked, the more she wondered why her cocoon had been kept separate from these. She'd been around no others, out in the open. Something carefully made and placed these in neat lines down the wall. Some were empty and ripped open from the outside as if the poor souls trapped in there had been cut out to be eaten whole. Some held animals who had died from hunger and thirst. Even more held dried corpses waiting to rot.

It wasn't until she was far enough to feel surrounded by death, did she hear voices.

Evren darted behind a swaying cocoon and held her breath. The silk creaked low with every little sway, but over that she strained to hear the voices. Two? Maybe more. They were whispering. She thought she caught the low hissing of a Weaver between every other word, and the clicking of pincers. And then a voice distinctly not weaver stood out, rough and raspy and achingly familiar.

Arke.

Evren didn't allow herself to hope. Not even when all voices she thought she heard faded to just his. He was muttering to himself in Goblin. He never spoke it around the others if he could help it, but there was no mistaking that throaty, guttural language, as his voice bounced from web to web.

She counted her breaths, making sure she wasn't hallucinating him, before she stepped out from her hiding spot. And there he was, a few rows down from where she stood. His cocoon was noticeably smaller than the rest of them, and he hung upside down with his head peeking out from the bottom. His white puff of hair blended in with the silk, and his ears flopped with every shake of his head.

"Arke!" she hissed, and his whole cocoon snapped at her voice.

Those wide, yellow eyes were as big as dinner plates when he saw her, and his grin was even bigger. "Kid! You made it out!"

She nodded and jogged over to him. She put her hands on his cocoon to keep him from swaying too badly. "You're alive."

He chuckled. "You too. How'd you get out?"

Her stomach rioted at the mere memory. "Long story," she said hurriedly. "Let's get you out of here. Where's everyone else?"

The elven blade was old, but the steel was still sharp as she dug into the silk. She started saw at it and, bit by bit, the strings parted under the sharp edge. Underneath, Arke was hesitating.

"It's all right if you don't know," she said quickly, and another string snapped. "We can look together. They'll be here somewhere, and we'll get out together."

"Kid . . ."

"They took your spellbook, didn't they? Took my weapons too. Shouldn't be too hard to find, though."

"Evren."

She stopped sawing through the cocoon. The tone in his voice was odd, like he was trying to tell her something without using the words he needed. She stepped back to look him in the eye.

"What is it?" she asked. "We don't have a lot of time."

Again, Arke hesitated. It was only a brief second, but the conflict in his eyes was stark enough for Evren to understand. He was hiding something, and he was afraid.

Before she could press him further, his eyes snapped to something behind her and widened even further. He shook his head. "No—"

Evren whirled around, her stolen dagger in front of her. A Weaver stood behind her, eight legs bristling with tiny hairs and all eight black eyes fixed on her. At the glint of the dagger, it snapped its pincers and hissed lowly.

"Stay back!" Evren said and put herself between it and Arke. "I won't let you have him."

The Weaver's legs pattered anxiously as it looked between her and the dagger. It wasn't a large one; it only came up to her waist in height. The little blue iridescent hairs on its thick abdomen might've been pretty if they belonged to another creature. And it was hesitating, floundering between running and attacking.

Evren couldn't let it do either.

"Stop!" Arke's harsh growl made her jump, and both her and the Weaver broke their stand-off to stare at him.

He was glaring at Evren with an impressive amount of venom, considering he was hanging upside down. "If you hurt her, I'm gonna be pissed."

Evren blinked, waiting for more until she realized he was talking to her. About the spider.

"Her?" she asked and looked back at the Weaver.

It, or she, hadn't moved. It seemed to wait on Arke, and was staring at him expectantly. No, hopefully. She was afraid.

"Kid," Arke huffed. "Neri's on our side. She's helpin' me. Put your fuckin' knife down."

Evren let out a strangled laugh and did not put down her knife. "A Weaver? Helping you? This has got to be some sick joke. Arke, they don't help anyone but themselves. Have you looked around here recently?"

"'Fraid I've been too stuck to explore," he retorted. "Neri's gonna fix that."

Neri the Weaver took a step forward, but shrank back when Evren lifted her blade again. She hadn't heard of Weaver's playing tricks on their food, but she wasn't about to blindly trust one now.

"What kind of game are you playing?" she asked the spider. "Why would a Weaver help us?"

Neri chittered anxiously, and her front two legs worried together as if she was wringing her hands. *I am not a Weaver,* she hissed lowly. *Arke speaks truth.*

"Not a Weaver?" Evren repeated. "What's that supposed to mean?"

"Cursed." Neri spat the word out like it was venom. Then, softer, *"I am not Weaverkind."*

Slowly, Evren lowered her blade. It wasn't that she didn't want to believe Neri, because Divines knew it was possible for someone to get cursed into another form. But she didn't know of anyone cruel enough to change someone into a Weaver.

"Who did this to you?" Evren asked. "Why?"

Behind her, Arke growled in frustration. "Does it fuckin' matter? She's offerin' to help."

"It does. We have no idea who she is or why she ended up like this."

"Anyone evil enough to curse someone into somethin' like that don't care who they are," he said. "They do it 'cause they can. Trust me, I've been around enough Fey to know."

Evren turned back to the spider, who was still regarding her warily. No, not warily, fearfully. She was afraid of Evren, who was weak and small and armed with nothing but a dagger. Neri was afraid and hesitant, where all other Weavers would've jumped at her despite the blade in her hand. That, or she was just cowardly. Either way, Evren couldn't find another argument against her. So she stepped aside.

"Get him out," Evren demanded.

If Neri nodded, Evren couldn't tell. She scurried over to Arke with such animalistic quickness that Evren had to keep herself from lashing out. Her pincers were sharp and oh so close to Arke's throat as she started to cut through his cocoon. Evren's death grip on her dagger didn't go away, and her tightly wound muscles wouldn't relax. Even when Arke slid free from the cocoon unharmed and trailing silk, she still couldn't force herself to ease her anxiety.

Arke picked himself up off the ground and dusted himself off. Neri hovered close by, clicking her pincers as she looked him over. Any time she caught Evren's eye, she shied away.

Arke scowled. "Stop that."

Evren looked back at him. "Me?"

"Yeah, you look like you wanna murder her."

It wasn't far from the truth. It would be safer to kill Neri. She might not act like a Weaver, but the spiders had proven to be especially good at traps. There was nothing to stop Evren from thinking that this was all an act to have them killed later down the line. But Arke trusted her, and Evren knew from personal experience that kind of trust didn't come easily. That was the only thing that kept the spider alive.

Judging from the look in Neri's many eyes, she knew it, too.

"Where's everyone else?" Evren asked the spider. "Gyda, Abraxas, Sol, and Sorin?"

More nervous chittering from the spider. She looked at Arke for confirmation, and when the goblin nodded, Neri turned back to Evren. *"Separated. We must keep looking."*

Evren ground her teeth. It was smart to keep them all separated. With every minute spent searching, they risked being discovered. But, hopefully, Neri could be more useful than just cutting them down from their cocoons.

"Do you know where to find them?"

Again, the spider hesitated, and then finally said, *"Yes."*

"Lead the way, then."

It wasn't Evren's words that Neri followed, but Arke's nod of reassurance. As the spider turned and started walking down the corridor, with much more grace and balance than Evren could ever manage, she narrowed her eyes a little at Arke. It wasn't common for the goblin to be soft and reassuring with anyone, especially not a stranger. Never mind that that stranger was a spider bigger than he was. But if he noticed her questioning stare, he didn't let on as he followed Neri, and Evren followed him.

The cocoons came to life the farther they walked. Muffled crying and moans of pain slipped through their silken walls. Some swayed as if they were rocking themselves to sleep, and others rocked and screamed as she'd done not so long ago.

Arke cast them all regretful looks. "We can't help them."

Evren blinked down at him, a little ashamed that the idea hadn't crossed her mind yet. "I know."

"Later, kid. We won't forget about them."

"Yeah," was all she said.

With every passing cocoon, she expected Neri to stop and point out one of their party. She found her eyes looking for a cocoon large enough for Gyda, or one with a sea shanty spewing desperately out of it. She found none.

"You really trust . . . her?" Evren struggled with not calling Neri 'it,' and it showed.

Arke scowled up at her. "Yeah, I do. She's been helpin' me the past few days. Bringin' food and news."

"Days?"

"You've been out a while, kid."

Evren's already torn-up stomach twisted itself into knots. How much had she missed as she slept? What if she was already too late?

Why was she still alive?

They walked a little further, and Evren's grip on her dagger had slackened until she felt the webbing underneath her feet dip. The previously still air whispered past her ears. Evren pushed Arke to the side and dove in the other direction just as something large crashed into the spot they'd just been standing.

Evren got to her feet as quickly as the bouncing silk would let her and came face to face with a much larger, much more aggressive Weaver. This one was at least twice the size of Neri, and pitch-black, save for the knobs on his legs that shone a sickening yellow amber. Its eight eyes fixed on her with the type of rage that Evren shared in her gut.

She knew those eyes. The same ones that had stared at her gleefully as the toxins kept her from fighting back. The same spider that had ambushed her.

"Little elf blood," it hissed and circled her. *"Out of bed. Very naughty."*

She flipped her dagger up so that the blade shone in the light. It chittered as its reflection glittered back at it. "You should've killed me first."

"Yesss." It plucked at a string by one of its feet. *"I ssshould've."*

The Weaver launched itself at Evren faster than her eyes could follow. It crashed into her in a blur of black and yellow. She was dimly aware of Arke screaming, but all she could feel was fear and an all-consuming rage she'd pent up since she was a child. Her back hit the spongy floor, the Weaver's pincers mere inches from her face.

With a cry she jabbed the dagger between the pincers. She meant to stab into its soft flesh, but the blade caught the pincers and twisted until it was wedged in a way that the two sharp mandibles couldn't open or close properly. The Weaver reared up, a hollow screech echoing in her ears as something underneath it glimmered sharply.

Evren barely rolled out of the way as its stinger came streaking towards her. It struck inches from her face, dripping venom. The legs stampeded around her as it readied for another strike, and Evren glimpsed a small opening and rolled through the gap in its legs.

She got up on her feet as the Weaver rounded on her. It rushed her again, but before the webbing between them could dip under its weight, she leapt off it and up into the air. The Weaver darted underneath her; the surprise shining in its eyes until Evren's arc dipped back down. She twisted in the air, landing on its massive back with a jolt.

It hissed around her stuck blade in frustration and then bucked. She grasped at anything to hold on to. Bladed hairs cut into her palms. Its skin was slick as metal and smelled like death. She slid forward as its abdomen lurched into the air. Without thinking, she wrapped her arms around what would've been its neck had it been a normal creature. Her face was inches above its pincers and right next to its burning eyes.

The smaller legs in the front tried to pry her off. She twisted and bucked as they missed her again and again. She was at a spot it couldn't quite reach, no matter how much it thrashed and tore at her clothes.

Evren felt its whole body convulse as it tried to shake her off. She loosened her grip and let herself slide forward. As the Weaver's triumphant cry tore from its body, her fingers grasped the hilt of the dagger and tore it free.

She scrambled backwards to keep from falling off. Her legs straddled the Weaver tightly, and she raised the dagger above its head. A flame of triumph tore through her body. She was going to do it. Finally, she was going to kill a Weaver, a creature that had haunted her nightmares and her home for centuries. She would end it with the blade of a fallen hunter, and it felt so fitting.

And then the Weaver was running.

Evren yelped and struggled to keep her grip on the dagger and the spider as it tore down the corridor at a frightening speed. Bright sunlight was ahead, and what hope Evren might've had was squashed as the Weaver picked up speed and then launched itself into the open air.

For a brief, shining moment, it was just the two of them

suspended in the hot, spring air. The sunlight made the webs glitter like silver, the green leaves rustled in the breeze, and everything was gilded and gold. But all too soon, they started to free-fall.

The weaver was heavier and fell faster than Evren. Her stomach lurched as nothing but air swept beneath her and she tumbled down, down, down.

The tree branches blurred past her, brimming with leaves. And then the webs got thicker and thicker. The sunlight faded away until it was cold and distant. Evren was still grasping for it when she slammed into a spongy web and it knocked out the wind of her.

She heaved more air and checked her grip on the dagger. It shone like a beacon of hope in her hand. Past it, the web that crossed the abyss between two trees was thin enough to see through, and the Weaver was tearing after her with enough speed to make Alkimos jealous.

A flare of panic went through Evren's veins. It was just a few feet from her, its pincers widening in anticipation, when she slashed wildly at it. It jumped back, but the blade had never been close to hitting it. The confusion only lasted until an audible snap filled the air, and then another. And then a dozen. If those eight eyes could hold surprise, Evren would've relished the look. Instead, she slashed the web one more time, and the whole thing tore in half under the Weaver's weight.

The Weaver fell through the open air once more. The web underneath Evren gave too, but she kept her grip tight in her other hand. She dangled from a moment and gave herself time to catch her breath. She couldn't force herself to look down or think about climbing up. Not yet.

Just as she was relaxing, a string of newly formed web hurled up at her from below and latched around her leg. A second later, it ripped her from her grip on the cut web and sent her shooting down to the forest floor.

There was no fear in Evren now. She angled her body so

she'd fall faster. The air rushed past her ears like a scream, and the wind picked at her eyes until she had tears streaming down her cheeks. Before she knew it, she was rushing towards the Weaver as it tried to slow its own fall.

She crashed into it with a cry of rage. The wind tore at her blade as she tried to plunge it into its side, but the spider twisted, and the dagger glanced off its leg instead. As she tried to go for another blow, they both lurched as they slammed into another web and tore through it. Their fall began anew, but slower this time. It tried to move in the air to grab at her, but she kicked out of its grasp. The air fluttered around her, lifting her hair as she almost hovered above it for a second. And then it yanked the web around her foot and pulled her back down.

She aimed the dagger at its underbelly, soft and patterned. The point was mere inches from it. And then they slammed into another web. This one was strong enough to hold them for a bit. The two wrestled and tried desperately to find each other's weak spots. She slashed her dagger out at one of the smaller legs and cut the tip clean off.

The weaver screamed in pain. It launched at her and her blade went flying into the open air. The spider's glistening pincers were inches from her throat when the web finally snapped, and they fell again.

This time, the fall was abrupt and ended hard. Evren slammed into the ground and heard her ribs crack more than felt them. She laid on the forest floor, still littered with webs, for a moment to catch her breath. A few feet from her, she heard the Weaver getting up, and she knew her time of rest was over.

Ignoring the pain in her side, she jumped to her feet. Across from her, the Weaver was doing the same. It was bleeding, and one of its legs was bent oddly. But it kicked up the dirt, and without hesitation, closed the distance.

Evren let out a final battle cry and, weaponless, went to do the same. But before she and the Weaver could crash into each other, two powerful arms wrapped themselves around her and pulled her out of the way.

The weaver rushed past her. When it turned to go for another pass, another one came out of nowhere and blocked its way.

"Out of the way!" The injured weaver screamed. It darted around, trying to get to her, but was being blocked by the faster spider.

Evren's bloodlust wasn't done. She thrashed against the arms holding her and tried to pull herself free to finish her fight.

"Let go!" she growled and bucked against her capture. But they wouldn't budge.

Across the way, more spiders were crowding her injured opponent and forcing it to stand down, even as it howled and tried to move past them.

"Enough." A voice hissed in her ear. Gyda. "Enough, Evren. It's over."

And just like that, the fight melted out of her. She slumped against Gyda's arms, her chest heaving as she tried to catch her breath. The injured Weaver was corralled away by a dozen others, and soon its bloody cries were swallowed by the ground and silk.

"I'm going to let you go," Gyda murmured, her lips brushing Evren's ears. "You will not fight. You will harm none of these creatures. Understood?"

Not in the slightest, but Evren nodded anyway. It was the only way Gyda would let her go, and her feet needed solid ground more than her rage needed to be sated.

Slowly, Gyda set her down on the floor. When her legs wobbled, the warrior kept a hold of her shoulders. Evren didn't push her away.

She cut Gyda a glare. "What is going on? How are you free?"

Gyda's lips tugged into a deep frown. Besides the telltale silk clinging to her and the puncture wound on her stomach, she looked unharmed. And completely unfazed by the Weavers.

"There is much we need to talk about," she said softly.

As she did, a figure emerged from a silk tunnel. He was dressed casually, and his weapon was gone. His hair was a black mess on his head, and a few strings of silk were the only things that hinted at his captivity.

"Ah." Barrion smiled thinly. "Looks like you freed yourself after all. I owe Anep a snack."

10

"I don't understand," Evren said, but found that she couldn't finish. She didn't understand any of what was going on.

All around her, Weavers scurried by. Some as large as the one she fought, many a little smaller. They all gave her a wide berth, and some even hissed in her general direction. But they didn't attack. They didn't string her back up and lock her away. They let her be with Gyda and Barrion.

On the other side of what Evren could only assume was a crossroads for the nest, Neri carefully picked her way down with Arke balancing on her back. When she got on even ground, he slid off and eyed Evren with a look of enormous relief.

"That was some dumb shit," he said as he walked up.

Gyda shook her head. "You didn't see the half of it."

Evren glared at the two of them. "Can someone please explain to me what the fuck is going on?"

Gyda started to speak, but Barrion beat her to it. Despite his casual appearance, he looked exhausted. "We will explain it in due time, I promise. We were talking to everyone individually so as not to cause a panic."

"Panic?" Evren asked hotly. "Individually? What do you mean we? I'm assuming you and Gyda."

"Not exactly." He winced. "The Matriarch of this nest and I have been in negotiations. When your party came in—"

"They tricked us into coming here!" she argued. "Ambushed, because of one of your people."

"I'm aware," he said flatly. "That was not on mine or the Matriarch's orders. And you were never to be harmed. The idea was to talk to you each one by one and explain the rather delicate situation. However, you somehow broke free before we could send Neri to you."

Arke elbowed her to get her attention. "He ain't lyin'. Neri explained it all before you came in. I woulda told you but you looked like you were gonna kill her."

Evren scowled, because she probably would've, and then turned back to Barrion. "So, what? That thing attacking me was just an accident? You can ask Arke, it came after me."

"He," Barrion corrected. "Anep is not an 'it,' he's a 'he.' And, much like you, he's acting on instinct and anger."

"Instinct?" Evren sputtered.

"You notice how he didn't attack Gyda?" Barrion asked. "Or even Arke, for that matter? He sees you as a threat. The biggest one in this group, actually."

"Why? I'm no more dangerous than Gyda."

"You are, actually." Barrion regarded her with something close to pity. "You were raised to hate his kind, much like he was raised to hate yours. That sort of thing goes beyond strength or skill. Hate can make villains out of the weakest among us."

Evren scowled. "You expect me to believe that he was kind to everyone else? That he didn't try to kill Abraxas or yourself for being elves?"

"We are not of Orenlion," Barrion said with raised brows. "And I don't expect you to believe anything, only to listen. Trust me when I say that Anep's aggression towards you will be dealt with, but you must attempt to temper your own."

She wanted to protest. She wanted to shout until she was blue in the face that he couldn't trust these creatures; none of them could. All she could see were the lines of cocoons, silk-wrapped victims just waiting to be eaten and then left to rot. How could Barrion stand in their nest and tell her to control herself when it was the Weavers that started all of this?

She looked him up and down again. It had all started with the Weavers taking him. "How did you get out?"

"I talked, Evren," he said. "And then I listened. You'll find that does wonders on a host's good will. Now, come. You were meant to be last, but I suppose we can do you and Arke together and get this over with once and for all."

He turned, and without another word of explanation, went back into the tunnel he came from. Evren looked at Gyda, hoping to see some distrust or unease there. Something to hint at Evren's gut feeling of being right. But she found nothing but worry in those eyes. Worry for her? Or for what she might do?

Evren swallowed her discomfort. "I follow you," she said hoarsely.

Gyda nodded, but instead of leading, she walked beside Evren and kept her hand on her back. It was warm and comforting, despite how much the nest made Evren's skin crawl. She wanted to lean into her touch and sink into the familiarity that it held. But Gyda only held her fully when she was doing something stupid or was about to die. Apart from that, Evren had to be content with the hand lying flat on her back.

The tunnel was dark, but not suffocatingly so in the way Serevadia had been. There was always light to be found somewhere. Near the corners were bright balls of fireflies clumped together and seemed content despite the large predators roaming by. The webs evened out the forest floor so that she wasn't tripping over roots or falling into little valleys of leaves.

And the nest was brimming with life.

All around her, the silk trembled with passing feet. Above her head, she could tell there were layers and layers of tunnels just like this one. All of them were easily twice as large as Anep, so the spiders could walk side by side or pass by each other with ease. None passed Evren and her group, and the tunnel was almost laughably big for all of them and Neri. But the sound of hissing and the chattering of mandibles soon became overwhelming. It wasn't from those around them, but ahead of them. It wasn't until she stepped out of the tunnel and into the next room did she realize why.

The tunnel fell away into a massive chamber. It was draped in enough silk to soften every harsh edge. Sunlight glittered warmly through the trees above. Pockets of fireflies nestled along the walls, and as Evren looked up, she could see the openings of more tunnels, each stacked higher and higher up. Those openings held chittering Weavers, their beady eyes fixed on the floor and the creature it held.

Evren's feet froze, and a strangled cry barely escaped her numb lips. Standing before her was the biggest Weaver she'd ever seen. A pale ashen-grey, flecked with ancient white hairs, its legs stretched across the entire massive chamber. Its body was shivering as if cold, and nestled deep within mounds and mounds of soft silk. And it's eyes . . .

"She's blind," Gyda murmured and nudged her closer. Evren barely registered her feet moving. All she could see were those eight filmy eyes staring sightlessly through her. "And she is kind. She will not harm you."

Every bone in Evren's body screamed otherwise. She wanted nothing more than to turn tail and run, dragging Gyda and Arke with her. But Gyda's hand at her back kept her moving steadily forward. Arke beside her looked somewhere between fear and awe, and he worried the hem of his tunic in his hands. His ears pricked up when they both heard a familiar laugh.

"Sorin." Evren breathed a sigh of relief as they climbed a little rise to be nestled between the Matriarch's front two legs. At the top was . . . well, everyone.

Sol, Abraxas, and Sorin were sitting together, looking a little tired and small without their armor and weapons, but otherwise unharmed. Sorin's worg was running between him and Lieutenant Kester, who was tossing a twig back and forth idly with a small smile on her lips. Behind her, all of Barrion's people sat unharmed. Many looked weak and terrified of the creatures around them. They relaxed only when Barrion came into view.

Barrion stopped before the Matriarch's feet and bowed low. "Matriarch Shelis, I bring you two new guests."

Shelis's body dipped low, her long legs quaking with effort until she righted herself again. *"Prince Barrion, we are beyond sssuch formalitiesss, are we not?"*

Her voice was a whisper in the wind and yet Evren felt it thrumming in the marrow of her bones. To her astonishment, Barrion straightened his back with a warm chuckle. "My fair lady, it is hard to put formalities beneath me in your presence."

"Flatterer."

"So I've been told." He smiled and opened his arm for Evren and Arke to step forward. Again, it was only Gyda that kept Evren moving forward as she corralled her up to Barrion's side and closer to the Matriarch. "Might I introduce the last of the Wandering Sols? Esteemed wizard, Arke of . . ."

He faltered and looked at the goblin questioningly.

Arke shrugged. "Just Arke."

"Right. Just Arke. And the brave leader, Evren Hanali of Orenlion."

A chorus of angry hissing erupted around them. The Weavers along the wall chittered angrily at the mere mention of Orenlion. All of them looked at Evren with varying postures of hate and distrust. A few even dared to climb down the walls, mandibles clicking as they ground out profanities.

Matriarch Shelis sighed heavily, and it echoed like a swift breeze in the chamber. All at once, the angry voices stopped. The Weavers climbing down scurried back up into their respective tunnels, still eyeing Evren suspiciously but keeping back for now.

"Daughter of Orenlion," Shelis breathed. *"I know who you are."*

Evren struggled to swallow the lump in her throat before speaking. "You do?"

"You were Xun Evren first."

Evren might've fallen if Gyda wasn't there to hold her up. She gave her a concerned look. "Xun?"

Evren was shaking. Every breath felt like a fight. Out of all the times she imagined hearing that name again, never did she expect to hear it from the mouth of the Weaver's Matriarch. "My father's name." She explained. "I . . . took my mother's last name when I left Orenlion."

Finally, Evren found the strength to leave Gyda's arms. She was colder for it, her skin still tingling with the echo of the warrior's touch. But she couldn't think with Gyda hovering over her. She took a step forward, meeting the Matriarch's eyes as fear played a delightful tune down her spine. Shelis might be blind, but Evren could've sworn those eyes were fixed on her.

"How do you know me?" she asked, her voice wavering. "How do you know my name?"

"You are a hunter."

"I never hunted you," she spat. "Which is more than I can say for your kind."

"Your father did."

Was it fear or grief that had its vicelike grip on Evren's throat? Whichever it was, she struggled to break free, to breathe. Her vision was blurry with tears she refused to let fall as she forced her words out, one by one. "What do you know of my father?"

An eerie, uncomfortable silence settled over the chamber. The only one who seemed unbothered with it was the worg pup, who gnawed noisily on the stick Mira had given up tossing. Everyone was staring at her and the Matriarch. No one seemed to dare to breathe.

"Xun Yuhan," Shelis said. *"Hunter of my people. Butcher of*

the Wood. Thief and Guardian both. I knew him well before he was lossst."

Evren's breath caught in her throat. "Did you kill him?"

Another chorus of hate and hissing rose in the air. This time it died down without the Matriarch's guidance. The ancient Weaver shuddered as if an icy breeze had swept through the chamber. The warm air did not stir.

"*No, child. No harm came to him here.*"

"Don't call me child," Evren snapped. Barrion held out a cautious hand to her, but she shrugged him off roughly. "You say you know me. You say you knew my father. And yet you resort to violence and darkness to bring me here. Your people look at me as if I've been the one hunting them down and killing them for centuries. You take me, imprison me, attack me, and then bring me here to, what? Lecture me? What is the point of this peaceful act if not to confuse me? I know what you are, and no amount of pretending you knew my father, who wouldn't have hesitated to kill you, will make me trust you."

Another shaky, weary sigh crept from the Matriarch's massive body. "*There isss much you have forgotten, whether intentionally or not. Sssit with your friendsss. I will sspeak again.*"

Forgotten.

As if Evren had done this before. She knew she hadn't. She knew in her gut that Weavers were intelligent monsters that her younger self wouldn't have dared gone to for answers. But . . .

She looked at her friends. Sol and Sorin with their barely bridled hope that she'd swallow her pride and sit with them. Arke and Gyda sharing a look of confusion, but also agreement. They thought she was acting irrationally; that one more sharp word would set off the nest and they'd die with no weapons to defend themselves. And Abraxas.

Abraxas had a familiar look in his eyes, one that mirrored her own not so long ago. In the belly of an icy ship, when she stood between him and something he thought was evil. Something he swore would turn around and kill them if given the chance. And she'd promised it wouldn't, because some part of her still trusted Keres despite their actions. She'd asked Abraxas to stay his blade, to trust her where he couldn't trust Keres.

And he had.

The message was obvious. She needed to trust him. Moreover, she needed to swallow her hate, even if it was just for a little while longer.

And so, Evren sat, begrudgingly, among her friends, nestled between the legs of something that her body screamed was an enemy, but her friends swore wasn't. She sat, but didn't relax when Sol hooked her arm through her own and held her tightly, or when Gyda and Arke sat on her other side. Friends surrounded her, but she couldn't get her stiff muscles to stop shaking.

Matriarch Shelis settled deeper into her webs when Barrion sat. When he whispered they were ready, Evren felt like a little kid waiting for the local storyteller to weave a ridiculous tale. Something her little brain would've eaten up and thought about for weeks on end. Something her adult mind would've seen for what it was, a pretty story with no truth.

"*You call uss Weaversss,*" Shelis began. "*A name Orenlion usesss in ssspite of knowing the truth. We are the Hisrachi, and the Wood was our home long before Orenlion wass built.*"

Evren frowned and started to protest, but Sol tugged her arm and Shelis kept talking. This was not a story she could argue with.

"*We are the Keepersss of the Wood. We lived here first. And when the elves came to make a home, we gave them a piece of our land. The Wood was meant to be respected, but above all, it was meant to be sshared. We were new to sssuch creaturesss. We knew not the fear in their heartsss.*

"*They built a grand city. They tamed the wild wyvernsss. They learned the magic of the treesss and hid their precious city within. Thisss they did with the help of the Hisrachi. Help we gave freely.*"

Evren couldn't keep quiet anymore. "They taught me that the Horizon Walker gave the elves Orenlion. She built a sanctuary so that none could find them if they weren't worthy. And then you attacked from the dark of the forest."

Something akin to a laugh whispered through the Matriarch. "*We know of thisss Elder. She wasss desssperate when she came here. She did not ssee us Hisrachi already living. But sshe was not the problem. When her death ssshattered the goodwill of the elves, they turned on us.*"

"Why would they do that?" Evren asked. "You said you were their allies."

"*That we were. We knew nothing of war, of violence through blades and arrowsss. Our fights were of survival against the witches of the wood, of the wyverns who would ssteal our young and the dragon who would hunt uss for sport. Thessse threats we knew well. It did not prepare usss for Orenlion'ss wrath.*

"*The elvesss saw a pale shadow at the hand of the Elder's death. The high priesssst, once a friend, saw usss as the only enemies in the Wood powerful enough to kill his goddess. We were the only intelligent beingsss who knew of her, who knew of Orenlion. Their wrath turned to usss, and the Wood burned for it.*

"*We sssuffered for centuries. Hunted near to death. Eggs sssmashed before they could tasste air and sssee ssunlight. The Archdruidsss of the Wood protected usss by hiding uss. But even their magic wasn't enough to temper sssuch hatred. We Hisrachi ssserve the Wood. We sserve the Archdruidsss. Our only true alliesss were them. But, when the dwarvesss came from the mountainsss and offered an end to the elves, we were bitter. We had sssuffered and lost and hid in our own home. Many Hisrachi took wrath into their heartsss and followed the dwarvesss into war. But not all.*"

Sol's grip on Evren's arm tightened, but the dwarf didn't say a word. She'd heard this story. Instead, Evren spoke again. "The

War of Widows. Orenlion nearly fell because of the dwarves and their alliance with you."

"*But the elvesss did not fall. They called for help. For the kingdomsss of the sssurface to tie the dwarvesss into treaties of peace.*"

"They didn't care about you," Evren said. "The dwarves at that time only cared for conquering. They would've turned on you when the fight was done."

"*Sso the child of ssstone said,*" Shelis said and gestured in Sol's general direction. "*Sso ssaid the Archdruidss before her. Asss I mentioned, Xun Evren, not all of uss fought. Many remembered why we were made. To protect to Wood, to sserve the Wood. Not to fight.*"

"You keep talking of the Archdruids," Evren said. "I've never seen them."

"*Ssso, you do not believe what you can't ssee?*"

"I didn't say that." She scoffed. "But why didn't they help you?"

"*They hid usss.*"

"But why didn't they do more? If you truly served them and the Wood, why didn't they fight for you?"

"*It iss not their way,*" Shelis insisted. "*They hide us, protect uss, but fight they cannot. Their bodiess are tied to the Wood. They cannot fight any more than the treesss can.*"

"So, you're telling me you're completely innocent?" Evren said. "That you've never done wrong to Orenlion and hurt their people?"

"*We are predatorsss, Xun Evren. Like yourself, we hunt to live. We mussst feed, the way any spider must. Why is it monstrous becausse we prey on larger things? Your people teach you about uss well. Well enough that you don't often stray into our webss.*"

"But you don't just trap us," Evren argued. "You don't just lie in wait. You hunt us in return."

"*Only thossse in our territory.*"

"It's grown since I last left."

"*It iss our home. There were no bordersss before Orenlion came.*" Shelis shuffled, as if she was trying to get comfortable, and the whole chamber shook as her legs tugged at the webs. When she settled, her clouded eyes looked tired. "*I will not spread liess. We are an angry people now. Many eggs hatch, and the children are filled with the ssame hate the elves harbor. It iss difficult to quell when we are treated as monssters in return. You have sseen our wrath. You bear your own. Have we done personal wrong to you?*"

Evren opened her mouth.

"*Before you returned to the Wood,*" Shelis added. "*Before you lead the kind prince here with bloodlust in your eyes.*"

Evren hesitated. She looked down at her scarred hands. "No. I never . . . hated your kind before. I was afraid, yes. My father taught me the signs of your nests and how to avoid them. He told me stories of what you did to hunters who strayed too far into your lands."

"*Xun Yuhan taught you respect, not hate.*"

Evren's head snapped up. "My father also left me to rot in Orenlion and never came back. Did you have something to do with that?"

The words felt raw as she spoke them. She'd locked them inside her hollow chest for so long that saying them aloud felt like she was tearing off her armor in the middle of a battle. Her father had left nearly ten years ago, and it had been so long ago she didn't think she was still angry about it. But she was angry at everything now, and Yuhan had more than earned her rage.

"Ten years ago, he leaves on a hunt and never comes back." She bit out every word like it was poison. "Ten years ago, he doesn't even say goodbye when he walks into the Wood and leaves me to fend for myself in a city I don't belong in. Tell me you had nothing to do with his death when you're so familiar with him, you know his name and what you think he taught me."

Her friends had stilled beside her. Even the Weavers, the Hisrachi, watched like statues. But Shelis didn't look phased. If a spider could show pity, her eight eyes gleamed with it. And Evren despised her for it.

"*Me and my kind had no hand in Xun Yuhan's disappearance, asss I have told you before.*"

"You didn't tell me that," Evren retorted.

"*Not thisss time, but before. When you came here reeking of desssperation and duty. You were much different then, ssstill whole, I think. I told you our ssstory then, just asss I have now. You took it as truth once, will you not once more?*"

Evren faltered. "I . . . I never came here before. I've never seen you. I knew nothing of your kind before now."

"*Your friendsss sspeak of your failing health. Gyda of the ice thinksss you do not remember all that you think you do.*"

"I don't," Evren admitted. "I thought I left Orenlion to escape a cage. But I lost something." Her fingers found the laces of her blouse, and she tugged them open enough for her to graze the top of her scar. Shelis couldn't see it, but Evren had the feeling that the Matriarch felt the scar in the air.

"*Your heart.*"

Evren blinked in surprise. "Yes."

"*You are much changed, Xun Evren. When you came here before, you were whole and ssseeking truth. You sssought a tassk even the Hisrachi could not complete.*"

"The Heart of the Wood." Evren shook her head even as she said it. The memory of her and Aster hiking through the Wood, hope in their lungs and autumn air, came to her like a tidal wave. "No, that was a fabrication. Gail was playing with my mind."

"*Magic cannot make ssomething out of nothing. There isss a give and a take. A measssure of ash to create fire, or ssstatic to churn lightning. The goblin tears magic-laced paper and ink to weave hisss ssspells. Would not thiss Gail tear through memoriess to create a falsse reality?*"

Evren's chest was tight again, and she gripped Sol's arm to stay steady. Perhaps too tightly but the dwarf didn't protest. "But if that's true . . . did I give my heart to the Wood?"

It had been dying then. Not all at once, but she remembered how tense Orenlion had been when autumn lasted longer than it should've. When the trees lost their warmth and the animals started dying. They thought it was because her father had left, and that his bloodline was all that kept the forest alive. Evren, to save herself and Aster from a marriage that would do nothing for the forest, had tried to find the source of the illness.

Only now, she didn't remember if she did. All she had was Aster screaming at her for turning her back on him, for not even trying to see if the wedding of their families would help. She felt Ainthe's claws digging into her chest again and sucked in a sharp breath. What was real? What was fabricated?

And in the end, would it even matter?

"I do not know what you did at the Heart of the Wood," Shelis said solemnly. *"But whatever it wasss, you healed the Deep Wood. And, desspite your anger, we of the Hisrachi owe you a debt."*

"What?" Evren exclaimed.

"We are creaturesss of the Wood. If you healed what we could not, you sssaved usss."

"Will I have to use that debt to let us all go free?"

Murmurs rose from a previously silent and transfixed crowd. Across from her, Barrion shook his head. "That was worked out while you were, ah, asleep."

Evren cocked her head quizzically, and he continued.

"The Matriarch heard that I was heading to Orenlion. She seeks peace between her people and the elves, in the same way I seek aid for my people. It's a bit of a complicated agreement, with a lot of extra amendments for Etherak and Hisrachi both, but they've agreed to let us go so long as we try to broker peace between Orenlion and Hisrachi."

Evren struggled to breathe again. Did Barrion even know

what he was asking? Forging an alliance with Orenlion would be difficult enough, but trying to get them to forget thousands of years' worth of fear and blood would be impossible. At best, they'd laugh in his face. At worst, they might actually kill him for even suggesting such a thing.

But she looked at him, and the resigned peace in his eyes, and she knew. He was aware of how difficult it would be. Maybe he even realized it was impossible. But, whether out of fear for his own life, or perhaps a sense of honor that few in the world seemed to have anymore, he was going to try. Even if it jeopardized his own plans.

She turned back to Shelis. "What about my father? Do you truly not know what happened to him?"

"*Assss before, I wish I had the answersss you seek. The only peace I can offer you isss that he did not fall by our websss and venom.*"

It wasn't much of a comfort, but she knew deep down that the Matriarch wasn't lying. She had no reason to, after all. Evren could be as discontent as she wanted to be, and Barrion would still carry out his mission. The Matriarch owed Evren no lies, no comforting words. But her truth was a far cry from what she needed.

11

Night had fallen and the Wandering Sols were still in the Hisrachi nest. Not that they weren't allowed to leave, it was just that Barrion was being a thorough diplomat and refused to leave until he had everything ironed out.

No matter how many promises the Matriarch made, Evren didn't feel safe in the nest. Even when Neri had shown her to a very private spot where she swore no Hisrachi would bother them, she still felt like her skin was crawling and that she didn't belong. The area they'd been allowed to stay in was high in the trees and made completely of sturdy webbing. But there was fresh, open air, and the floor felt like a hammock that moved gently in the breeze. Her party took their time finding their spots to rest and started passing out food. Evren stayed near the back, weaponless and still very much afraid, as Neri turned to leave.

"Did you lie?" she asked the spider suddenly, without turning back to look at her. Her eight legs froze, and the web bounced to a stillness as she hesitated.

"No," Neri finally said. *"I never lied to you, or Arke. Or anyone."*

"So, are you cursed?"

"*Yes. One of the witches of the Wood turned me into this, and the Hisrachi took me in as one of their own.*"

Evren looked at her slight form and where she'd started to anxiously rub her legs together again. "What were you before? An elf?"

Her mandibles moved slowly, as if she was chewing on the question. "*It's been too long . . . I don't remember.*"

"I see." Evren turned away. Neri's story was likely, and probably common. Evren had never dealt with a witch before, and the spider acted differently than the others in the nest. Arke trusted her, which meant Evren should too. But Evren, no matter how hard she tried, couldn't find it in her to care.

She didn't see or hear Neri leave, but when she turned back, the spider was gone. She crept into the space they'd been given, quickly finding her bag with the blankets, potions, and food she'd packed. No weapons or ammo, though. The Hisrachi didn't trust them. Evren didn't blame them.

She took her bag and settled a few feet from the edge. Her view of the forest was unrivaled. It was still black as pitch, but the leaves were sparse enough this high up she could see the stars and the moon. Silvery moonlight made everything shine. The air was a little sweeter this high up and felt cooler as it swept across her hot skin. Evren tried to let that calm her as she cleaned off the scrapes, dirt, and silk she still had stuck to her. She ate little, the hard cheese and bread a far cry from the silk of the cocoon, but the memory was still close enough for her to put them away after only a few bites. She spread out her bedroll, shook out her dwarven blanket and . . .

She sat.

The weight of the Matriarch's words wouldn't leave her. Being alone made her feel like she was swimming in a river with stones tied to her feet; only inches away from sinking and drowning. Her friends were only a few feet away, chatting happily and helping each other rub off the silk. But she couldn't bring herself to go to them, because then she'd have to smile and laugh with them or sour their mood. Beyond them, Barrion's soldiers relaxed and eagerly waited for his arrival. Mira even gave her a curt nod. Chayne was in the very back, refusing to look at her.

She could go to them. She could talk to Chayne at the very least and tell him she didn't hold a grudge for what he did. It couldn't have been easy lying and leading them into a trap. He probably thought Barrion's life was forfeit if he didn't. He was a soldier, young and scared, who'd done what he could to survive. She couldn't fault him for that.

But she couldn't bring herself to talk to him, either.

Evren turned away from both groups, hating the solitude but not being able to force herself closer to her friends. They would leave her alone, she knew. After everything that was said, they probably thought she wanted to be alone. And didn't she? Alone, she couldn't lash out and hurt someone. Alone, she didn't have to worry about if she was acting right. She could sink deeper into the ever-growing pit in her chest until morning came, and then she'd drag herself out and try to be better.

Evren rubbed her face, trying to force some feeling besides pain into her skin. She pushed her hair back and looked up at the stars. Everywhere she went, they followed her.

The Horizon Walker's death seemed to sink into the soil of Eith and taint everyone. Her death had caused the Shadow Dancer to hide away Serevadia, and for them to grow in power in the shadows, bitter and restless. Her death had caused Orenlion to war against the Hisrachi for centuries. How many elves and Weavers had died in the wake of that slaughter? How many dwarves had fed the fires of war for a taste of more blood? Evren was only mildly surprised that there wasn't an Elder causing the Long Night in the Reino Terminan, but even then Nerezza had shown her hand and stolen power. A daughter of Serevadia thrust on the surface and grabbing at more power than she could handle.

For what? A way to bring Serevadia into the light again? What was that if not another effect of the Horizon Walker's death?

Evren traced the scar on her chest again, her breaths feeling far too short and shallow to fill her lungs. Viggo's clue about the crown being in the Wood now seemed less like a far-fetched idea, and more like something to look for. Especially if—if Evren's gut was right—she had given her heart to the Wood. She still couldn't remember why, or how, but she knew for certain there was no taking it back.

Not unless she wanted to watch the Deep Wood die all over again.

The web dipped deeply to her left as Barrion settled beside her, cross-legged. He sighed, mussing his hair as if to relieve the tension in his scalp. The bags under his storm-grey eyes were heavy, and his shoulders hunched in on themselves in a very un-princely way.

"Quite a view," he said, his tone cheery despite his worn body. "It beats sleeping on the ground, no offense."

Evren wasn't up for small talk. "Orenlion won't go for peace, Barrion."

He sighed, all cheer draining out of him. "I feared as much."

"You could lose your own alliance if you push it," she warned. A chilling wind broke through the trees, hinting that winter still had grasping fingers even in the late spring. She drew her blanket over her shoulders, even as she instantly began to sweat. Her fever still hadn't left her.

"I gave Shelis my word I'd try." he said, ignoring the chill.

Etherakian, she thought. *Snow runs in their veins nearly as much as the Ikedree.*

"Orenlion nobles aren't known for being flexible," she said. "They have a council made up of the families of those who first fought against the Weavers. These are men and women proud of that heritage. You'll be asking them to shove their pride down and ignore the history they've fabricated. You'd have better luck talking a dragon into giving her egg up to scramble."

"It can't be all bad," he said with a small smile. "You turned out all right."

Evren snorted. "It doesn't feel like I did."

"Gyda told me why you're sick. If I can help—"

"You can't," Evren interrupted. "Even if you somehow could, you still couldn't."

"Why not?"

She eyed him knowingly. "You can't help everyone, Barrion. At some point, you have to choose your battles, pick a side, and put all your coin on one bet. If you don't, you'll lose everything."

He sighed and rubbed his eyes. They shifted away from her and back to the forest. Westward, where Etherak laid waiting for him. "If I don't try, then what's the point? There's so much to fix, and I have enough power to do it. Why can't I be the one?"

The longing in his voice tugged at her own. That need to fix, to stand between the threat and what he loved. She shared that and had the scars to prove it. And hells, she still had that longing, no matter how cold the hole in her chest became. She still wanted to fight, to protect, to fix. She just had no energy anymore. The world had bled her dry.

"Why are you doing this?" she asked in a hushed voice. "The alliance with Orenlion, the treaty with the Hisrachi? Why try to do the impossible?"

Barrion thought for a while as the wind tussled his hair and his black curls danced around the points of his ears. When he spoke, his voice was a whisper. "Because I was born into war and hate, and it broke the world. Because of my father, people died. More than that, they lost their homes, their livelihoods, and their cultures. The Divines are gone, the world is broken, and I feel like if anyone should fix it, it should be me." He finally met her gaze, his grey eyes solemn and dark. They were eyes of someone who mourned a father long before he'd truly died. "I will not be my father. And if I must break myself to prove it, then that's a small price to pay for the blood he shed."

Evren nodded; her words stuck in her throat. Because what could she say to that? A heavy legacy was nothing she wasn't familiar with, but Barrion carried the weight of everything his father had broken. Vernes, Gratey, Terevas, and even Etherak suffered. And then there were people like Abraxas, living with the stains on their hands and souls. How many other knights roamed Eith endlessly in hope for some redemption? How few found it?

Barrion was trying to stitch rock together with string. It was admirable, if foolish. And a part of Evren she thought had died sparked to life, just a bit.

"When we get to Orenlion, take Sol with you," Evren said, and Barrion looked at her with a puzzled expression.

"Why?"

"She's an excellent diplomat. She spent her whole life in the dwarven court, and she can help. Another voice can't hurt. Maybe Sorin too, if he's willing to try his magic again."

Barrion. frowned. "But you said you wouldn't go into Orenlion. Gyda said you needed to find a cure."

"I do." She nodded. "But I have no idea where to look. And if my gut is right, a cure for me could spell the end for the Wood." She looked out at the trees, as if she could see the glow of Orenlion from there. "No matter how much I've changed, I'll never put myself above this place. It was more of a home than Orenlion could ever be."

Barrion studied her for a while, as if she was a puzzle he couldn't quite sort out. In the end, he gave up with a massive sigh that shook his whole body. "I can see there's no fighting with you."

She smiled ruefully. "I'm afraid not, Your Highness."

He rubbed his chin thoughtfully. "Maybe there's a cure in Orenlion? Someone who could help you put together your missing memories."

Aster.

Evren swallowed nervously. If anyone knew what happened to her, it would be him. But was she ready to face him again? After she'd abandoned him the same way her father had her? Who was to say he would even help after so much time apart? Maybe Orenlion had finally poisoned him too, and he was just another snake waiting for her to get close. But maybe not . . .

"You should get some sleep, Your Highness," Evren said. "You look like you haven't slept in days."

"As a matter of fact, that's nearly true." He pushed himself to his feet and gave her one last look. "You as well, Evren. You wear your hollowness well, but it is weighing you down."

"I can't decide if that's a compliment," she said, puzzled. "But it doesn't sound like something sleep can fix."

"Sleep, a proper meal, and maybe a pleasant talk with your friends?" He shrugged. "Just a thought. I bid you goodnight." Ever the gentleman, he bowed low before carefully making his way back to his waiting bedroll.

Evren didn't give herself time to think. She gathered up her own roll and bag and awkwardly made her way to her circle of friends. They'd left a spot open for her, between Gyda and Sorin, as usual. She started to apologize and explain, but Abraxas held up an understanding hand, and they all gave her varying smiles of warmth. As she settled down, they went back to eating and tossing the pup scraps of food. Evren settled in, and no one breathed a word about her isolation.

12

Evren was happy to discover she had slept the entire night. She was happier to wake up how she fell asleep, with no cocoon or ambush waiting for her. She was less sure how to feel waking up mere inches from Gyda, as if she'd moved closer to the warrior in her sleep. There was a strange comfort in being closer to her that Evren couldn't quite name, although it could be the very same thing that drove her across the frozen Expanse crawling with the undead to save Gyda. She hadn't thought about it. She was just glad that Gyda had come back.

Evren scooted away from her, back to her own bedroll, and started packing up. A few minutes later, Gyda stirred, and if she knew how close Evren had crept in the night, she made no mention of it.

The Wandering Sols woke up on their own, some more gracefully than others. Sol somehow never looked unkept and woke up bright eyed and chipper as she dished out everyone's breakfast. Arke, on the other hand, was a mess of bleary eyes and wild hair.

Sorin snickered. "You look like you got struck by lightning."

The goblin scowled. "Ain't matter to me."

"Oh?" Sorin grinned devilishly. "So, you don't care how you look?"

"Nah." Arke gathered the crust out of his eyes and flicked it over to Sorin, who easily dodged their normal morning routine.

"Not even for your crush?" He waggled his eyebrows, and Arke froze mid-flick.

Abraxas stopped tying his hair back. "What's this about a crush?"

"Nothin'!" Arke said quickly.

"Someone said crush?" Sol hopped back to her spot. She studied Arke for a few seconds and then gasped. "You're blushing!"

"Am not!" The goblin still covered his cheeks, which were turning a darker shade of green by the minute.

"You are!" Sol bounced and the whole web did too, sending Evren's stomach churning. "Who is it?"

"Nobody."

"Oh, you haven't guessed?" Sorin turned to Sol as if they were sharing a particularly coveted piece of cake. Arke's yellow eyes went as wide as moons.

"Don't you fuckin' dare, you little salt demon."

"That's new," Sorin said with a raised eyebrow.

Abraxas smiled and finished tying off his hair. He never smiled wide enough to cause his entire face to lift and brighten, but it softened his usually hard-set mouth. "I don't suppose you have any particular fondness over our guide, Neri, then?"

Arke made a small squeaking sound. And then Gyda burst out into rolling laughter that shared kindred with thunder. It shook the whole web, and Evren felt her chest lighten by the mere sound of it. Unlike Abraxas, when Gyda smiled, it was everything. And she smiled often, despite her icy demeanor towards most things. She laughed at Sorin's vulgar jokes and his worse antics. She smiled when Sol was talking about something she was so passionate about that the dwarf was bouncing on her feet and waving her hands around. She smiled on the battlefield with Abraxas, her laughter chilling to all those opposing her and a rallying call to any who called her friend.

It was quickly becoming Evren's favorite sound.

"You do." Gyda's grin towards Arke somehow made him relax, although he didn't stop scowling. "That little spider and you talked for hours last night before she left."

"She ain't a spider." Arke put up a finger. "She's cursed to be one."

"Looks spidery to me," Sorin muttered, and then stifled a yelp as Arke elbowed him in the side.

Weary and still aching from her fever and fight with Anep, Evren forced a smile towards Arke. "You really like her?"

He hesitated and then nodded curtly. "It's odd. I just met her, and she's . . . different. But it's like I can see what she was before, ya know? What she's tryin' to be."

"That I can understand," Gyda said softly. "But she is cursed."

He snorted. "Many are. It's common in Terevas. Maybe . . . Bah! Never mind."

"You want to break her curse." Evren said what he couldn't, and again he nodded.

Abraxas whistled. "That's a tall order."

"I can find a way," the goblin insisted. "Even if this don't lead to nothin', I can help her. Someone should."

"I said it was a tall order, not that it was impossible," Abraxas corrected. "I'm not sure how we can help, but I'm sure while finding Evren's heart and healing a few centuries' worth of bad blood between two people, we'll find a way."

Arke narrowed his eyes at Abraxas. "That's awfully optimistic of you."

"I have my moments." He cocked his head to the side, as if remembering something, then rummaged through his bag. "Just because my romantic comings and goings have failed doesn't mean I wish it on others. However, it would be best if you cleaned yourself up." Abraxas finally found what he wanted, and with a flash of silver in the morning light, handed Arke a cracked silver hand mirror.

Arke took it and combed through his hair, while Sol scooted over and tried to help him. Sorin eyed Abraxas instead.

"I guess I should've known you'd have a fancy mirror in your bag with all the time you spend on your hair."

Abraxas scoffed. "It was a gift." He gestured towards Gyda.

Gyda shrugged. "Sahar insisted that it'd be useful and powerful. She called it a Fey gift."

"And you gave it to Abraxas?" Sorin blustered.

"Why not?"

Before Sorin could argue more, Arke stopped fixing his hair. "Fey gift?"

Gyda nodded. "What does it mean?"

He looked back at the mirror in his hands. "Dunno. Could be anythin'. But Sahar was right, it'd be powerful in its own way."

"Powerful is a puppy that can shoot lightning out of his eyes," Sorin muttered.

Evren smiled. "And yours can?"

"I'm holding out hope."

"Hope for what?"

Arke got even greener as Neri picked her way over the web to him. Now that Evren was looking for it, she could see the way Arke's smile softened around her, and how his shoulders stopped hunching, so he looked more relaxed. She wasn't sure about Neri, since giant spider body language was beyond her, but she could've sworn Neri's eyes glistened excitedly when he turned towards her.

"Nothin'." Arke put the mirror in his lap. "Sorin and his pup again."

Neri's eyes followed the mirror though and her legs danced excitedly. *"You have a Fey gift!"*

Arke's ears perked up. "You know what it is?"

Her mandibles started chittering with her newfound energy.

"Yes! I've seen a few before . . . well, I know them. Maybe I used to study them."

Evren couldn't help but smile sadly as she watched Neri try to dig through her memories. Why she could remember an object of magic, but not even what she used to be must be hard. "Do you know what it can do?"

"I think so . . . May I?" She held our two of her legs questioningly, and Arke gave her the mirror without hesitation. She cradled it, as if it were a newborn child she held in her legs and not a silver mirror. Her eight eyes danced across the surface as she studied it. *"I think it needs to be broken."*

Sol frowned. "Broken? But it's beautiful. Why would we break it?"

"It's already cracked." Neri pointed out. *"I think it's a clue. Fey like their gifts to be puzzles as well, so you have to work for their power. They have a different way of giving gifts than we do."*

Abraxas tapped his chin thoughtfully. "It's rumored that the Fey have their own world beyond ours, like the Divine Realm and the Hells. It's said to be a mirror of our own, an Eith with unbridled magic and light, where ours is darkened."

"Mirrors and mirrors," Arke muttered and took back the mirror when Neri offered it. Without looking up, he squinted at the bright, cracked surface, and then he dug into it with his long claw.

Evren watched with bated breath as he tried to pry up a piece. She wasn't sure why she was nervous, but it wasn't until Gyda chuckled beside her and whispered, "Remember to breathe, Evren," that she even realized she wasn't.

"Right," she muttered and sucked in a breath.

After a few minutes of fiddling, Arke let out a cry of triumph, and a shining shard of glass winked in the sunlight. "Catch!" he said, and flicked it over to Evren.

She barely did that, and the sliver of mirror bounced from hand to hand until she cupped both hands around it. "Thanks?"

"What do you see?" Neri asked with unbridled curiosity.

Evren frowned at her but unfurled her fingers to look down at the mirror shard. It was nearly as long as her hand, and sharp enough to hurt if used properly. But she squinted at the widest part. At first, she saw nothing but tree limbs and leaves with sprinkles of silk here and there. And then she caught sight of a wisp of white hair and a yellow eye.

She gasped. "Arke, look at your mirror!"

He did, and suddenly all she could see was him staring back at her. His eyes widened, and he jerked away from the mirror. "You!"

She looked up, grinning. "You!"

Sorin looked back and forth between them. "What's going on?"

But instead of answering, Arke passed out chunks of the mirror. In the end, there were exactly six—one for each of them—and they took turns looking at each other. It was hard to work at first. Evren's mirror always showed pieces of all of them, unless she and one other exclusively used their mirror. But she felt thrills of excitement go through her, regardless of how much time it would take them to learn how to use the mirror.

"I wonder if you can talk through them," Arke said excitedly. "Splitting up wouldn't be so hard anymore."

Neri seemed to smile, although it was hard to tell. *"I think time will only tell. You still have a long journey ahead of you."*

And just like that, Evren watched Arke's face fall a little. Neri wasn't there to chat and help them with their Fey gift, she was there to lead them out.

"We're leaving?" Evren asked, instead of *We're free to leave?*

"Matriarch Shelis wishes you good fortune on your journey and quest. Your armor and weapons will be returned to you once you leave."

Evren exchanged looks with everyone in the party, as if asking for a vote. But there was no point in staying past their welcome, and Evren was glad to leave. Even if it was just exchanging the nest for Orenlion, one thinly veiled threat for another, she was sure she'd never feel comfortable with the Hisrachi, no matter Shelis's promises.

It took no time to gather the rest of their things to leave. Barrion and his people were quick to pack as well, and before long, they were all following Neri through the winding tunnels of the nest. It was a quiet walk, and one that no Hisrachi interrupted. It was if they'd rearranged their whole nest to avoid their guests. Evren wasn't surprised or disappointed not to see any as they walked.

But it was strangely bittersweet for everyone else. She could see Abraxas pausing to look down every corridor they didn't take before he walked away from it, as if he was afraid he'd miss something amazing. Sorin alternated between letting the worg pup run ahead, and then chasing after him when he got too far. The pup was trailing more silk from his mouth by the time Sorin decided to just hold him the whole way through.

Evren could hear Sol talked to Barrion animatedly about different tactics and arguments they could use from their spot in the back. She turned to glance back at her friend and smiled. Sol's entire body was relaxed in a way that Evren hadn't seen since Heliodar's betrayal. Her grin was blinding, and her good mood seemed to rub off on Barrion as well, who was waving his hands in the air as if demonstrating their strategy in front of them.

Evren turned back around as they entered another winding tunnel leading to the forest floor.

At the head of their little pack, were Neri and Arke. And if Sol looked relaxed, Arke looked like he was about to melt into his clothes from lack of tension. They whispered back and forth, spider and goblin. It was almost heartwarming to watch.

If Evren had a heart.

"They somehow fit," Gyda murmured as she watched them.

Evren hummed in agreement. "He's going to be a grouch for the next couple hours," she said.

"Perhaps."

Evren looked up at her questioningly and the warrior shrugged before explaining, "Maybe he'll focus on removing the curse and spend all day with his nose in his book. Maybe he'll be excited he got to spend more time with her. Not everything ends sadly."

Evren tried not to frown. "No, it ends more bittersweet. Leaning on bitter a lot."

"Some people don't like sweet things."

"Oh?"

Gyda nodded, her eyes thoughtful and not looking at Evren when she said. "There is a unique kind of love for something that doesn't make it easy to do so. You must fight for it, and sometimes yourself. Sometimes it's not good for you. Sometimes it hurts more than it loves, and you must walk away. But, for those that prefer it, it is the best kind of love. Hard earned, finding beauty in pain. An acquired taste, as Sol would say. Perhaps Arke prefers to work through the bitterness for a taste of sugar at the end."

Evren hadn't heard Gyda talk about love before. She wanted to ask her what kind of love she preferred, but couldn't get the words out. She turned back to the tunnel. "Maybe he does."

The rest of the walk through the nest was quiet. When the ground turned from spongy to hard, she felt herself sigh in relief. Neri led them through the ground level, until the webs thinned out, and all their weapons and armor waited for them there. Neri watched them closely as they quickly grabbed what was theirs. Gyda swung her sword a few times and checked the runes along the hilt. The new one glowed brighter than the others. Abraxas took a while to put his armor on, and Sol went to help him along while Sorin and Arke dug through the pile to find Arke's spellbook.

Evren hefted her bow, checking for any damage and content to find it unmarked. Besides the damage she'd done, of course. Her quiver was still mostly full, and her armor intact. She didn't bother putting it on; her skin was far too hot and tight to entertain the mere thought.

Out of the corner of her eyes, Neri shrunk back a little. That was all it took for Evren's anxiety to go through the roof. Her fingers were still fumbling for an arrow when she snapped around towards the entrance of the nest. They froze when she saw Anep's massive form dangling from the web, now in front of her by mere feet. She didn't draw an arrow, but she didn't let go either.

Her eyes watched him as Anep carefully slid down to the ground. He was just above her eye height when he straightened up, and she bristled at the fact that she had to look up to him. Behind her, everyone was deathly still, as if they were waiting for one of them to snap.

Evren was ready to. She didn't even have to fire the arrow; she could just jam it into his eyes when he leapt at her. She'd have to make sure he couldn't catch the arrow like he did with the dagger. It wouldn't hold up like Orenlion steel under the pressure of his mandibles.

A thick, dark silence stretched between them. Neither bothered to break it by talking or moving. The entire forest seemed to hold its breath.

And then Anep held out one of his legs.

Evren tensed and took a step back, but he made no move to hurt her, even though his tight muscles suggested he wanted to. Perched on the end of his leg was the wyvern dagger.

She frowned at him. "You'd give me this after I tried to kill you with it?"

Anep hissed and drew back a little, but the dagger remained on his extended leg. *"I would give it to the elven rat crawling back to Orenlion. The Matriarch requiresss it of me."*

Evren smirked and let her hand drop from her quiver. "She really forced you to apologize, huh?"

"Ssshe did no sssuch thing!"

"Oh, but I do accept your apology, Anep," she said as she

took the dagger back and watched him bristle at the use of his name.

He drew himself up a little taller, and his shadow fell over Evren. *"No apology, rat. If it were up to me, you would not be whole and pulsing with life. I do not forget what your kind hasss done to me, or my family. The losssses we endured, the torn corpsssses of loved ones we find after you desssicrate them and leave them like they are filth, that I do not forget. That I will never forgive."* His mandibles clicked audibly as he stared at Evren with enough hate to make her feel like she was bathing in fresh blood. *"Centuries of killing will not be erasssed because of your prince. And we will alwaysss remember those who wrong usss."*

With that, he turned and left as quickly as his legs could move him. Evren knew better than to think fear drove his speed. Anep was not afraid of her, or any of them. It was hatred and disgust that carried him away and settled in the hollow of Evren's chest as she turned away from the nest.

She clutched the wyvern dagger and suddenly felt that Orenlion was far too close for comfort. She could almost smell it in the air. It made her sick, so she put the dagger away and the feeling lessened.

"Time to go," she said.

Arke and Neri said a hurried goodbye before the march of anxious people took him away. Evren didn't look back as the nest faded behind them, but she saw Arke look over his shoulder time and time again, until the webs disappeared and took Neri's small form with them.

13

"I told Chayne you wouldn't come back for us," Mira said as they walked side by side again. She'd taken up her normal spot at the head of the group with Evren, and their slow march through the vast trees made it feel like the Hisrachi nest was all one bad fever dream. If it wasn't for Arke's sullen mood and Sol and Barrion loudly talking about their plans for peace, Evren could pretend it had been.

The wyvern dagger weighed heavily in her bag.

She looked over at Mira. The lieutenant wasn't paying her any attention, or was going to great lengths to appear like she wasn't. Her brown hair stuck to the back of her neck, slick with sweat, and she wiped the perspiration off her brow as she continued not to look at Evren.

She was angry.

"You did?" Evren asked, because she didn't know what else to say.

Mira cut her a knowing look. "You don't strike me as the type to dive into danger for strangers."

Evren was inclined to believe her, but the problem was, she *was* that type. At least, she used to be. And she used to be proud of it. Now, her mouth was dry, and she struggled to swallow enough to speak. Was it shame or the fever that made her skin hot? Her friends telling her she'd changed was one thing, but someone she barely knew was different. They saw Evren exactly how she felt; hollow except for all the nasty things that had been festering inside her. She wasn't hiding herself well anymore.

Then again, she never asked to be a hero. She never asked to be the wall between chaos and order. Eith killed its protectors, slowly but surely. It was killing her, and she was tired of pretending that she was even marginally the same woman that stepped into the Yawning Deep.

That woman bled herself dry. That woman turned pain into a power that cost far more than she ever expected. And, in return, she was rotting from the inside out.

"You're not a stranger," Evren said finally and turned away from Mira. "And I did come for you."

"Your party did," Mira corrected. "You just tagged along."

Evren didn't try to correct her. After all, she was right. Evren would've left them. So, she pushed herself a little harder, ignoring how lightheaded she got, and walked away from Mira.

Mira didn't keep up with her.

They took a break at midday, from which Evren barely got up from. She ignored all the stares of pity and confusion as she lingered at the camp site hissing in pain. With the bruises all over her body from her fight with Anep finally coming through, deep red and purple against her sweating skin, they probably thought he hurt her worse than she let on. Her whole body felt like it was burning from the inside out. Every muscle screamed in pain. After leaving the nest and setting out for Orenlion, the fever had come back with a vengeance, and Evren didn't bother to cover it up.

She thought about nicking herself to give herself a brief break from the pain. Something to clear her head and give herself a rush of strength. But she knew better than to try outside of a fight. So, she drank her water and ate when Abraxas told her to. She allowed Gyda to take the lead while she muttered directions from behind her. She pretended not to notice how many times Sorin loudly professed he or the pup had to use the restroom, so everyone would have to stop and she'd get another break. Evren didn't want any of it. She didn't want Sol's little comments on how beautiful the Wood was to cheer her up, or Arke's experiments with the mirror shards. She wasn't even sure what she wanted, but it wasn't this.

By sunset, they were setting up camp and Evren was leaning against a tree trying not to puke up the food Abraxas insisted she needed to eat. Her body couldn't decide if the warm tree was what it wanted or if it was still too hot to handle any more heat. The bark pressed into her forehead as she took in deep breaths. When she closed her eyes she felt like she was falling, so she forced them open and focused on the brilliant orange of the sunset deepening the shadows to a rich black at her feet.

Evren didn't even hear Sorin or his pup approach until the worg was running around her boots to chase his tail. She murmured a weak hello to Sorin, who stood just behind her.

"I thought you were getting better," he said quietly. Not that anyone would hear them. Sol and Barrion kept the whole camp busy and loud to prepare dinner.

Evren sucked in a sunset-stained breath. "It comes and goes."

"Yes, but you looked good this morning."

"Thanks."

She could hear him roll his eyes. "That's not what I meant. You looked like you weren't sick."

"I was," she said and pushed off the tree. She could feel the imprints of the bark against her forehead and her stomach didn't settle, but Sorin liked it when people looked at him while he was talking. She could at least do that for him. "I always am now. It didn't get bad until we started moving. Abraxas says that's normal."

"Normal?" Sorin laughed humorlessly. "What about this is normal?"

The worg tired of Evren's legs and bounded over to Sorin.

He barked impatiently until the Vasa scooped him up into his arms. His belly was rounder, almost comically so. Sorin was spoiling him. He rubbed the fat belly while he stared at her worriedly.

"Tell me what I can do, Evvie."

"Nothing."

"That's shit, and you know it."

"I don't, actually," she said bitterly. "I don't know a damn thing anymore, Sorin."

"Doesn't that bother you?" he asked, frustration seeping into his words enough for the pup to whine a little.

Evren chewed her lip. "It used to."

"And now?"

"It worries me more that I find myself not caring."

He sucked in a breath like she'd punched him in the gut. His eyes looked like liquid gold in the sunset, and they were wide and unbelieving. "We've fought worse than this."

She shook her head. "It's not a matter of fighting. It's just . . . searching. And hoping."

"You're not doing either."

She smiled a little for him, feeling her chapped lips crack as she did. She could always count on Sorin to call her out on her shit. "You can do something for me, actually."

He instantly perked up, and the pup mirrored him with alert ears and hopeful eyes. "What? What can I do?"

"Sing," she whispered, so as not to scare him off. His eagerness flooded right out of him, and he fell back on his heels. "You haven't sung in so long."

"I sang for the funerals in Direwall," he offered weakly.

"I don't want you to sing because you're sad, or because you have to, Sorin." She sighed heavily. "I want you to sing because you can't keep yourself from the melody."

"I-I can try. I haven't really since Heliodar . . ." his voice broke, and he looked away. "But I can try—"

Evren took a few unsteady steps towards him and put her hand on his shoulder. "Not now. When you're ready."

"I don't know when I'll be ready," he said. "Or if I ever will be."

Evren shrugged. "Whenever you're ready, I'd love to hear it again." She didn't want to add *before I can't anymore.* Sorin was strong, but resurrection had left a dark mark on him he hadn't recovered from. He was still the light in the Wandering Sols, and she wouldn't darken him with her thoughts of a short future.

Before either of them could say more, a shrill cry pierced the still, darkening air. They jumped apart, eyes to the sky. The orange was fading fast, and the rest of the Wood was eerily quiet.

"What was that?" Sorin hissed. He was clinging to the pup tightly, enough for the worg to squirm and whine to get out of the grip. Or maybe he was just afraid.

The cry sounded again, and the pup went stock still. The source was close.

"Wyvern," Evren said, eyes combing the tree line. "It's a hunting call."

"But we're not in their territory, right?"

Evren shook her head, and she didn't know if she wanted to smile or run in the other direction. Instead, she turned to Sorin. "We're not in theirs's, but we must be in Orenlion's. Get the others and break camp."

"What? We just set down!"

"This could be our only chance to get into the city," Evren said as she picked up her bow. "Now go get everyone before I change my mind."

She was about to. She was about to tell Sorin *Never mind! I got it wrong* and go to sleep for the night. But she knew the Khama wouldn't stick around for long. They'd finish off whatever they were hunting, and they'd disappear back to the city.

But if they saw her . . .

Evren threw her fear aside and ran. Which her body hated, and so did her throbbing, overthinking mind. But she did it anyway. She heard confused shouts from behind her; her friends possibly trying to catch up to her. Even if they couldn't, the sounds of the wyverns were easy to follow. They pierced the air like a siren's call, leading Evren one hurried step after the other closer to them.

If she was the poetic sort, she might've said it was a sudden rush of nostalgia or longing that drove her through the trees and their darkening shadows. Because, in a moment like this, she could almost forget everything she hated about Orenlion in favor of the things she loved and missed. But the heartless do not forget, and she was not a poetic soul. With every footfall closer, she wanted to turn back. With every tree passed, she was relieved to find only shadows.

It wasn't longing that kept her running. It was the promise of an end. No matter how much she dreaded it.

That promise kept her going. It kept her from thinking of her faltering body. The way her lungs cried out for more air than she could give them, and her legs trembled to the point of nearly crumbling beneath her. For one bright and shining moment, her focus made her feel whole again.

Until she stopped, and everything came crashing down on her at once.

The rough bark scraped against her palms as she tried to slow her fall. All it did was drive her to her knees and not her face. Her bones rattled at the impact. The air was too hot and thick. She pressed a dirt-caked palm against her head to ease the pounding that brought tears to her eyes and left her gasping.

Too much. She did too much, went too far, pushed too hard.

Evren was barely aware of the wyvern's calls right above her now. The rushing beat of their wings tossed leaves on her skin that cut. The smell of poison and brimstone hung like a heavy cloud.

At least she found them before she collapsed.

She forced herself to sit back on her haunches just as Arke

appeared beside her. He steadied her with a hand. "You all right, kid? We almost lost—"

His eyes snapped away from her, and then his spellbook was out faster than Evren could track. "Hey! Back off!"

Evren tried to clear her throbbing eyes enough to see. He was already pulling a paper from his book and crumbling it in his hands. The surrounding air chilled, and it was a balm on her struggling lungs, her flesh prickled in goosebumps. He hadn't used ice in a while, especially after Direwall. Fire was much more his speed. He remembered her lecture on wyverns' weaknesses then.

Evren held out a hand to stop him. "Arke, don't," she gasped.

"They ain't hurtin' her!"

Finally, Evren looked ahead.

There were five wyverns in total. Great scaled beasts with two muscular hind legs and thunderous wings. Both the wings and the legs ended with jagged claws, perfect for climbing. Their slender necks ended in viscous snouts bristling with teeth and rows of spiked frills to protect their face and neck. Two were perched on the trees, powerful limbs poised and ready to jump. The other three were circling in the air, and their cries of triumph sent Evren's head reeling again.

It confused their prey as well.

A lone Hisrachi stood in the middle of it all. Legs bunched up tight in fear, all eight eyes wide and trying to track every wyvern at once. It kept turning in circles, but every angle had its back exposed to another wyvern. It was smaller than most Hisrachi, and utterly familiar.

Neri.

Evren didn't remember drawing her bow. She barely remembered pulling the tight bowstring back or looking down the shaft of her arrow. But she recalled changing her aim from the eye of the closest wyvern to the rider sitting on its back.

The wyvern shrieked in alarm and jerked away from the

arrow. It glanced off the armor of the rider, who whipped around to face Evren.

The Khama were just as beautiful as she remembered. Their lovely armor glittered in the fading light, the same color as the scales of the wyverns. Some a deep bronze, others a green so pale it looked like jade. Their helmets obscured their faces, all but their eyes. The longbows in their hands were tall and thin, and the arrows tipped with the same poison their wyverns carried.

And they were all staring at her.

Evren forced herself on her feet and nocked another arrow. She tried to calm her breathing and look strong. She didn't want to look like she was a stiff breeze away from passing out. Her arms shook anyway as she gripped her bow. Her voice did too.

"That was a warning shot," she said, and felt all the recovered air rush out of her. "Leave the Weaver be."

The rider she shot at narrowed their eyes down at her. Their wyvern clung stubbornly to the neighboring tree and raked its claws up and down the trunk to send bark flying. It hissed at her, and the smell of heated poison crept thicker in the air as it gargled in the back of the wyvern's throat.

"You dare interfere with a wyvern's hunt?" the rider asked. Female then, her voice strong and clear even as her steed buckled underneath her.

"Only this one," Evren said. She eyed the other wyverns. Two of the riders had aimed their bows at her. One of them was smart enough to focus their efforts on Arke, who was still hanging onto his spell as frost coated the ground around him. "The spider is under my protection. Unless you'd like an ugly fight, I'd suggest you stand down."

This time it was another rider who spoke up, his words lacing with laughter. The wyvern under him was smaller than the rest, and her scales were fresh and unscarred. The unhinged look in her eyes did not mirror her rider's confident nature.

"And who are you to stand between us and this creature? Do you have any idea who you're dealing with, mutt?"

He's new, she thought with a small smile. *Very new.*

Evren drew back her arrow and aimed it at him. His wyvern hissed at her audacity, and the frills along her neck puffed up to make her look larger.

"I wonder how well you've done training your mount." Evren asked. "She has a wild streak about her. Wild enough not to know better if I say, shot at your leg and missed. If I hit her flank, will she still lash out at the arrow and take your leg off? Or are you a more competent hunter than you look?"

As if to prove her point, Evren moved her aim exactly where she threatened. A twinge of satisfaction blossomed in her belly as his leg moved to the side.

"You wouldn't dare!" he hissed. "Attacking one of us means you attack all of us. We have you outnumbered."

"Not for long," Evren said coldly.

"Enough!" The first rider cut off the second before he could retort. With a snap of her legs, her wyvern leapt from his perch on the tree and onto the ground. Neri scuttled away as fast as she could and stood behind Evren and Arke as the rider jumped off her wyvern's back. The wyvern was older, a massive knot of scarring on his shoulder free from the bronze of his scales. Saliva dripped from his jaws as Evren lowered her bow.

The rider sauntered up to Evren and was only a few feet away when she took off her helmet and tucked it under her arm. Ink-black hair tumbled free, and long ears slipped well past the strands. A face as pale and as cold as the moon stared back at her. Plump lips and high cheekbones gave her the look of a high noble lady, but the fire in her brown eyes and the scar cutting one of her eyebrows in half said otherwise. Those lips turned up into a knowing smirk as she looked Evren up and down.

"Well, well." She shook her head. "Here I thought I'd never see your face challenging me again."

Evren couldn't help but smile back. "Song Mei." She bowed her head. "You're a better rider than the last time I saw you."

"And you," Mei pursed her lips, "look like shit."

Mei's eyes flickered over Evren's shoulders just as her own wyvern hissed a warning. Evren turned to see the rest of her friends catching up. Gyda and Abraxas with their swords drawn, Sol sandwiching Barrion between her and Mira. Sorin was closer to the back, trying to wrangle his worg into his bag as the pup tried to run from the wyverns.

Evren held a hand up to them, and Arke, who still hadn't stood down. "It's fine. Put down your weapons."

A tense moment tightened between the two groups. Even with Barrion's soldiers, fighting the wyverns and their riders would be a slaughter fest. The Khama were the best fighters Orenlion had to offer, and their bond with their steeds made them even more dangerous. But that was something Abraxas could sense without being told. He sheathed his sword, and then Sol put away her daggers. One by one, the soldiers did the same. Arke folded his spellbook back into side, and the frost dissipated. Only then did Gyda lower her blade, but she did not sheath it.

Mei flicked her hand to tell her Khama to do the same. The other riders started to relax a little. Their bows lowered, and their wyverns snapped at each other rather than at Neri or the newcomers. But the young one was still not giving up.

"Song, what are you doing?" he asked. "She attacked you."

"Even looking like death, Evren wouldn't have attacked and missed me," Mei threw over her shoulder. "Unlike you during training, she can hit a target."

"Only when I'm not thinking about it," Evren said wearily.

"Evren?" The surprise in the rider's voice was thick. "Xun Evren?"

Evren winced. New enough not to know her face, but not so new that he didn't know her name. Then again, it hadn't been so long since she'd been in Orenlion. A little over three years at most. Why did it feel like decades since she'd last sparred with Mei, or heard the calming lilt of her accent?

Mei looked back at the rider. "Lady Xun, if we're being proper. Which we are, Gao."

"But she—"

"I'm well aware of what she did." Mei shrugged, and her armor clinked delicately as if it couldn't deflect off a dozen well-aimed arrows. "Which brings me to my next question. What are you doing here?"

There was more to it than that, Evren knew. Mei wanted to know everything, always did. Starting with why and how, and ending with who the hells are these people? Evren didn't blame her, so she motioned for Barrion to step forward.

"I was asked to guide someone important to Orenlion," she said as Barrion fell in place beside her.

He bowed low, lower than a prince should. Mei regarded him cautiously. "I am Prince Barrion Rhys, first of my name and heir to the throne of Etherak." He straightened up and put on a warm smile. "I was hoping to meet with your leaders and make history."

Barrion's smile would've melted anyone else. It made people want to trust him. But Mei became even icier, if that was possible. "You are a prince?"

"Yes. Although, I'll admit, I've seen better days. A bath will turn me into royalty in no time."

She snorted, and so did her wyvern, which was a strange sight, and Barrion drew back as if the beast was going to snap at him.

"Royalty isn't in the way you look," Mei said. "It is in the way you hold yourself. You bowed to me."

"Out of respect," Barrion defended.

"Respect I did not earn. You don't know me; therefore, your respect is as good as perfume on a pile of worg shit. Useless." Mei turned away from Barrion and back to Evren. Her disregard of the prince couldn't have been more obvious, but the way she regarded Evren sent more than a few tongues wagging behind her.

"You ran and came back to bring us a prince?" she asked. "What is your game?"

"No game." Evren held her hand up. "Believe me, I didn't want to come here. But Barrion is who he says he is and is working towards something greater than us."

Mei frowned at her. "Many things are greater than us, Evren. That has never stopped you from turning your back on them in the past."

"Consider this an apology." Evren took a breath. "And a surrender."

The fierce Khama rider had never been a close friend, but Evren knew her well enough to see the smart of surprise in her eyes, as well as the doubt. During the hopeful years Evren had buried herself in training to be a Khama, Mei had been her instructor. She knew how Evren fought as well as she breathed. She knew her words carried the weight of mountains.

Mei turned back to the rest of the riders sharply, and her Elvish words stung like the bite of a whip when she addressed them.

"Fly back to Orenlion and tell them the news. Lady Xun has returned to us and brought an Etherakian prince with her. Their retinue is not to be harmed on my order."

There was no hesitation or questioning as the riders took off to the sky and left. They left only a hurricane of leaves and dirt in their wake. Mei went over to her wyvern and murmured a few words to him. The beast snorted indignantly, but eventually took her words and flew off as well.

When she turned back to them, her face was stony and serious. "My name is Song Mei, and I will now be your guide to our sacred city. But, before we go further, I would know your names and purpose."

Her eyes fell on Evren's party rather than Barrion's soldiers, and it wasn't hard to see why. The soldiers were obviously just that, with their uniforms and close eyes on Barrion. The

Wandering Sols were a strange assortment of people who didn't quite fit; Evren felt proud as she looked back at them.

"These are the rest of my party," Evren said. "The Wandering Sols."

"Party?" Mei's eyes flashed curiously. "Adventurers then?"

Abraxas was the first to step forward. "Yes. My name is Abraxas Kain. I, as well as my friends, stand with Evren. This is Gyda, of the northern Ikedree clans. Beside her is Solri Amet of Dirn-Darahl and Sorin of . . ." he sighed, exasperated. "Sorin, what are you doing?"

Sorin was not paying attention. He and the worg pup were still wrestling over the bag situation and, despite being a fraction of the Vasa's size, the pup was winning and had all but one paw out of the bag.

"I'm fine! All good. Would you just—OW! Come back here, you little turd nugget!" Sorin leapt after the pup as he wiggled free of the bag and ran for Neri's still shaking legs.

"Just Sorin." Abraxas waved him off.

"Of course." Only the slight twitch of Mei's lips showed she was amused. But her eyes darkened when she caught sight of Neri again. "And what of the weaver?"

"She's got a name," Arke growled.

Mei's eyebrows rose. "The goblin speaks?"

"The goblin does a lot more than that." Arke took a menacing step forward until Evren held him back.

"Arke is also part of our party" she explained. "He's an accomplished mage, and Neri is under his protection."

"Neri?" Mei's face twisted into a disgusted frown. "Pretty. For a Weaver."

"She's not," Evren said, before Arke could say something foul. "She's not actually a Weaver. One of the witches cursed her in this form, and Arke promised to break the curse."

It wasn't a lie, but she still felt Arke's stiffness beside her and Neri's surprise. He hadn't told her, and Evren swallowed down her regret before it could burn her up. Mei wasn't a savage, and she wouldn't cut down someone who was cursed with a fate she'd consider worse than death. Better to live with the regret than Neri's corpse.

Mei's eyes roamed over Neri's form, and just as Evren expected, a flicker of pity found its way into her dark gaze. She nodded and finally shouldered her long bow. "Very well. If you claim she is harmless, then I'll see what I can do about her safety in the city. But I can't promise she won't be harmed."

"If she's with me, you can." Barrion stepped forward.

"You'd protect her?"

Barrion smiled again. "Of course. My people and I have grown fond of her. She'll be well protected in our ranks. And should she be harmed; I'd take it as a personal offense."

The threat was obvious, and Mei took it as she took all threats, with a wintry smile and icy resolve. "Very well, Your Highness. Let us hope the High Sovereigns are as open-minded as you. In any case, you've brought a great gift to compensate for your strange guest."

Barrion frowned. "Have I?"

Mei turned away as the last of the sun's rays disappeared. A paper lantern was in her hands in minutes, the blue glow making her look more like a ghost than a woman as she looked back at him. "Yes. You've brought Xun Evren home."

Walking behind Mei in the Wood was strange for Evren. She hadn't followed anyone in years. But whether it was her exhausted mind, or her unworthiness to see Orenlion, Mei's steps were far surer and swifter than hers. Barrion kept up with the Khama and tried more than once to offer conversation. He was met with crisp, short answers and nothing more.

Evren was relieved she didn't have to lead anymore. She fell in line with everyone else, unsure whether she was physically sick or her stomach was rioting because of nerves. Beside her, Neri kept close and Arke muttered furiously.

"What were you doin' out?" he asked. "You knew it was dangerous."

"I know. I just wanted to help," Neri chittered uncomfortably. *"I haven't left the nest in years. Following you seemed like a good way to stay out of trouble and make sure you were safe. I didn't mean to get caught by the hunters."*

"They coulda killed you," Arke shot back. "They coulda killed her, right Evren?"

Evren didn't spend the air to answer. She just nodded.

Neri's little spider face fell, as did her voice. *"But I helped you find them, didn't I? That means Barrion can help the Matri-arch, and you can help Evren."*

Arke shook his head. "Yeah, sure. You still shouldn't have done it. Barrion's gonna have a hard enough time makin' peace without . . ." he stopped himself. "Never mind."

Neri rounded on him and nearly tripped Evren. *"And you don't have enough to do without taking on me and my problems?"*

He faltered. "I . . ."

"I didn't tell you I was cursed to ask you to fix me, Arke," she said. *"Maybe I don't want to be fixed. Or maybe I need to do it myself."*

"I never meant to—"

"You don't have to worry about me. I won't burden you or Barrion simply by existing the way I am. I'll help, and I don't need your protection to do it."

Neri scampered off, the little hairs on her back the only thing giving away her anger. Evren looked down at Arke, who was staring after her, completely stunned.

"I was tryin' to help," he muttered.

"Word of advice with women," Evren rolled her shoulders and nudged him to continue walking. "Don't assume. Just ask. Consent is always better than an unwanted surprise."

She forced herself to walk because she'd stop and fall asleep right there if she didn't. Arke said nothing except for the occasional confused muttering. He looked up at Neri frequently, where the spider had taken up walking beside Barrion. Mei looked less than thrilled, but regarded the spider with the same attitude she did Barrion.

It was a start.

They walked for another hour before Evren's feet drug on the ground. A warm arm enveloped her shoulders as Gyda corralled her further. Evren didn't want to admit how thankful she was that the warrior had moved up from her spot in the back to help her. Until she realized Arke was far ahead of her, as was everyone else.

"Sorry," Evren muttered and started pulling away.

It took very little for Gyda to keep her inside the circle of her arm, and Evren eventually relented. "Don't be. You're ill, you can ask for help."

"We're almost to Orenlion." Evren yawned. "Soon there will be nothing but help, and I'll want none of it."

"That is what we're here for." Gyda nodded to the party ahead. "Wyverns or no, we won't let them do something you're not comfortable with."

Evren smiled but didn't answer. Because the reality was the High Sovereigns could do whatever they wanted to her, and there was nothing Barrion or her friends could do. She'd escaped Orenlion once, and just as she predicted, she wouldn't be doing it again. So, she let herself sink into Gyda's embrace more. She let her help and didn't feel guilty for doing so. She savored the walk, no matter how much it hurt, because it would likely be the last they had where they were both at peace.

The night was calm enough for her to feel safe. And where she felt safe, her mind wandered. The High Sovereigns wouldn't let her leave again, purely out of spite rather than anything else. Barrion couldn't fight for her, the Hisrachi, and Etherak all at once. They'd use her against him and Sol, and there would be no peace or alliance. They were vipers, and Barrion was a mouse seeking their aid. He would give them whatever they wanted, or they'd end him. Evren wasn't sure the hopeful prince knew what he was getting into with his plan, but she knew he'd have to leave her for his kingdom, and she didn't fault him for that.

But what of her friends? They'd fight for her. She could picture Sorin's ridiculous escape plan, Abraxas's soft but sure words giving everyone hope. She could see Sol's drawings of the plan as clearly as she could see Mei's blue lantern. Arke would try to burn the whole city down. And Gyda . . .

A massive root acted like a wall in front of them. Gyda left

Evren to climb easily up to the top. She held her hand out, with that same soft smile that she seemed to only give Evren. Evren took her hand and her stomach fluttered when she was pulled up to the top. Her boots caught the root where her reflexes couldn't, but she clung to Gyda's arm anyway and let out a shaky breath.

"I used to do that on my own." Evren breathed heavily.

Gyda squeezed her arm reassuringly. "You will again. Until then, I have you. I won't let you falter."

Evren looked up at her, and her words died in her throat. Gyda was a lot closer than she realized, which was ridiculous because Evren was holding her arm like a lifeline. Her other muscled arm circled around her to keep her from falling off the other side. She was close enough that all Evren could smell was her. Her breaths whispered between them. Gyda was so steady and sure now, less like a thunderstorm and more like a mountain. Something solid to hold on to without feeling guilty. Someone strong enough to hold her but gentle enough to melt into.

With a jolt, Evren realized she wanted to be closer. Suddenly, the few inches between them felt like a canyon. It would take nothing for her to lean in and . . .

What?

What did Evren want from her? Why did her chest feel so tight and her throat as dry as the desert? Why couldn't she look away from those glacier eyes? Those eyes she chased across an icy tundra to see again. Why did she, now of all times, finally realize she felt whole next to Gyda?

Didn't she need a heart to look at Gyda like this? To feel like this?

"Evren?" Gyda looked at her quizzically.

All hells, she thought. *Why did it have to be you saying my name like that? Why did it have to be now? Why couldn't I have seen you sooner?*

She mustered up what little strength she had and took a small step away from Gyda. Enough to break the warrior's hold on one of her arms. Enough for the canyon to become large enough that she could breathe again.

"I'm fine," she said, forcing a smile. "Just winded."

Gyda nodded. "I'll help you down."

Gyda let go of her and jumped down as if she was hopping down the last couple of stairs on a staircase. She looked up at Evren and held her hand out again

Evren knew then that it didn't matter how she felt, or why she was just realizing it now. It didn't matter if Gyda would even return those cursed feelings. Because, in the end, once she stepped into Orenlion, she wouldn't be the same person. She wouldn't be allowed to leave, and Gyda would have to go.

Gyda still had a heart. Evren would not be the one to break it.

Evren took her offered hand and slid down the rest of the way. When she got back on her feet, she took her hand back.

"Thanks." She smiled thinly. "I can walk on my own now."

Gyda frowned. "Are you sure? I don't mind, truly."

"I know. But I can't be seen as weak where we're going." She nodded again. The blue light of Mei's lantern was far ahead of them and was catching the shapes of the trees. Farther ahead, there were more lights. Some bobbed between the trunks, some stood still. Others gathered around the massive silver archways that announced the beginning of Orenlion. They'd pass through nine of them before the city came into view. "We're almost there. Let's go."

Gyda looked like she wanted to argue, but just clenched her jaw and nodded. It took some time, but eventually they caught up to the rest of the group just as they passed underneath one of the arches.

Evren shivered as she passed under the first of the nine Heavenly Gates. It had been too long since she'd walked the road under her feet. As much as she despised Orenlion, the gates held a beautiful tranquility. The blue paper lanterns cast an ethereal glow and glinted off the curling silver carvings of the round gates. The Keepers of the Gates floated like ghosts past them with their long white veils and robes. They did not acknowledge Mei or the rest of the group following her. Mist seemed to cling to their feet as they walked, reminding Evren of Viggo.

Nothing but the sounds of the quiet Wood and the soft humming of the Keepers broke the awe-filled silence. One gate passed, and then another, each carved and wrought just a little differently than the other.

"These are exquisite." Sol breathed, craning her neck up to catch the artwork of the fifth one. "What do they represent?"

"Many things," Mei said. "But originally they were built for the nine heroes that stood between Orenlion and the Weavers. The virtues that they stood for are highly respected to this day, and their descendants rule our city as the High Sovereigns."

"Except for the four families that are considered lesser," Evren added.

Mei gave her a withering look at the same time Sol turned to her with unbridled curiosity.

"What happened?"

"The nine that originally ruled together fell apart during the War of Widows." Evren made her voice gentle to Sol, but the dwarf didn't seem to care. "They couldn't decide on how to deal with the dwarven army. Four wanted to surrender and make peace. Five wanted to fight. They got their war, and when it was done, those four families were removed."

"You make it sound so terrible," Mei snapped. "They still have more power than most in Orenlion."

"Just not a say in how to rule," Evren muttered.

"Would that have made you stay?"

She pursed her lips and looked away. "No."

Neither Evren nor Mei commented when they passed under the Xun gate. The gate of guardians, hunters, and those that called the Wood home. It was no more tarnished than the others, for the Keepers wouldn't let it fall to ruin. But it held an air of neglect anyway as she stepped under it.

The last and final gate was larger and grander, but completely overshadowed. Because at this point, Orenlion was in view. The city rose high above them, the glittering windows and walkways suspended high above the ground. Lanterns of all colors hung from the branches. Bridges of immense size and beautiful scrollwork art connected tree to tree, building to building. In the shade of night, it was hard to tell where the buildings began and the trees ended. But Evren knew there was no end or beginning. The trees enveloped the buildings as if they were their own. Branches as thick as roads supported walkways. Canopies of leaves shaded pavilions where couples walked under the silver hue of silk umbrellas. Curved roofs glinted like sword points in the moonlight as wyvern statues glared down at the forest floor. Round windows let out the smell of cooking food and string music.

Not a single building was built less than twenty feet up from the ground. What had once started as a safety measure had turned into a show of magic and opulence.

"Welcome to Orenlion." Mei smirked at their dumbstruck faces. She softened when she looked at Evren. "Welcome home."

Sorin whistled. "I'll say it before Sol does. Exquisite." He mocked her tone perfectly, and the dwarf swatted him on the knee. "But how do we get up there?"

"A lift," Evren said wearily.

Sorin started wheezing with laughter. "Oh man! You're so fucked, right? You hate being up high and the entire city is—"

"I know, Sorin."

Mei frowned. "What's this new fear?"

Evren sighed. "A lift I was using fell and the fall nearly killed me. Now heights make me uncomfortable."

"Oh, that is bad luck." Mei shrugged. "Anyway."

She walked past the gate and started shouting in Elvish for the lift workers to bring it down. It would take a few trips to get them all off the forest floor. The lift itself was a thing of beauty and art, as were all things in Orenlion. There was a tall rail to keep anyone from falling off, and the metal used was light but sturdy. Evren knew some enchantments were involved, but she put them from her mind as she, her party, Neri, and Barrion climbed on.

Mei closed the gate behind them. "I'll come up with the rest of your people, Barrion."

The prince didn't have any time to acknowledge her. The lift suddenly jolted upwards, and the forest floor fell away beneath them. Evren watched Mei turn to Mira, and the two exchanged curt words, two warriors from vastly different worlds. It was almost serene to watch. A human from Etherak, brash and bold and stubborn, next to an elf of Orenlion, fierce and patient and cold. It was a scene she never would've pictured happening in her lifetime.

Evren turned away from them and to the city they were rising to. Her palms were sweaty on the cool metal of the railing as she held onto it like a lifeline. Beside her, Neri was as stiff as a rock, as if moving would attract attention and the elves would rain hellfire upon her. Which they very well might. On Evren's other side, Barrion was looking up at the approaching city, his eyes widening with every passing minute.

The lift didn't stop at the bottom of the city, instead it rose through the levels as if to give them the time to admire it. Orenlion fell around them in a steady grace. Curving bridges and twisting staircases coiled in the air, connecting pathways of thick branches and glittering houses. The curled edges of roofs held guardian wyvern statues staring down at everyone with their gleaming eyes. Bards played on every corner, and the music lilted a sweet melody that paired beautifully with the smell of baked sugar rolls. The air was lit with multicolored paper lanterns, and they hung from strings across the trees and walkways. Children scurried back and forth with them dangling from long, bent poles. Ornate gardens held gurgling fountains and streams, water pouring from one level to the next in streams of moon-colored silver. Couples in shimmering silk walked in the flowers, their heads bent and their whispers soft.

"Okay, I'll say it so no one else has to," Sorin piped up, and everyone tore their eyes away from Orenlion to stare at him. He grinned wickedly. "This city is . . . disgusting."

Barrion blanched. "Surely you don't mean that."

Abraxas nodded thoughtfully as he tapped his chin. The twinkle of amusement in his eyes was brighter than any star. "No, he's quite right. I find everything about this place to be remarkably dull. Sol?"

"Oh, I don't know." The dwarf cocked her head up at a passing house. "Dull seems a little soft for this place. It's just awful, right?"

Gyda nodded solemnly. She caught Evren's eyes and winked. "Too delicate, like glass. I'm afraid I might break something just by sneezing. It's horrendous."

Barrion shook his head, looking between them and the city. "You . . . we're seeing the same thing, right?"

Arke rolled his eyes. "Of course, we are, princeling. We're looking at garbage." He elbowed Barrion and jerked his head to Evren.

Realization dawned on the prince's face. He spared a final look at a tumbling fountain filled with golden fish before turning back to her. "It truly is . . . well, atrocious. Just ghastly and wicked."

Arke barked out laughter. "There ya go!"

Barrion nervously chuckled with him and joined the party in pointing out everything they didn't like about Orenlion. Soon, the lift was filled with snickering and bad jokes, and the elves they passed gave them dirty looks. It didn't matter to them though, and a bit of Evren warmed at what they were trying to do.

"*It's beautiful,*" Neri whispered beside her.

Evren nodded, drinking in the sounds and smells of her old home, as bitter as they were. "Yes, it is."

The good mood on the lift evaporated as it came to a stop in front of a line of bristling soldiers. The red and silver of the armor was harsh and intense compared to the rest of Orenlion's soft ambience, and their spears bristled in the moonlight like the spines of a wyvern. At their head was an elf no older than Mei, but whose presence and lifted chin betrayed his rank. His black hair was tied severely from his angular face, and his armor had more silver than red. He opened the gate of the lift as it came to a stop and found Evren instantly. His smile was neither warm nor welcoming.

"Lady Xun." Sovereign Shao looked her up and down. "Looks like you made your way back to us."

Evren smiled, but felt more like she was baring her teeth. "Much to your disappointment, I'm sure."

He shrugged. "What can I say? You make my life exceedingly more difficult than it needs to be." His eyes flickered over Barrion, the Wandering Sols, and Neri. "A habit you have not shaken, I see," he said, frowning.

"Neri is under the protection of Crown Prince Barrion." Evren waved off his dark look as the spider cowered behind her legs.

"Yes, an Etherakian prince. Because we bow to those." When Evren looked at him sharply, he held up a hand. "I have my orders. I am aware of what Mei has done to bring you forward, even if I would've done differently to keep this sacred city from undeserving eyes."

"You seem to have an unfavorable opinion of me." Barrion stepped forward. "I'd like to remedy that."

Shao sniffed indignantly. "Yes, I'm sure you would."

"Someone gonna introduce this asshole, or is he just gonna stay asshole number four?" Arke growled.

Shao sneered down at the goblin. "I am High Sovereign Shao Ruogang, General of Orenlion."

"Oh boy, he's got titles," Arke said.

Evren could've pointed out that Shao Ruogang was the

newest and youngest Sovereign in Orenlion, having only took his father's spot eight years ago. So much to prove, and so little time. It was a wonder he took off his armor at all. But bruising his ego so early into their arrival would do nothing but make their lives harder, so she kept her mouth shut.

Shao held his hand out and beckoned her forward with two fingers. "Come, Xun. The others want to speak with you." He glared at her party. "Without you companions to badger us."

The spike of fear in Evren came and went like a strike of lightning—quick and horrifying, but gone in a flash. No matter how much she despised the idea, she knew it was coming. She swallowed uncomfortably, but walked forward. She was halfway there before Gyda took a step forward and all the spears snapped towards her.

"Xun, tell your overgrown dog to stand down before I toss her to the forest floor," Shao drawled, completely unconcerned with how he was courting death by uttering those words.

"Oh, please try," Gyda growled. "I haven't wetted my blade with elven blood in months."

"I am not surprised to find a heathen like yourself in Xun's company." Shao looked unconcerned.

As Gyda went to take another step forward, Evren laid a hand on her bicep. "Don't."

Gyda spared her a soft look of concern. "You don't want to go alone. I won't let them force you. None of us will."

"What I want is no longer a concern," she whispered. "Please, Gyda, understand this. They won't hurt me."

"You hate them," the warrior hissed. "I can see it in your eyes. Why don't you fight them?"

"I have," Evren insisted. "It's gotten me nowhere. This talk is just that, a talk. They'll crow and demean and demand, but that's all. Without it, Barrion stands no chance. None of us do."

Gyda turned away. It was easier for her to stare down Shao, an enemy, than it was to look at Evren. Evren's chest was tight, and under her hand Gyda's muscles were tightly wound. She wasn't giving up.

"Gyda, please," Evren pleaded. "Do this for me."

The warrior stilled, and after a long moment, rocked back on her heels. The spears fell away from her in sharp unison. Her jaw was tight, and she was still staring at Shao with unbridled disgust when she spoke. "If she is not returned as she is now, I will tear this city apart. Understood, small general?"

"Yes, because she looks so well now." Shao rolled his eyes. "But of course, guard dog. My fellow Sovereigns and I wouldn't dream of hurting the last of Xun's bloodline. However . . . diminished she is."

Gyda stepped back and Evren let out a sigh of relief. "Thank you." She said nothing, so Evren turned back to Barrion. "I'll do what I can for you tonight. Take care of my people."

He nodded solemnly. "Of course. Do stay safe."

Evren left the lift and somehow felt more on edge next to Shao than she had in the Hisrachi nest. He swept a hand out, and the soldiers parted and let them pass. Evren didn't look back, no matter how much she ached to, but she heard the snapping footsteps as the soldiers closed back into formation as she and Shao walked away.

Shao ushered her around a corner and down another street before Evren could hear her friend's comments and protests fade, and she tried to ignore how irritating Shao's efficiency was.

"You look like worg shit, Xun," he said crisply as they walked over a bridge. The air was cool so high in the forest. If she looked past the disgusted glances from the passing nobles, it might've been a pleasant night.

"And you still look like you're padding your father's armor in order to fit into it," she said smoothly. "What's your point?"

For the first time all night he bristled, and Evren felt a twinge of satisfaction. "I don't want to catch whatever illness you've got," he snapped.

"It's not contagious."

"Good." He marched on, always keeping his pace quicker than hers so she had to hurry to keep up. All around her, Orenlion looked exactly as she'd left it. The same shops and bakeries, the same tired bard playing a dented silver flute. She wondered if she'd find the same fat goldfish in her favorite pond if she looked. Not that Shao was giving her the time to linger on anything.

"You really fucked us when you left," Shao hissed.

"The Wood seems fine." Evren shrugged. "Doesn't look like marriage or another heir was needed."

"Your disappearance resulted in an uproar of rumors about the Sovereigns," he said. "Had you exited more gracefully—"

"I tried," she snapped. "You all wouldn't let me go."

"So, stealing a wyvern and launching yourself into Weaver-infested territory to keep the Khama from following you was the way to go?"

"I don't remember stealing a wyvern," she muttered.

"Well, you did. And it cost us. Without the support of the Xun house, many in the city saw it as the beginning of the end. As if we were unfit to rule."

"Aren't you?" Evren raised an eyebrow.

Shao cut her a frosty glare. "I know it is all a game to you, always has been. If things aren't your way, you burn it all to the ground in a fit of rage. Only, now you drag a group of strangers into our streets. Barbarians and zealots looking like they'd kill for you."

"They would."

Shao rounded on her, his face furious. "Is that a threat?"

"No," Evren said. "It's confirmation. My party took down two separate governments, countless monsters, and faced horrors you'd wet your pretty armor just thinking about. If anything, it's a warning. Gyda fights because she loves it and the more blood, the better. Abraxas has more experience and blood on his hands than your father ever did, which is saying a lot. Solri could make this whole city crumble with a well-aimed blow at its supports and leave you at her mercy. Arke is by far the best mage on this continent simply because he enjoys proving people wrong. And all Sorin has to do is bat his eyes and say some pretty words, and you'll do anything for his approval. So don't talk down about them to me. Because, in the end, I'd choose them before I'd choose you and your sick control over this city, and that should scare you more than them."

Shao's nostrils flared as he stared her down. "I had hoped you were dead. Did you know that?"

"I could've guessed."

"I curse the stars for the fact that you're here now. But be warned, Xun, you are much changed and so is Orenlion. We are more aware of your trickery, and you will find it harder to leave these gates now than it was before. And, you made a mistake."

"What's that?" she asked.

He leaned forward as if he was about to share a juicy secret, and whispered close to her ear. "You brought leverage, and we will use them against you. Be sure of that."

15

The High Chamber had been a place of hellishness for Evren in the past. She'd hoped the soaring ceiling and cold floor would feel different now that she'd been away for so long. But, as she stood in the shadow of the five thrones, she felt nothing but the same creeping embarrassment she always had.

At least in years past, she was healthy and dressed nice. She'd wear one of those pretty silk dresses her father always urged her to put on before such a meeting. She would've smelled like flowers and not like death. But now she felt akin to a dirty stray who came begging for scraps. Her fever still raged like a wildfire, but her spite kept her standing.

If she couldn't be seen as weak in Dirn-Darahl, she certainly couldn't afford to even breathe heavy in the presence of the five Sovereigns.

"It is good to see you again, Xun Evren."

Evren blew a piece of hair out of her eyes and stared up at Sovereign Wasanthi, who'd been the first to break the silence after Shao had delivered her and took his own throne. Wasanthi, as one of the five families and pillars of Orenlion, represented piety and faith. An old elf, showing his age behind a long graying mustache and balding head. He had the look of a grand-father, but Evren knew he could be utterly cruel and cold to those who didn't share his views. She'd been at the brunt of many of his lectures before.

Evren raised her chin up. "Is it?"

Shao let out a snorting laugh that echoed in the large hall. "You see this? She's been like this since I got her off the lift. Made only worse by the ragged band of cutthroats she brought in her wake."

"Peace, general." Sovereign Liang held up an elegant hand studded with moonstone rings. She was a plump woman, who would've had a pleasant face if her eyes weren't so cold. "We should see this as a blessing. An opportunity, at least. Lady Xun brings us allies from Etherak."

"Yes, a dying kingdom floundering like a fish without water." Shao shook his head. "Only you would see that as an opportunity, mage."

"Prince Barrion means to secure an alliance," Evren said to Liang. She could start working for Barrion and Sol and weakening the Sovereigns' resolve. "He comes with only peace and hope in his heart."

"The son of a butcher will be a butcher himself," said the next elf. Out of all of them, Yikao was clothed the simplest. No finery or jewels, just a simple robe and a tired look on his face. It always had been this way with the elf in charge of safeguarding and keeping knowledge and history. "The line of Rhys has not stepped foot in this Wood for many generations. The boy is bold, but foolish."

"That boy's name is Barrion," Evren corrected. "And he's trying to undo his father's mistakes."

"One cannot heal a severed head with honey balm, child."

"Sure as all hells beats acting like the beheading didn't happen," Evren said.

The woman beside him scoffed, her strawberry blonde hair effortlessly piled high on her head and tinkling with decorations.

"Such a distasteful tongue you wield," Sovereign Fen muttered. "Have you no respect or humility?"

"Only for those who don't press me into arranged marriages with their sons," she snapped back.

Fen scowled and her eyes glittered darkly in a way that used to make Evren shiver with fear as a child. Aster was good and pure, but his mother and father were far from that. While other Sovereigns worked in the light, Fen worked in the shadows. She snatched whispers and lies to use them for her own gain, and had eyes all over the city. Evren wouldn't be surprised if her Crows had found their way past Orenlion's borders, for Fen's ambition was large, and never held in check. Her intelligence had served Orenlion well.

"You broke his heart, you know." Fen pursed her painted lips together.

"I wasn't the first," Evren said, to ignore the sting of truth. "But we're not here to discuss me."

"Oh, we are," Fen said. "The little prince can wait. You have been needing punishment for a long time."

"I feel like being here is punishment enough."

Yikao waved her off and snapped to get Fen's attention. "Fen, do not harass her. It is your judgment that drove her away."

"I sought to solve the problem that was killing our home," she protested.

"And how did that turn out?" Evren asked. "No marriage. No little Evrens running around, thank the moon. And yet, the Wood seems to be in the clear, anyway."

"Aster says you had a hand in it," Fen said. "Tell me, what dark magic did you use to leave us without consequence?"

"All magic has a cost. If I used any, you'd be sure there was a cost, and a high one."

Liang clapped her bejeweled hands giddily. "Oh, she remembers my lessons! The little runt who had no magical talent remembered better than my fellow council."

Shao pinched the bridge of his nose. "Sovereign Liang, must we go down this road?"

"Indeed." Wasanthi nodded. "Whatever magic might've been at work isn't of consequence. As I said when the green returned, our Lady of the Heavens looked out for us. Whether through Evren's hand, or by another, we have been saved. And we can put the business of the marriage of your two houses at rest, Fen."

"Yes, I suppose we can," Fen agreed slowly.

Evren felt herself deflate with relief. It had been one thing she was terrified of, but now it didn't matter. She didn't have to marry Aster. She was safe. She was free to . . .

Do what, exactly? The same threats still applied. Evren put Gyda from her mind.

"That still doesn't excuse your neglectful actions to this city," Fen went on. Those keen eyes bored into Evren as if she was taking in every shift of her shoulders, every bruise and spot of grime on her body. What did she make of the fresh scars? Or the new look of exhaustion in her eyes? What did Fen, or any of them, see when looking at Evren? Disappointment was common, even a little disgust too. But this . . . triumph in Fen's expression was new.

Evren had crawled back to her, just as she'd always said she would. Only now, instead of a hopeful and defiant girl with her mother's human spirit, she was little more than a hollow husk that had seen too much and was leaning on pillars of support that could easily be broken.

Fen pushed herself up from her throne. Her robes fell like pools of silken water around her arms and legs, the chunk of moonstone dangling from her belt was nearly as big as Evren's fist. As Fen stepped down to her level, the jewel glinted in the blue light like another eye. It took everything Evren had not to back away from her.

"For as long as this city has stood, there have been nine families," Fen said, speaking as if Evren was a toddler who'd never heard the story before. "Five large pillars to hold, four smaller ones to support. By removing yourself instead of taking your father's place, you endangered Orenlion's very existence with your selfishness."

"The city looks fine to me," Evren muttered.

"Only a fool would think 'fine' was enough. We are a beacon of civilization in the Wood. We protect it, and nurture it, and wait for our Lady's return. But we cannot do that without the Xun bloodline to act as our guardians, to show us what the Wood needs and how to provide it."

Fen's fingers were cold on Evren's fire-hot skin as she laid a hand on her shoulder in what would've looked like a motherly gesture from the outside. The Sovereign even smiled, her painted lips cracking under the strain. Only her eyes betrayed her true contempt.

"You are the last of your name, Evren," she said. "We only wish for you to fulfill your destiny as you were born to. As your father before you, and his father before him. Orenlion needs you."

Out of all the things she expected out of Fen's mouth, attempted softness was not one of them. She hadn't used honeyed words on Evren since she'd learned how to shoot a bow. Did the Sovereign really think she was so weak that she'd buy that sort of gesture again?

Evren's shoulder started to shake underneath Fen's icy hand before any noise came out of her mouth. It started as a little wheeze at first, just enough to get all the Sovereigns to look at each other with varying levels of confusion. But when the wheezing turned to laughter, Fen's mouth twisted down into disgust.

"You're a fucking parasite," Evren wheezed. Fen tightened her grip on her shoulder, but Evren knocked it away before she could. The little sidestep sent her head spinning, and her chest ached from the laughter, but she couldn't stop. She looked at the Sovereigns each in turn.

"You're all fucking parasites." Her harsh voice echoed in the cavernous hall. "The Deep Wood was never yours to protect and manage, and it never will be. You've stolen it, and killed the ones who lived in it, just to stake your claim. You're leaching this forest dry the same way you did to my father, and his before him, and his father before him. Over and over, the same tireless speech of protection and support, and for what? What are you waiting for? What are you so damn scared of that you cower in an ancient forest, surrounded by magic, so that none could find you?"

Shao stood to his feet so fast he was merely a blur of shining armor. "You should hold your tongue!"

"Will you make me, little general?" she asked. "All those years of isolating me and force-feeding me your ideals didn't work before. It didn't keep me silent then, and it won't now."

"You are young, Xun," Yikao said gently, as gently as one who was obviously irritated could be. "You know less of the world than you believe."

"Do I?" Evren asked. "Because out of everyone here, I'm the only one who's left these borders. I've seen the world outside these trees with my own eyes, and it's not whatever picture Fen's spies have painted for you. Eith is shattered and broken. You say Etherak is dying without its gods? You're right. But that's the entire world right now. Giants wake from their mountains in fits of rage and destroy thousands of lives before they're put down. Leadership falls and corruption spreads in every city. Dark magic has no one to hold its leash anymore, and it's tearing the world apart.

"I have seen things that will never leave me. Great civilizations hidden in shadows and biding their time before they take their place in the light, even if it's on the graves of every living soul on the surface. Lonely boys turning into monsters and commanding necromancy in a way that nearly destroyed a whole way of life. I watched a King die at the hands of my friend and felt nothing. I've seen monsters who had more heart and purer motivations than most people I know. And you sit here on the same thrones that your families have taken and speak of a world you do not know."

Evren's hand was shaking as she raked it through her hair. Her breathing was far too fast, but she couldn't stop. Now that she was talking, all she could see were the horrors she witnessed. Ainthe's torture for her missing child, Viggo's map and lies, the wreckage of Gail's ship and his carved journals of madness on the walls, the fall of Direwall and Drystan's bloated corpse. All she could hear was Sahar's screaming over his body, the cries of the undead, Alkimos's war cry over his nest.

Viggo's ghost didn't haunt her now, but she swore she could feel it at the nape of her neck.

"Eith is crumbling," she said. "And the more you sit here and do nothing, hiding behind your pretty lies and magic, the more you'll be caught unawares when the end comes for you. You call Barrion desperate and grasping because he seeks an alliance for his people. I'd say you're the desperate ones, and if you're as smart as you claim to be, you'll hear him out."

She sniffed and took a small step back. "Then again, you have a habit of making shitty mistakes and calling them fate. I wouldn't be surprised if you let your one chance of salvation walk away."

The silence was deafening, but it was all Evren had to hold on to as her vision blurred. She blinked rapidly and scowled when it was Fen who came into focus first.

Those talon-like fingers curled into a fist. Evren didn't need to see her face to know she was seething.

"Our decisions are beyond you, Xun Evren." Fen's voice was like ice. "You have no right to judge them, as if you know better."

"I don't know better, you're right," Evren agreed. "But my father taught me early to stay away from fools." She let herself smile and cocked her head to the side. "And you wonder why I was gone for so long?"

"Enough!" Wasanthi raised his hands before Evren, or

anyone else, could continue. He sighed heavily and Evren felt a smidge of satisfaction at the look of disappointment reappearing in his eyes. "Xun Yuhan taught you many things, Evren. He tried to teach you how to best carry on his legacy. It seems that our warnings of fickle human nature were correct."

"In more ways than one," Fen hissed.

Evren ignored her. "And? What's your point? What do you want to do with me?"

Wasanthi steepled his fingers and frowned. "We only want you back on your destined path, child."

Evren didn't have time to utter a word of argument before Liang cut in. "You place is here in Orenlion. Despite your human habits, you're still Yuhan's daughter. There has always been a Xun guarding Orenlion, and there always will be."

Evren's stomach lurched. She knew this would happen, but hearing it was different. It was all she could do to keep her meal down as she glared at Fen.

"Satisfied?"

"Hardly." Fen arched an eyebrow. "There is much more work to be done to repair the damage you caused."

Wasanthi shook his head. "A conversation for another night. The swelling moon will make light of muddy waters. Do not fear. In the meantime, we will deal with the prince you brought us and his demands."

Shao scoffed. "There is nothing Etherak could give us that will make an alliance worthwhile."

Liang shook her head. "That remains to be seen. But that still leaves Lady Xun." The mage's washed-out eyes looked her over. "You have always been ready to flee. Will you run away while the young prince distracts us?"

Shao answered before Evren could. "She won't leave so long as her friends are here. The Khama will watch them if Xun thinks they're so capable."

"Do as you wish," Evren snapped. "I stay with them."

"And when they leave?" Fen leaned forward. "How will you watch them ride off without you?"

Evren smiled, caught between believing her body wouldn't last that long, and longing to cure herself and escape once again. She wasn't sure which path she'd be forced to walk when the time came, but if it robbed Fen of her victory over her, Evren didn't care. She'd die in spite, or she'd leave in it.

"With bated breath and a dagger, Lady Fen," Evren said softly. "Just as you taught me."

16

The ancient house of Xun was exactly how Evren left it, shadowed and lonely and aching to fill its grand halls. It *had* been grand once, and no amount of time could diminish that. The golden arches, the elegant yet still extravagant curve of the roof, the open-air balconies with unrivaled views of the forest, and the once lavish garden in the center that had withered without a nurturing hand. The magnificent tree it was built into curled around the house in a fierce grip, as if it was afraid it would lose it. Evren could see new vines curling along the circular windows and new branches supporting the foundations. The tree had grown much in the years she'd been away, or had she just been too busy to notice the growth before? The house hadn't been home after her father left, just a place to lay her head and lock everyone away for a few hours.

And here she was, crawling back to it as if the past years hadn't changed her.

Her fingers brushed over the new leaves as she passed through the gate and closed it behind her. The overgrown path felt wild and almost fitting, and by the door she slipped off her boots, just as she had for twenty-two years of her life. A new vine, baby green and still flexible, was curling around the wyvern door knocker. Evren let it stay there and pushed her way inside.

Stepping inside was less like coming home and more like walking into a living memory. Nothing had been touched since she'd left. A thick layer of dust coated everything, from the carved forest scenes on the walls to the scrolls and maps scattered across every surface. Her toes flexed on the woven mats under her feet, seeking grounding and comfort and finding none. The windows had been opened, filling the air with the smells of wood and sap, and keeping the musty smell of neglect at bay. Soft moonlight filtered in from the skylights, dappled by the swaying shadows of leaves.

As Evren stepped down into the sunken gathering area, she could feel the weight of her ancestor's eyes. Her gaze flickered to the wall where they were all immortalized, guardians and hunters and nobles with a cause, all bearing great deeds and deaths that made their legacy harder to shoulder. The space for her father was bare, because Evren had refused to accept his death, and her mother looked far out of place with her dull, rounded ears and a serene expression that Evren somehow knew she didn't carry in life. She'd never met the woman, but it didn't seem to suit her. Whoever had immortalized her with the rest of the Xun family hadn't done so correctly but that carving was all Evren had to go on when she was growing up.

Her feet lead her back to it, despite how she wished to walk the other way. Her fingers found the smooth, rounded curve of her carved cheek. She remembered being so small she had to stretch to the very tips of her toes to do the same. Now, in what felt like a lifetime later, the wooden carving of Jordiana Hanali was at eye level.

The shadows clung to the hollows of her eyes until warm light cut into the room. Evren backed away from the wall, unsure why her cheeks were burning, as her friends were slowly trickling into the room. Sorin was carrying his Luminstone, apparently unsure of how to work the paper lanterns dotted around the house. The sunlike light was enough to breathe a little life into the heavy room.

"You're back!" Sol's smile didn't quite reach her eyes. "Gyda didn't think they'd let you go. We were already planning a rescue mission."

Evren refused to look at Gyda, because if she did, she knew the rest of the house would fall away and she'd just want to be closer to the warrior. Instead, she kept her eyes on the ground, her toes picking at a stray and withered blossom that had fallen from the courtyard garden.

"Mei led everyone here?" Evren asked instead.

"Not entirely," Abraxas said. "She took Barrion, Neri, and the rest of his retinue to a different guest house. We were told to stay here."

"Nice place," Sorin said, trying to force some cheerfulness into the room like he was with his false sun light. "Needs a little dusting. I mean, for a guest house, it's pretty nice, just a little let go."

"It's not a guest house." Evren shook her head. "It's my home."

Sorin's jaw hung open a bit and when he spoke, his voice was squeakier. "Your home?"

Arke rolled his yellow eyes. "You didn't hear them callin' her Lady Xun?"

"Well, yeah! But I thought it was a joke." He swung back to Evren. "No offense, of course! You're a really great lady."

"It was a joke, Sorin," she said. "I'm a lady by right and bloodline, but nothing else."

"I really thought you just lived in the woods your whole life," he said. "Seriously, all this is all yours?"

"My family's." She shrugged. "Which I'm the last of so . . . yes, I suppose it is all mine."

Gyda finally spoke for the first time since entering, and she was still wearing the hurt and anger she had on the lift. "There is a lot you haven't told us."

"A lot I didn't think was important," Evren argued. "I had no plans to come back here but, now that we're here, you're right. I have a lot to talk about."

All Evren wanted to do was curl up and go to sleep on the floor, but her friends needed answers. More importantly, they needed to know the dangers of Orenlion and just how hard it was to leave the viper's nest.

They slowly got everything needed for a solemn midnight talk together. Food and drink and minds emptied of expectation. Evren made tea, partially out of habit and partially because Sol had already gone through the effort to clean everything in the kitchen and set up their rations. The cups were small and stemless and ancient, but Evren had never known them to break and crack. The teapot was a little older and delicate and filling it with hot water almost felt like she was stepping back in time. The fragrant green tea was brewed, and then poured carefully. As she normally did, Evren kept a little left for the final part of the tea set. The stone carved 'tea pet' she'd found when she was five and fell in love with was just as she remembered it. The worg was carved to look friendly and plump, curled up into a ball and sleeping peacefully. Evren drizzled the last of the tea over his stone body, and then carried the tea outside.

The courtyard garden was overgrown and dead. Weeds tangled around her ankles and covered the carefully laid path. Bushes and flowers were brown and neglected. The only thing living was the slightly bent and withering weeping star tree, its white blossoms littering the ground in a carpet of decaying petals.

There were many paths through the garden. One would lead to a wide, dirt-packed arena used for training or games, another would lead to a now green and still fountain for meditation. But the one Evren used, and her friends followed, led to a wide, covered gazebo. They swept away dead leaves and twigs as seats were taken and tea passed out.

Evren's whole body ached when she sat down, and her lips burned when she sipped her tea. The air smelled of dying flowers and too-bitter tea. And all her friends waited for her to speak.

She told them everything.

Mei's history lesson at the gates was enough of a foundation to build on. She told them the five families that ruled, and how they did so. Fen, for secrets and shadows. Shao, for armies and defense. Wasanthi for faith and rituals. Yikao for knowledge and how it is given to the people. Liang for magic and its shroud on the city.

The Xun legacy was a lesser one, thanks to Evren's great-grandfather. He had refused to fight in the War of Widows, and in return, the Xun family had lost their status as rulers. Instead, they focused on the Wood. Guarding, hunting, listening, and learning. The Khama and their wyverns were built because of Evren's family, and they were a big enough asset that most forgot their refusal to fight.

All but the Sovereigns, who never forgot a single detail.

The Xun line, as her father always told it, had started to die long before Evren's time. Yuhan was the sole heir remaining until he met a stubborn human in the Wood and had fallen in love. That, above all, was rumored to be the true fall of the Xun legacy.

"Because of a human woman?" Sorin snorted. "That's stupid. What did she do?"

Evren looked him dead in the eyes. "She had me."

"Oh . . ."

Evren drained the last of her now lukewarm tea and set the cup aside. Elven birth is hard on humans. Often as a child she'd imagined that if the roles were reversed, and her mother had been an elf, she would've survived. But the birth had killed her and left Yuhan with a half human child and an empty home.

"If the Sovereigns had been hard on him before, they were

harder after I was born. They overshadowed those precious days in the Wood with my father by months of him gone on dangerous hunts. I was tutored and taught how to be a lady, which turned out fantastically well, as you can see." Evren gestured to herself with a rueful smile. "My father would come back each time darker and colder than the last, until one day he never came back. The hunt went on for months and months, until I was begging the Khama to search for him and the Sovereigns to bring him home."

A cool breeze carried the scent of weeping star blossoms in the air, and Evren breathed deeply. "They never found a body, and suddenly I was the head of the Xun house. Half human and bearing all the qualities they wanted gone. A quick temper and fast way of living were human things that needed to be bred out, of course. Once my father was gone, they could focus on me."

Across the gazebo, Abraxas hadn't touched his tea. He watched her thoughtfully, and she was relieved to see no pity in his expression. "Bloodlines and successions are important in Etherak. It seemed Orenlion has a lot in common with its rugged neighbor."

"More than they'd like," Evren agreed. "And I leaned on that while I was here. For everything they made me do, I made them work twice as hard to get me to do it. I tried to become a Khama, a soldier instead of a noble lady they could marry off. It didn't work. They cut off my training to 'preserve my bloodline.' As you can imagine, I didn't have many friends. Only one. Fen Aster, son of the spymaster, who didn't have a bad bone in his body. At first, they were thrilled to see us together. They thought he'd be a beneficial influence. In reality, it was Aster who needed a friend more than me. A boy too scared to become his father or to stand up to his mother found solace in the half-breed bastard of Orenlion. And it was . . . fine, until the Wood started dying.

"No one knows how it started, or why. The trees started dying, the rivers were drying up, and the animals were becoming sick. The Sovereigns blamed me because I wasn't upholding my father's legacy. To fix that, Aster's mother thought she'd marry us to combine our families and weed out all my impurities over the generations. It was supposed to get me back in line and do my duty so the forest would heal. But I wasn't stupid enough to think that a wedding would fix anything, so I convinced Aster to help me find a way out, a way to heal the Wood."

Evren gestured to the green, thriving forest they could see beyond the dying garden. "I guess we succeeded. I don't remember anything, and all the Sovereigns said about the matter was that Aster claimed I fixed it before I fled."

"So, the Matriarch was right," Sol said. "You went to her to find the Heart of the Wood and fix it."

"Apparently."

"Well, that's simple then!" The dwarf perked up. "We just need to find Aster and figure out what you did to fix the forest. Then retrace your steps."

Evren pressed her lips together, and the sound of crickets nearly drowned out the light tinkling of wind chimes on the wind. "No, Sol."

She blinked. "What?"

"If Aster and I thought the Heart was the source of the problem, and I fixed it, then curing me could be impossible," Evren explained. "Whatever I did must've cured the Wood, and in doing so, I don't have a heart."

"You're saying you think you gave your heart to the forest," Gyda said.

Evren hesitated before nodding. "Yes."

"So . . ." Sorin stumbled for his words. "We get it back, right? Like Sol said."

Evren said nothing. She'd promised them she'd try to fix herself, but the more she traveled into the Wood, the more she realized it wasn't possible. Had her past self been so desperate for a way out that she'd been content with a long, suffering death? Now that she was in the same cage as before, was she still ready to accept that fate?

"We won't know anything until we meet this Aster again," Gyda said, and stood up. Evren could hear the determination lacing her words together like bits of string.

"The Sovereigns are going to make things difficult here," Evren said. "Barrion will be fighting an impossible battle."

"He won't be alone," Sol said.

"They won't like you, Sol. They won't listen to much."

"Oh, boohoo, that's politics." She rolled her eyes. "I can deal with it. In the meantime, we need to figure out how to help Evren. That's why we're here."

"That starts with the ex-fiancée," Arke said. "He still a friend?"

"I think so, yes." Evren put Gail's vision out of her mind. She hoped so. Aster was all she had before the Wandering Sols. If he turned his back on her, she would deserve it, but she would hate it all the same.

Abraxas sighed, looking up at the swelling moon. "There will be little rest in the coming days. Sol, you and Sorin will stick with Barrion and work on peace."

Sorin laughed. "Right! Because they love humans so much."

"You grow on people." Arke shrugged.

"The rest of us will work on Evren's heart and retracing her steps." Abraxas looked at Evren. "So long as you think we can."

The more time passed, the less Evren was sure. But she forced a nod anyway. She wasn't quite ready to die yet, since her will to live came in spurts every other hour, but she wouldn't damn the Wood she loved for her own life. She may hate Orenlion, but she wouldn't burn her family's legacy like that.

The night was dark by the time everyone trickled back into the old house. Evren helped everyone find their rooms. Someone must've been keeping it in order since she'd left, because besides dust and stuffy air, it was pristine. She knew Sorin and Arke would want the one with two beds, and that Sol would gladly take the one with the massive view of the Wood from the balcony. Abraxas found the smallest, barest room to call his own, which was still opulent by most standards. When she meant to show Gyda to her room, the warrior shook her head and instead started walking her way.

"What are you doing?" Evren asked, half fearing the answer.

"Walking you to your room."

"I know where it is."

Gyda cut her a knowing look. "You don't fool me, Evren."

If Evren had a heart, it would've stuttered in her chest. Instead, she swallowed the lump in her throat down as they descended the sweeping staircase. "What do you mean?"

They weren't quite at the bottom yet when Gyda jumped the last three stairs and rounded on her. Evren stopped short, her hand still clutching the banister. She wasn't nearly eye level with Gyda now, but she was closer than she ever had been before.

"You will not let yourself wither away," Gyda said firmly.

Evren shook her head. "Gyda—"

"I saw your face." The warrior cut her off. "I know that look now. If it means this fucking forest survives, you would kill yourself for it."

"At least then I'd be following in my family's footsteps," Evren said bitterly. "That's how things are here. I have one purpose, one duty, and whether or not I remember it, I've already made that choice."

"Then unmake it," Gyda growled.

"If it was that simple, I would!" Evren snapped. "But we don't always have a choice, do we?"

Gyda blinked. "What do you mean?"

"Have you forgotten Lostwater already?" Evren asked. "Did you forget that I stood between you and death, and you shoved me aside without a second glance?"

Evren watched Gyda's hard resolve fracture. She took a small step backward but was still too close for Evren to think properly. And those eyes . . . the amount of guilt in them made Evren's stomach twist into knots.

"Evren, I . . ."

"Don't talk to me about death and family when you walked away from me twice and broke me both times." Evren's eyes burned. She needed to get away. If Gyda saw her tears, she would see through the rest of her. And hells below, Evren couldn't bear to hurt her more.

Without thinking, Evren put a hand on Gyda's chest to push her away. The warrior took an unsteady step backward, but before Evren could slip past her, Gyda's hand fell on top of her own and held it against her chest.

Evren was frozen, but her hand was tingling, as if Gyda's touch was enough to make her feel something other than pain and despair. She stood there, breathless, her hand caught in a trap she didn't want to escape from with Gyda's eyes looking at her as if she held the answer to an impossible riddle. It was so hard to meet those eyes, and when she did, her knees were weak.

It should be a crime to have eyes stare at me like that.

"Evren," Gyda breathed. "Don't do this. What I did was a mistake. Please don't go down the same road I did."

As her words tumbled in the still air between them, Gyda's thumb brushed over Evren's knuckles. She shivered at her touch. Inside her was a war. The side that had realized how much she cared for Gyda wanting the damn the future and to give into whatever this was, whatever it could be. And the practical side whispering that in this house, in this city, giving in would just cause more pain.

Wanting Gyda was harder than any battle, because she could never let herself fall into her completely. Love had ruined her father; she would not follow his example.

Evren wrenched her hand free from Gyda's grip. "The third story has a room you'll like. No communal bathhouse, but I'm sure you'll manage with the private tub."

Evren refused to look at Gyda as she stepped around her and walked towards the familiar shadowed hallway of her childhood. Behind her, she heard Gyda struggling for words before turning around.

"Evren, please . . ."

Gyda never begged, and it knocked the wind out of Evren. She was glad to be facing away from the warrior, so she didn't see the tears beginning to fall down her cheeks.

"Goodnight, Gyda," she said, and walked away.

17

Evren woke up with blood on her lips.

She couldn't get to the water basin quick enough. The tacky sheets stuck to her skin as the blood dribbled freely down her chin. Her whole cheek was sticky with it. It splattered a crimson trail across the floor as she stumbled for the porcelain bowl, and the crystal water turned red the moment she hung her head over.

Evren's reflection shimmered with every drip, drip, drip of blood from her nose. The blood sank to the bottom, the red tendrils curling and grasping at every new drop. Evren simply stood there, praying for it to stop. Her arms shook as she hugged the bowl, her mouth tasted of copper and for once it didn't give her any strength. Her body was still heavy and aching from the sleep she'd jerked it out of. Too late to save her sheets, she noticed. Her pillow was slick with blood.

She bowed her head lower until her nose almost touched the water's surface and she shuddered. Nothing about the bleeding hurt but there was an inherit wrongness about it. The bleeding was too fast and sudden, and showed no signs of stopping. The blood looked black in the bowl.

It looked like her body was finally falling apart without a heart.

"You're running out of time."

Evren tried to swallow more blood. "It's a little late for you to be showing up," she muttered to the ghost.

He stayed out of her vision, but the cooling mist was welcome on her skin. "You need to find the crown," Viggo insisted. "If you want to live, you must try to search for it."

"I know," she snapped. "I'll try as soon as I'm not bleeding anymore."

"Then why haven't you told your friends?"

Evren paused, and the only sound that filled her old room was the steady dripping of blood in water. Finally, she took in a sucking breath. "I don't know if I can trust you. I don't know if the crown can help me. I don't know a lot of things other than my heart is tied to this forest and taking it back would kill it."

"Your friends are willing to risk it for you."

"I'm not."

Viggo, or his ghost, scoffed. "Are you so willing to die?"

Evren thought for a moment before speaking. "No, not really. But I think I'm going mad, and if I am, then you're nothing but an illusion to give me false hope. So, I'll let them look for the Heart. I'll look for the crown. Either way, I don't see a way out of this."

"If you would just—"

"Do you know for certain that the crown can save me?" she asked. "Is it known for curing someone without a heart? Or are you guessing?"

His silence was all she needed. The crown might cure her, but there was a mystery around it that could do many other things, too. And if the Horizon Walker's crown was in the Wood, it would've been found. Thousands upon thousands of years worshipping a martyred goddess and the priests of Orenlion clutched whatever baubles they had of her. Her crown would be a precious prize. One that would be guarded but also displayed.

It would be concrete proof that she existed, and Evren wasn't sure she was ready to believe that.

Dawn was a dim awakening by the time she stopped bleeding and Viggo was gone. There was more blood than water in the basin, and her hands shook as she stepped away. The light of the approaching morning turned everything dull and grey. The blood on the sheets and the floor had dried brown.

Evren did her best to ignore it all. She stripped her bed of its bloody sheets and scrubbed the floor clean. It took her a while. Every time she moved too much or too fast, her vision would swim and her body would flare with dizziness. She had to sit back down and wait for it to pass before picking back up her task.

She peeled off her sleep clothes and sank into the tub to scrub off all the blood and grime she'd been too exhausted to wash off the night before. Her scalp ached when she washed her hair, her arms trembled with every repeated movement. By the time she crawled out of the tub, she was wheezing for breath and ready to curl up on the floor.

She forced herself to get dressed instead.

There was a line of silk dresses waiting for her in her old wardrobe, but she ignored them. The nicest, and cleanest, things she owned while traveling were the clothes from Serevadia, so she slipped those on. As sunlight poured in golden from the skylights, it picked up the floating dust motes careening in the air. They shifted in waves and whorls as she passed. She hadn't bothered to look at the room much last night, but now that she could see it, she felt like she was walking in a dream.

The vanity was exactly how she left it, stuffed with makeup and jewelry she never felt comfortable using but adored too much to give away. Only the bloody basin made it new. The bed was bare now, the white sheets stained and tossed in the corner carelessly. The gauzy net to keep insects out hung like a veil around it. The walls were covered with pieces of fabric, a child's attempt at weaving tapestries. They were all too blocky and comical to take seriously. Some showed fat dragons flying with impossibly tiny wings, others were attempts to recreate the peace of the garden by stitching the blooms and trees by hand. There was one where her tea pet came to life and chased her around the gardens. Another looked like she'd tried to stitch her father together from memory.

It had been a long time since she'd been that child. Evren missed her.

The old bedroom was lonely as she left it again to find break-fast. She picked at her nose and chin subconsciously, as if trying to find any missing flakes of blood as she came into the main living area.

It always amazed her what daylight could do to a place. Where night softened and condensed, sunlight widened and illu-minated. Dust motes reflected light back like floating lanterns. The shelves of baubles and walls filled with retired, ornamental weapons glittered in the morning rays. The stairway where she'd left Gyda looked the same, and she tore her eyes away from it before the memory came back too strong. From the wall, the wooden eyes of her ancestors followed her as she walked past.

It was quiet, save for the sound of some rustling and growling across the room. Evren picked her way over to find Sorin's worg pawing at a closed door. When her shadow fell over him, he immediately perked up and looked at her with hopeful eyes.

Evren cast her own gaze to the carved door, although her face felt more like a scowl. "You don't want to go in there," she told him.

He whined in protest and, as if to prove his point, pawed it hard enough to leave a scratch on the soft wood.

"My grandfather would've had your head for that," she muttered. "Well, he would've had your head, regardless."

She leaned down and gently pushed him away from the

door. He struggled only for a bit before giving in and trotting away. Almost immediately, his ears perked up in alert and he zeroed in on some other poor target. His round belly swayed as he trotted away with his tail held high and the door was forgotten.

But not for Evren. She lingered.

Her fingers brushed against the worn bronze latch, and her thumb found the same indent it had since she was a toddler. How many hours had she spent like this? Waiting for her father to come out of his study and just be around her? How many days had she spent in there after he left trying to piece together why? The puzzle she never solved.

The tinkle of windchimes from inside the study made her pull away. From there, it was easy to leave the door behind.

Passing an open window into the courtyard, Evren could hear the clashing of swords and the muffled shouts of encouragement. She frowned, edging closer to get a better look. Just a glimpse was all she needed.

The garden path closest to her cut through the foliage for a clean line of sight. For a moment, there was nothing but white sand reflecting the morning light. But then there was a flash of black and the glint of a blade swinging through the air. In an instant, it was caught and deflected with a much larger sword, and Abraxas fell back with a chuckle.

"It says wonders about the craftmanship of that blade seeing how quickly it moves," he said. His hair was pulled back, and he was dressed in nothing but his causal shirt and trousers. Not for battle. As he circled the sand, Gyda's form came into sight.

All Evren could see was her back, but that was really all she needed. The well-toned muscles shining under the sun and a soft sheen of sweat. The black ink covering her shoulders and down her spine were painted thicker this morning, and far more intense than usual. Gyda spun her great sword in the air and Evren could hear the smile in her voice.

"Part craftsmanship, part skill." Gyda shrugged her shoulders, and Abraxas came back into view as they continued circling each other. "You could be just as quick if you took off your armor more often."

Abraxas let out a laugh, one of his rare and genuine ones that completely transformed him. "My friend, it is as much a part of my intimidation as your scowl is to yours. You invite people to try to hit you. I show them it is impossible."

"I've seen you stabbed, Kain."

"Lucky blows. Now, are you going to try that new rune out on me again or are we chatting the rest of the morning like nobles over tea?"

He'd barely finished his sentence before she was swinging at him again. Instead of just a length of sharpened steel though, the blade was glittering with a field of blue light. Abraxas deftly dodged the first swing, his smile in place and his eyes glittering. At the next swing, he brought his blade up to parry her away; a tricky thing with such an enormous weapon, but the elf knew more about fighting than even Gyda. His experience and skill tempered her raw power. He should've easily stopped the blade and turned it aside.

When her sword met his and then passed through, Evren saw genuine fear in Abraxas's eyes and felt the same reflected in her chest. Gyda's blade passed through Abraxas's like it was a phantom and sped towards his unprotected chest. He ducked out of the way just in time, rolling in the sand as Gyda pulled her blade up short.

"You said you'd be ready this time," Gyda panted. She flicked her sword, and the light went out.

Abraxas shook the sand from his hair and touched his hand to his ear. His fingers came back red, and he showed them to Gyda. "Useful trick. A sword that knows the difference between steel and flesh."

Gyda rolled her shoulders before offering her arm to help him up. He clasped her forearm and pulled himself to his feet while she shook her head. "I still need to a control it. These runes are almost beyond me."

"Perhaps you can ask Arke for help."

Evren didn't need to see Gyda's face to know she was scowling. "He only wants me to mess with souls more. I have little interest in Gail's gift."

"Admittedly, though, another useful trick." Abraxas patted her shoulder. "Come, let's go another round. You're favoring your right side again, and I intend to beat it out of you."

He picked up his sword and Gyda laughed lowly. "We'll see, old man."

The two picked up their sparring again, and Evren fell away from the window. It felt wrong to watch them, even though she knew they wouldn't mind. Just like Sorin and Arke, Gyda and Abraxas had a special bond that only warriors seemed to share. She didn't want to intrude on that.

She also didn't want to look Gyda in the eye again.

Evren searched the rest of the house, finding nothing but stuffy rooms and haphazardly made beds where her friends had slept. She ate her breakfast, looking over a note the other three had left. Barrion had taken Sol and Sorin to the Sovereign's already, and Arke was checking in on Neri. There was a very helpful tip at the bottom of the note.

Find Aster.

"As if it's that easy," she muttered, but forced herself to eat the rest of her breakfast. Evren didn't want to be in the house when Gyda and Abraxas got done with their training, and what else could she do? She'd only hinder Barrion by appearing with him, and Arke would want to talk to Neri alone for a bit.

Aster it was.

Evren checked her dagger and her mirror shard before getting to the door. She pulled it open and froze mid-step at the threshold.

Aster had grown up since she'd last seen him.

His hair remained the same, the long fall of strawberry blond tumbling down his back unhindered by braids or ornaments. But his face was more defined, his cheekbones and jawline standing out more than when they were hidden behind rounded cheeks. His already long, pointed ears were made more so by simple, but beautifully wrought silver ear cuffs. Those straight brows were furrowed into a worried line that got deeper when he laid eyes on her. His robes were nice, a bold color choice of maroon and sky blue unmarred by mud or leaves. The moonstone she'd gifted to him when they were kids still hung from his belt.

And she was frozen. Evren couldn't move from the doorway. Aster too, also seemed rooted to the spot. His eyes looked her up and down, taking in the strange clothes, the scars, and the unhealthy pallor of her skin. He opened his mouth to speak once, twice, and then three times before clearing his throat.

"You look . . ." he shook his head. "Moon above, what did they do to you?"

They could've been a broad term. He could've meant all her enemies, to which she would've rolled up her sleeves and began listing out every injury and the story behind it, if only to fill the silence. He could've meant the Sovereigns, if his opinion of them had fallen lower than it'd been when she'd left it. But, worst of all, he could've meant the Wandering Sols.

"Who?" she rasped.

He flinched, as if hearing her speak was as painful as a punch in the gut. He met her eyes. "I suppose the more accurate question is *what*. What happened to you, Evren?"

She sucked in a breath and loosened her grip on the door. Only then did she realize her nails had dug into the wood. "Lots of things. Found some people, lost some people. Got jobs, got betrayed. Saved one city, watched a village burn. You know, adventuring things." She looked him up and down again. "And you?"

He pursed his lips in a way that looked too much like his mother. "What it always is, Evren. The betrayals are softer, the burning is covered up, and losing people only matters if they're of noble blood."

Evren let out a sigh of relief. Not because of the words themselves, but because of the bitter tone of Aster's voice. He hadn't changed so much then. He still hated the Sovereigns like she did. He was just a lot closer to them than she was.

"I need your help," she said. "I know I have no right to ask, but I have no one else to turn to. No one else can help me."

Aster's face twisted into an odd expression somewhere between surprise and hurt. Even as she watched him smooth it out into a mask of neutrality, it remained in the depths of his eyes. If anything had changed about him, it was those eyes. They were colder, emptier than she left them. Was that her fault? Did her leaving hurt him that much?

Evren found herself wanting to care, but such a soft emotion wasn't welcome in the jagged thornbush of her chest. It was shredded before it had the chance to bloom.

"What do you need?" he asked, his words careful in the way that he hadn't quite decided whether he was going to help her or not.

"A lot. Let's start at the beginning." She stepped over the threshold and closed the door. When she looked back at him, she noticed he'd taken a small step back from her. "First, I need to know what happened at the Heart of the Wood. And from there, I'm going to need a lot more."

Aster nodded stiffly, his eyes flashing. "One condition."

"What?"

"You first. Tell me everything."

~

ASTER LISTENED MORE than he talked, which wasn't anything new. What was new was how heavy his silence was. It weighed on Evren's shoulders like a bulky fur coat she couldn't shake off. So, she talked instead.

She told him what she remembered about leaving the Wood, and no surprise made its way past his cool mask of indifference. She told him about Dirn-Darahl, about Serevadia and the elves that lived there. Evren told him about the Reino Terminan, Gail, Direwall, the Ashen Bond, with every terrible detail she couldn't leave out.

She told him everything. It was like tearing off the scab of an infected wound.

They walked while she talked, and when she was done, they were on one of the many gilded bridges near the top of Orenlion. Aster leaned on the railing, his hands clasped together and his eyes fixed on the forest beyond the buildings. Evren rested her elbows next to him and tried not to pant.

"That's a lot to take in," Aster said, and his voice startled Evren after so long of silence. He still refused to look at her, and a knot formed between his eyebrows. "A secret race of elves living underground. A Vasa boy who ate souls and commanded the dead." He shook his head. "I wish I didn't believe it."

"Why do you?" she asked.

"Because you don't lie," he said. When she snorted, he looked at her out of the corner of his eye. "You don't lie well, I should say. Especially not to me."

"I've never lied to you."

"But you keep things secret, thinking I can't handle them. I bet you do the same to your new friends."

Evren swallowed down her discomfort as the memory of her bloody morning and Viggo's ghost came back into mind. "Some things aren't meant for others."

"You've always feared what people thought of you," he said. "That's why you act like nothing bothers you. Why you'd keep an all-knowing figure from your friends while you followed its orders."

Evren bristled and pushed away from the railing. "That's not why I keep secrets."

"Oh? Then please, enlighten me."

"It's to protect them."

"How is that protection?" he asked, finally rounding on her. "Didn't your friends deserve to know that something was behind sending you to Serevadia? Didn't Solri deserve to know your suspicions about the people who ruined her life?"

"You weren't there. You didn't see how delicate everything was."

"But if you'd told her, and everyone else in your party, couldn't you have formed a trap of your own instead of playing right into Heliodar's hands?"

She scoffed. "That's easy to say, looking at it from a wyvern's-eye view. But if it makes you feel better, yes." She hissed the word out between clenched teeth. "Yes, and I know that now."

"So, no more secrets?" He looked like he didn't believe her, with his eyes narrowed and his fists clenched.

Evren paused. For a moment, she let the sounds of the city fill the silence. The leaves rustling in the breeze, every shrill flute note that sounded in the air. Eventually, her shoulders sagged, and she fell back against the railing.

If there was one thing that hadn't changed about Aster, it was his hatred of secrets and lies. What his mother used as easily as breathing, he abhorred. And he knew Evren better than the Sols did, maybe better than they ever would.

"I said there's been no sign of that figure and I meant it," she said. "But there is something else. Something I'm not sure is real."

"What is it?"

"A ghost." She shifted from foot to foot. "Viggo's, I think. It looks like him, and talks like him."

Aster frowned. "How long have you been seeing him?"

"A couple days after we left Keld's Outpost," she said. "You have to understand. This started once I got really sick. I think I'm just losing my mind. If I told Abraxas, or Sol, or any of them I was seeing his ghost, they'd panic. They wouldn't listen anymore. They wouldn't trust me to lead them."

"I think it's less about your madness and more about Viggo never being trustworthy to begin with," Aster said. "From what you've said, he wasn't the most transparent person."

"No," Evren admitted. "But he knew a lot about the Elders, and he's been telling me about them."

Aster leaned forward a bit. "What has he said?"

"Not much. It's always about the Horizon Walker."

"You said he didn't know much about her, even after years of study."

"Without the Convocation to pull him away, he would've gone deeper into his research," Evren argued. "He mentioned before that each Elder had an artifact of power, each represented in their murals. He thinks the Horizon Walker's crown is here."

"Okay . . ." Aster hummed into his next words. "We would've found that by now. With the way Wasanthi's ancestors had been scouring ruins, we would've recovered it."

"I mentioned that to Viggo, but he didn't seem to care," Evren said. "He seems to think that the crown can help me."

Aster took a deep breath that wavered in his chest at the end. "Can it?"

"I don't know." She turned back to him. "That's why I need your help. I can't remember what happened to me and how I ended up like this. Tell me what happened."

Evren expected him to because it was Aster. No matter how much time had passed, he was still a good person. He wouldn't keep it from her out of spite. She watched him frown again, and he looked like he'd rather be anywhere else in the world except at her side.

"What do you know?" he asked instead, carefully, as if he was stepping through the remains of a shattered mirror.

Evren scowled. "I told you what I remember, Aster. Nothing. Shelis claims we went to her for help, and I'm not even sure that's true."

"I didn't go there," he muttered, and Evren's irritation flared up again.

"Then tell me where you went!"

He didn't even flinch, and Evren didn't know what to make of it. It used to be that even the slightest edge to her voice, or anyone's really, would shut him down. It wasn't something his parents seemed to notice. Or, if they did, they didn't care. Evren had picked it up easily when they were children and had vowed never to raise her voice at him.

She swallowed down the sudden rush of shame. "I'm sorry. I didn't mean to snap at you."

His eyes flicked over to her, and she wasn't sure what was churning in their depths. Nothing she recognized; she was certain. "I know," he said, and those two words sounded more like an ending than the beginning of something.

"You're not going to help me," she said, once the reality hit her.

Aster winced now, as if she had hit him. Her voice hadn't been above a whisper. "You told me not to."

She shook her head. "The fuck I did."

"You did," he said firmly. "You made me swear that if you, or anyone invoking your name, came to me for help, I wouldn't say anything."

"But you—"

"You made me swear on my family name, Evren." He cut her off as his voice strained with a dozen emotions at once. "Don't look at me like I'm the villain when you forced this on me."

"So, you won't help me find the Heart?" she asked.

"No. You'd hate me if I did."

"I'm getting there now," she muttered. Evren couldn't remember a time when she could've hated Aster for anything. She dug her fingernails so hard into her cuticles she could feel the skin break under the pressure.

Aster sat back on his heels. "I won't take that as personally as you meant it because you're not yourself. But if we're sticking together, I won't put up with anymore words like that."

A part of Evren that was maybe still her was genuinely

impressed with his strength. Three years ago, Aster wouldn't have spoken those words, let alone with so much force and strength. He meant them, and that caught her off guard.

"I thought you said you wouldn't help me," she said.

"I said I wouldn't help you with the Heart. We did that once, and it's done." He looked her up and down and suddenly a flicker of the sunset-soft Aster she remembered bled through the cracks in his mask. "But I don't want you to die, and certainly not acting like you are. So, we'll find this crown and we'll heal you. Together."

Evren struggled to breathe as the sudden, heavy emotion slamming into her crushed her chest. He meant to help her. She hadn't lost him at all.

"Kind of like old times, right?" she asked with a shaky laugh that sounded more like the precursor to tears.

Aster shook his head. "No. We're very different people now. But I wouldn't mind helping a hero with the memory of my best friend."

"I wouldn't mind the help of the ghost of mine."

18

"No." If Mei's tone wasn't a wall enough, her body cutting off the way to the High Chamber was. Evren could easily see the massive, ornate doors beyond her, but Mei made it impossible to get to. Even without her wyvern, she was immovable and deadly. And her hands hadn't even found their way to her spear yet.

"Mei, this is absurd." Aster shook his head and his ear cuffs flashed in the golden sunlight. "As an heir, I'm allowed in the Chamber."

"You are," Mei agreed. "She isn't."

Evren scoffed. "All this effort to keep me here only to lock me out."

Mei cut her a haughty glare. "You don't get a say in how things are run, Xun. Your great-grandfather made sure of that, and you only confirmed it when you left us. Your friends and the prince are fine without you. You have no place in there."

"I'll vouch for her," Aster said.

"As you always do." Mei stood firm. "No. Your judgment is clouded around her."

"I assure you; I'm thinking clearly." When Mei didn't agree with him, he folded his arms. "What's wrong with you, Mei?"

"It's Khama Song," she corrected him.

"It hasn't been for us for a while. Why the need for formalities now?"

Evren watched the two of them with raised eyebrows. Aster was still as calm as he had been a few minutes before, even if his jaw was a little tight with frustration. But Mei wasn't a noble, and she didn't make a habit of wearing masks. She scowled the moment Aster argued, but it wasn't her normal kind. Evren had been on the receiving end of many of Mei's terrible facial expressions and knew them well enough to know that the Khama wasn't angry.

She was embarrassed.

"Perhaps we should go back to such formalities, Lord Fen," Mei told him pointedly.

Aster leaned back on his heels. "Huh. I see." Evren thought he was masking his hurt, but when she glanced over, his eyes were twinkling. "Very well, Khama Song," he drawled. "Please give Sovereign Wasanthi a message that I need to see him whenever he's free."

Mei blinked as if she hadn't expected him to give up on both the formalities and getting Evren into the Chamber all at once. She narrowed her dark eyes at him.

"The Sovereigns won't be free all day, thanks to the visiting prince."

Aster shrugged. "When there's a recess, then. My mother will always make herself comfortable on days like these. She'll call for one within the hour. Just let Wasanthi know I wish to see him after sundown."

"You and Lady Xun?"

Aster cut Evren a quick look before shaking his head to Mei. "Just me."

"Fine." Mei's tone was less than formal. "I'll do as you ask, Lord Fen."

"Thank you, Mei," Aster said with a shit-eating smile and a bow, before whisking himself and Evren away with a flick of his robes. Behind them, Mei hissed in annoyance and muttered a few foul curses that were certainly not formal at Aster's back.

"That was amusing," Evren said, once Mei was out of sight. "And pointless, as I thought it would be."

"We need an expert on the Horizon Walker, right?" Aster asked. "Who better than the head of the family in charge of religious studies?"

"Yes, but we're not talking to him right now, are we?"

Aster rolled his eyes at her and cut another corner. The already thin crowd of people on this level of Orenlion was now nonexistent as they took the little staircase up another level. "Moon above, you've gotten thick."

"I hit my head a lot recently," Evren wheezed, one step at a time.

He waved her explanation off. "This is hardly the first time they have barred you and me from the Chamber. I could've pulled rank on Mei, but she's no fun if she's in a foul mood. And it's been a while since I've snuck in and spied on my mother."

It hit Evren all at once where Aster was leading her now. The rickety wooden staircase with moss clinging to its unused banister, the quiet breeze carrying no sounds of people or music, just rustling leaves and creaking branches. This high in Orenlion, the floor swayed gently as she walked. The leaves had thinned out, and the sunlight warmed her face, as comforting as an old friend. As they reached the top of the landing, she leaned against the railing to catch her breath and Aster waited for her. The curving rooftops of Orenlion sparkled in the sunlight where they weren't blanketed by fallen leaves. She could see the grand tiers of the Sovereign's Chamber in all its glory now.

"I thought your mother blocked this off the last time she caught us." Evren's chest clenched with every breath wasted on a word, and by the last her voice was barely a whisper and she gasped for more air.

Aster nodded and waited until she was done. "She did until you left. I have no reason to sneak in by myself, you know."

Evren huffed. "In my defense, we weren't allowed to when we were younger."

He grinned at her. "And when we were older?"

"I liked how much you mother looked like a toad when she found us."

Aster chuckled softly, and the beads on his robes clacked together in time with his breaths. "You almost sound like yourself again."

It was easy to hate Aster's mother. It was even easier to fall back into old habits with him. But inside, she knew nothing was the same. Even if she wasn't rotting from the inside out, Evren was nothing like the girl who'd dragged Aster into every bad idea she could come up with, a giant grin on her face and a chip on her shoulder. Heliodar had made sure of that, as had Gail. Her friends, too, and it was for the better that way.

"I'm sorry I'm not the same," she blurted, before she lost her nerve.

Aster stared at her for a while, before breathing deeply. "As am I. It would be easier if we were those kids again."

"You changed a lot," she said, and he nodded.

"I had to fight my own monsters." Aster held out his arm for her. "Are you ready?"

She took it with a crooked, grateful smile and tried not to lean on him as they walked on the deserted tops of the city. The branches were thinner here, woven loosely into springy catwalks that went between and over roofs. A few workers were patching a broken roof, guiding the fast-growing tree limbs together to hold the tiles as they worked. They paid Evren and Aster no mind as they walked past.

The two skirted from rooftop to rooftop until they'd circled all the way around to the back of the Chamber. Mei would be several stories below them on the opposite side, and probably still fuming. The thought made Evren laugh.

The Sovereign's Chamber was taller than the rest of the city, and its roof was a foot over Evren's head.

"Is it still here?" she asked.

"Well, I paid off the workers my mother sent to patch it and I doubt she came up here herself." Aster tiptoed around the top of the window, keeping his robes up so he wouldn't block the sun. On the other side, he let the silk fall back down like a graceful cascade, and his hands went to the wall. First just along the side, but then he trailed further up.

"Moon above, where is it?" he hissed.

Evren cocked her head to the side. "Right."

"Which right?"

"Your only right."

"There's nothing here, Evren."

"There is."

"Well, I'm fondling the wall and finding nothing so—"

"I think I'd remember where I put my own trapdoor."

"Well, it's not here, so I'll go to the left."

"It's not—"

With a plume of dust and plaster, the trapdoor swung open violently. Aster grabbed for it to keep it from banging on the wall of the Chamber, but it slipped through his fingers. The door raced for its loud reunion with the wall, ready to announce their misconduct before it even began.

Until Evren darted forward and slide her hand against the wall just in time to soften the blow. The wooden trapdoor crunched her finger bones, but she barely let out a hiss of pain, and stood stock still.

Neither she nor Aster moved for a handful of breathless minutes. Evren waited to hear raised voices through the window, or some cry of alarm. But the minutes ticked by, and all she could hear was the same dull, muffled voices coming from inside.

She slid her hand out from under the trapdoor and gently let it rest against the wall.

Aster let out the breath he was holding. "See? Told you it was left."

"Just get up there."

It took quite a bit of folding, cursing, and maneuvering for Aster to squeeze up into the crawl space Evren had found and hidden so long ago. His robes caught and snagged on everything, and he looked like a butterfly trying to squeeze back into his cocoon with all the wiggling he was doing. When the way was finally clear of his silks, Evren hopped up and grabbed onto the lip of the opening. She hung there, swaying slightly, before heaving herself up.

She got her top half into the musty attic before her vision started being peppered with black spots. She wheezed something that might've been 'help' but was more likely 'fuck,' and then Aster was grabbing her under her armpits and hauling her up.

One leg at a time, she wiggled up with Aster's help, until finally she was breathing hard on her hands and knees and crawling away from the trapdoor. She sat down and leaned back against the wall, huddled in an uncomfortable crouch from the ceiling being so low. "You know, this was a lot more fun when we were kids."

Aster covered his laugh and shook dust out of his hair. "I don't remember it being so small in here."

"We're bigger."

"I am. Not you."

"Ass," she muttered, but laughed too.

They took another few moments to catch their breath before starting the slow crawl through the attic space. It wasn't ever intended to be used, just some space between the ceiling and the roof for support beams and the like. Rough branches grew next to smooth beams, and they crawled under and over each one. It was a forest all on its own, and Evren could still pick her way through the beams and avoid the creaky ones as if she was twelve again. This was her place when she was little; the one spot in Orenlion that was hers before it was anyone else's. She couldn't count how many times she'd hidden up here to escape nannies, nobles, and punishers alike.

But now she'd changed. Even Aster, who'd spent more of his time in the dusty, cramped space was out of place. They'd stopped using it when they were fourteen and had been caught eavesdropping on a Sovereign meeting. This was the first time they'd been back in ten years.

They were both vastly different people now.

"So," Evren whispered. "You and Mei?"

"What about me and Mei?"

"Why the need for formalities now?" she mocked his tone. "You were flirting."

"Good of you to notice. I've been flirting with Mei for years." He shot a grin over his shoulder.

"Oh, I know. But she was blushing this time." Evren snickered. "What did you do to her while I was gone?"

"Nothing so base as that." His tone made it clear that he was scrunching up his nose, even if Evren couldn't see his face.

"Aw, why not?"

"Moon above, I'm not talking about this with you."

"Do you need help wooing her?"

"I can woo just fine on my own, thank you."

Evren snorted, but kept her mouth shut. The truth was, he was right. Mei obviously felt something for Aster, even if it was currently frustration. A couple years ago, Evren might've been a little peeved at not cracking Mei first. But now . . .

Well, even when she wasn't thinking about Gyda, she was somehow always thinking about Gyda. It explained a lot of her feelings in the Reino Terminan, at least. Stupid, irrational, terrible feelings. She'd get rid of them if she knew where they were rooted, but since she obviously didn't have a heart, she'd have to settle with picking at her nails until something distracted her again.

In front of her, Aster stopped and held up a hand for her to as well. He put the same finger to his lips, but she knew better than the tease him now. The muffled voices of the Chamber below were becoming solid, coherent sentences, and none of it sounded good.

Evren stepped around Aster, and carefully picked at the tiles at their feet before her nails found the right one. She motioned for a little help, and together, she and Aster carefully removed the loose ceiling tile and set it to the side.

Cooler, fresh air wafted up to greet them. A dizzying view below showed the Sovereign's Chamber from a bird's-eye view. The five thrones staring down at the dais in the middle looked small from where they were squatting, and the elves in them looked even smaller. At the dais, Barrion, Sol and Sorin weren't given any comforts. They had to stand, as everyone addressing the Sovereigns did. The long hours had not been kind, judging from their shifting feet.

From above, Evren could see Fen rubbing her temples as if she had a nasty headache. "Must I repeat how insulting this request is?" she asked, with the air of someone who never expected to even utter the words.

Barrion, to give him credit, was doing a good job of looking at ease. He'd cleaned up nicely, with his traveling clothes washed and pressed and his hair neatly combed. He hadn't shaved, and looked more rugged than princely, but it suited him.

"You may, of course," the prince said with a coy smile. "But only if I can reiterate how distasteful your blatant uncompromising nature is."

"Again," Sorin drawled. He looked incredibly bored and uncomfortable, and it leaked into his voice.

Shao's armor clanked and echoed in the grand hall as he shifted on his throne. "The human is unnecessary and intentionally distracting."

"Oh, you find me distracting, do you?" Sorin perked up.

"You are interrupting this process."

"By breathing? Speaking? We're here to talk, aren't we?"

"And I'm sure that's all you want to do," Shao shot back.

Sorin laughed. "What's that supposed to mean? I'd like to sit my ass down and eat a cake, if that's what you're getting at."

Liang's glittering hand waved in the air as she talked smoothly over both. "Sovereign Shao, it is rude to assume the human has no self-control over his base instincts."

Sorin guffawed. "I beg your pardon. My *what?*"

"It is well known that humans find it easy to be . . . attracted to all manner of species. This has resulted in many crossbreeds such as half-elves, half-orcs, and the occasional and unfortunate half-dwarf."

Evren winced as Sorin's voice went up a whole octave.

"I will have you know I find *none* of you all that attractive!"

"Uh, Sorin." Barrion cleared his throat and tugged on Sorin's sleeve, but the Vasa shook him off.

"Maybe if you all reached up and collectively pulled your racist heads out of your wrinkled, sagging assholes, you could resemble something I'd give free food to. But not a single one of you are worthy of a dinner date with a prize such as myself. So, jot *that* down, Scribbles!"

Sorin waved an accusing finger at the poor hunched scribe in the corner, who was dutifully taking notes. They jumped whenever he turned to them and then looked at the Sovereigns, questioning if they were to actually take the Vasa's request.

"It's going well, I see," Aster murmured.

"He's fine. Sol's got him."

Sol pulled Sorin back and whispered furiously to him as Barrion stepped between them and the Sovereigns. Sorin's wide hand gestures were impossible to hide, and his voice bounced incoherently off the walls.

"Prince Barrion, control your council or we will have them thrown out," Fen said coolly. "I've executed a man for less."

"You insulted him first, and I will not apologize for his just reaction." Barrion drew himself up straight.

"This is not a debate," Shao argued.

"You're right, it isn't." Barrion narrowed his eyes at the

general. "We're here to discuss peace, not human physiology and nighttime habits. If you're so distracted by Sorin, might I suggest a blindfold?"

Shao surged to his feet in a flash of armor, but before he could take a step away from his throne, Wasanthi grabbed his arm and pulled him back down with more strength than she expected from the old elf.

"Enough, all of you." The priest sounded exhausted. "Let us get on with this, lest time move on without us."

Everyone settled down a bit, and the wildfire of anxious, angry energy simmered down to a contained blaze. Sorin continued to pout behind Barrion and glare at Shao. Evren half expected him to stick his tongue out at the general and inflame the fire all over again. But he shuffled aside with his arms crossed as Sol joined Barrion at the front of the dais.

"You've heard our proposal," she said in a loud, clear voice.

This time Sovereign Yikao leaned forward. "Which one, young lady? The desperate plea to save a drowning kingdom? Or the blasphemous attempt to open our gates to death itself?"

"The Hisrachi people want nothing but peace," Sol pressed.

"They are monsters, not people," Fen said dismissively.

"If they're monsters, what does that make you?" Sorin asked.

Another murmur of outrage swept through the Chamber, and Scribbles the scribe dutifully wrote it all down. Aster gave Evren a questioning look.

"What are they talking about?"

"The Weavers," she explained, watching as a flicker of fear crossed his eyes as she did. "The Matriarch asked Barrion to speak on her people's behalf."

"Speak?" he hissed. "For what? Your prince willingly serves monsters now?"

"Not my prince," she corrected him. "And I don't know if they're all monsters."

"We have thousands of years of violence and bloodshed to prove that they are."

"And even more proof to do the same for us."

That shut him up. He rocked back on his haunches, his face grim.

Evren sighed. "Look, I don't know if I trust them. I grew up the same way you did. But they let us go, and my friends think they're genuine. The Matriarch said that Orenlion attacked first, unjustly, and that they've been here since the Deep Wood was still young."

"And you believe her? We have our own records."

"Controlled by one family for generations and kept from the public." She shook her head, feeling the same war of emotions inside her that she'd had in the Hisrachi nest. "I don't know what to think, Aster. But I trust my friends, and they seem to trust Shelis. Barrion is risking his entire kingdom for this."

Aster watched the prince with keen, curious eyes. "He's a fool."

"Yes." Evren sighed. "But a good one. Believe me, those are rare these days."

Aster spared her a funny look before they both focused back on the argument below.

"The Hisrachi aren't asking you to leave," Barrion said. "They simply want peace. They want clear, respected borders in the Wood, and they want to make sure their children are protected. That your hunters don't destroy their homes."

"And what about all the innocent elves they've killed?" Wasanthi asked. "Shall they go on with no justice to give their divine souls rest?"

"If we're going to stand here tallying murderers for both sides, we'll be here for a while," Sol announced. "The Hisrachi will forgive pass transgressions so long as Orenlion agrees to meet to discuss further peace."

"We will not meet with the monsters who haunt the woods we call home." Fen dismissed her argument with a wave of her hand.

"You would not even try?" Barrion asked. "They've reached out to you!"

"Yes, that means it's a trap."

"They want neutral ground where both parties can meet and terms everyone can agree with. They want to coexist peacefully instead of slaughtering each other in some vain attempt at constant vengeance. I will gladly be an escort for both parties to make sure nothing goes wrong."

"And what is your word worth, prince?" Fen asked.

Barrion froze, as if something in her tone or expression was a brick wall to his passionate voice. Evren thought she saw him shiver.

"I don't take your meaning."

Fen stood up, and she was a vision in golden silks and delicate jewelry. Her ear cuffs were framed with butterfly wings as black as onyx.

"We would be remiss not to remember your bloodline," she said smoothly, and Evren knew exactly what terrible grin Barrion faced now. "Tell us, did King Eldridge keep his word to the people of Vernes to spare them before he slaughtered their families and burned their homes? Did he promise the Queen of Terevas freedom and then jail her until she withered away to nothing, and her children had to hide from his wrath? What about the kingdom of Gratey? All those proud and powerful cities never had a chance to unite against Etherak because he turned them against each other with promises of safety, riches, and favor. So, it's only natural to wonder . . ."

Fen stepped down until she was nose to nose with Barrion. His fists were clenched at his sides and his jaw was tight, but he didn't back away from her.

"Are you your father's son?"

Fen's question was soft in volume but echoed in the Chamber like a stone falling down the stairs. The other Sovereigns watched with unnatural stillness from their thrones. Sol had taken a step back and was pale as she kept Sorin's seething form from going any closer to Fen.

"I think the fact that I'm here with a small retinue of my trusted guards and not an army is answer enough to what I am," Barrion told her.

"You also came with the Wandering Sols." Fen's attention turned to Sol and Sorin. "King killers and serpent slayers. Mercenaries playing at being heroes. You'd put your kingdom on the line for them? For monsters in the shadowed forest that haunt the nightmares of every child here? You act so noble and honorable, but find company with the darkest of creatures. I wonder if your father started out the same way."

Evren wanted to strangle Fen, and she couldn't imagine how Barrion felt. She thought she could see his hands twitching at his sides, but before he could do anything insulting—but likely satisfying—Liang clapped her hands and the two were forced an extra foot apart by an unseen force.

Fen whirled around with fury pinching her cold features, but she did nothing but glare at Liang.

"I think it's time for a break," the mage said lightly, as if they were discussing the weather or what to wear that evening, rather than trading insults.

Wasanthi stood and stretched. "Agreed. The guests could use this time to cool down. Let's say, an hour before we return?"

Barrion gritted his teeth before nodding. "That sounds agreeable."

"And when we return, we will speak no more of alliances with monsters," the priest said. "We'll go back to Etherak's issues, and whether or not they are worthy of being Orenlion's ally. A much more pressing matter for its crown prince, don't you think?"

Barrion's hesitation was barely a second long, but it was enough for everyone in the room to know where the prince stood. "Yes, I agree. We look forward to the discussion."

Evren sat back with a heavy sigh as everyone noisily exited

the Chamber. She wanted nothing more than to climb down and tell Sorin, Sol, and Barrion that she was sorry they had to endure such insults. Instead, she settled for ignoring her headache and rubbed her eyes. "It's worse than I thought."

Aster laughed humorlessly. "You knew they were trying to stick up for Weavers, and thought it would be better than that? The only reason they're not in prison for such an idea is because of Barrion's title. Even that won't last for long. If they grow tired of him, they'll just keep him and everyone else here. Anyone in Etherak will think he's just another casualty of the Wood."

"Barrion's tougher than that. He'd fight."

"Then he'd die."

"Yes," Evren said. "But he'll keep pushing. He's trying to be a better man than his father, and that means healing where he could hurt. He won't give up on the Hisrachi."

Aster chewed his lip, an old childhood habit she'd thought his father had beat out of him. Apparently not, and Evren warmed a little at the tiny bit of defiance.

"Your friends won't either."

Evren shook her head.

"You do realize this is impossible, right?" He raked his hands through his hair. "On top of two alliances, we have to try to see if Wasanthi has some information about the crown. Preferably before you wither away."

"Thanks."

Aster ignored her. "He's got no clue how to talk to any of them. He can't be so forward with my mother. He can't win with Wasanthi at all unless he converts to the Horizon Walker. He has a chance with Liang, but she's got minimal pull in this and will side with whoever speaks before her. Shao is an imbecile and seems to personally have it out for him, and Yikao is just bored. He stands no chance unless he starts working with them!"

Suddenly, Evren was grinning. Which was unsettling to feel after a rant of impossibles, and even more unnerving because she was, in fact, dying. Aster was somewhere between scared and intrigued when he finally noticed.

"What?" he asked. "You have that horrible look on your face. That means I'm going to hate whatever comes out of your mouth next."

"Oh, don't be so negative."

"Spit it out, Ren."

Evren faltered at her nickname. First her father's name for her, and then the one Aster insisted on calling her whenever he was too drunk to stumble through both syllables of her name. It became a sober tradition not long after. She smiled despite herself.

"You could help him."

"If I wanted to commit suicide, probably."

"Aster, come on," she begged.

"No!" He was so furious at her that he started taking off his ear cuffs. His ears were red and flushed, like they always were when he was upset. "I'd be going against my mother to help a foreign prince who's backing not one, but two lost causes."

"Three." Evren pointed to herself.

"Not helping!" He groaned and tossed the ear cuffs in his lap. "This will ruin me."

"Maybe not. Even if Barrion doesn't get his alliances, with your help he'll walk free. And so will my friends. On top of that, you'll finally be able to speak up in there." She pointed down at the empty Chamber. "Regardless of whether you win or lose, you're showing your mother that you have a voice and will use it. That you're not a puppet for her to use, but your own man. The other Sovereigns will see it as you preparing for her throne. She'll see it as petty rebellion. And the whole time you'll be closer to Wasanthi."

Aster continued to glare at the Chamber below. His mother's throne sat empty and cold, drenched in shadows where daylight bathed the rest. He started chewing his lip again.

"I hate you," he finally muttered.

Evren perked up. "So you'll do it?"

"Yes." The word was hard and as final as a gravestone. He looked away from the throne. "On a few conditions."

"What?"

"I make the rules, and you, your friends, and the prince listen to me."

"Done."

He sighed and looked back down. "And when this is done, I leave, too."

Evren gaped at him for a full minute before stuttering out a single word. "What?"

"I want to leave," he said, as if it wasn't a revelation that rocked the foundations of their very lives. "I want out of Orenlion and away from that fucking throne. I want to destroy my reputation so thoroughly that you look like a saint. And I want to do it my way."

19

Barrion took Aster's first piece of advice about as well as Evren thought he would. In that, he essentially threw it out the window without so much of an ounce of consideration and had the gall to be offended at Aster for even mentioning it.

"In what world did you think I'd betray the Hisrachi?" asked the prince. "Does anyone in this gods forsaken city not understand what I mean when I said I gave them my word?"

Aster looked at him, completely unfazed. While the prince paced the length of his spacious guest quarters, he stood as still as a tree, his eyes trailing on the agitated man with increasing curiosity.

"By giving up the Matriarch's nest, you'd be proving yourself a valuable ally to Orenlion," Aster explained calmly. "Etherak would have its alliance without a fight. Is that not what you wanted?"

"I wanted to be listened to," Barrion shot back at him. "Not looked down upon like a child who has no idea what he's doing."

"That's exactly how the Sovereigns see you," Aster said.

Evren winced and focused on the cup of bitter tea Aster had

forced into her hands. He insisted it would help her feel better. Really, all it did was make her tongue feel fuzzy and her head heavy, but she was on her third cup of the day to keep him appeased. Abraxas had bought the tea in bulk.

"You're not helping," Evren muttered to Aster.

He didn't pay her any mind. Instead, he unfolded his arms and marched across the room to Barrion. The prince stopped his pacing to glare at him, but Aster didn't stop until he was mere inches from him.

"You can't have both your kingdom's alliance *and* peace for the Weavers," Aster said. "There is compromise in all alliances, and the Sovereigns will make sure that it is you compromising and not them. That is the only way you win, Barrion. You must keep your priorities in mind. Are your people worth risking it all for a thousand-year blood feud?"

There was a long and heavy silence between the two men. Evren shifted uncomfortably in the corner. It felt like she was intruding on something private with how they were glaring at each other. The two argued like they'd known each other for years. But she supposed dealing with the Sovereigns could make mere days feel like a lifetime. And there was no doubt that Barrion looked at Aster and saw his mother, not an ally.

Evren drank the dregs of her tea. It was going to be a long road.

"Don't call me Barrion," Barrion finally said. "You haven't earned that right, yet."

Aster chuckled. "So, what should I call you? Your Highness?"

"It's appropriate."

"You are not my prince." Aster flicked an invisible piece of lint off Barrion's shoulder, and the prince reeled back as if he'd been hit instead. Aster smiled. "I'm here at Evren's request, not for your comfort. You should listen to me."

"And if I did?" Barrion seethed, his voice barely a whisper.

Aster lowered his voice to match, but his words were lost on Evren. She leaned back against the wall and rested her head against the door. Watching the two of them whisper furiously to each other, their eyes bright and burning, was entertaining enough. If only they could see that they each had the same goal, they would get along. How long would it take for them to trust each other? They needed to be united, or Fen would tear them apart.

The walls were thin enough and Evren's ears were keen enough to pick up on the creaking of floorboards just outside the door. Barely a whisper of movement, but enough for panic to flare in her chest.

"Shut up, both of you."

The two turned to her with mixed glares of anger and confusion, but they had stopped talking, and that's all she needed. She set her cup to the side and made her way carefully to the door. She barely opened it; her face pressed against the crack to peek into the hallway. Bit by bit she opened it, seeing nothing but an empty hallway drenched in sunlight from the windows, but her anxiety didn't ease.

She turned back to them and shut the door.

"Snakes, the whole lot of them." Evren shook her head. "Someone was listening."

Aster pressed his lips into a firm line, bleaching the color from them. "Expected but concerning. Any clues?"

"You mother's Crows aren't so sloppy. I'd bet Shao's people."

"So, they heard an argument, so what?" Barrion crossed his arms. He was still seething and had taken a few long strides away from Aster.

Aster rolled his eyes. "Shao is an idiot, but if it was him, he knows about this alliance. Which means we have no advantage of surprise, and they can start working on how to undermine us. And if we're arguing, we're weak. This is bad."

Barrion's cheeks reddened. "I see."

"I told you this place was awful," Evren said.

"You did." The prince sighed. "I wish you'd been wrong."

"Me too."

"Awful or not, we need a better place to talk," Aster said. "This is obviously not a secure house."

Evren shook her head. "Mine won't be either. We need somewhere we can get lost in, where our voices won't carry." She paused, thinking a bit. "Somewhere no spy would want to go."

"I take it from that look on your face you already have a place in mind?" Barrion asked.

"Yes. I suggest you keep your hands in your pockets from now on. Unless you want to lose them."

THE KHAMA'S wyverns weren't exactly tame, which meant no one with a desire to live went to their nests on the southern edge of the city unless they were truly desperate. The Khama lived and trained there as well, but they also raised their wyverns from hatchling to adults. They were family, so the creatures didn't give them any trouble. Anyone outside of that needed Khama escorts, permission, and a hefty amount of courage.

Evren hadn't been to the Roost in years. Her training to become a Khama was short lived and there was no reason for her to stay there. But it still felt a little like coming home, stepping into the enormous aviary. It housed dozens wyverns and their riders, and each needed to be kept separate from all others. Wyverns don't like being crowded and weren't fond of walls in general. Their roosts were grand things that could easily have room for a tavern full of people and were open to the vast green wilds of the Wood. Where their roosts allowed Khama access, it looked a little like a very large, sturdy beehive. The aviary was the center of the Roost, with branching hallways leading to where the riders slept, ate, and trained.

It was a grand place that had a significantly wilder feeling than the rest of Orenlion. The air smelled of the acid stench that hung around wyvern scales. Off duty, Khama laughed and joked with each other as they oiled their saddles or picked up their spears for sparring. Those that paid the trio any attention simply waved to Aster before letting them pass. Several levels up, a wyvern was being fed, and the noise of tearing flesh and snapping bone echoed in the vast chamber.

Barrion shivered. "This is safe?"

"We're not staying in here," Aster explained. "They routinely bring the wyverns through for bathing, saddle and armor fitting, as well as medical checkups. And they are creatures of habit. They despise new faces. As pretty as yours is, I doubt a wyvern would leave it intact."

Barrion snorted, but Evren didn't miss the way he flinched at the sound of snapping teeth a few roosts above them. "Thanks for caring about my pretty face."

"Of course, Your Highness."

There were many paths Aster could've taken them through the Roost. He chose the nicest option, and before long, they were out in the open-air training platform teeming with Khama. Racks of weapons lined the fence that kept anyone from accidentally slipping off and falling to their deaths. Several training pits dipped down for private sparring and were filled with the same fine sand wyverns used for bathing. She knew from personal experience that the sand did little to soften falls.

She lingered at the edge of one pit, her fingers itching for a sparring staff and her body already tensing for a fight. It was empty, the sand smooth and combed over. But she could almost see the memories imprinted in the pit. So many long hours with Mei, fighting for her approval and for Evren's own freedom. And getting thoroughly demolished by Mei's superior skills.

The Roost had almost been a place she'd belonged. She could still taste the excitement as she waited for a new clutch of eggs. She could still feel the way the saddles felt against her legs on the wooden training wyverns. The camaraderie between fellow Khama was achingly familiar to the Wandering Sols, so much so that Evren could envision this other life as vividly as a fever dream.

But she hadn't stayed. They had torn her away before new eggs were hatched. Her training armor and favorite staff were put aside. Someone else filled the spot when the Sovereigns had dragged her away.

Evren turned away from the pit and tucked the memories away.

The Khama paid them no attention as they went about their drills and training. Evren didn't see Mei, and was silently thankful.

Aster stopped at the edge of the platform and leaned casually against the fence as if there wasn't a terrifying drop just below him. Above them, similar platforms dotted around the Roost where wyverns sunbathed and landed from their flights.

"I can't help you if you won't let me," Aster said.

Barrion tore his eye away from the wyverns to stare at him evenly. "I won't go back on my word. Your mother thinks I'm a copy of my father. Betraying the Hisrachi would be my first step in becoming just like him. Find another way."

Aster didn't bristle at his demands. He seemed genuinely intrigued. He chewed on his lip, his eyes shifting from Barrion to the wyverns as he plotted.

"You will not take Orenlion all at once, so we'll need to start small," he said. "Get the Sovereigns on your side one by one."

"How difficult will that be?"

"Extremely. Liang will be the easiest to win over, but she's the one with the least amount of power in the Chamber."

Barrion frowned and looked truly baffled. "But she's a mage. Shouldn't she have more say in how the city is run?"

Evren shook her head. "It's not about magical strength, not like Etherak. In the grand scheme of things, Liang's bloodline has done little but protect the city from wandering eyes. Since a few outsiders still manage to find their way in and she's created no new ways to stop them, her overall voice in things is dimming. That, and she finds Etherak fascinating."

Barrion brightened. "She does?"

"Like a particularly interesting bug, yes." Barrion made a disgusted face while Aster continued to muse out loud.

"Offering her access to the Greyreach Conclave would easily get her to support you," he said. "Of course, she's likely to steal and leech knowledge from your library. We can prepare for that. But Liang's support alone is laughable."

"Who else then?"

"Well, your gods have been gone for several decades. How do you feel about converting to a new deity?"

This time Barrion looked like he'd sunk his teeth into a rotten apple. "I'd like to keep my throne, and my people wouldn't take a King who serves a foreign god."

"Etherak is touchy about religion,." Evren reminded Aster.

He shrugged. "Fair enough. Then I suppose Yikao would be the next easiest, the foul bastard."

"What does he want? A master of knowledge, right? He would have access to our histories, maps, notes on past cultures—"

"I assure you, none of that is enough to buy his support," Aster said. "He seems like a plain man, but in truth, he's got terribly decadent habits, and most are not fitting to be said in the light of such a beautiful day." He wrinkled his nose. "I've got a lot of filth on him I had been saving to use on a different day. But perhaps a little extortion is all we need to get his support."

"Force him?" Barrion blanched. "Won't that do more harm than good?"

Aster smiled wickedly. "It'll keep a disgusting man on a leash; a very short one, so long as I'm holding it. Trust me, you can't buy him. Unless you have a few pretty children you're willing to sell to him."

"Absolutely not," Barrion hissed. "It sounds like I'd rather kill him."

"Get in line. Now, let's see. That leaves Shao and my mother." Aster tapped his chin. "My mother will not easily support us. In fact, she'll oppose us out of spite more than likely. Shao will be difficult, though. In a similar fashion, he'll disagree with us just to do it. However, if I can find out what he wants, we can use that to our advantage."

"You don't already know?" Barrion asked.

"A few years ago, I could've told you, but he's changed a lot since taking his father's place. And he doesn't like me around because he fears I'm my mother's pet. He won't let me near him, so that's another problem."

"So, we make a situation where he doesn't see you coming." Evren finally spoke up. Both the men looked at her as if they'd forgotten she was there. "A crowd, something pretty to distract him."

Aster delicately cracked his knuckles. "Alcohol would help as well. And if we caught him in a compromising position . . . well, we could buy his support with our silence. If we can pull that off, then that'll give us most of the Sovereign's in our favor. Wasanthi and Fen will have no choice but to go with the majority vote."

None of them mentioned that this would work only once, and that Barrion was still going to have to choose to fight for the Hisrachi or save his people. It wasn't a situation Evren envied, and she still wasn't sure what he'd choose in the end. All she knew was that it was his decision, and she couldn't make it for him.

"Is there nothing we can do about your mother?" Barrion asked. "I'd feel better if she wasn't against me."

"A wise feeling." Aster and Evren shared a knowing look. Fen would never be a true ally, but it was better to have her passively despising Barrion than waiting to order one of her Crows to slit his throat and frame it on some poor Etherakian noble. Winning her over would take nothing short of a miracle or a sacrifice.

Evren knew which one to bet on.

She turned to Barrion and felt the setting sun warming her back. The golden light fell in greens and golds on the prince's face, which was pinched with worry. What did he see in those trees? The anchor of an impossible cause dragging him down? Or perhaps the wall of trees obstructing his view home? She hoped he got to see it again one day. She would've liked to see Whitestone herself, Terevas too.

"We'll handle Fen, don't worry," Evren said, and she knew it did not convince him because she didn't sound confident at all. She didn't try to smile because it didn't matter if he believed her or not. She'd promised to help him, and heartless or not, she'd do it. "We'll get all of them in one place, handle them separately, and maybe get drunk doing it."

Barrion blinked at the two of them. "You're planning a party," he said flatly.

"This is Orenlion, Your Highness." Aster pushed away from the edge. "Parties are honey traps, and we have five snakes to catch. This'll either be the end of us, or our winning move."

He nodded, and for a moment, his eyes turned from silver to gold in the sunlight. He looked at Aster with a softer expression, the one of a man laying everything he had in the hands of a stranger.

"All right. Where do we start?"

20

It took three days to set up Xun Manor for Aster's party, and Evren spent all of it somewhere between falling apart and completely numb. She drank her bitter tea as the gardens were refreshed and brought to life. She endured Abraxas's prodding as the house was cleaned until the lacquered wood shone and every corner smelled of fresh blossoms rather than neglect. She coughed up blood in the mornings, followed Aster as he brought his grand plans to life in the afternoon, and slept restlessly in the evenings.

The nightmares were nothing but fever dreams; she knew that. It didn't help to remind herself of that every time she woke up drenched in sweat and feeling like a frail skeleton held together with nothing but hot skin. The bad dreams were about Gail and the White Cairn. She saw the same writhing mass of bodies, and the mirrored sea of souls where Drystan watched her. She fought Gyda over and over again until she wasn't sure if she remembered the fight correctly. Surely, she hadn't been the one holding the sword to Gyda's chest, watching her beg.

"You don't need to do this," Gyda would beg, and Evren could never look her in the eyes. The sword was far too light in her hands. It felt like she was holding nothing. "You're not alone.

You have all of us waiting for you. You have me. All you need to do is take my hand."

It was always easy to take the hand in the dream. It was even easier to drive the sword through Gyda's heart. But it was impossible to wipe the memory of her dying face from Evren's eyes, even after she'd been awake for hours.

The other dreams didn't hurt as badly, but they sent terror down so deep into her bones she couldn't shake it free. The figure in the Wood that had lured Mira out, that had controlled the infected worgs, was always there. Shadowed, beckoning, screaming. The claws on its hands were wooden and rotting. The white mushrooms growing on its shoulders puffed out noxious gas that Evren could swear she smelled in her dreams. It always screamed at her, silent and unyielding. Somewhere between reaching for her and pushing her away.

Evren always woke from those dreams bleeding.

By the fourth day, she must've looked truly awful because Sorin stopped by her room three different times to apologize about something before giving up and walking out. Only Arke would talk to her normally, bluntly. But he pitied her, and she hated seeing that in his wide yellow eyes.

"Kid's scared comin' here did more harm than good," Arke explained. "He thinks you're gettin' worse by bein' here."

"Am I?"

Arke hesitated and looked away. "Hard to tell what looks healthy or not with you lot. You're all ugly as hells to me."

The lie was sweet, but a bad one nonetheless. Evren was grateful for it.

Abraxas was a dark shadow at all times, and his expression grew more and more grim each day. Evren told him she didn't want him praying over her again, and he'd agreed. Whether that meant he was just allowing her this one request because he didn't want to argue with her, or he'd finally started to lose faith, she wasn't sure. Neither was a good option.

Gyda was never around when Evren was. A part of her was

grateful, because her nightmares were bad enough without having to face the warrior every day. But she missed Gyda, and the house felt emptier without her. Abraxas always said that Gyda went off to explore the city with Barrion's soldiers. Evren felt like she was distancing herself from her so she wouldn't be around when everything went to shit.

Evren couldn't find it in her to blame her.

She saw very little of Sol in those days. The dwarf had taken up as Barrion's official voice in the Chamber and spent all her time in there. Aster said that his mother left more frustrated than normal each day, so that meant Sol must've been getting somewhere. But she was exhausted every time she came back to the manor and hardly spoke to anyone before falling into a hard, deep sleep. She was always caught between exhilarated and exhausted, but the Sovereigns were wearing her down. Aster's party couldn't come soon enough for her.

By the fourth night, Xun Manor was alive again. Lanterns lit up the halls, each room, and the spacious garden. Food and flowers made their air sweeter, and the house gleamed like a polished jewel. She was hosting it as the last of her line, but Aster had done everything that was necessary to build a party. From the decorations of golden paper stars to the specially selected food, to hiring cooks, servants and the like for the night. It had his name all over it, and he made no attempt to hide it. That was, after all, the point.

Evren was sure none of her friends realized how crucial that detail was. The party was more than a trap; it was a show of unity. She hated every minute, and when no one else was looking, she could tell Aster did as well. Neither of them had a choice though, and if Barrion kept to the plan, it wouldn't matter.

The cage was getting comfortable for Evren, the way it did for all dying animals. She didn't have the strength to rage against it anymore.

THE MOON WAS at its highest point once the party had reached its capacity. Xun Manor saw more life and laughter in a few hours than it had since Evren was born. It was brimming with people dressed in their finest picking at the food, or walking through the softly glowing gardens. The music that floated lazily over their heads nearly drowned their conversations and debates.

Barely anyone in attendance mattered. Petty lesser houses and bloodlines were let in to make sure the bigger fish got lost in the sea of silk. Barrion was the guest of honor and looked stiff and uncomfortable in his borrowed finery. Aster's clothes looked good on him though. The flush of navy blue and silver was meant to show Barrion's allegiance to the Rhys name, but they were good colors for Orenlion as well. Colors of luck and trust and purity.

Mira and the other soldiers mingled and stood out like sore thumbs. Their eyes were only on Barrion. But he'd let them know the plan just like Evren had the Wandering Sols. Mira gave the slightest nod to Evren as they passed each other.

Evren's dress swirled between her legs like gossamer wings. She had a hard time reminding herself that the pretty green and bronze silk was just another form of armor when it felt as flimsy as it did. She had worn nothing like it in years, and she felt like an impostor. The long, wide sleeves and sweeping neckline were comfortable in the evening heat, but did little to cover her scars. The weight of her guest's stares was heavier than her dress.

"I thought I'd hate this less," she muttered into her cup as she and Aster skirted around a throng of nobles.

He smiled thinly. "I knew you wouldn't. You've changed, but not that much. It's all still poisonous air and predators pretending to play nice for you."

Aster looked like he belonged. His simple ear cuffs were gone, traded out for an elaborate set studded with topaz and dangling chains of gold that brushed his neck. His hair was all tied up in a formal knot. He looked too much like his father for her to be comfortable.

"Isn't it for you?"

He shook his head and leaned in close as if they were sharing a secret. Another part of the show. "I see them as they are now, obstacles and opportunities. I think that's worse."

Evren forced a laugh as if he'd told a joke and drowned the last of her drink, more of that damn tea, and she swallowed without tasting it as Aster pulled away. Three years alone had drastically changed Aster. He'd armored himself up and made himself colder. If he hadn't shown Barrion and herself some kindness, she would've thought Fen had finally worn him down.

But no, this was just Aster surviving. She couldn't fault him for that.

"Everyone's here?" she asked. It was no use combing the crowd.

Aster nodded. "All except Yikao. Don't worry, I talked to him this morning. Your friend Gyda was extremely persuasive in getting him to see our side. It was a good idea for you to send her."

Evren frowned. "I didn't. I haven't seen Gyda in days."

"Well," he shrugged, "she helped, nonetheless. Yikao's leash is in hand. Liang will make her way to Barrion soon, and he's no fool. He'll get her on our side."

"That just leaves Fen and Shao." Evren wrinkled her nose. "Unless you have something up your sleeve for Wasanthi?"

"I'm playing all my cards to get him to help you," Aster said. "Asking that man to favor Barrion would earn me nothing but a laugh in my face. I'll cash in what secrets I must to get what we can on the crown tonight. In the meantime, we can't hope that he'll like us enough to oppose my mother. We'll need to work on Shao and hope for the best."

"Sorin's on it," Evren said, remembering how eager Sorin had been to knock the general down a peg. "It's risky though."

"We know what it'll take to get my mother's vote if Shao

fails." Aster looked at her pointedly. "Are you sure you're up for it?"

She almost laughed. Evren felt so close to death that thinking more than a few hours into the future felt like a joke. Everything she ate or drank tasted like blood. If she moved too fast, her vision blackened to the point of uselessness. She didn't know if she could make it through the night, let alone to whatever sacrifice she needed to appease Fen.

"Whatever it takes," she said finally. "This party is statement enough. And if it comes to marriage again . . ." she shrugged. "You'll make a handsome widower and inherit all my secret ways of sneaking out of the city."

He squeezed her arm gently. "If it comes to marriage, you're not widowing me. We'll live. And when we've caused enough trouble here, maybe we'll make a run for it together."

Together.

Her throat tightened with tears she couldn't afford to shed. This wasn't the end she wanted. Agonizing death drowning in her own blood, stuck in an arranged marriage all over again. But what choice did she have? Orenlion wouldn't readily let her go. Barrion needed all the help he could get, and another friendly face in the Chamber couldn't hurt.

If she lived, she could do some good. She could tear down the thrones and change things. She could forge a strong alliance with Etherak to keep it on its feet until Barrion was King. Evren could even work on undoing the generations of damage and hate between her people and the Hisrachi. She could do it with Aster by her side, too. Never loving each other, but partners regardless. He'd have Mei once she got over the sting of betrayal, because Evren wouldn't take that away from him. And Evren . . .

Evren would have no one. She'd get the Wandering Sols to leave with Barrion once everything was finished. She'd argue with Sorin until he broke. She'd hug Sol until her ribs cracked. Arke wouldn't say goodbye because he hated it. Abraxas would be reasonable and get everyone out because he would see what she did and why. Gyda . . .

Her gut twisted like someone had punched her.

Evren would endure Gyda's silence and her anger. She'd take it all because it was better than the alternative. Orenlion was no place for a warrior like her, and Evren couldn't stand it if she stayed. Evren would let her go, and keep all those terrible feelings locked deep down because it would hurt less for Gyda that way.

All stories came to an end at some point. Whether by death or marriage, Evren Hanali's was always meant to end in Orenlion. Maybe Aster could get out. Maybe he'd take Mei with him. But Evren knew when she stepped back into the Wood that she wouldn't be leaving again.

"I'm going to find Shao," Evren said, once her throat had cleared up. "This night has gone on long enough."

Aster nodded. "I'll check in with Barrion. Once we have Liang settled, I'll work on Wasanthi."

"Let me know when he's ready to talk. I want to be there."

"Of course. Good luck." He bowed a little to her before walking off.

Aster's freedom relied on how cooperative Shao could be, and that hinged on how much wine Sorin had been funneling him. And, in the end, it all relied on how Evren could get him to their side.

As she roamed through the manor, she became increasingly aware that it no longer felt like hers. As with all parties, the familiar rooms felt smaller and far too warm. But more than that, it was as if the lonely imprint of her childhood memories had been wiped away when Aster ordered the place cleaned and refurbished. It was good to see the manor alive again, but it was not hers. The house had moved on. It shouldn't have hurt as much as it did. She'd abandoned it first, after all.

Evren only saw glimpses of people she cared about as she walked. A flash of Sol's golden hair as she talked passionately to a minor noble. The deep cackle of Arke's laugh from the kitchen seconds before the worg pup came tearing through the doorway with his tail smoking. She thought she saw the telltale glimmers of Mei's armor, but when she looked closer, it was simply another Khama she didn't recognize talking to Abraxas in a cool, professional manner.

She caught his attention, and moments later, Abraxas excused himself and made his way to her.

"Have you seen Sorin?" she asked.

"Not since this all began. Have you asked Arke?"

She shook her head. "He's holed up in the kitchen, no doubt with Neri."

Abraxas frowned. "Barrion said she wasn't coming to the party. Did she change her mind?"

"I don't know, but I hope so. It's safer here with Arke."

To be honest, Evren hadn't seen the spider since they'd arrived in Orenlion. Arke hadn't talked about her or said if she had spoken to him again. At least, she couldn't remember if he'd mentioned it. Aster's tea made it hard to remember the small things.

She wanted to ask where Gyda was, because it couldn't be hard to miss a seven-foot-tall woman, but she thought better of it and went back to scanning the crowds. As angry as Sorin was at the whole of Orenlion, he loved a good party. He'd stick out, eventually.

She let Abraxas go and wormed back into the crowds. Eventually she found herself in the gardens, where the air was sticky sweet with humidity and fallen petals. It was marginally quieter outside as people gathered underneath the gazebo and on hidden benches to whisper quietly to each other. Her skirts whispered along the path as they gathered up dirt and leaves in their wake.

Just as she was about to give up, Sorin rounded the corner so fast he nearly tripped himself on his long legs. His version of dressing up was a cleaner shirt, tastefully unlaced at the top, and stolen jewelry from Evren's own collection. He wore gold better than she did.

"There you are!" he exclaimed, and stumbled over to her. He grabbed her shoulders to right himself, and the heavy smell of wine poured off his skin. "I've been looking everywhere for you."

Evren lowered her voice, and hopefully his, as she brought him back to a darker corner of the garden. "Is it done?"

He laughed nervously. "Funny thing that."

Panic shot through her. "What?"

"See. I have Shao . . ." He trailed off, twiddling his fingers like a naughty child.

"And?" Evren pressed.

"It was going fine! The man can drink like a sailor, but he doesn't have the tolerance for it. Evvie, I didn't even have to press a cup into his hands. He was halfway there before I found him. Which is great, yeah? Works with the plan swimmingly."

She waited for him to elaborate and motioned for him to do so when he didn't.

"Right! So, you know, it's kind of hard for me to feel bad about what we're doing to this guy, right? He's a total dick and a complete hypocrite. I know we said not to do anything to him, just to get him drunk enough to make him think we did . . . ya know." He waggled his eyebrows. "Which, I want to stress, I would never do under normal circumstances."

"Sorin." Evren knew all this. They'd been through it before. The morality of it and whether it was right to even ask Sorin to pretend to be what Shao had accused him of being. The Vasa had agreed easily. There was no reason for him to explain himself.

"Right, well," he winced. "I got him alone and everything was going according to plan. Major hypocrite this one but . . . Evvie, I can't do it."

Evren stared at him. "What?"

Sorin rubbed the bac of his neck nervously. "He babbles when he's drunk. You know, like Sol does. He started talking instead of feeling me up, and I started listening. I still don't like him, but this is just wrong. He's a wreck. It's not right."

If she'd been able to drink that night, she would've thought she'd had too much, and that this was one big wine-fueled misunderstanding. But Sorin was looking at her with dead serious eyes, completely sober, just like her. He'd drawn a new line, and he was refusing to cross it.

"Where is he?" she asked. "Is he still alone?"

He nodded. "Yeah. He's not going anywhere. I'll show you."

Sorin led her through the manor and up to the second story. There was plenty of room for mingling up there, but there were few people around. He led her over to one of the empty guest rooms and opened the door for her, squeezing in after her and shutting the door.

The room was dark, save for one of the blue lanterns in the corner that had been tossed carelessly to the side. It reeked of wine, and Evren nearly tripped on an empty bottle on her way in. The glass bottle rolled merrily across the floor and stopped just shy of a fallen boot.

Shao was crumbled against the wall on the ground, nursing an already half-empty bottle of wine and looking exactly as Sorin had described, a wreck. His hair had fallen free of its severe knot, and his clothes were wrinkled. One boot was across the room, the other was mere inches from his feet. His neck was bruised with love marks, and Evren gave Sorin a questioning look.

His cheeks darkened and he shuffled around. "I might've gotten carried away. He's a decent kisser, for a prick. But we didn't go any further than that."

Shao let out a dark chuckle from the floor. "Not for lack of trying. Although . . . stars above, I can't remember who was trying harder. Pathetic." He choked on another laugh before drowning it in wine.

This was not the Shao she knew and despised. There was nothing carefully groomed or sharp in this man. He was rumpled and discarded here, reeking of wine and desperation and possibly sadness. The gleam in his eyes was far too wet to be anger. These eyes were clouded and thick with wine haze.

Someone this drunk didn't have a choice but to be anyone but themselves.

"I may be fucked up, but I know where this is going," Shao said bitterly. "You used your human to frame me."

Sorin let out a sound of protest, but it died quickly. Without saying anything, he left the room. Shao's eyes watched him until he was gone and then landed back on her.

"This is where you tell me that you'll keep my secret if I do what you want." He waved his free hand at her as if he was giving her lines to a play. "I can see it now. You've changed. Funny thing, Aster warned me. Said you would do things now that you wouldn't have dared before. Finally one of the big fishes now." He bared his wine-stained teeth in a feral intimidation of a grin. "So, what do you want? Don't make me guess, I'm far too drunk to tolerate such games. Something to do with the little princeling?"

Evren was rooted to the spot, back to her strangely numb sensation and hating it. She barely forced herself to speak. "Yes."

Shao laughed again and went to drain the last of his wine. He got about halfway through before he started coughing and had to pull the bottle away before he choked to death. He sputtered and spat, dark red wine staining his shirt like blood. Evren knelt and took the bottle from him.

"I'm still using that," he wheezed around his coughs.

"Later." She waited for him to recover before handing it back.

"You know, it's a little funny." He laughed to himself again and leaned his head against the wall. "I always I knew something like this would happen to me. I mean, it's inevitable, being who I am. But of all the people I expected it from, I never thought it'd be you." He looked at her from the corner of his eyes. "That's the worst part. You left here thinking you were above our games and came back just to sink as low as we are. How does it feel?"

She answered truthfully. "Like I'm dying."

His laugh was feverish, like a man on the edge of the gallows waiting for the axe to come down. When he stopped, his cheeks were wet, and the tears never stopped.

"Fuck you, you melodramatic saint," he hissed. "You were supposed to be different. I was supposed to be able to rely on that, and you've fucked it all up."

Evren let him be angry rather than notice his tears. He'd just lose himself if he realized he was crying in front of her. "Had a grand plan?"

"Me? Not really. I was going to kill a few people and blame it on your thuggish friends. I'm afraid that's out the window now, yeah?"

"Yeah. Who did you want to kill?"

He swallowed hard, but didn't reach for the rest of his wine. "Does it matter now?"

"Yes."

"Fine." He spat the word out with traces of wine and saliva. "Yikao, for starters."

She tried to cover the gasp that left her chest, but he heard it anyway.

"Does that surprise you, Xun?" he asked. "There's a lot of men who want him dead. Aster, soft as he is, wants the same. I was going to kill him for what he did to us, and then I was going to see if his brat of a son was the same way and kill him, too."

Shao drank the last of the wine, and the bottle rolled out of his fingers to clink merrily with the other one. "Fen too, for letting it happen. She knew, you know? She knows everything. Still not sure why she didn't kill Yikao first. Maybe that's why he always sides with her. He knows he's a knife's edge away from oblivion. She gets to rule the city, he gets to live. Well, fuck that. Both of them can rot."

He finally noticed the tears and wiped them away so hard she thought he was going to tear his skin off. "Fuck every single one of them. Do you know how dirty they all are? I thought I did until I took my father's place. I didn't want to be like them. I wanted to be a respected equal. All it took was a dreadful night and a few terrible lies, and I was their puppet. Just like my father, just like yours."

Shao grabbed her wrist with so much strength she thought the bones were splintering under his grip. He pulled her so close she could taste the wine in the air with every hurried breath.

"You know what happened to him, right?" Shao asked. "That's why you left. Better to leave than stain that pure soul of yours."

"Know what?" She tried to wiggle out of Shao's grip. "Shao, what the fuck are you talking about?"

"My father knew something was wrong," he said instead. "When Yuhan vanished, and you were screaming for help, he dug. As much as a soldier can because that's all he fucking was. I remember him saying, 'Yuhan's destroyed this city with his neglect, but he's the only man with any honor left in Orenlion. I need to find him.' And I tried to help. Every night I pulled out maps and read through old letters that made no fucking sense. For him. Not Yuhan, not you, for my father. Until one night, I had everything ready. It was all laid out right where we left off and easily folded to be put back in its hidden shelf. But when he came through the door, he was different. The other Sovereigns had forced him to step down. The title fell to me. He told me it was because he dug too far, that Wasanthi had found out and warned him to stay away."

Shao's grip tightened, but Evren couldn't feel it anymore. She couldn't think of anything beyond his words.

"Do you remember when you came into the Chamber for what must've been the fiftieth time, and I was there? Do you remember me voting to help you, to send out another band of soldiers to search? Of course you don't. You were too clouded with hate to see that. I was doing what my father had tried to do, and when I came home, he was sick. The healers said it was a common disease for a soldier his age, that his mind and body were poisoning each other. But I knew better. I knew they'd hurt him to get me to shut up. I watched him wither away, unable to speak or feed himself or wipe the drool off his face. FOR YOU!"

Evren finally wrenched her wrist free and tumbled back on the floor a few feet away from him. He was sobbing now, clutching his head in his hands, and rocking back and forth.

"I couldn't do a damn thing! And it was all your fault. When you left, I sent soldiers out to kill you, but the Khama were on your trail first. I just know Song let you go. All I could hope was that Etherak killed you one way or another."

She was shaking so hard she couldn't stand if she wanted to. "Shao . . ."

"Why did you have to come back?" he wailed. "Why did you have to fuck everything up again? I'm ruined now. I am your puppet, just as I was theirs. I will never be an equal, or my own man. If this is what my father's legacy is, I want none of it."

Evren sat there for what felt like hours while he cried. She held her wrist, feeling the indents in the skin that would become bruises soon. And her mind wandered.

Her father had gone missing, and Shao's father had tried to find him. She remembered little of the man, other than he was a brute who favored battle more than sense. More than once, his ability to lead was questioned because of the amount of head trauma he'd suffered. He and her father were not friends, but they shared one thing in common.

Honor.

Shao's father suspected a conspiracy. And then he'd been removed from power. Putting his son in his spot was an obvious threat. But Shao himself had pushed, and the threat ended up being a double-edged sword he hadn't seen.

She didn't like Shao, and never would. But she did pity him. The weight of a father's legacy was a terrible thing to shoulder. They were both too young for it. Neither'd had a choice. And if Shao and his father had been right, then it was the Sovereign's fault.

"Shao," she started gently. "Do you know who would've killed our fathers?"

There was no doubt about it now. Xun Yuhan was dead, and it had been covered up as a disappearance, or the Hisrachi's fault, or his own shirking of duties. With one death, they'd ruin the Xun name, wage more war on the Weavers, and give themselves an out. The only question besides who, was why? And she intended to find out.

"I have my theories." He sniffed and looked up at her. His hair was ragged and torn at his temples, and his face was red. There was no covering up his breakdown. "But I figured it was all of them. I didn't dare pick up my father's research. My cousin . . . she just had twins. I couldn't let them hurt her too without being sure."

"Let's do it then."

He let his hands drop to his lap and eyed her suspiciously. "Do what?"

"Kill them," she said easily. "Destroy them. Force them to give Barrion what he wants and then leave them nothing but ash behind."

He laughed bitterly. "As if it's that simple. How do you propose we do it?"

"Easy," she said, and stood up. Her skirt caught on her shoes, and she wobbled until her head cleared. Then she held a hand out to him. "We work together. You, me, and Aster. They've had us divided and blind. Not anymore."

"You don't give a shit about me, Xun."

"I don't," she agreed. "I fucking despise you and everything you are. But it's not all your fault, and I owe your father. So now, I owe you. They'll never see us coming."

He regarded her hand for a while before looking back up at her through wet eyelashes. His grin reminded her of Gyda's in battle, red with wine and far too sharp to be friendly. "I do love a surprise attack."

His hand clasped hers.

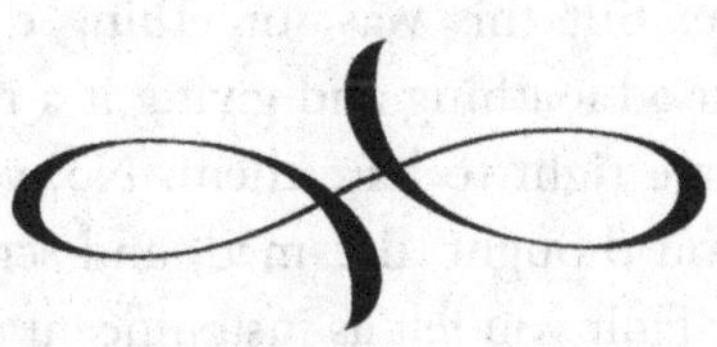

21

Evren left Shao to clean himself up, with Abraxas waiting on him. People would start to notice if their general was gone too long, but he was a mess few could fix. Abraxas was a soldier and a commanding presence. Hopefully, Shao wasn't too drunk to listen to him.

She didn't have much of a plan, but that didn't nag her as she made her way back through the gardens with more purpose than she'd had in days. Despite this, she could feel her hands quivering as they hid in her sleeves. She knew the Sovereigns were foul and corrupt people. But to have killed her father and Shao's? To cover it up and threaten a grieving boy until he shut up? That was cold. More than that, it was evil.

Was there a purpose behind it? Had her father done something that threatened their way of life more than marrying a human and having a half-breed child? Was it all of them or just one? Why did she want it so heavily to be Fen when Wasanthi was their closest clue?

The only thing she knew for certain was what she was going to do when she found out.

Evren thought she knew evil. The bloodthirsty warmongering of Heliodar, the calculating torture of Ainthe, the tearing of souls from Gail. But Heliodar, however awful, sought to bring her people up in a stronger unity. She didn't see any other way but war. Ainthe was the type of powerful mage that nightmares were made of, but she did it all for her child. Gail was nothing but a scared child with far too much power for his broken mind to handle.

She understood all of them. Even Velcros's betrayal in Serevadia made sense. But this was something different. This was taking her childhood loathing and giving it a reason to lash out. As if, yes, you were right to hate them. No, you didn't make it up. Everything you thought, dreamed, and screamed about was fair. And it's their fault you felt as insignificant as possible.

The only thing left to do was figure out who it was and destroy them.

"Evren!"

The voice that stopped her wasn't anyone she'd planned on seeing, like one of the Sols. Nor was it someone she sadistically hoped to run into, like the Sovereigns. Instead, when she turned around, she saw Mei marching up to her.

Grand parties were not a good fit for the Khama. She looked like she just got out of a hunting party with her wyvern, her hair askew, her cheeks flushed, and her armor spattered with leaves.

And she did not look happy.

"What the hells is this?" the Khama asked when she got closer.

Evren fought the urge to pinch her nose. "A party?"

"Where's Aster?"

On a different night, Evren might've responded with something barbed and entirely unhelpful. But there was something laced in Mei's stoic voice that gave her pause.

"Why?" Evren asked instead and watched the hunter bristle.

"Because I'm looking for him, obviously."

Evren had half a mind to repeat her question, but thought better of it. Weaponless or not, the Khama would snap her in half if she kept pushing her.

"Aster was looking for Wasanthi last I saw him," Evren said.

Mei breathed a little like she'd been struck. All at once, she seemed to notice that they weren't alone. Her eyes flickered around the crowd surrounding them. The nobles were watching with unbridled interest as Mei had not tried to keep her voice down. They turned away when she glared, giggling behind their fans and whispering into their cups. Mei seemed to shrink a few inches and drew closer to Evren. As she did, her eyes were filled with disgust at the audience she'd accidentally gathered.

"What are you planning?" she whispered. "What is all of this? And why did you drag Aster into it?"

"This was mostly his plan," Evren said. "I didn't push much, only asked for his help with Barrion's case."

"Of course, it's the fucking prince." She seethed. "Why would it be anything else? Everywhere he is, you are, or someone working with you."

Evren didn't think she was that far up Barrion's ass, but it could be hard to tell from her position. She didn't try to argue with Mei, she just let her believe what she wanted. In the end, it didn't matter.

"Why are you so worried?" Evren asked. "You came in here like you were looking for a fight."

"I was," Mei said. "I thought better of it." She glanced around at the nobles, who were slowly but surely losing interest in them, and leaned closer so her words were for Evren alone. "What's this really about? Aster despises these events, and so do you. Neither of you tried to cover that up before."

At the moment, nothing but Shao's confession mattered. All she could think about was what she planned to do and how she'd tell Aster. There was so much to be done, but she felt close enough that she could almost sink her teeth into the hope that finally her father would get some justice. It must've shown in her eyes, because Mei took a cautious step back.

"You're planning something else," the Khama said. "What is it?"

It couldn't hurt to tell her, but Evren was tired of telling the same story more than once. Better to kill two birds at the same time. She gestured for Mei to follow her and walked back into the manor without a word. The Khama followed closely.

They could've wandered for an hour or two trying to pick Aster's form out of the sea of jewels and silk. But he found them first.

Aster stopped short just in front of them, his eyes darting between the two of them as he swallowed down whatever news he had for Evren.

"Mei," he started. "I didn't think you'd come."

She shifted from foot to foot. "I wasn't. But Gao ended up taking my shift for some extra practice and I . . ." she glared at a passing couple. "I thought I'd see what you've been working on."

"This really isn't the best time." Aster grimaced. "I'm sorry, but I—"

"I think it'll be fine," Evren said.

He finally looked at her. "Did you get Shao?"

Mei let out a strangled noise. "Get what?"

Evren ignored her. "More or less. He's with us, quite willingly I'll add."

"Sorin did well then."

"Willing *completely*." Evren pressed the word and hoped he understood. His eyes widened a fraction. "Not without a price, but it's one I think the three of us can agree on."

"What in the hells is going on?" Mei hissed.

Again, Evren and Aster ignored her. A very brave, but stupid, thing to do to a woman who spent most of her time with wyverns.

"We should take this somewhere private," Aster said. He turned to walk off and then paused next to Mei. "And Mei—"

"Absolutely not," she snapped. "You're not leaving me here while you do something stupid and secret. I'm coming with you."

The flash of hesitation in his eyes was as quick and intense as lightning. But whatever protests he had, he swallowed them down quickly and nodded to her. "Okay, you'll come with us then." He turned back to Evren. "Wasanthi is waiting for us in the study. Let's get him out of the way first, and then we'll enact whatever terrible plan that's building in your head."

Evren had forgotten Wasanthi in the sense that she'd forgotten about the crown. For a brief, shining moment, she didn't have to feel like she was dying. She still was, and her body wasn't letting her forget it, but talking to Shao had eclipsed everything else. It was the first motivation she'd had that didn't revolve around her heart and the crown. Having it all come crashing back to her was like stepping into a puddle of cold mud after a nice bath.

Aster took them through the house to the study. Almost as if the guests knew they weren't allowed, no one stayed around this area. There were no signs, and no one was told to stay away. In every way, this part of the house should've been the highlight. The ancestral wall was one to marvel at, and all the candles Aster had put up made it gleam like gold. It was common for guests to pay respects to the ancestors of their host, but no one was around. It was if the manor had taken this part of itself and warded anyone else off. This was where the hallway to Evren's room branched off, and where her father's study had laid quiet and undisturbed since he left.

Aster had asked to unlock it when he was prepping for the party. Evren had been too numb to care at the time, but as she stepped in, she'd wished he'd left it alone.

The study was large and felt secure in the way a vault would. There were no windows, just deep brown wood which made her feel like she'd stepped into the very heart of a tree. Maps of the Wood, ancient and incomplete but stunning in their delicate beauty, were framed and hung on the walls. Ancient ancestral weapons blanketed what parts of the walls the maps didn't. Bows and spears, swords and daggers, and pieces of burned Khama armor were carefully displayed, the scales old and rusty but still gleaming like copper coins in the soft candle-light. The desk was just as ancient and imposing as the men and women who'd used it in ages past. Evren had never seen it clean and not covered in scattered notes and scrolls. Aster had made it perfectly bare, like it hadn't been touched since it was carved.

That made her feel a little better at finding Wasanthi sitting behind it and sipping wine. He was staring at the art and weapons on the wall, but his eyes were fixed on the piece hanging from the ceiling in the corner. The handmade wind chime didn't belong next to ancient artifacts, but it hung there with its sea glass chimes twinkling in blues and yellows nevertheless.

"Such an odd piece," Wasanthi mused.

Evren let the door slam behind her enough for Aster to jump.

"It's a family heirloom. Leave it."

Wasanthi looked over at her with a raised eyebrow. They were shockingly white and curled up like horns. "I meant no disrespect. I find it quaint that you father wanted to add a human novelty to his collection. He was always a very generous man."

"It keeps evil spirits away," Evren said weakly, reciting what her father had told her.

"Ah, what a human superstition." He shook his head. "Only they would think spirits are evil. The only things that are truly evil are the hearts of mortals. We are corruptible and fragile. Our Lady has always said that."

"We didn't come here for a lesson." Aster stepped forward and leaned on the desk.

Wasanthi regarded him coolly. "No, you didn't. Although I do find it odd that you have cornered me out of all people. Wouldn't you have a better chance of persuading your mother to help you support the little prince?"

"This isn't about that," Evren said and turned away from the wind chimes. "Before I left, the Wood was dying and nothing could stop it."

"I remember." Wasanthi nodded. "I prayed day and night for our Lady to answer us and give us the means to keep our home alive. She must've answered in a way that I hadn't heard."

Mei snorted. "That was your way of helping? Prayer?"

His eyes flashed at her before returning to their normal, bored glare. "General Shao slaughtered Weavers, thinking they were the cause. Yikao locked himself up in the library for days on end, nearly starving himself to find the answers. Liang nearly killed five apprentices trying to use magic to heal the forest. Fen reverted back to her old line of thinking and blamed you." He pointed a finger at Evren. "Of course, a divine marriage could've worked. The Xun line was supposed to be our connection to the Wood. You had no such connection, child, and your father left us with no choice. It is fortunate that the Wood recovered, though no amount of Weaver blood or Liang's magic did it."

"You still think it was the Horizon Walker?" Evren asked.

"Well, of course. My faith is all I have, child." He sipped his wine slowly. "I will say I was looking forward to the wedding. You were so close it was bound to happen, eventually. But, alas." He shrugged. "Youths will always rebel. I see you're done with that now. Have you come to ask for my blessing?"

Evren and Aster shared a look. Behind them, Mei hissed a curse. It would've been truly cruel to bring her in here to witness that. But Evren didn't deny it, and neither did Aster. Shutting that door before they were sure they didn't need it would be foolish.

"We're looking for something that belonged to the Horizon Walker," she said. "During my travels, I found a lost race of elves. They worshipped their own Elder, the Shadow Dancer."

Wasanthi nodded. "I have seen his likeness on the temple walls."

"Then you've seen his sword."

He frowned and rested his elbows on the desk. "Depictions

of it, yes. Each of the Elders had a special item, from what we could tell. There are scarcely any holy texts about them, but they were a piece of the Elder's powers. Why do you ask?'

"The elf I talked to said he thought these pieces were in Eith. Whatever drove the Elders away, some had time to leave a trail, even instructions. These elves had instructions from the Shadow Dancer to stay hidden."

"Just as we had orders to stay in the Deep Wood," Wasanthi added.

"Yes." Evren nodded.

"Did your friend ever find his Elder's sword?"

"No," she took a breath, "but he believed the crown was in Orenlion, or somewhere in the Wood."

Wasanthi seemed to freeze like a statue for a moment, his fingers steepled together and his eyebrows scrunched together in thought. Then he laughed.

"Child, that's ridiculous! My entire bloodline has spent every waking moment of their lives looking for our Lady's artifacts. We've come up with very little. Surely we would've found something with so much power by now."

"The texts he found said that we would find it by the 'light of the swollen moon and the fall of silver.'" Evren continued, even as he laughed over her, "It's only a few more days until the full moon. We need to find the fall of silver, and quickly."

"Fall of silver? That could mean anything." Wasanthi waved her off. "Assuming your friend got the translation correct, the Elder's spoke in riddles. Fall of silver could mean anything from a vein of metal in a mountainside, to a strike of lightning, a waterfall, the light of the moon reflected in the silver of a bowl, anything."

He stood up and shook out his robes. "If this is all you had for me, Aster, I must say that I got the better end of the deal. I thought you learned to trade secrets like your mother. But it seems you have more to learn still."

He moved around the desk and swept by Aster, who was too

stunned to move, and Evren, who was too angry to do anything that would keep him from leaving. But just as he was reaching the door, Mei stepped in front of him.

"We're not done, Sovereign." Her tone was crisp and professional, but Evren could hear the barely bridled rage underneath.

"Khama Song, stand aside." Wasanthi sounded tired. "This is no way for a hunter of your stature to act."

Evren turned her back on the desk and looked towards Wasanthi. Whatever Mei's reasons for keeping him here, she'd milk it for what it was worth. She couldn't live up to her promise to Shao if she was dead.

"Why did you warn Shao's father to stay away from mine?"

Wasanthi froze. Everyone in the room did. Mei's face was a carefully controlled mask, but her eyes darted to Aster to see if he knew what angle Evren was playing. But he didn't. Aster looked up at her with nothing short of fear.

It was one thing to frame, bribe, or blackmail a Sovereign. It was another to threaten one. And there was nothing but malice in Evren's voice.

Wasanthi turned slowly towards her. His smile was still there, but it was strained. "I have no idea what you're talking about. From my understanding, the two men couldn't stand each other."

"That's my mistake." She laughed as if she'd tripped over his feet. "No, what I meant was, why did you tell Shao's father to stop looking for mine? Why did you, when he didn't stop, force him out of his seat and put his son there? And then, why did you kill him?"

"Shao's father died of natural causes. A warrior such as himself should've taken better care of his body."

"Oh, spare me another halfhearted lie," Evren spat. "You warned him to stay away. Why?"

"The same reason I told you to stop looking," he said. "There is no use chasing the dead. It's clear you haven't moved on, and neither has Shao." He shook his head sadly. "I should've seen this. He was too young for the weight we put on his shoulders. My child, I can help you grieve—"

"Call me child one more time and I'll rip your spine out through your mouth."

That shut him up. She closed the gap between them.

"Whatever your involvement with my father's death, and Shao's, I will find out," she said. "I'll rip out whatever secrets you have tied to your heart and bare them to the light of day. How I do it, how gentle I am, and if you survive the aftermath, is entirely up to you. You will tell me where the crown is."

"I told you I don't know."

"And I think you're lying."

"Evren . . ." Aster cautioned behind her. She ignored him.

"You should've jumped at the idea of finding such an artifact. Instead, you laughed it off. I think you know where it is, and if you tell me, I'll see what I can do about keeping you alive."

Wasanthi was hard to read. Evren meant every word, but she couldn't tell if they were hitting home. She was so angry that her vision was blurring. She couldn't tell if the red haze she kept seeing in the corners of her eyes was a new symptom or if she was actually seeing red.

"You have become what your father never could, Evren," Wasanthi said. "Yuhan was always too honorable to see what needed to be done. Too much heart, too much conscience holding him back. You were the same. And yet, I see that you have become one of us. So willing to get to your goal that you'd destroy everything and everyone in your path."

"We aren't the same," she growled. "My reasons are good."

"As are mine. You just haven't seen it yet. I am not an evil man. I warned your father that his little quest would destroy him. It wasn't me that did it, so please keep you weapons to yourself. I simply knew his path would end in death and tried to steer him in a different direction. And I'm doing the same for you.

"You're dying, and you will die if you keep to this path. I think you need the crown to live, and I would give it to you if I knew where it was. But I can say with absolute certainty that it is not within the Wood. It never was. You will die, Evren, whether by your hand or another's." He smiled sadly, as if she was a starving kitten he pitied. "It is not a threat. It is the observation of someone who has watched many people pass on. But, you are your father's daughter. You won't wither away. I suspect you'd like to go out fighting and doing something important. A shame the only way you'll meet the end of a blade is by your own hand."

There was no time to process what he'd said. A threat? A confession? Something between sympathy and relief to see her go? Before anyone could do anything, there was a thunderous boom that rattled their bones. The wind chime clicked merrily in the corner.

And then there were the screams.

Evren had only a second to relish the horror on Wasanthi's face before she was shoving past him and out the door with Mei. The Khama bolted through the house, and it was all Evren could do to keep up. She didn't bother to look to see if Aster was following.

The manor was thick with fear, made worse by the amount of wine and the lack of room. The panicked crowd parted easily for Mei though, and Evren slipped behind her and out the door.

At first there was nothing to see. It was so dark she nearly ran into Mei. It wasn't until she saw a plume of fire that she realized something was very wrong.

Orenlion shouldn't be dark. All the lights in the city were out.

The fire was a quick plume, and then it was gone. Magical and hotly burning, but none of the buildings or city had caught fire.

Yet.

Mei said, "That's near the Roost."

Evren didn't need to look at her to know she was afraid. Fear had a vicelike grip on her throat and her voice was strained. But Evren knew she'd push through that feeling.

"Who would attack the Roost?"

There was another flash of fire, bright enough that Mei's face lit up and the flames were reflected in her wide eyes. She wasn't looking at Evren, her eyes were only on the Roost. Mage fire, Evren had been around Arke enough to know. It disappeared as quickly as it came. She couldn't see any lingering flames from where they stood.

"I don't know," Mei said and set her jaw. "But I'm going to find out."

And then she was gone, tearing down the street in a desperate run. Without Mei beside her, the screams of the frightened were all she could hear. Despite the heat, all she could think of was Direwall. The dead piling up and clawing at the living, the snow and ash mingling so thickly in the air it was hard to breathe, let along see.

She had nothing. No bow, no arrows, let alone the strength to use them. The wyvern dagger was tucked up her sleeve but practically useless in her hands. She licked her dry lips. She couldn't watch Orenlion burn.

"Evren!"

She turned to see Aster shoving his way out. There was a throng of horrified nobles crowding the door and they were all staring at the Roost as if it was a part of some awful light show. Aster couldn't quite get through, and she couldn't see any of her friends.

It was the time for terrible ideas then. And she wanted to make something bleed.

"Something's happening at the Roost," she said. "Whatever Khama are still in the manor, get them out and tell them to head there. The wyverns could be in trouble."

"Evren, listen!" Aster shouldered a noble who just shoved him back. "Most of the Khama are at the Roost. If it's under attack, we have no defenses elsewhere. And Liang's mages seem to already be fighting."

Orenlion hadn't been attacked in ages. They stayed hidden. That was their defense. The next were the Khama, and then the mages. Outside of that, the city was as fragile as spun glass. All in one decisive hit, it could be broken.

Aster saw it too, just as he saw the empty space beside her where Mei should be.

"Get her out of there," he begged.

She was already rolling up her sleeves. "Get my people, too. Get out of the house and figure out what the hells is going on. I'll get Mei out and meet you back here."

He nodded, and before she could regret her decision, Evren was running after Mei into the fiery dark.

She made it around the corner and across one bridge before she nearly passed out.

Evren grabbed the railing as she fell to her knees, gasping for air that did no good. There was another burst of fire, and she should've worried that it didn't go out. But she couldn't fit another breath into her failing lungs, let alone see where the fire was coming from.

"Oh, fuck you," she cursed her weakness. Then she brought out the dagger out, traced the back of her hand with the point, and dug it in.

The pain, as always, was temporary. It was sharp and refreshed her view of the world, which was getting fuzzier and more out of focus by the day. Suddenly, she could feel the wind on the nape of her neck. She could feel the blood trickling down the hairs on her arm. Every breath counted, and her lungs expanded and contracted with ease. Her bones weren't so brittle anymore. She felt strength where she'd only known frailty for so long.

Evren stood up, easily this time and with no dizziness. The wind carried the smell of smoke and brimstone. There was a growing light of hellish fire burning brighter near the Roost.

Against the flames she could see the silhouettes of wyverns flying from the burning Roost. Some had riders. Many didn't. One tumbled to the ground, on fire, crying out as it fell.

Evren gathered up her skirts, bloody dagger in hand, and ran.

She didn't know how long she had before she crashed, so she willed each stride to be longer than the last. She hopped over garden fences, cut through shops, and took stairs two at a time. She needed to be strong enough to fight whatever was out there and drag Mei out. The Khama wouldn't go willingly. And if there was anything wrong with her wyvern . . .

Evren put that thought out of her mind.

The stairs leading to the bridge that connected to the Roost were wide and littered with bodies. The firelight flickered and deepened the shadows to the point where they looked like they were jumping from the bodies out at her. Blood soaked the stairs, and the smell of burned flesh and poison was noxious.

Khama were cut open and looked like they were thrown aside like trash. Liang's mages hadn't lasted long. Evren could see the scorch marks from their spells, the ashes from their burned spell pages floating lazily from one body to another.

Evren crouched next to one of the mages and turned her over. Her eyes stared glassily at nothing and her clean white robes were nearly black with blood. Where her robes were torn, her flesh was green and peeling. The smell of acid overtook the blood and Evren's veins filled with ice.

She scrambled to her feet just as a large black shape leapt at her from the shadows. She dodged out of the way, falling back a few steps before landing in a crouched position and holding her blade before her.

The Hisrachi loomed over the bodies like a nightmare. The fire crackled behind it, and she watched the blood drip off its pinchers.

"What are you doing?" Evren cried. "You said you wanted peace!"

The hairs on the Hisrachi stood up on end, gleaming like thorns along its body. *"Traitor!"* it screeched. *"Murderer! You killed the Matriarch."*

Evren faltered. "What? No! We wouldn't. Barrion didn't give you up. He gave his word."

"Liessss!"

The Hisrachi leapt at her with all the fervor of a wild animal. Hate shone brighter than any forest fire in its eyes. Evren jumped back and slashed wildly at its legs. The blade glanced off the thick hide and only seemed to enrage the spider more. It took a couple of steps back and picked up the armored body of one of the fallen Khama. Then, with a cry of great effort, it threw the body at her like a catapult would a rock.

Evren tried to dash up the stairs to dodge, but the body clipped her back as it fell. The weight took her to the ground with a painful, jarring impact. The stairs dug into her ribs and the armor cut into her silk. She could hear the skittering of legs coming for her and tried to crawl out. But her dress was caught under the body. Dead weight and armor both kept her pinned.

She slashed at her dress, not caring that she nicked her own legs as she did. The fine silk tore under the flash of silver and when she gave it one more tug, the train came free entirely. She wiggled her leg free and rolled over on her back just in time to see the pinchers eclipse the night sky above her.

"Traitor!" the Hisrachi screamed, and she felt in her bones the grief in its voice.

Evren screamed too as the pinchers came down. It was not a cry of fear or pain, but one of rage and years of pent-up bloodlust. She shoved the dagger past the pinchers and into the Hisrachi's mouth before it could tear her throat out.

The spider's cries turned to wails. The pinchers snapped around her forearm but barely grazed her skin. Her arm was coated in blackish-green blood. She pulled the blade out and the spider reeled back, spitting blood, and gurgling its hate.

Evren surged to her feet and brought the dagger down on its

head. Once, twice, and then again. Until it was still on the blood-slick stairs and her arms were coated in it.

She stumbled up the stairs; her breaths heaving and her eyes blurry. The wide bridge to the Roost was worse than the stairs. Hisrachi swarmed over grounded wyverns. Where one spider went down by blade or teeth, another five would take their place. The walls were blackened, and the spiders scurried along the edges. They were coming up from the trees and it was a sea of legs, hateful eyes, and venom. Above, wyverns screamed. Both pain and battle cries pierced the air. Orders were shouted but lost in the din of battle. Evren watched in horror as a wyvern tried to take off from the Roost far too late. Its legs got caught in silvery webbing. It tore free just as the Hisrachi jumped on it. It dove into the air, but more leapt on it and tore at its skin. The wyvern screamed as it fell to the forest floor.

She tore her burning eyes away. What was this for? Hadn't the Hisrachi wanted peace? This wasn't even an assault. More Hisrachi bodies piled up than she could count. This was just blind, unrelenting rage. How did they even get in?

Where was Mei?

"Mei!" Her voice was lost in the cries of the dying.

Evren tightened her grip on her dagger. She didn't have much longer left, but she'd be no good with just a dagger against a gauntlet of foes eager to tear her throat out. She scanned the battle for anything she could use—a dropped bow, a broken spear—anything to make her more of a threat.

The only thing was a bloody spellbook.

She grimaced. Time for bad idea number two.

And then she ran.

There were fighting Hisrachi and Khama between her and the book. She slid underneath one spider, slashing its legs as she went. It buckled as she got to her feet. As she got back up, the Khama fighting it ran it through with his spear.

He turned to her with frightened eyes. "What do we do?"

She didn't have an answer for him. "Where's Mei? Khama Song, where is she?"

"I don't . . ." he sobbed. "I don't know. All my friends are dead. I don't know what to do."

"Go."

He blinked at her. "What?"

"Do you have your wyvern?"

He shook his head. She pushed him back towards the stairs. "Go! Spread the word. There could be other places under attack." As he turned, she grabbed his arm. "Find the Wandering Sols at Xun Manor. Tell them exactly what you saw here. Do it now."

She pushed him away, and he ran as fast as he could. He slipped on the bloody stairs, and then the smoke swallowed him up.

Evren turned back to the Roost. It was a bonfire everywhere except the very top. Wyverns and Hisrachi alike were on fire. Through the haze of smoke, it was hard to tell if any more wyverns and their riders were escaping. None were coming from the main entrance, which was an inferno of snapping flames. It wouldn't be long before the whole structure fell and took the tree with it.

She couldn't do anything about the fire. Evren needed to get survivors and get out. She needed to get to Mei.

Evren dove into the thick of the fighting again. She leapt on top of a Hisrachi and drove her blade into its skull until it stopped moving. She jumped off its body just as another leapt at her. It took her down, but she rolled onto her back and kicked it up and over her. The spider slid off her and over the edge of the bridge. She got on her knees just in time to see another one charging her. Without thinking, she flicked her wrist out. Her dagger soared through the air and landed right in one of its eyes. It skittered back, screeching in pain. She ran over and took the knife out, then swiftly cut again until the amount of blood leaking from its body made a river. She dashed away before its body hit the ground.

She wanted to be sad. She wanted to hate this. If she lived, she would. But now all she could hear were the sounds of dying wyverns and the cries of their riders.

One cry pierced the smoke enough to part it. It stopped Evren dead in her tracks and she looked up.

Through the flames and spiders, she saw Mei. She was at the top of the Roost, riding her wyvern. The old beast had bloody foam in the corners of its mouth. One of its wings hung limply at its side. Mei wielded her spear in a deadly arc, knocking back any Hisrachi that got close. But there were too many spiders, and the Roost was finally collapsing.

Evren couldn't keep from gasping as the roof buckled and Mei's wyvern dropped a foot. The beast pulled itself upright into the waiting fangs of a Hisrachi. The wyvern spat a steaming wad of saliva at the spider and then whipped around to fling another two off with its tail.

They had to jump. Bad wing or no, there was no safe landing in a fire. Evren watched the same thought process on Mei's face. She watched the hunter lean down and whisper to her wyvern. The beast understood. It even seemed to nod. There were tears in Mei's eyes from the smoke. Evren watched her bury her face in the scales of the wyvern's neck and close her eyes, and then it jumped.

Both wings, good and bad, flared out to catch the wind. Hisrachi leapt after them but fell short and into the fire. Their fall was fast, uncontrollable. Their landing shook the whole bridge.

Mei's wyvern's legs snapped underneath it, and it rolled to a stop with a pained cry. Mei leapt off the saddle to avoid being crushed. But the moment she was on her feet, she was running back.

"Mei, no!" Evren shouted, but it was useless. Even if she could be heard, Mei wasn't leaving behind her wyvern.

The Hisrachi focused on the injured wyvern now. The few remaining Khama took their chances and ran, scooping up wounded comrades as they went. Mei was running against the tide. She picked up another spear and threw it at the spider trying to chew at the wyvern's neck. Then she took her place between them and the wounded beast, her face smudged with soot and tears but set with determination.

Evren gripped her dagger and started running after her. The spellbook was just a few feet between her and Mei now.

Mei fought like a devil. She was as quick and precise as lightning and lashed out with enough force to shear legs off her enemies. More and more piled up at her feet, dead and dying and coating the floor with oily blood. But the Hisrachi had numbers, and it was far too easy to swarm a lone hunter and her wounded mount.

A stray Hisrachi slipped past Mei's guard. It flung itself at her, and Evren watched in horror as the hunter went down in a spray of blood.

The wyvern became unhinged. It tore the Hisrachi off and ripped it in half. Others started climbing on its body, biting and tearing through the scales. It simply curled itself around Mei's prone form and endured.

Evren picked the fallen spellbook out of the dead mage's fingers. Half the spells were gone, the rest were partially smudged or burned from the fighting. There were only a few blank, usable pages.

If she could use a spell Nerezza prepared, she could use one she made. Theoretically. But she'd never done so before. She'd only flipped through Arke's spellbook a few times. She knew symbols, but not what they did.

She looked up at the wyvern's bleeding, swarmed form shielding Mei.

She also didn't have a choice.

Evren pricked her finger for good measure and then tossed the dagger aside. It clattered to the ground like a warning bell.

With her bleeding finger, she traced the arcane symbols from Arke's book that she remembered. With each one, she felt the page quiver under her finger. The blood fizzled and burned as the page drank it in. Her finger was numb and tingling painfully by the time she was finished, and she tore the page free from its bindings.

"Hey!" she shouted as she marched steadily forward. The paper crumpled in her fist started to smoke. One by one, sets of eight burning eyes snapped to her. She spread her arms wide, dripping with the blood of their friends. "Don't you want someone who can fight back?"

They chittered their fangs and started jumping off. None of them noticed the ash falling from one of her fists. They were slinking ever forward. Behind them, the Roost gave a great heaving crackle and sagged further down. But there was still hesitant Hisrachi bent on killing the wyvern. She needed all of them.

"Your Matriarch trusted me, you know. She sent me here on her behalf. And look how many of you I've killed. I'll kill more before I die. Who wants to be the one who finally puts me down?"

Evren backed away a little shuffle at a time. She tried to feign terror, but she was too angry for it to come naturally. She didn't think they cared. Like any good predator, they saw prey moving away. They gave chase.

The ones on the wyvern scrambled off. The crowd of legs and fangs scurried after her at an alarming speed.

And Evren smiled.

Wasanthi was right. She would like to go out in a blaze of glory.

The ashes fell from her hands just as the Hisrachi surrounded her. The fluttering flakes were soaked in blood but didn't fall to the ground. Instead, they swirled around her legs and upward. The glowing glyphs they formed burned a deep, bloody red. The column of ash encircled Evren entirely and then froze solid in the air.

She took a deep breath and waited. When the first Hisrachi leg touched the ash, she screamed, and the ash exploded outward.

The bloody flakes turned to spears of white-hot metal and they flew out in every direction from her. Hisrachi were impaled and hurled backward. Oily blood sizzled around the heated metal. The smell of burning meat and hair filled the air. The shock wave that followed tore through the bridge, buckling its supports and battering bodies off the side with an ear-popping snap of wind.

And then it was still. And then it was quiet.

Evren's ears were ringing. She tasted blood and bile at the back of her tongue. All at once, the wonderful strength she'd had was gone. She was a husk, burnt and empty. She swayed as her vision blackened, but she didn't feel it when she fell to her knees. Evren blinked, wheezing in one breath at a time. The fire of the Roost grew dim and blotchy. She watched it fall, and then she fell. The ground beneath her cheek was uncomfortably warm, but all she could do was breath and try to blink.

Was Mei alive? Was the wyvern?

She blinked.

She breathed.

A shadow in her vision moved, but she couldn't see what it was. She just saw it come closer and hover over her.

She blinked.

She breathed.

And then everything faded to black.

22

Death had come for Evren twice now, and each time it felt different. In Serevadia, after Ainthe was through with her, there was a black and comforting numbness to her world. Things were too soft for her to pull away on her own. Death lulled her away like she imagined a mother would a rowdy child fighting sleep. Gently, tenderly holding them until they slipped away.

This wasn't like that.

There was nothing calm about this death. Her blood was on fire. Every inch of her marrow shivered with a deep, unrelenting agony she couldn't shake. Her lungs bubbled with every shallow breath she took. She was shorn apart from everything, but she could still feel every painful twitch of her spent body.

Death was not kind to Evren a second time. Maybe that was why, against all odds, she fought against it.

THE SMELL of damp earth hit her first. Strong and pungent, laced with rotting leaves and roots pulsing with life. Her cheek was pressed into the soil and leaves fell against her parted lips as she breathed. It was all her body allowed. That and the slight twitch of her fingers. She curled them into the dirt and relished the moist soil gathering under her fingernails. She could feel it through all the dried blood. Life against death. She might've sobbed if she had the strength.

She couldn't open her eyes. Every time she tried, the sun blinded her with a dagger of light digging into the back of her skull. She gave up and listened.

The voices came to her slowly. Exhaustion and desperation laced their words. One was furious, and the sound of her voice was enough to make Evren forget her pain.

". . . an idiot! Only one would've kept that a secret. You could've prevented this if you'd just opened your mouth."

There was sobbing now in the background. Strange and gurgled as if it came from a mouth that wasn't used to such action.

And then someone else spoke up. This voice she recognized, too. It broke at the end of his words, as if he was one bad breath away from tears. "Moon above, what have you done? Why would you—"

Gyda cut him off. Evren could almost see her turning on him in that moment.

"What has she done? She reacted to what *you* were doing. She thought her people were going to die."

"So, the response was to attack Orenlion? The city burned! It may never fully recover."

"It still stands. Which is more than we can say for the Hisrachi nests we've passed."

"Mei almost died because of her!"

"Because of you! And your fucking plots."

"I was never going to give the nest to the Sovereigns. Barrion wouldn't let me even if I wanted to. It was a gamble, a bait to lure them in. That's politics. That's how this bloody works."

"And it is war now. You threatened, they responded. And now everyone is dying. This is how war works."

Evren groaned, and the fighting stopped. The strange sobbing didn't. She'd had enough of listening to them argue. She wanted answers. And for them to talk quietly because the yelling was just giving her another headache on top of the one she always had.

Evren kept her eyes shut against the sunlight and pushed herself up inch by inch. Her arms shook and screamed in protest. She felt herself falling back down to her elbows before powerful arms gently hoisted her up and propped her up against what felt like a thick wall of roots. The comforting scent of crisp ice and sword polish left her shaking, or maybe that was just the bag of bones she called a body now. A shadow passed in front of her eyelids, and Evren knew she had to open them even if it hurt.

Little by little, she forced her eyelids to open. Everything was fuzzy. All except for Gyda's face, which came back into focus first. She eclipsed the sunlight, and it lit up the stray hairs of red peeking out of her scarf like strands of fire. Gyda's face was pinched with worry, and Evren nearly melted when the warrior's callused hands brushed her hair out of her burning eyes. Her fingers lingered on her cheeks a moment longer than they should've.

"Hi," Evren muttered weakly.

Gyda's breath came out of her chest all at once, like some pitiful imitation of a laugh that she was too exhausted to commit to. "That is what you lead with after everything?"

Everything could've been a number of things. The battle at the Roost, her spell that nearly killed her, her and Aster's plan, the party, the long days of avoiding Gyda.

"It's open-ended. Can't really go wrong with it," Evren said.

"How do you feel?"

"Like death beat me with a few hundred spiders. I take it that wasn't a dream?"

Gyda's mouth twisted into a frown. "No, it wasn't."

Evren looked over Gyda's shoulder. The glare made her

wince, but she pushed through it. They were far into the Deep Wood now. The roots were almost as tall as normal trees in some areas. They were tucked into the alcove of one, and off to the side were two other figures. Aster was a mess. His robes were torn and blackened with soot, and somewhere along the way he'd lost his jewelry. His eyes were bright with tears, but his hard-set mouth was quivering with the effort to hold them back. Far away from him, trying to make herself as small as possible, was Neri.

"What happened?" Evren asked. She didn't aim the question at anyone in particular, but Gyda moved back so she could see everyone easier. Her icy glare was set on Aster.

"Tell her what you did."

He swallowed hard and wouldn't meet her eyes. "It was nothing. Just a rumor to pull the Sovereigns in."

"Aster . . ."

"They wouldn't meet with us!" he protested. "The party wasn't going to work, not for the ones we needed. I had no cards left to play because they refused to let go of the notion that Barrion was a Weaver ally."

"He was," Evren said. "He told you as much."

"I know!" Aster seethed and tore down his already falling hair as he paced. The leaves under his shoes crunched like tiny bones with every step he took. "He didn't know about the rumor. It was just me. All I needed to do was just get everyone in, and then we'd be fine. I didn't mean for anyone to get hurt. I wasn't going to give Shelis to my mother, no matter what she—" he pointed an accusing finger at Gyda "—thinks."

And that's when Evren turned her gaze to Neri. The spider was quivering, and her legs were bunched up as if she was trying to fold in on herself. "You were the one spying on us," Evren said.

"I-I didn't mean to," Neri said softly. *"I overheard Aster talking to Prince Barrion and trying to convince him to hand the Matriarch over as a sign of goodwill. But I . . . I couldn't hear*

much after that. And then I ran before I could hear anymore. I wanted to believe that Barrion wouldn't betray us, but I followed Aster anyway. When I heard his rumors, and the deals he made, I thought everyone I knew was going to die. I couldn't . . ." she buried her face in her legs. *"I couldn't watch them do that."*

"Why didn't you come to us?" Evren tried to keep her voice soft. "We would've helped."

"I thought you knew." Neri sniffled. *"You tried to kill Anep. You only kept me around because I'm not a true Hisrachi, and Arke liked me. And the Sols, they follow you. If it came down between you or the Matriarch, they'd chose you."*

"Maybe." Evren shrugged and winced. "But I make a lot of stupid decisions they catch me on. A lot more than normal lately."

"Did you know?"

She shook her head. "No, I swear. And neither did the rest of us."

It didn't seem to relax Neri. Aster was looking far away, as if he could make out Orenlion's scorched husk through the foliage. Finally, it was Gyda who spoke up.

"I noticed Neri acting strange closer to the party. Arke and I had little to do in the last few days, so it was easy to notice. We thought it would be best if I followed her instead of him."

Evren frowned. "Why? I mean, no offense, but you don't exactly give off non-threatening vibes."

Gyda smiled as if it was a compliment. "Arke had not worked up the courage to talk to Neri again. He thought she was still mad at him."

"I was."

"So, I went instead," Gyda continued. "She found a way out of Orenlion, and I lost her in the Wood. When I realized where she was going, I got to the nest too late. The Hisrachi had already marched, and it was too late for us to bring them back. Neri and I settled on trying to get to Orenlion first, but we were, again, too late."

Evren's eyes flicked back over to Neri. "You told them how to get into the city, and where to hit first."

The spider shuffled, but nodded. *"The mages had let their magical wards go. I figured out how to disrupt one enough to keep the city 'still,' as it were. From there, it was easy to see where Orenlion's strength came from."*

Aster whirled on her in a flurry of burned silk and tears. "You destroyed the Khama! Countless innocent riders and wyverns are dead because of you. Any that survived may never fly again."

"You would've done worse if the roles were reversed," Neri said.

Gyda interrupted before Aster could argue further. "And it would've been worse if Neri hadn't gotten the rest to retreat. Your city still stands because of her."

"There were more?" Evren asked.

Gyda nodded. "Many more. It is only by sheer luck we were able to convince them to turn back and defend their nest."

"But the Hisrachi I fought called us murderers," Evren said. "They said we killed the Matriarch."

Gyda's eyes fell to the ground, and she nodded again. "Shelis was dead by the time I got there. It could've been old age, or an illness. But the Hisrachi took it as a poisoning and assassination. Anep used it as fuel to fire their hate."

"Of course." Evren leaned her head back against the warm root. When she closed her eyes, all her injuries came to her at once and it felt like her whole body was tearing itself apart. She forced her eyes back open.

"How did you get me out? What about Mei?"

Gyda scowled. "We didn't. The Roost had fallen by the time we got there. Barrion was in the thick of the fighting and had pulled you out. He tried to get Mei too, but her wyvern wouldn't let him close. Aster had to do it. She's . . . alive," Gyda finally admitted. "For now. There was a lot of damage."

Mei was alive. That had to count for something. Evren's

fingernails pressed into her blood-crusted palms, and she struggled between feeling relieved and broken. She didn't want to think about 'for now' and the way it sounded like a death sentence on Gyda's tongue. She didn't want to see the hopelessness threatening to overwhelm Aster. Mei would live because death wasn't an option for a fighter like her.

"Next question." Evren cleared her throat. "Why are we out here instead of back in the city if it's still standing?"

"Simple." Gyda's eyes bore into her own. "We're curing you."

Manic laughter bubbled up from Evren's chest, all splintered and bubbly as it fought through the blood she kept swallowing back. Every chuckle turned into a cough until she felt like her ribs were going to snap and had to force herself to stop.

"I think we're past that," she tried to tell her, but the warrior's frown deepened. Evren knew that look. Gyda never put up with her shit when she had that expression.

"We're going to the Heart," Gyda said. "We're curing you, and then we'll fix the mess he made. Now, can you stand?"

"Do I have a choice?"

"You're not staying here. You can walk yourself or I can drag you through the Wood."

Evren ground her teeth and then sighed heavily enough to feel every rib. "Fine. Help me up."

Gyda made sure to get her on her feet too fast for her to hesitate or think about. The warrior held her arms and kept her standing as her legs threatened to give out. Evren blinked away the dizziness but didn't let go of her.

She was still in her torn gown, but the emerald green had turned black from the soot and blood. The silk was stiff against her skin, and Evren could feel bandages on the few wounds she'd picked up. These weren't the worst injuries she'd left a battle carrying. Everything that was wrong was internal, but she tried to pretend that it was just another dangerous wound she could recover from.

Gyda turned to Aster. "Now, tell us where the Heart is."

Aster's eyes flicked over to Evren. "I can't."

Gyda stiffened against Evren. "You won't?" she asked, and her voice was dangerously calm.

Aster heard the threat and took a step back. "No, I can't. There's a difference. I don't want to see her die any more than you do, but I made an oath."

"To who?"

"To her! She doesn't remember, but she knows it's true. I wouldn't lie about this. Would I?" He turned to Evren, pleading.

She squeezed Gyda's arm gently. "He's not lying. If I forced him to swear, he wouldn't tell me. He couldn't, no matter how much he wanted to."

"Fuck your oath," Gyda snarled. "Do something good. You want to save your city? Save her first or I'll burn it down myself."

"Gyda—"

Aster took a very brave, very foolish step forward. "Even if I told you, it wouldn't make a difference. She wouldn't get her heart back; she'd just die in a different spot. It won't do any good."

"Do you have any other ideas?"

Aster froze, his mouth slightly open, but no words fell out. He looked at Evren and she saw nothing but defeat in those warm eyes of his. Their only other hope had been the crown. Wasanthi was either telling the truth about it not being in the Wood, or he was lying. Evren believed him. If the crown was here, it would've been found. Her visions of Viggo were just grasping at a hope that never stood a chance, like morning fog trying to cling to the ground as the hot sun burned it away.

Aster's shoulders slumped, and he shook his head. "No. We thought . . . but no."

"That would be the crown you've been chasing after?" Gyda asked bitterly. When Evren looked at her, startled, the warrior just rolled her eyes. "You talk in your sleep. You should've told me, all of us."

Shame burned the points of Evren's ears. "I know."

"But that's a lecture for another day. I don't feel like yelling at you when you're a strong gust of wind away from your grave." Gyda turned back to Aster. "The Heart or leave. Your choice."

Aster just stood there, looking helpless, and Evren wanted nothing more than to hug him and tell him it was all right. She didn't blame him; she saw the truth in his eyes. There would be no answers in the Heart. But this wasn't her quest anymore. It was Gyda's. And there was nothing she could do to stop her.

"I can take you."

They all turned to Neri, who had unfolded herself from her legs and was inching closer.

Evren shook in Gyda's grip. "You know where the Heart is?"

"I know where to take you. All Hisrachi do. I can make this right," Neri said. *"If we can heal you, will you stop this? Can you get everyone to stop fighting?"*

Evren hesitated. In truth, no, she couldn't promise that. Even at her peak, stopping a war once it began was nearly impossible, and she had no say in the power struggles of Orenlion. The only leverage she had was Aster, and no one would take them seriously. But, truthfully, she wouldn't live long enough to matter. So she nodded her head.

"Yes. Show us."

～

ASTER RETURNED TO ORENLION. He couldn't follow them, and while Gyda was happy to send him back, Evren was sad to see him go. It was the last time she'd see him, and she wanted that goodbye to mean something. But she couldn't do much besides squeeze his hand and smile through the tears pricking at the corners of her eyes.

"It's okay," she whispered. "I don't blame you."

"It would be easier if you did," he choked out and squeezed her hand back. "If you . . . If I don't see you again, I want you to know that you were the closest thing I had to true family. And I'm sorry I wasn't enough for you."

"I'm sorry I left you."

He let out a strangled laugh. "Me too." He stepped back from her and looked at Gyda. "I hope you're right, for what it's worth. I hope you bring her back alive."

"I will," the warrior promised, and then she hooked her arm around Evren's shoulders and turned her away from Orenlion.

Evren leaned on her heavily, each step dragging and feeling like her last. Her eyes blurred with tears, and she was glad she wasn't watching Aster walk away. Focusing on Neri's form in front of them was easier.

"Don't be angry with him, Gyda," she begged. "An oath is bound in blood. It's not simply a promise. If he broke it, he'd be damning his soul and the souls of everyone he loved."

Gyda was quiet for a while. When she spoke, Evren felt the vibrations through her chest. "Souls are fragile things. All are damnable, regardless of a broken oath or not. I would damn mine a thousand times before I let anyone I loved die."

"That's the difference between you and Aster. You've watched nearly everyone you cared about die, and you couldn't do anything about it. He's never had to before."

"That's changing now."

Evren chewed the inside of her cheek. "Yes, it is." A part of her selfishly hoped she wouldn't make it back to Orenlion. At least then she'd avoid seeing more bloodshed.

The trek into the Wood was painfully slow. Evren couldn't keep up a steady pace and they had to stop frequently. With each break, Gyda forced her to drink water or to eat something. She barely kept the food down, and it all tasted like ash. The water did nothing but slosh in her stomach and make her sick. By the time the sun was setting, they'd taken another break and Evren couldn't get up.

She gripped the root she was sitting on so hard she felt her nails crack, but no matter how much she tried, she couldn't get her legs to hold her. Every time she tried to put her weight on them, they spasmed and tiny pricks of white-hot pain shot up and down her body.

She collapsed back on the root, gasping and cursing as she held back tears. She didn't want to cry, but she was close to giving up.

Suddenly, she was being scooped up. Her stomach lurched a little as Gyda cradled her in her arms and started walking forward.

"This feels familiar," Evren said weakly and tried to ignore how close they were.

Gyda snorted. "You were unconscious the last time."

"Bleeding out, if I remember. You used your scarf to try and stop the bleeding."

"It didn't work."

The trees passed one by one as the shadows grew, and Evren laid her head on Gyda's shoulder. She was far too exhausted to feel guilty about having to be carried. Dying in her arms wouldn't be such a bad way to go.

"I know I said I'm sorry for ruining your scarf, but I still am." Then Evren laughed enough to draw Gyda's questioning gaze. "You always find me at my worst. I keep dragging you down."

Gyda swallowed and shook her head. Evren thought she felt her stumble. "You don't need to apologize. I don't mind following you into the shadows. I'd do it even if you told me not to."

"That's not very healthy of you."

"Eith is full of dark places. Better to walk them with someone you care about than alone."

Evren searched for something witty to say for a while. But, before she could, she started to doze off. She should've been worried then, that that was it. That death was reeling her back and the whole day of hiking was the last one she'd ever have. But the air was sweet and cool against her fevered skin, and she couldn't be bothered to care about anything while she was in Gyda's arms.

Nothing could hurt her there.

~

WHEN EVREN WOKE AGAIN, everything was blue.

The ground was hard and cold against her back. The air was heavy and wet. She watched the lights flicker against the ceiling, rippling like water. The ceiling wasn't smooth. It was a deep black, and long tendrils hung down from it as if reaching out to her. Roots, she realized dimly. She was underground.

"Evren." Gyda's hand was on her cheek again and she was shaking her gently. Her cheeks were wet. Where had her scarf gone?

"Your hair is showing," Evren rasped.

The warrior didn't seem to notice or care. Something shifted behind Evren, just out of eyesight. The smell of damp, decaying earth was suddenly overpowering. And Gyda looked up at whatever it was with barely bridled desperation.

"You'll help her?" The question that would've once been a demand. Things were really fucked then.

"There is little I can do . . ."

Evren grasped Gyda's forearm with enough strength to startle the warrior. She looked down at her, bewildered, but Evren wasn't looking for an explanation. She was trying to sit up.

She knew that voice.

Gyda helped her sit up. Then, despite the blood threatening to choke her, Evren pushed herself on her knees and turned around. The very motion of it sent her head reeling, and she coughed up a wad of blood. It was black against the slick stone floor. She wiped her mouth with the back of her hand and sat back on her legs.

The cave was wide, but the roof was low. If Gyda was standing, she'd be crouching down. A glowing pool of water lit up the room with a soothing luminosity. And, standing before it, was the figure from the forest.

It was just like her nightmares. Wreathed in decaying roots, caped in mushrooms, and the cloak torn and dirty as it covered its face. She couldn't see past the shadows in the hood, no matter how much she stared.

"Take off your cloak," she said, with far more strength than she really had.

The figure hesitated. She saw his fingers twitch at his sides as if he was fighting within himself. But, slowly, she watched the clawed hand rise, grasp the hood, and slide it back.

Xun Yuhan stared back at her. The same black eyes and wild black hair tumbling down his shoulders. The same dark circles under his eyes. The same jagged scar down his temple to his cheek. But he wasn't the same. The roots around his hands cradled his face as well. They curled around his head like horns. Moss grew along the tops of his cheeks.

He was her father, and he was not.

The cry that left Evren's mouth was that of a pained, dying animal. She tried to cover her mouth to keep it back, but the more she stared, the more horrified she became. Gyda held her as if she was afraid of what she would do, and it was all Evren could do to keep from falling apart. Those eyes were the same that crinkled in the corners when he smiled. Those hands were the same that tucked her into bed and held her steady when firing her first bow. She saw his face and saw all the memories of her childhood. Him waiting for her at the end of the mirror maze with sugar rolls and a handkerchief to dry her panicked tears. His laughter as he chased her around the trees outside her mother's old cabin. The flour from his cake turning his hair white. The long nights where he'd fall asleep in his study and she'd drag a blanket over his slumped shoulders, ignoring how her mother's wind chimes had been torn down from the wall again.

Evren finally pulled her hand away, her chapped lips crusted with salty tears.

"You . . ." she sobbed. "It was you."

Yuhan faltered. He reached out toward her but saw his hands and thought better of it. He hid them in his cloak and then knelt. He was still a few feet away, but having him at eye level was worse. She couldn't look away.

"It was me, little Ren," he breathed. "I . . . I am so sorry."

She couldn't speak. What could she say? She spent ten years looking for him, grieving for him. Only last night did she finally accept his death, and she was willing to kill to put his soul to rest. Now he was there, some twisted form of him, and nothing made sense.

Gyda spoke for her. "I remember you. You controlled the worgs."

His eyes flickered over to her. Now that he was closer, Evren could see there was no more white left. They were all black, like that of a Hisrachi.

"Yes. I pulled them away."

"Why did they attack?"

"The truth is irritatingly simple," Yuhan said. "They were already dead when my spores infected them. In a way, they were under my control. It is difficult to explain to someone unfamiliar with the Wood. I meant to have the worgs drive you back to the prince and the Hisrachi. My control slipped when the worgs saw their pup."

He turned back to Evren. "I'm so sorry. I never meant for them to hurt you."

Evren didn't care about the worgs. She just stared at him, dumbfounded. "What are you?"

His face fell a little, and Evren was struck by just how expressive he was. When she was growing up, he always wore a mask. He smiled rarely and frowned often unless they were alone in the Wood together. The people expected the Xun guardians to be stoic, and it was easy to keep unwanted nobles away when he looked like he wanted to skin them.

This was the face of a man who hadn't had to school his facial expressions in a long time. Evren could see the hurt clearly in his eyes.

"You don't remember . . ." he nodded as if it made sense. "I should've known you'd block it out. It was easier that way."

"What was easier?"

He sat down cross-legged on the floor. The mushrooms on his shoulders let out a little puff of spores and he waved them away. His eyes were dark when he spoke.

"It is difficult to know where to begin. So much of this was decades in the making, long before you were born, even before I met your mother. But, the simplest way of explaining was that I stumbled on the truth and I died for it.

"The Sovereigns kept me busy hunting Weavers. There were times where I didn't think I'd come home to you. One hunt went terribly wrong, and I found myself in a nest. But, instead of killing me, the Matriarch kept me alive. Moon above, there were so many times I tried to kill her. Again and again I was paralyzed, restrained, and put away. And even more times I'd cut my way free. After so long, I questioned why I was alive. And instead of killing, I asked to speak with Shelis.

"She was . . . kind. Forgiving. Like a grandmother trying to help her grandchild realize he'd been raised wrong, and she was there to right it. She told me the truth about the Hisrachi, as she told you and your friends, and asked for my help the same way she asked for Barrion's. I accepted, like a fool."

"You did?" Evren asked.

"I did. And to ensure my loyalty, they introduced me to the Wood's most ancient being, or one of them. That Archdruid had been there since the trees were saplings. She'd been watching for centuries as the blood stained the soil. She could do nothing to help the Hisrachi, but she'd seen enough of me to think I could be persuaded. It's . . . very hard to tell a creature with that much age and power no. She taught me a lot on my way back to Orenlion, and when I got back, I promised I'd see her again. I wanted to learn more, and I'd need all the help I could get to persuade the Sovereigns."

"This sounds a little too familiar," Gyda grumbled.

Yuhan ignored her. "For months I tried to steadily work for peace. Whenever I pushed too hard, they sent me back out. I'd find the Archdruid, and I'd learn some more, and then I'd go home. But the others caught on."

"Which one?" Evren rasped. They could all burn for all she cared, but she wanted a face to blame. She needed a name to hate.

"Fen's Crows spotted me. I know she was the one who knew something was wrong first. But it was Wasanthi who confronted me. He warned me that the path I was walking was riddled with darkness, that I was abandoning the Horizon Walker by pushing for this peace. I didn't see what faith in a dead Elder had anything to do with ending a feud between two species. But Wasanthi wouldn't let it go. I should've been more careful the next time I went out to the Archdruid. I should've watched my back. But no one knew the Wood better than me, so I thought I was safe."

Yuhan clasped his hands together, and Evren watched as a new vine curled around his ring finger. The wedding band gleamed a tarnished gold there.

"Wasanthi found me, and I'm a little ashamed to say, put me down. There was poison on the blade; I'm not sure what kind. He was a sloppy killer, but anyone who stabs you enough with a poisoned knife will get the job done. I remember little of that night, but I do remember him praying over me." Yuhan chuckled humorously. "Guiding my tainted soul back to the stars. Funny then, when he left me in the Wood to die."

Yuhan stopped. "You needed a break the last time I told you this. You're shaking again."

She was. Anger could make a normal body stronger. But she

was too far gone for that. It filled up her frail bones and hummed in the black cavity of her chest until the only thing keeping her still was Gyda's muscular arms.

"Finish it," Evren said around her tears. She needed to get the image of her dead father out of her mind. "Tell me what happened next."

For a moment, she thought he'd deny her the same way he used to when she begged for sweets before bed. But then he started speaking again.

"The Archdruid found me near death. She offered a way for me to live, but warned that I would never be the same. I agreed because, at the very least, I could watch you grow up. The process was excruciating. If I'd known what she was doing, I would've told her to stop, I think. But I didn't, and she didn't, and then it was too late."

Gyda let out a heavy breath. "She made you like her. An Archdruid."

He nodded to her. "Yes. There are rules to being this. Our lives our tied to the Wood, so we live as long as it does. We can prevent disasters that would normally destroy the forest, so long as they're natural. We have some influence over the beasts that live here. We can keep those we choose out and keep whoever we want in. But what we can't do is interfere with mortal affairs. The war between Orenlion and the Hisrachi is a sore spot among us Druids, but there is nothing we can do. The few who have tried have destroyed themselves in the process. It is mortal's nature to destroy itself, and because it won't destroy the Wood if they did, it is beneath us." He worked his jaw, and she saw a flash of old irritation in his eyes. "Something I've struggled with for some time."

"But that was ten years ago," Evren said. "It's only been three years since I left. What happened?"

Yuhan's eyes softened as he stared at her. "You recall the Wood dying before you left?"

"Yes."

"That was me, dying a second time," he explained. "There is no one Heart of the Wood. Every Archdruid is a separate, beating heart. As the Wood gives us life, we do the same for it. Wasanthi's poison didn't leave my body when I was remade. It continued to infect me over the years, and eventually spread to the rest of the Wood. Mortal poisons were not something any of the other Archdruids knew how to heal, and they couldn't find a cure in the wild. Any cure in Orenlion that was made by mortal hands was just as likely to poison me now that I wasn't fully mortal anymore. And that's where you came in."

He smiled fondly. "You tracked me down with this insane quest to heal the Heart of the Wood. You went all the way to Shelis, and she pointed you to me. And we sat, very much like this, and we talked. You cried, and you raged, and more than once you threatened to walk out. You were so angry at everything . . ."

"You left." Evren's lip quivered around her words.

"I never meant to . . ."

"But you did." Evren angrily wiped away another tear. She was so sick of crying and the empty feeling it left her. She was so damn tired and this . . . this was not the ending she wanted. "You left me alone in there. For ten years, I waited for you to come back. I didn't let them carve you next to Mother because I knew you were alive. And you were! But instead of coming back or sending me any sort of sign, you hid away."

Yuhan slumped into his cloak. "I am sorry . . ."

"I was in the Wood alone so many times!" she cried. "You didn't bother to reach out to me then. Why?"

"You were being watched. I didn't want Wasanthi to hurt you—"

"He did!" She shrugged free of Gyda's grip. "Every single one of them did. They never laid a hand on me, but they pushed me, isolated me, forced me to do things I never wanted to do. There was nothing I could do because I had no one to help me. No one to guide me or tell me if I was doing right or wrong." The tears fell like rivers now, and she couldn't be bothered to stop them. She was just so fucking tired. "You left me all alone in that house, and I was so scared and confused. I thought you left because you didn't want me anymore, because I reminded you too much of Mother."

This was a scar that would never heal, and she'd ripped the scab off to let it bleed out. She buried her head in her hands, for once not caring at how weak it made her, and she sobbed. For her mother, who she never met. For the child she used to be, and the little boys like Aster and Shao, who were forced to grow up too fast. She cried for Gail, Drystan, and Vox. She cried for Viggo. For Sorin, who'd lost everything and still smiled every day. For Sol, who could never go home to her mother, and Abraxas, who would never be accepted by the people he fought for. For Arke and all he suffered to keep them all alive. For Gyda, who thought she deserved to die and was still trying to live.

She cried for her father, finally and completely, and it broke her to do it.

Evren felt long, clawed hands cradle her face, alien and comforting all at the same time. Yuhan brushed her tears away the same way he used to and smiled through his own.

"Little Ren, no." He smoothed her hair out of her face. "I never loved you less for what you looked like, or what you did. Your mother was everything to me and seeing her in you every day made me feel like she was still there. I was not the father you needed, and I wish I could be now. Oh, my little girl, I wish I'd had the strength to tell you no before. Then we wouldn't be here."

"What do you mean?" she choked out.

"Wasanthi's poison was a matter of my own heart. I was dying when you found me last. And the only way to stop it, to save me and the Wood, was to give up your own." Tears spilled down his cheeks, caught and soaked up by the moss. "I tried to stop you, but you were always so stubborn, just like your mother. Your heart is mine now. It beats in my chest as strong as before and keeps this forest alive." He laid a hand over his own chest and then pressed one to hers. The scar prickled under his fingers. "There was no replacement for you, as you now know. The magic from the ritual gave you something in return, power for sacrifice. But it wouldn't keep you alive."

Evren was struggling to breathe, and she couldn't tell if it was because of the weight of the truth or her time running out. "Why didn't I remember? I wouldn't have let them take me back if I did."

"I don't know." He shook his head. "Maybe you thought it was easier not to know. You're here now, though. I get to see you again. If only it was under better circumstances."

Gyda cleared her throat behind them. She was sitting awkwardly in the back, her cheeks red. "You can't do anything? Not even make her like you?"

Yuhan shook his head firmly. "Her lack of heart would make the Wood reject her. Even then, she'd hate it."

"And . . ." Gyda winced like she was about to regret what she said. "There's no way to give her heart back?"

"No." Evren answered first. She turned back to Yuhan. "No, please don't. I can't lose you again."

"Little Ren, I am your father." He tucked her hair behind her ear. "I am not meant to outlive you."

Panic seized her like an icy fist around her lungs. She pushed him away and scrambled back. "No! No, if you do, you'll die. The Wood will die!"

Yuhan calmly got back to his feet. His face had taken on a familiar mask, one of determination and calculation. Both those eyes didn't fool her. "The Wood can survive with one less Archdruid. They've prepared for this since you came back. I'm sorry."

"No . . ." she tried to get to her feet and run. It was a laughable thought, even if she could run. She'd never outrun the Wood itself. But she didn't get a chance. Just as she was getting to her knees, Gyda caught her.

"Evren, please don't fight," she begged.

But Evren fought. As much as her frail, wilting strength would allow, and she struggled against Gyda's arms. It was too much for her body. Her strength gave out, and Gyda's arms cradled her collapsed form even as she still twitched towards the exit. The tears were back now, and it was getting harder to breathe. She could see her father getting closer.

"Don't do this!" she sobbed. "Gyda, please, don't make me."

The warrior was trembling now. Her eyes were red and watering as she held her down. "I cannot lose you. I don't care that you'll hate me after this, but I need you alive."

Her vision was fading. Her arms weren't doing much besides flopping uselessly at her sides. All she could see was Gyda, and that ever-encroaching shadow of her father. She gasped another breath and with what little strength she had left, she brought her hand up to cup Gyda's face.

"Please," she said. "If you love me, don't do this. I can't . . ."

A thousand words died on the tip of her tongue as the shadows overtook her vision and Gyda faded away.

23

The shadows broke under the weight of a strange ethereal light. And with the light came something foreign; it was jarring and welcome all at the same time. Something that had been missing for so long that living without it was easy, and having it back was overwhelming

A heartbeat.

Blood rushing like the river rapids. Beats thumping like the song of a thousand spears on the ground. Shaking her bones, who were so used to the stillness that they quaked and shivered with each passing thrum of life.

With that came strength. Not borrowed from blood magic, but true unbridled strength she'd been starved of for months. The world came back to her. The flickering blue light was blinding and a little too like Gail's sea of souls for comfort. She was cold all over and . . . floating.

She was underwater. Not cradled by Gyda's arms, but instead by soothing, healing water. Her torn dress tugged her down. The depths muffled any sound. The water kept the pain at bay, and she was half tempted to stay down there in spite of it all. But as she opened her mouth to swallow the water, the heart thumped loudly. The blood rushed in her ears like a roar, and before she knew it, she was clawing for the surface.

She broke the surface, gasping for air. Maybe she was sobbing in between, but the water running down her face could've been anything. She ignored the idea of tears.

She grasped the rough edge of the pool and dug her broken nails into it as she clutched at her chest. The heartbeat was strong, far stronger than she remembered. It felt too big for her chest, like her scar would split open under the pressure. Had she really been so long without a heart that the feeling of having one was so alien? Would she ever get used to having her own heart back in her chest?

Would it break before she had the chance?

With a jolt, Evren looked up at the rest of the cave. Her father stood near the edge of the pool; his face pulled in a worried, almost pained grimace. He looked at her as if a dozen different apologies were circling around his head, but none of them would do the job. She wanted to scream at him and hate him some more. How much longer did he have before he died? Would he wither away slowly, like she had? Choking on his own blood until his body finally caved in? Or would he do something very reckless and brave, again, to end it quickly? Evren couldn't handle either.

She started to pull herself out of the pool, sopping wet and shaking with anger and newfound strength, when she stopped.

"Where's Gyda?"

Her voice was hoarse, like she'd been screaming. She didn't remember screaming.

Yuhan took a step back, pain flickering across those black eyes as he looked not at Evren, but behind her.

She whipped around and sent a wave of sparkling water across the pool to meet Gyda. The warrior was slumped to the side, half in the water and breathing hard. Her armor was torn, her hand at her own chest, coated in dark blood. It stained the water like a storm cloud.

"No." Evren's voice broke, and Gyda's eyes met hers. "No. What did you do? *What did you do?*"

She lurched across the pool to Gyda's side. The warrior didn't try to pull away. With shaking hands, Evren pulled Gyda's away from the wound on her chest. More blood oozed from the deep gash, so much like her own that it made her chest ache. Tears blurred her eyes as she tried to stop the blood, and Gyda slipped further into the water.

"What did you do?" Evren cried.

Gyda's laugh was breathless and her hand grabbed Evren's. "You asked me not to . . ."

"This isn't what I meant, you fool!"

She didn't look at Gyda. If she did, she'd have to watch the light die from her eyes and she couldn't, she wouldn't. Instead, she tried to stop the bleeding even after the wound slipped under the water and the blood was so thick, she couldn't see her hands anymore. Evren's breaths were too quick, and her heart, Gyda's heart, was beating far too loudly for her to focus.

Evren could feel the wound, and the jagged tears of skin and flesh. She could hear Gyda's soft sighs. She wasn't fighting Evren, or anything. She was . . . content. Out of all the times Evren needed her to fight, and this was when she gave up?

No. No, she wouldn't allow this. She wouldn't let Gyda slip away because of her mistakes and choices. Not when she still had so much left to say.

Evren didn't know when the blood cleared from the water. She was so focused on Gyda that she hadn't been paying attention. But she noticed when the open wounded stopped being a wound and turned into a scar. The skin puckered and then smoothed out. Pink and a little raw instead of grey, but . . . healed all the same.

Evren held her breath, not daring to hope. Her hand went to the side of Gyda's neck, where the warrior's pulse jumped up to meet her fingers. Swift, a little shaky, strong.

And it beat in time with Evren's.

"It seems that Gyda had enough heart for two . . ." Yuhan murmured behind her, but Evren wasn't paying attention.

She was staring at Gyda, into those eyes which hadn't left hers since this all began. Her hand fell away from Gyda's throat, but her own heartbeat quickened. She knew Gyda's did too. The water darkened her hair to a deep, almost bloodlike red. It stuck to her face in wet curls. Evren drew away before her fingers brushed the hair out of the way.

As the color returned to her face, Gyda sat herself up a little more. Her hands were shaking underneath the water.

"You asked me not to," Gyda said. "I found another way."

"I . . ." Evren's throat closed and she couldn't get any more words out. Her hand went back to her chest. The scar was still there, as were all the others she'd collected, but it had the same pinkish hue that came with newly healed skin. Beneath the scarred skin was half of Gyda's heart, beating strongly despite the pain.

Evren glanced at Yuhan, desperate for answers. He shrugged, a mushroom toppling over.

"The experience was painful. You chose to forget the first time, just as Gyda asked to this time. There was no need for you both to suffer more, especially if there was a chance it wouldn't work. But . . ." He let out a heavy sigh. "You both made it."

Evren didn't know what to say. Was this somehow wrong? She'd asked Gyda to let her go and instead she'd given her half her heart. How would that affect them? If one died, would the other follow? Did they share the same feelings, the same rush of emotions?

Evren's ears burned. She hoped not. She didn't feel any different emotion wise, but she didn't need Gyda finding out her feelings towards her like that.

Suddenly, Yuhan's strangely clawed hands were extended towards both of them. The pain in his eyes was gone, and while he still regarded Gyda as if she would collapse any minute, there was a palatable air of relief around him. And something else. As Gyda took his hand, he smiled and squeezed her hand gently.

Thank you, he seemed to say, and then he pulled them both out of the water.

They sat shivering on the cave floor, too stunned to move and too scared to try. The air of fragile silence didn't hold long, however.

"What now?" Evren asked, looking up at her father. He smiled gently, as if he understood how she was feeling. The strange first steps into a future she didn't expect to live long enough to see. And there was still so much to do.

"Now, I'd think you'd better make good on your promise to save Orenlion and the Hisrachi from each other." Yuhan flicked a hand towards the cave entrance. It was shadowed with night, but Evren could just barely make out Neri's form waiting for them.

Stop a war that's already begun. Hells, what had she gotten them into?

"Orenlion won't let the Hisrachi live," Gyda said, and her voice was gaining more of its old strength back with each word. "How do we even start making peace when they're both ready to burn the forest down so the other cannot have it?"

"You assume there's only two parts to this play," Yuhan said. "The Hisrachi and the Sovereigns. There is you as well, and the good prince,"

"Is that enough?" Evren asked. "We stopped a war once, and it ended in one of our own dying. Even then, we had more of an advantage."

Yuhan shook his head. "But there is another player that has been pushing everyone from the shadows, including yourself, isn't there? Something more tangible masquerading as a ghost, or a memory."

Evren's blood went cold. "Viggo."

Gyda's head snapped around. "What?"

Evren winced. "I've been seeing Viggo's ghost for a while

now. Or something like it. It's how I got the idea for the crown. He wanted me to find it and said it would heal me."

"The Horizon Walker's crown isn't here," Yuhan said. "It was hidden somewhere in Etherak."

"Viggo wouldn't know that," Evren protested.

"Or he did, and he's tricking you again," Gyda said.

Evren didn't have an argument. What she'd thought was a figment of her dying mind had turned out to be another trick? Hadn't they gotten past that, her and Viggo? She'd thought after their parting that they'd ended on better terms. She even felt guilty for leaving him.

"Why would he want the crown?" Evren asked. "Or whatever it is that he's looking for."

Yuhan waved Gyda off before she could argue. "Whoever he is, if it even is him, we've felt his presence for months now. Lingering on you, some of the Hisrachi, and someone in Orenlion. They want something in the Wood, and pitting everyone against each other must be a way to do it."

"But, you said it yourself. The crown isn't here."

"Ah, yes, I did." He grinned. "But that isn't the only Elder artifact of power in Eith. Another resides in the Deep Wood, one far more valuable to the ambitious. The Eternity Keeper's dagger, stowed here long ago to keep it from falling into unworthy hands. It's been lost to the Wood for ages, bound to the same shifting magic that kept Orenlion hidden."

"It moves," Evren said.

"Yes, but always comes back to the same place when the timing is right."

"By light of the swollen moon and the fall of silver," Evren recited. "That's what Viggo said."

Yuhan nodded. "Then that is what he wanted you to find. Likely, he wanted you to complete the trials and get the dagger for him. By the time you'd completed it and found no healing crown, it would've been too late. A dagger of that power in the hands of someone unworthy would break Eith, not just the Deep Wood."

Gyda stood up, and the water fell off her like soft rain. She wobbled slightly before grabbing for her sword, which had been waiting for her on the ground. She strapped it across her back, a familiar expression of rage settling into her face. Her scarf hung from loose fingers.

Why had she taken it off? Evren eyed the bright fabric as she got to her own feet.

"So, we just need to stay away," the warrior said. "If we don't find the dagger for him, he doesn't get it. Simple."

"No." Evren shook her head. "He's got others looking for it, too. They likely don't know what they're doing and won't stop unless we keep them from doing it."

"Or find it ourselves," Gyda finished. "That's what you were going to say."

Evren recoiled. "No, but now that we know his plan, we can trap him. Make him think he's getting what he wants until the end. By then, we will have figured out who all is looking for the dagger and can stop this war."

"Assuming that it's actually this Viggo you speak of," Yuhan pointed out. "This being has lied to you before and probably has done so multiple times. I doubt it is what it appears to be. But," he sighed, "you are both right. To trap this being should give you the edge you need to prevent Orenlion and the Hisrachi from destroying each other, and that will only come with a great deal of subterfuge. Luckily, you aren't working alone. I'm sure the rest of your friends and allies in Orenlion will have ideas. You work better as a team."

Evren and Gyda shared a look. Their friends would be furious, most likely, but . . . well, this was a better plan than building a sled ship to go into the heart of a glacier teeming with undead. And far better than walking into a dwarven army camp with no idea of what was going on.

Evren felt her ears burn again. Arke might've figured out

Viggo's ghost if she'd told him. Sol would've seen the manipulation from a mile away. Abraxas and Sorin would've found out about the dagger through sheer force of will. None of this would've happened if she'd opened up.

She'd promised Sol to be more open with everyone, and she failed. Aster had been right about her. She'd kept her secrets because she was afraid of how her friends would see her. Insane for seeing strange figures and weak for seeing a dead man. Hells, she should've told them about Keres, too. Now, Gyda had given her a second chance. She had to be better.

No more secrets.

Gyda went towards Yuhan, towering over him but strangely reverent. "Will you not help us?"

He shook his head sadly. "Until the Wood is threatened to a point of destruction, I cannot. All I can offer without breaking my bonds is advice and counsel, and I don't know if it's worth anything."

"It's worth everything," Evren said, drawing his gaze. "We'll figure this out, I promise."

A fond smile touched his lips, and he was suddenly less Archdruid and more her father, beaming at her as she strung her first bow by herself. "I know you will, little Ren. If I have faith in nothing else, I do in you. And the company you keep."

He bowed to Gyda, and she made a clumsy, embarrassed attempt to do the same before marching out of the cave. Evren could hear her talk to Neri as they moved further out, but she ignored them for a little longer to face her father.

"I'm sorry I forgot you," she said.

He put his hands on her shoulders. "I'm sorry for leaving you. Furthermore, I'm sorry that you must be the one that cleans this mess up. This was not the legacy I meant to leave behind."

She put her hand over his. "You know it ends with me, right? The Xun line won't go on."

"I knew it died when your mother did," he said carefully.

"But, I think, it has been dying for a long time. We are creatures of the wilds, Evren. We aren't meant for gilded walls and thrones. Sacrifice is in our nature. The legacy you leave behind will be new, and I have a feeling it will change the world."

Evren laughed a little. She didn't feel like she had the right to change anything anymore. "No pressure, right?"

He grinned, his canines a bit too long. "Eith needs a good change. How you do it once you leave here is entirely up to you."

Then, hesitantly, as if he was embracing a wild animal, he hugged her. Evren melted into him, even as the moss pressed into her cheek and the mushrooms made her eyes water. Her father squeezed her tight enough to almost make up for all the lost hugs he'd missed.

"Go," he whispered in her ear. "I'll be watching."

Evren pulled away from him as fresh tears spilled down her cheeks. She thought she'd spent all her tears, but her new heart was shattering as she walked out. She looked over her shoulder at Yuhan one last time.

I love you, she mouthed.

He pressed his fingers to his lips. *And I you.*

She tucked those words close to her chest and walked out of the cave, torn between a vigorous wave of grief and fresh determination.

The fresh breeze hit her first. Scented with sweet sap and damp soil, it smelled like home. The air was warm and comforting as it embraced her. She didn't shiver in her soaked gown. She took a deep breath, eyes wide, trying to soak in the world as if she was seeing it for the first time. And she was. Everything was sharper now, clearer. The path ahead didn't look like an impossible climb. It was a challenge she'd relish, as she had a thousand times before.

The stars overhead bathed the Wood in a silvery light, although they paled in comparison to the moon. It was nearly full. They had perhaps one more night to find the dagger; a slightly more daunting task.

Evren found Gyda easily. She was waiting for her just a few feet ahead, standing under a patch of starlight. Evren's breath caught in her throat, but she couldn't force herself to look away.

"Where's Neri?" she asked instead.

"She went ahead to scout. There's an intact nest nearby that she thinks will be good to stop at. They're peaceful and should be able to be persuaded to stand down once they understand what happened."

Evren nodded, suddenly feeling naked without her bow. "Right, well, we should catch up to her."

She marched ahead and made it as much as three whole strides past Gyda before her voice stopped Evren in her tracks.

"If you love me."

Evren's heart was racing. Or was it Gyda's? Hells, she couldn't tell. Either way, her skin burned as she turned back to face the warrior.

"What?"

Gyda stepped out of the starlight and towards her. "If you love me. That's what you said in the cave. When you wanted me to let you die." Her eyes flickered to Evren's chest and then back to her face. "What did you mean by that?"

Oh fuck, why did her chest hurt? Why was this heart, or half of a heart, beating so loudly? Could Gyda hear it? Evren was sure the whole damn forest could. And now Gyda had caught her. Evren wanted to curse herself for the slip. She'd been dying, but that was no excuse. How could she get out of this without royally embarrassing herself?

"Did I say that?" She tried to laugh, but her voice wouldn't cooperate. "I can't remember half of what I said. You know, dying and all makes things a little fuzzy."

"Evren."

"Besides, I wasn't in my right mind. I should never have asked that of you. What you did . . ." Evren swallowed nervously and gestured to Gyda's chest. "We have no idea how that's going to affect us. Who knows what the side effects are."

Gyda cursed, actually cursed, and tore her hand through her damp hair. "You're impossible sometimes."

Evren winced. "I've been told."

"I don't care about the consequences," Gyda snapped. "You're alive. I'm alive. Shouldn't we be happy?"

"All magic has a price, Gyda. Hells only know what this'll do to us. How many times can we cheat death before it changes us?"

"It has changed nothing. I still feel the same."

"Do you?" Evren asked. "Because you don't look like it."

Gyda stared at her breathlessly, and when she spoke, her words held something heavy behind them, like a dam keeping back a flood. "Tell me how I feel, Evren."

Evren sighed and crossed her arms. "I can't do that."

"Yes, you can." The words were hissed out in desperation, but the warrior didn't take another step towards her. There were still too many feet between them. "Tell me how I feel."

It was almost like a threat. Evren could see how tightly wound she was. Her hands were balled at her sides, as if she couldn't trust them to not reach out of their own accord. Her brow was furrowed and her jaw clenched tight. Every muscle quivered as they were forced to stay still.

Yes, Evren had seen Gyda like this before. Each time before battle, or even in the middle of it.

"You look like you're in the middle of a war," she whispered.

Gyda fell back on her heels and just stared at her. "I am. But you didn't tell me how I felt."

"I can't answer that for you, Gyda."

"Then tell me how *you* feel."

This time, it was Evren who wanted to move but was rooted to the spot. She couldn't look away from Gyda, but she was sure the Wood had grown its vines around her and kept her from moving.

She'd promised herself no more secrets but this . . .

"Gyda, I . . ." Her words died in her throat. Hells, what could she say to the woman she'd risked death for repeatedly? What words would be enough to show her? And if they were enough, would it ruin everything they already had? This friendship that was so strange but easy between them was all that she had. She didn't want to take it and shatter it in some vain hope of being more.

But if Gyda knew, and she was angry, then there was no point in hiding it.

Why couldn't she just say it?

Evren closed her mouth, unable to speak.

"If you can't speak, then I will," Gyda said as she walked over. They were less than a foot apart now, and Evren couldn't move. "Because I'm done suffering in silence."

"Suffering? Gyda—"

"Stop saying my name like that."

Evren was almost too baffled for words. "Like what?"

"Like a prayer." All the fight seemed to leave Gyda. Her shoulders slumped, and her face . . . Divines, that face nearly broke their heart. There was such a plain and vivid yearning in it, it took her breath away.

Gyda stepped closer, and the air was blissfully cooler against Evren's burning skin. "Let me tell you how I feel, if you cannot," she said again, and her eyes never left Evren's. "I don't know what you did to me, or when it happened. But, fuck, I don't care. All I know is that I . . ." She looked away and took a breath before coming back to her.

"Ever since I've met you, I have been unwilling to part with you. It's not that I can't. I've proven that I could in the mountains, but I don't want to. All I want, all I need, is to be by your side and for you to see me. To understand that this—" she took Evren's hand and placed it over her chest again. "—was not an accident. It wasn't a decision made solely for your survival. I have been trying to give you my heart for months now."

Evren couldn't breathe. Her hand was on Gyda's chest and suddenly she was back on that dark staircase, pushing her away. How had she been so stupid? How did she not see?

"You . . . I mean, I . . . Fuck." Evren cleared her throat. "You're telling me that you're . . .?"

"Yes." The word left with all the breath in Gyda's chest.

Evren shook her head. "No, but you never . . . I thought you didn't. Fucking hells, Gyda, why didn't you say anything?"

The warrior's cheeks flushed a pretty pink. "I did."

"You did?"

"Well, in my own way."

Gyda's grip on her hand tightened as if she was afraid Evren would leave. "I let you see my hair. I stayed with you after the Long Night. We bandaged each other's wounds after battle. These are all things lovers do."

Lovers.

Evren had missed it completely. All those small little quirks that only she seemed to see in Gyda were loud signs showing her how the warrior felt. She would never show her affections the way Evren expected.

Gyda looked like she was fighting because she was. She loved fighting, and she loved Evren.

Suddenly, the memories of the last week made her sick. She'd avoided Gyda. Then she'd made plans to marry Aster to secure Barrion's alliance. She'd let herself fall to the brink of death and refused help. And she'd done it all with no thought to how the warrior felt.

Evren's other hand went up to cup Gyda's cheek again. She brushed a drying red curl out of the way and ran her thumb along Gyda's cheekbone.

"I hurt you," Evren said. "All I've done this quest is push you away and hurt you without realizing it. I thought that by keeping you away, I could spare you, and myself, some pain. But now I see just how shortsighted I was."

Gyda melted into her touch and her eyes fluttered closed.

Her breath whispered against Evren's palm when she spoke again. "I told you how I felt, now tell me how you feel."

Like kicking myself until I pass out.

Like tearing the world apart for you.

Like kissing you because it's all I've been trying not to think about and your lips on my skin aren't helping to keep me focused.

"I feel like I'm falling short on words, so I'll try something else instead."

Evren stood up on her tiptoes, stretching as far as she could. She tugged Gyda down gently, and her eyes flashed open in surprise, then she leaned down. Evren's hand went to the nape of her neck and her fingers tangled in her hair. Gyda's breath was against her lips. If they were just a little closer—

"Evren! Gyda!"

Neri tumbled through the trees toward them in a panic and the two women rushed apart, faces flushed and lips still tingling with a phantom kiss.

Neri, for all her fear, didn't seem to realize what she'd interrupted. She was covered in soot and her chest was heaving.

Evren's embarrassment and disappointment turned to dread.

"Neri? What is it? What happened?"

"The nest," she wheezed. *"Come quick!"*

With that, the spider took off back to where she came. Evren and Gyda shared one last, longing look, before running after her.

THE HEAT it took to burn Hisrachi silk was nothing short of dragon fire. At least, that's what Evren had been told. Standing in the devastation of the nest told her otherwise.

The forest here was covered with ash. The grey destruction spread for nearly a mile before it faded to normal greenery. Ash fell in fat, heavy flakes from the levels above, and settled like snow over the charred corpses of the Hisrachi. The fire still smoldered in places where the webbing was thickest, and the flames were an unnerving green where it ate the silk. The air smelled like burning corpses.

It was the remnants of a massacre, and none had survived.

"Was this the only friendly clan you knew?" Evren asked, unable to tear her eyes away from the group of smaller Hisrachi bodies underneath the corpses of their mother.

"The only one I knew we could get to in time." Neri sniffled and stared at the dead. *"The others will go into hiding now."*

"Or to war," Gyda said. "There's only so much a people can take before they fight back. Orenlion has pushed them too far."

"They'll march straight to their deaths," Evren said. It would not be a war where either side survived. The destruction would kill both elves and Weavers.

"What do we do?"

Evren truly didn't know. Even if she rooted out Viggo's spy in Orenlion, that would still leave the Hisrachi to deal with. The plan only worked if she had all sides willing to stand down. She didn't want to bait another battle and lose friends.

Gyda tensed at her side just as Evren heard voices. Far-off Elvish, but getting closer. Executioners making sure the dead stayed that way.

She turned to Neri. "Find another nest. Tell them what happened."

Neri faltered. *"What if they don't believe me?"*

"Just tell them not to fight, Neri. Stay in hiding until we come and get you, and get as many Hisrachi with you as possible. My father should be able to help."

Gyda nodded. "We'll keep the search parties from you. Go."

The spider looked like she wanted to argue. Evren had spent enough time with her to notice her little facial tics now. But, at the sound of more Elvish curses, she nodded and scampered off.

Evren watched her go, covering her immediate tracks before turning back to Gyda.

"Ready?"

The warrior just frowned at her, as if the answer was obvious. It made Evren smile a little as she turned to meet the coming elves.

They emerged from the ash, spears and bows bristling, and their armor muted with ash and soot. Evren held her hands up in surrender and took a step forward.

"I am Lady Xun Evren of Orenlion, and I request to be taken home."

When Evren had been of an age that everything looked like a target to kick down, she'd made a habit of kicking down bee's nests. She liked the raw honeycomb inside and was smart enough to know how to avoid the angry bees after she'd snatched her prize. But she was still young and foolish, and with so many wins under her belt, she got the special kind of confidence that only came from foolhardy eleven-year-old girls with too much to prove. She'd knocked down a hornet's nest, expecting honey and clumsy little bees. All she got was rage and pain. Even after she'd run from the broken shell of the nest, the hornets continued to chase her. She'd never known true rage and bloodlust until she saw them swarming after her with no regard for their own health.

Orenlion reminded her of that broken nest and the gleam in its peoples' eyes was far too much like the simple, consuming rage she'd encountered before. The people were buzzing hornets, still seething over the burned husk of their city. It was only a matter of time before they gave chase en masse.

Evren was glad it wasn't her boot that had done the kicking, but she still waited for the stings as she and Gyda made their way back to Xun Manor.

The house was blissfully untouched by the destruction, although it looked a bit like a wilted flower with all its abandoned decorations. The only light came from the dusty sunlight streaming through the windows, and shadows still had a fierce grip on the corners and hallways. But it was as if something had changed in the manor. The shadows were still and waiting, but not threatening. The dust was not from neglect, but just a reminder that there were more important things to get to.

Xun Manor felt like a house again, not a cage or a tomb. She still wasn't sure she could call it home, though. Home, she'd learned, was a group of people she couldn't live without.

The Wandering Sols met her and Gyda's return with equal amounts of confusion and relief. Aster had told them about Gyda's plan, but also his surety that it would fail. And Evren, true to her new promise, told them everything. Her father's fate, the ghost of Viggo, the waiting dagger, and Gyda's role in saving her life.

The words the two had shared, and the kiss they nearly had, Evren kept to herself. She wasn't sure what to do with Gyda's confession or her own feelings. They hadn't been alone since then, and now had the overwhelming task of stopping a war. The end of that conversation would have to wait.

"That's . . . a lot, Evvie," Sorin said. He was still wearing the jewelry from the party, and the dark circles under his eyes showed he hadn't slept since then, but he'd changed into his usual faded blue coat. "We have to somehow get both sides to stand down while also finding out who else this ghost has been talking to *and* find this magic dagger before they do. I'm not saying I don't love a challenge, but a little smidgen of possible would be great."

"There's also the Sovereigns to deal with," Abraxas said darkly.

Sorin snorted. "What? You're up for toppling another government?"

"We did it once by accident. I imagine we could do a better job on purpose."

Evren cut him off with a wave of her hand, although that was on her list. She'd do it right, though. "Leave the Sovereigns to me and Aster. That's always been our fight."

Sol winced from her spot on the floor. The worg pup was curled up on her lap and snoozing as if they weren't talking about death and destruction. "Aster's been a little off since he came back. It's worse because Mei refuses to see him. He blames himself for what happened to her."

"As he should," Gyda grumbled.

"It was a mistake, yes, but I see his reasoning behind it." Sol shook her head. "It would've been a good plan if he'd been more open to us, specifically Neri. Speaking of which . . . is she going to be all right?"

Evren glanced over at Arke. The goblin had said little since they'd gotten back, and spent the whole talk gripping his spellbook and staring at the leather cover. He blinked up at her, asking the same question Sol had, but loaded with guilt.

Evren hesitated. "She's smart, and she's fast. Gyda and I kept the surrounding soldiers away from her, so she's got a good chance of getting to a friendly nest unharmed."

"Until Orenlion burns that down, too," Arke rasped. He looked back at his spellbook. "She ain't gonna make it."

Sorin rested his hand on the goblin's shoulders. "Don't think like that. She's smarter than that."

"She ain't just hidin'. She's tryin' to get the Hisrachi to stand down. Which means she's gonna be in trouble."

"She knew that going in. Hells, she knew that coming to Orenlion with us. Honestly, I don't think there's much she's afraid of, and if she is afraid, she doesn't let it get to her for long. Her people's lives are at stake. She's going to do whatever she can to get them through this alive."

Arke grumbled but didn't push Sorin away. Instead, he relaxed a little more. His ears still drooped in the telltale way that showed his anxieties, but Sorin had eased them a bit. Magic words or not, he knew what to say to his best friend.

Evren smiled

"So." Sol lifted her chin to meet everyone's eyes. "What's the plan?"

And then all their eyes were on Evren.

There was fear for a moment, thick and overwhelming, but underneath it was something else. Under the fear, the spite, and the anger was the small little seed of determination she'd been nursing since she was little. The drive to make her father smile, to prove the Sovereigns wrong, to survive Serevadia and to get Gyda back. She'd been missing it and was floundering without it.

But she couldn't do this alone.

"Viggo talked to me, so I'll work on figuring out his conspirators and where the dagger is. We only have until tomorrow night for that. Sol, you've worked with the Sovereigns well enough to read them, right?"

The dwarf nodded stiffly. "Most of them, yes. Fen is a bit of a mystery, though."

"Viggo is probably talking to one of them, and my bets are on Wasanthi. I need you to pull Shao away from his slaughtering and tell him what's going on."

"Shao?" she exclaimed.

"Asshole number four?" Arke asked, equally bewildered.

Evren nodded. "He's an ally, at least for now. Fair warning, he's going to want to kill Yikao. If he asks you to, make sure Yikao isn't our connection to Viggo."

"And if he isn't?"

Evren chewed her lip. "Let Shao do it. Trust me when I say he deserves it."

The dwarf nodded slowly, still scratching the worg's ears. "All right then, I will."

Evren turned to Arke. "My father says the dagger uses the same magic the city does to hide. Can you track it?"

The goblin's ears twitched. "This whole damn forest is magical. Hard to trace anythin'. But . . . Liang wanted my help gettin' the city defenses back up. I can see how the spell works and go from there. Might be our ticket if we can't get this on the full moon."

"Sounds like a plan. Sorin?"

"I'm not going to be seducing anymore mentally traumatized elves, am I?"

"No."

Evren's immediate thought was to send him after Neri and assist her in keeping the Hisrachi from attacking. Maybe he'd even find which one of them Viggo was talking to. But Heliodar flashed in her mind, and she shoved that idea out of the way. She wasn't ready to send him to do something so dangerous.

"How do you feel about making some new friends?" she asked instead.

He raised his eyebrows at her. "Depends. Are these the stabby sort of friends or are they actually nice?"

"Stabby as of right now. I need you to work some doubt in the remaining Khama and hunters. Get Mira and her people in on it, too. The Khama aren't stupid, they're just angry. But, above all, they know the delicate balance of the Wood. No matter their anger, some will already see this war as wrong."

"You want me to turn a bunch of pissed off wyvern riders against the city they serve?"

"No." She shook her head. "Just be there for them. Don't try to turn them against the war, don't even mention it. Help them with their wounded, repair their saddles and weapons. Let them see the Sorin we know and love. If they see you as a friend, as well as Mira and the rest of Etherak's soldiers, they're going to relax. And if a war breaks out and they have to choose sides . . ."

"They might choose us," he finished. "Or, at the very least, hesitate. But that's not set in stone, Evvie. It might not work."

"Maybe not. But it's the safest way we can use that silver tongue of yours."

Gyda stepped forward. "I'll go with him."

Evren paused. She hadn't thought of what to do with Gyda yet, but she didn't really want her to go so soon.

The warrior gave her a knowing look. "I'm good with Barrion's people. And Sorin will need help if he pisses off a wyvern."

"Okay," Evren reluctantly agreed. "You two on the Khama, then. Abraxas?"

His dark eyes flashed. "To Barrion, I'm assuming?"

"You and I, yes. We need a plan that doesn't get him killed and secures his alliance. Where is he?"

"The Sovereigns won't see him, so he's spent most of his time with us or Mei."

Odd. Evren brushed it off. "Aster will be with her, too. Two birds, one stone?"

He pushed away from the wall. "A good plan. And Evren?"

"Yes?"

"It's good to have you back."

His words struck her like an arrow, and all at once, she felt a flood of emotions threatening to overwhelm her. She looked at all her friends, mentally cursing herself for neglecting them for so long. How they'd stuck by her and put up with her shit all this time was beyond her, but she was so grateful for it.

"I've been a terrible friend lately," Evren said. "Truly, I have been for a while. I'm going to be better. I'm going to understand that I can't do everything on my own and that I need to trust you all with far more than just my life. From now on, no more secrets. No more hiding. You all deserve far better than that."

"You know," Sol mused, with a mischievous grin on her face. "That's not the first time you've promised no more secrets. Will you actually keep it this time?"

Sorin banged his fist on the table. "Cooking duty for every kept secret!"

Abraxas chuckled. "How will we know to put her on cooking duty if she doesn't tell us?"

Sorin's resolve wavered before he shrugged logic off his shoulders. "Easy. She puts herself on cooking duty and we suffer until one of us gets it out of her."

"And what do we do for suicidal stunts?" Arke asked.

"Worg babysitting."

They all laughed hard enough to wake the puppy up, who stared at them with bleary and confused eyes. But he immediately went over to Sorin, who tried to hand him off to Abraxas for 'passive suicidal tendencies.' Watching the older elf dodge the wiggling pup made Evren's cheeks hurt with laughter. So long as Sorin was content on chasing Abraxas, his attention was off her. Sol and Arke were even getting into it too, pushing chairs in Abraxas's way and cheering the worg on.

None of them noticed when Gyda leaned down far enough for her lips to brush the point of Evren's ear and whisper, "You'll be on cooking duty for a while, it seems."

Evren looked up at her, relieved to find no malice in her eyes. "You'd enjoy that?"

Gyda's hum sounded in Evren's chest as she pulled away. "Maybe. At least until this is done. Then we'll finish what you started."

Evren scowled as a red blush crept up her cheeks. "Technically, you started it."

"I will finish it then."

Before Evren could react, Gyda was walking away and pulling Sorin out of his chase.

"Come on, we have work to do."

"But—"

"Bring the worg if you must."

She dragged Sorin out the door and, after a few moments, Arke and Sol followed, quietly chatting about how they'd achieve their individual goals. Abraxas fell in beside Evren, hair tousled and the remnants of a smile disappearing behind his stoic mask.

"It's good to see them laugh again," he said and squeezed her shoulder. "And we will laugh more once this is over."

"Always so confident," she teased.

"I have—"

"Faith, I know." She rolled her shoulders. "Spare me some. We're going to need it."

~

THE HEALER'S building was a light, airy place filled with sunshine and linen sheets. It reeked of blood, infections, and the sharp tang of potions. The main room was filled to the brim. Khama who's armor was melted into their skin. Mages who wept over lost limbs. And bodies, so many bodies. They were covered with the white sheets, spots still sticky brown with blood.

Luckily, Mei was afforded a private room, and it wasn't difficult to find. It was the only door that held a prince arguing with Aster.

"That's not your decision to make," Aster hissed at Barrion. "How could you even think of such a thing? After everything—"

"How could I?" The prince's voice was deathly calm. "Let us talk about what you did before coming to me."

"It was a rumor! A lie. Nothing more."

"And you should've told me." Barrion rubbed his eyes, looking more exhausted than Evren had ever seen him. He was unkept, his hair a mess and his skin still spotted with ash and dried blood. When he dropped his hand, he noticed Evren and held up a finger. The message was clear; wait.

He finally turned back to Aster, and there was very little anger in his eyes. He was just . . . tired. The kind of weariness that was bone deep and no sleep could shake off.

"What you did is done now, and I'm trying to save your home. I am trying to fix this. Divines guide me, won't you just let me?"

"Not her," Aster croaked. "Anyone but her, Barrion."

The prince flinched and took a step back. "It was her idea. I don't relish hurting you. But Mei," Barrion shook his head, mystified, "she would right now. I'm sorry that I'm her chosen instrument for your pain, but that apology is all I can give you now. Your city is falling apart. Let her try to fix it."

With that, he turned and nodded to Evren. No more waiting. Finally, Aster noticed someone else besides Barrion. And he looked just as terrible as when she left him, possibly worse. Guilt was an awful look on him. He lightened a little when he saw her.

"You're alive," Aster breathed, looking her up and down. "Moon above, how?"

"Let's just say Gyda and I worked out an alternative," Evren said. "The Archdruid . . . he told me everything. He's still alive."

Aster blinked at her as if he was trying to hold back tears. "I never saw him. We knew what he would be, and you sent me away. You made me promise not to follow you or tell you how to get back there again. Please forgive me."

"There's nothing to forgive." She ached to tell him about Wasanthi and what he'd done, how he'd almost murdered her father twice. But that could wait. She turned to Barrion, who gave her a tired but relieved smile. "Thanks for pulling my ass out of the fire."

"Well, it's not every day I get to engage in daring rescues," he said, then leaned in closer and lowered his voice. "Tell me you have a plan."

"I do, but it seems you do as well."

He nodded. "A desperate one. Yours?"

"Abraxas will fill you in. I need to speak with Mei."

Aster protested. "She's not seeing anyone—"

"I'm not seeing *you* right now," a sharp voice came from behind the door. "There's a difference. Send her in, and no one else."

Aster winced as if he'd been hit, but stepped away. Barrion slid the door open and ushered Evren in with a strange look in his eyes, but it closed behind her before she could decipher his feelings.

Mei's room was small, and the air was stale despite the open window overlooking the city. Shadows of leaves dappled the twisted sheets on the empty bed and Mei's face as she slumped next to the window.

But she was not alone.

Sovereign Wasanthi stood and smoothed his robes. He placed a gentle hand on Mei's unbandaged shoulder.

"You needn't worry about a thing, child. I'll take care of all the preparations."

Mei said nothing, and he turned to leave. Evren was frozen in place, her heart beating erratically at the sight of him.

You killed my father, she couldn't help but think. *You killed him and still called yourself the better man for it. You took him away from me.*

"Ah, Evren." He smiled warmly and his wrinkles creased deeply. "It is good to see you healthier. After losing the Roost, I feared you were at our Lady's side. I see now that you must've found what you were looking for."

"I did," Evren forced out.

"Excellent." He reached out to pat her shoulder, and it took everything in her power not to flinch away. She endured the weathered hand as one would cut away dead flesh. Painful, but necessary. She didn't want him catching on to her knowing yet.

His hand fell away. "I'll see you both by the light of the full moon, then. Do get some rest."

And then he was gone, and the room felt lighter. Evren felt herself relax as she locked the door behind him. Then, finally, she got a good look at Mei.

Without her armor, draped in the white linen robes, she looked frail. She was far too pale, and her cheeks were sunken and sallow. Her right leg hung a little awkwardly to the side and was covered in thick, creamy bandages, just like her right arm and most of her chest. Her black hair fell in an oily, unkept curtain in her face.

"Are you here to ask me how I'm feeling, too?" Mei asked.

"No,"

"Then why? I thought you'd run away again."

Evren shook her head and sat down on the floor across from Mei. The smell of healing salves wafted off her like a cloud. The Khama still wouldn't look at her.

"What did Wasanthi want?" Evren asked. "What preparations?"

Mei didn't look good, but she didn't look like she was dying either. Surely it wasn't for a funeral.

Almost as if sensing her thoughts, Mei laughed. If there was any pain from doing so, she didn't show it. "Not a funeral, if that's what you're worried about. I'll live, oh yes. As much as this can be called living."

Evren looked down at her leg at the same time Mei drew her robe over it.

"It broke. They didn't set it right before shoving a potion down my throat." Mei said. "It healed crooked. Part of my lower spine as well. I'm lucky to have any use of my legs at all, and rebreaking the bones to set them again is apparently too dangerous. It hurts to walk, to stand, let alone to ride." She wiped her face, and a single sparkling tear was flicked away. "I'm not Khama anymore. Saros won't have a rider, and as stubborn as he is, he won't take another. He'll likely be put down. To put him out of his misery, they'll say. He's too old, they'll say. Fucking imbeciles."

Khama and their wyverns were bonded for life. The hunters who lost their wyverns rarely chose another to fly. Wyverns who lost their riders would rarely trust another to command them. But it was exceedingly rare for both wyvern and rider to survive and be torn apart. It was unspeakably cruel, and all Evren could picture was Mei's desperate attempt to save Saros through flames, fangs, and overwhelming odds.

"I'm so sorry." Evren could barely get the words out.

Mei's chuckle almost sounded like a sob. "Me too. My whole life has been Saros's, and his mine. Without him, without my duty as a Khama, I'm fucking useless."

"I tried to get to you."

"Oh, fuck off." Mei waved her hand at her. "Your nasty little spell kept Saros alive. Stars know that's all I can ever ask of you, so don't act like this is your fault. I'm tired of that look on your face."

Evren tried to wipe her expression clean.

"So, what was Wasanthi here for?"

"A wedding blessing."

Evren gaped at her, unsure how to act. Mei said it as if it was nothing, like she was still talking about Evren's terrible attitude and not a life-changing ceremony she'd had no inkling of ever taking part in.

"A wedding? Why?"

She shrugged her good shoulder. "An alliance. Barrion needed something to mend Orenlion and Etherak together, and marriage is the oldest alliance in the book. He's not happy about it, nor am I, but it's a purpose. With this wedding, Etherak's troops will march on the Hisrachi and save Orenlion. Again, not something he's happy about, but fuck it. They attacked first. I can save my home, even if I must live on Etherak's soil afterwards."

"Mei this," Evren struggled for words, "this is a massive step. You and Aster—"

"Aster can go fuck himself." Mei snapped. "For an entire three years, it was only me he had eyes for. I fell for his pretty words and soft promises like an idiot. And then you came, and suddenly it was back to what it was before. Another wedding, only this time he didn't even try to fight it. He was just going to let it happen and offer no explanation to me. Oh, sure, I could've been his mistress. I'm sure that's what he thought in the back of that scheming mind of his. But is it so bad to want someone entirely to yourself? To want him to fight for you against all odds?"

"The wedding wasn't set in stone," Evren protested. "It was just a backup plan."

"The same way his little rumor was just a lie?"

Evren shut her mouth and leaned back against the wall. All her life, Mei had been one of the strongest people she knew, but she never cared to check on her all those years of fighting against the Sovereigns. Evren didn't see the hidden feelings she had for Aster, or how she raged just as much as Evren had during the first engagement. And in the office during the party . . . If Evren had just denied wanting a blessing from Wasanthi, it could've been avoided. Mei had trapped him in the room because she was going to fight it if Evren wouldn't.

Hells, Evren had been blinder than she originally thought.

"I never meant to hurt you," Evren said. "You never treated me any different for what I was, and I just ignored you."

"Don't start with the self-pity again." Mei rolled her eyes. "You didn't use me either, which is more than I can say for some."

"You don't have to do this wedding. We can figure something else out."

"My home is burning down around me, Evren, and unlike you, I can't turn my back on it just yet. If that means I must bind myself, body and soul, to a man and kingdom I barely know, so be it. Some sacrifices aren't in blood. Some come laced in holy water and metal. I'll gladly drink Sterra's Tears with Barrion if it saves my home."

Sterra's Tears.

Evren sat upright so fast that it startled Mei.

"Fucking what?" the Khama hissed.

"Sterra's Tears!"

"Yes?"

Evren pushed herself to her feet. "Hells, how did I not see this until now? Fall of silver could mean anything, including the sacred fucking waterfall blessed by the Horizon Walker herself. All noble weddings happen there, like mine was supposed to be. Everyone else has the water brought to them. And everyone gets married on the full moon."

"What the hells are you going on about?" Mei's eyes followed her as she paced, and while the Khama looked like she was getting ready for a fight, Evren's steps were bouncing.

She turned to Mei with a blinding grin. "Mei, you're right. A wedding is the key to saving everyone."

"I know?"

"I'm looking for a dangerous artifact, one revealed under the light of the swollen moon and the fall of silver."

"Sterra's Tears . . ." Mei muttered as it sunk in. "They're supposed turn silver in the moonlight."

"Exactly! That has to be where it is."

"Wait, hold on." She raised a hand and, just like that, Evren stilled. "Why do you want this artifact?"

Evren shook her head. "It's not so simple. Someone else is manipulating others to get it for him. This is a piece of an Elder's power, the Eternity Keeper specifically."

"Oh, the chaotic time controlling one that supposedly went mad and tore himself to pieces?"

"Yes, that one." Evren paused. "How did you know?"

Mei grinned. "I actually paid attention to my theology lessons, unlike someone."

"Right. You see how bad this is?"

"In a sense. And you want to get it first, right?"

Why did everyone keep asking that like it wasn't obvious? "Yes. I think by getting the dagger, I can draw out whoever is behind this and stop the war before it gets worse. While our actions are our own, someone I know has been prodding from the shadows to get this dagger. He wants it, badly. And I know I can keep it from him."

Mei studied her for a long time before settling back against the window. "You really think this'll save Orenlion?"

"And the Hisrachi. And Etherak."

"Tall order."

"You're planning to be queen of Etherak someday, right? Best get started on all these crazy, world-altering decisions. And, who knows, maybe if I can stop Wasanthi in time, you won't even have to get married."

"You're fucking insane," Mei muttered. "And I don't care about the Hisrachi surviving this, but . . ." She thought for a while and then a smile crept up her face. The grin of a fighter facing heaping odds for a slight chance at success and the thrill of battle itself. "I suppose I should get that ring ready, huh?"

"A crown too."

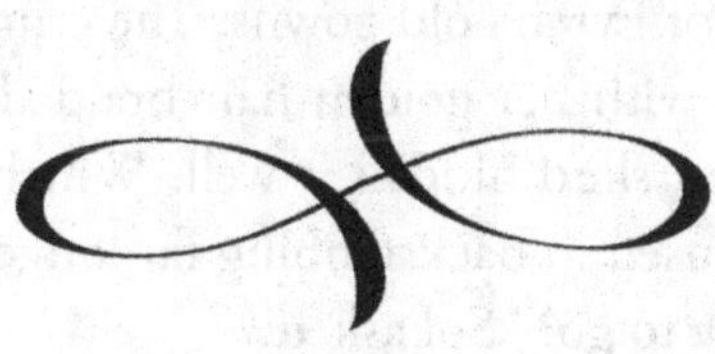

25

News quickly spread of the new alliance between Etherak and Orenlion. Whether or not people trusted Etherak's first outreaching of support in fifty years was irrelevant. With an alliance came an army, with Etherak came their war mages. The Hisrachi couldn't survive against that.

The people settled down into an uneasy waiting game, their rage still simmering underneath the surface but held back for now. They waited for a promise bound in silver and holy water rather than one forged in parchment and oaths.

As the sun was beginning its lazy descent into the horizon, Evren wrapped herself both in leather and silk. What she could afford to hide—and what was left—of her armor, she draped in a simple gown of moonlight grey. The billowing fabric whispered like the rustling of leaves, just barely covering up the sound of creaking leather. The long, wide sleeves hid her gauntlets. She fixed the sweeping neckline to cover any armor peeking through and tied it off with a deep purple sash around her waist.

She'd have to be careful. Even with everyone's eyes on Mei and Barrion, there would be enough worried eyes watching her. She didn't want to look ready for a fight.

She strapped the wyvern dagger to her thigh anyway. Mira

and a handful of Barrion's honor guard would carry all the weapons, Evren's bow included, but the weight of the dagger was comforting.

At a soft knock on her door, Evren swept the skirt over her leg. "Yes?"

The door opened just enough to allow Sol's form to slip through and she was quick to shut it again. She'd dressed up too, after altering one of Evren's old gowns. The crimson looked good on her, especially with her golden hair braided back. If she was wearing any armor, she'd hidden it well. Which made sense. Sol had been a noble used to backstabbing far longer than Evren.

"Are you ready to go?" Sol asked.

"As ready as I can be. Is everyone leaving already?"

"It's a long hike to the falls, apparently." Sol shrugged and walked over to the vanity. Her finger skimmed over the jewelry, discarded makeup, and glittering hair pins almost mournfully. "We have a little time, though. Enough to do something with that mop on your head that you call hair."

Evren combed her fingers through it. "I brushed it."

"Well, that's more than usual." Sol shook her head and then kicked the vanity chair out with her leg. "Sit."

"You know this isn't a nice wedding, right? I don't need to look too presentable."

The dwarf picked up the hairbrush like it was one of her daggers, twirling it over her fingers. "Either sit on your own or I tie you to the chair. You can call this payback for the last several months."

Evren reluctantly sat and let the dwarf comb through her hair. In the mirror, she was meeting the eyes of a familiar stranger. Plenty scarred, still too pale and shaking off the weariness that one night's sleep couldn't fix. But it was Evren, not a skeleton wearing her skin. There was color in her cheeks and her lips weren't stained with blood. She was both a little girl wrapped in silk and an adventurer bound in armor.

"If we make it out of this alive, what's the plan?" Sol asked.

"Terevas. Nerezza, if we haven't lost her. Or . . . wherever we want to go."

Sol picked up one of the ear cuffs. It was too big for Evren's ears, and the delicate metal wind chimes that dangled from it made a little melody in Sol's fingers.

"You'd give all this up?" Sol asked. "The house, the title, all of it?"

"Why wouldn't I?"

"You found out what happened to your father, Evren. He still lives. When we're done with this war, Orenlion is going to need someone to guide it through its changes. You've got the right name and vision to be the person to do that."

Evren hadn't thought about that. Staying there, while no longer a cage, felt wrong. The Wood had both her home and her father, but her family was the Sols. If there was ever a part of her that wanted to lead Orenlion, it had died when she'd left. She had promises to keep and a world to see, perhaps even save, and although she'd cut away all the festering guilt and wrongness that came with Xun Manor, she couldn't picture herself staying.

She grabbed Sol's hand gently and put the ear cuff down. "My home is with my friends. No matter where you are, I follow. We still have work to do."

Sol nodded, taking a deep breath as she did. "I guess I can't imagine leaving again, so I thought you'd stay."

"Would you go back to Dirn-Darahl if you had the choice?"

Sol's hand went to her braid, and she tugged a strand loose so it hung by her face. "I can't picture a world where I do have a choice. But even still, it would be hard. I miss my home and my mother. The steady heat and vibrations of the stone. My slippers too, funnily enough." Her eyes cut back to Evren. "I'd miss you all more, though. Regardless of what I want, my place is by your side, as always."

Evren smiled. "One day we'll come back home. When Eith has nothing else to give us and we can't stay away. Then we'll be the stubborn old adventurers who make everyone's lives more difficult, so the days pass by faster."

"I like that idea. But first." Sol held up Evren's hair. "What do we do if we're going to both a wedding and a war?"

Evren's crooked grin got wider in the mirror. It was time for a change. "I've got an idea."

~

THE EVENING AIR was cool against the nape of Evren's bare neck and her exposed ears. As she followed the winding path through the silvery Wood, her hand kept going to her shortened hair and smiling. All her life she'd tried to hide or downplay her ears. This felt good.

Far ahead, the wedding procession was led by the bride and groom themselves, and was trailed by the small army that accompanied them. Mira and her soldiers, the Khama who were strong enough to walk, the Sovereigns, and the Wandering Sols. It was a slow march. The roughhewn steps cut into the ground were made of root and stone alike and were winding and steep. Barrion and Mei had to lead everyone there to show their devotion to the wedding, and no one could help them.

Mei was struggling. The swaths of airy silver fabric concealed her injuries, but even as far back as Evren was, she could see the Khama's pained expression and gritted teeth. Barrion kept the slow pace with her, never offering help that would bruise her ego, but staying by her side all the same.

Trailing behind Mira, Aster couldn't take his eyes from either of them, and there was no masking the raw hurt on his face.

A whisper of silk along the ground was all that announced Fen's presence as she fell in step with Evren. She held one of the blue lanterns in her long fingers like Evren imagined a dragon would hold its egg.

"If this is part of some grand scheme of yours, you should know it won't work." Fen kept her voice to a respective murmur.

Evren hummed a little laugh. "This wasn't my idea. Not like this anyway."

"I suppose you're tremendously happy that it's another poor soul forced into a loveless marriage other than yourself."

"I take no joy in this. Mei was something of a friend to me before I left Orenlion, and Barrion is a good man who had no plans of tying himself or his kingdom down so soon. I feel for them, but it's their decision."

"That's what any queen would say about her pawns sacrificing themselves."

Evren cut Fen a strange look. The Sovereign's posture was stiff, and her mouth drawn into a tight, disapproving line. Either her mask was cracking, or this was another facade.

"You give me too much credit," Evren said. "I'm no mastermind. You, on the other hand, have the whole city on puppet strings. I haven't accidentally cut some in my fumbling, have I?"

The sound of rushing water trickled into the conversation and the path took a steeper turn. The ground turned mossy and rocky, the air sweet with cool mist.

Out of the corner of her eye, Evren saw Fen's grip on the lantern grow tighter.

"I have far less control than you think," the Sovereign whispered. "But I still have enough secrets to know that this is a trap."

"Of course it is, but for whom?"

"Don't be so flippant. The entire Wood could be in danger from Wasanthi's ambition, and believe me when I say he is far too smug about this alliance, considering how much he abhors Etherak's beliefs."

Fen's dress snagged on a rock, and she cursed as she stopped to save it. As she did, Evren stopped a stair up and let others pass her by. Abraxas gave her a questioning look, but she waved him on. Then she extended her hand to Fen.

The Sovereign looked up at it with a measure of both disgust and distrust. Her narrowed eyes found Evren's face as if she could see a hidden motive there. When she found nothing, either because there was nothing or Evren was better at masks than she was, she reluctantly grabbed her hand.

Evren helped her up the next step, leaning down as if to check her gown. "What do you know, Fen? And be quick about it."

As Evren shuffled her skirts, the Sovereign whispered. "Wasanthi claims to have visions from the Horizon Walker, that she's pushing him towards something that'll change the course of history itself."

"And you don't trust it? Not very faithful of you."

"I've known that man for centuries. I can tell the difference between faith and madness."

"And?" Evren straightened and met her gaze dead on. A shiver slithered down her spine, but she ignored it. "What aren't you telling me?"

Fen's face pulled into an ugly grimace. For a moment, Evren thought Fen would toss her down the stairs for spite and surprise alone; something close to their old relationship. But her eyes flickered up to Aster, still hopelessly following Mei like a shadow, and she softened.

"As a mother, you'd do anything for your children. I . . . have been wanting, to say the least. There was a time where I didn't see what he wanted, only what I thought he needed. What I needed, what the bloodline needed." She turned back to Evren. "I pushed for the marriage between you two for many reasons, but above all I did it because I thought it would save the Wood. A spymaster can do little against failing magic, but bloodlines and marriages? I know them well. The most potent magic is mixed in blood, our blood. Wasanthi thought so too. He convinced me that the marriage was the right choice, despite how much it broke Aster away from me."

Fen looked at Evren with an expression so nakedly guilty it made her feel uncomfortable. "My actions are my own. But something in Wasanthi has changed. I recognize that look in his eyes. Whatever he wants in those waters will not be the salvation he expects."

"I know what he wants," Evren said slowly. It felt good to have confirmation about her fears. "I know because I was pushed towards it, too."

Fen hissed. "What?"

"He's seeing something, an illusion, driving him towards its goal. Whoever is behind it is behind my own visions, and one of the Hisrachi as well. They appear as someone trustworthy, seeking to help, but they are someone else. Someone powerful enough to think playing with pieces of gods is wise."

Fen took a horrified step back. "And that doesn't concern you? That we will be falling right into this specter's plans?"

"More than one of us is looking for the same thing. Me, Wasanthi, and likely one of the Hisrachi. One of us will get it, regardless. I know what's coming, and I never said I was going to let this trap be our tomb."

Evren pulled up her sleeve enough for Fen to see a flash of leather armor and then covered up again. "Whatever happens, you'll keep Aster safe?"

Fen's mask slipped back on, cold and confident and calculating. "If it's the last thing I'll do, I'll be the mother he needs."

Evren turned her back on Fen to continue up the steps, something she wouldn't have done a couple days ago out of fear of a dagger in her back. But Fen was afraid, and it was enough to bolster Evren's own courage.

Sterra's Tears was heard before it was seen. Thundering water was followed by a thick, heavy mist that glowed blue in the lantern light. The path turned slick, and then cut right and down, then, out of the mist, they emerged at the bottom of Sterra's Tears.

The waterfall tumbled from a jagged cliff and into a glittering pool at the bottom. A ring of weathered arches encircled the pool, covered in moss and vines, but achingly Elder in design. A path of well-worn steppingstones stood just above the pool's lapping waters and led to a small island in the middle. The only Elder archway still complete stood on that island, right before a basin of clear crystal brimming with water.

There was no silver, though. Evren craned her head up to find the sky choked with clouds and winced. She hoped she wasn't wrong.

Evren found herself by her friends as Mei and Barrion picked their way over the stones, followed by Wasanthi. The rest of the witnesses gathered around the rim of the pool, watching in hushed anticipation.

Arke elbowed Evren's leg. "The fuck was that with Fen?"

"Truly," Abraxas whispered and gestured for Arke to lower his voice. "I'd like to know as well."

"Fen's scared. She thinks Wasanthi has gone mad. We shared some information, and I'm convinced he's the Sovereign we need to watch."

"Not Liang or Yikao?" Sorin asked. "Or even Shao? He might not even realize he's seeing things."

"Or Fen is playing you," Sol added.

Evren shook her head. "No, I think she's right. But, regardless, we have all of them here tonight. Once something happens, we'll be able to see who all reacts."

"I hate waiting," Gyda grumbled under her breath. She hadn't bothered with finery like the rest of them, but Evren found it hard not to stare at her.

"Ah, but you're so good at it," Evren said.

Gyda's lips twitched up into a smile. "Few things are good enough to wait for."

That sent a little thrill through Evren, and it was hard to keep her smile at bay even with the palpable tension in the air.

She made note of everyone around the pool. Shao, who barely acknowledged her, Mira whose curt nod showed she and her people were ready for anything, and Aster, who looked uncomfortable and somewhat less pained beside his mother.

At one point, Mei and Barrion were almost to the island

when her bad leg gave out. She stumbled, and he easily caught her and brought her back to her feet. When he went to pull away, she kept her grip on his hand, and the two kept walking side by side. If Evren hadn't known better, it would almost seem like a good match. Like the wedding was just that, and not gamble for survival at best, or a trap for a piece of an Elder's soul at worst.

She wished, just then, that they could be happy. If anyone deserved it, wasn't it them? Both Barrion and Mei were good people, duty-bound to protect their people. Was it fate or cruelty that had them stepping next to that bowl now? Could it have been any different?

Barrion stood on one side of the bowl and Mei on the other as they let go of their hands. Wasanthi stood behind it in full view of everyone. She could barely pay attention to his words as he blessed the union in the Horizon Walker's name. All she could see as he took the two rings and dripped them into the water was her father's murderer. It had been him the whole time. He'd comforted her and offered guidance without an ounce of guilt. Two men were dead because of him and his twisted version of what was good.

She'd have to make sure his list didn't grow. Shao could have Yikao, but Wasanthi was hers.

The rings sparkled as they were slipped onto Mei and Barrion's fingers. Simple bands of silver dotted with moonstones. Nothing grand like a royal wedding would normally call for, but strangely suiting for the two of them.

Evren could see Barrion's hands shaking as he put the ring on Mei's finger. The Khama took his hand to still it and guide the ring. Once it was on, Wasanthi clapped his hands.

"Where metal binds you in body, water will bind you in soul. Drink of Sterra's Tears, our Lady's most sacred waters, and know that your souls move as one from this night forward, until all the stars fall from the sky and the night is eternally black."

Mei dipped her hands into the crystal bowl and cupped the

water even as it fell through her fingers. She lifted them to Barrion's lips and he drank deeply, then he did the same for her.

But Evren had gone rigid.

Where metal binds you in body, water will bind you in soul.

Souls.

Evren looked up at Gyda and squeezed her arm. "Souls."

"What?"

A conversation on an icy, wrecked ship flashed in her mind. The sky blooming blue and green, the biting ice on her skin. Nerezza at her side, calmly talking about the magic she'd studied.

"I am a scholar, Evren. I scour the world for new magics every day. I'd found little. Things unattainable to mortals that shaped Eith, anyway. But now, I've found two."

"Two?"

"Souls and blood."

"It's not Viggo, it's Nerezza," Evren hissed, and she watched as all the blood drained from Gyda's face.

Just then, the clouds parted and the moon hung bright and swollen in the night sky. The blinding light reflecting from the pool was nearly painful. Evren had to squint to see clearly. But once her vision cleared, she could see Sterra's Tears look like they were turning to molten silver, and it felt like the air itself had changed. The arch behind Wasanthi was glowing as brightly as the moon itself.

All of Evren's confidence vanished. Viggo she could deal with, but Nerezza was a different story. And if she got a piece of a god's soul to eat . . .

"We have to get the dagger," Evren breathed, her hand going to her own dagger. "Now."

Before she could even step forward though, a chorus of bone-chilling hisses erupted in the air.

"WEAVERS!" Shao yelled.

They sprung from the forest, all black legs and bared fangs. They tore into the few they surprised, blood flinging in the air.

Mira called her people to arms, her face furious as she charged after the Hisrachi that killed one of her men.

Shao rallied the Khama as well, but it was too late. The Hisrachi had everyone scattered and separated. One spider was holding a noble under the water, ignoring the sting of weapons as the Khama tried to get it off.

And leading it all was a familiar Hisrachi.

"Anep!" Evren shouted.

He snapped away from his pursuit of a wounded Khama, and his eyes gleamed with a familiar hatred. He scurried over to her but paused at the steppingstones, and all eight eyes flashed towards the island.

The archway was glowing like a mirror now. It didn't show the other side of the pool anymore, just bright light, like the water itself. Evren watched as Wasanthi turned to run to it, but Mei slung her good arm around his neck and put the older man into a chokehold. The old priest kicked at her leg and sent her crumbling to the ground. But when he got up, he was quickly met with Barrion's fist.

That, at least, was taken care of.

Anep took off towards the island.

Evren gathered her skirts. "Mira!"

She knew what to do. With a shout towards her fighters, Mira and another four tossed the Wandering Sols their weapons over a bloodbath. Sol's daggers flashed briefly in the silvery light as she tore them from under her dress and gutted a stampeding spider. Sorin's sword splashed in the water, and he dove after it. Seconds later, Abraxas's sword impaled the shore, followed quickly by his shield. Even without his armor, he was a menace on the battlefield and surged into the fight as if nothing could touch him. Arke caught his spellbook at the same time Gyda caught her sword. Her runes glowed an eerie green just as Arke sent a wave of ice towards the nearest Hisrachi.

When Evren's bow landed in her grip, she felt complete for the first time in months.

"Don't just bloody stand there!" Mira yelled and tossed over her quiver. She smiled when Evren caught it easily. "Go be a hero! We'll hold them off here."

There wasn't many Hisrachi now. Maybe there never had been. The surprise had been the bloodiest part of the attack, but now that the soldiers and the Khama were getting their bearings, they were beating them back.

The real threat was Anep. He tore across the steppingstones, getting halfway unchallenged before Sorin leapt from the water and grasped onto his leg. Anep hissed and tried to shake him off, but he wouldn't let go. Sorin got his feet under him on the stone and, with a great heave, pulled Anep off balance and into the water.

The way was clear for now, and the Wandering Sols took their chance.

The steps were dangerously slick as Evren ran across them. The water was turning a deep red and sloshing over the stones and her feet. As the island got closer, Sorin's head suddenly popped out of the water. He barely had time to gasp for air before Gyda snatched him by his collar and hauled him out of the pool. Anep's form floundered at the surface, seething.

Evren didn't know if she wanted him to survive the swim or not.

The stones blissfully turned to grass as Evren scrambled up to the arch with her friends just behind her. Wasanthi was on the ground, clutching his face where Barrion's ring had cut him. Barrion himself was helping Mei stand as she growled profanities.

She looked up, panting. "Took your fucking time."

Barrion's worried eyes were combing the battlefield. "Divines, why would they do this?"

"Anep," Evren hurriedly said as she walked over to Wasanthi and put her boot on his chest. "He's Nerezza's pawn just as much as Wasanthi is, and I was."

"Who?" Barrion asked.

Wasanthi spat before Evren could answer. "Lies! Our Lady would not consort with monsters and non-believers."

"You saw a lie," Evren said, then turned back to Mei. "Can you keep him here? He can't follow us."

"I'm sure I can think of something." The murderous glint in her eyes only confirmed her threat. "Go. You're running out of moonlight."

Evren jerked her head towards the portal and her friends, dripping enemy blood and silver water alike, fell into it. Gyda was last and hesitated. She was waiting for Evren.

Evren knew she had little time, so she knelt to Wasanthi's level and whispered. "The Wood remembers what you did, and your stars will not save you from its wrath."

She stood up and slammed her boot on his face for good measure and then turned towards Gyda and the arch. It haloed the warrior in the light, waiting for her with bated breath. So willing to follow her into whatever oblivion the dagger lived in without question or judgment.

Evren had a list of things to do once this was over, and kissing Gyda was at the top.

She stepped up beside her and, without a second thought, took her hand. She looked at the silver portal, and then back at the gleaming battle behind them. Anep was crawling up the shore, one leg bent and broken, spitting water. He charged past Barrion and Mei, his eyes only for the portal.

Evren closed her eyes and stepped into oblivion with Gyda.

26

Evren emerged in the dark alone.

For a while, she was aware of nothing but her shallow breathing echoing back to her. Her empty hand flexed out to where Gyda had just been and found nothing but stagnant, still air. She gripped her bow instead and found comfort in the familiar worn grip and smooth wood.

Slowly, the shadows took shape as her eyes adjusted. Massive black walls rising beside her, a ceiling she couldn't see through the haze of swirling mist, and a dead end behind her. The corridor went ahead for what seemed like miles with no end.

Evren took a cautious step forward.

"Gyda?"

Her voice was small but bounced along the walls in a strange symphony before being swallowed up by the mists above.

"Arke?" she tried louder, to no avail. "Sorin!"

Only silence remained.

Evren's fingers fumbled in the folds of her dress until she pulled out the shining mirror shard. It gleamed brightly for what little light there was, and Evren clasped it as she walked forward.

"I don't know if any of you can hear me," she said. "But if you can, let me know where you are."

A few more moments of silence trailed her like shadows as she followed the corridor. She passed her knuckles along the wall, finding nothing to grip onto. The stone was as smooth as glass but seemed to swallow light. She kept contact with the wall, counting each slow step, until her knuckle found a corner.

She looked up to find a split in the corridor. One path going sharply left, and another going right. She rocked back on her heels.

"This isn't what I expected from these trials," Evren muttered, more than a little cross for not thinking about them at all. She only had thoughts of the dagger and getting it first.

"Kid, you there?"

Evren nearly jumped out of her skin at the sound of Arke's voice. She whirled around, looking down both corridors for a sign of the goblin and finding nothing but waiting stillness down both.

"Arke?"

"Mirror, dumbass."

Right.

She brought it up to her face and caught glimpses of his yellow eyes and pointed ears. "You all right?"

"I ain't dead, so yeah. Where are you?"

"I don't know. All I see are black hallways. It went straight for a while before splitting off in two directions."

He grunted. "Pretty much the same here. Been sittin' at a three-way fork for a while."

"But the walls look the same?"

"Yeah."

Evren tapped the glass on her chin, eyeing the walls thoughtfully. It reminded her of the White Cairn with the twisting paths leading into the unknown. Just far darker and warmer. To this day Evren wasn't sure how she got through the Cairn, or how they found their way back out. It felt like sheer luck. Walk with one hand on a wall and hope for the best.

"It's a maze," Arke finally rasped, but there was no joy in his revelation.

"I was thinking the same thing. The dagger must be at the end."

"Damn portal got us all separated. How the fuck are we supposed to get back to each other, let alone through this?"

"We've got the mirror. Hopefully, the others remember it as well. Maybe we can guide each other."

"Hate to break it to you, kid, but we're not walkin' the same path. Left for you could mean the way forward, while left for me is just a dead end."

Evren chewed her lip. "The only good thing is that any who follow us will have the same challenge. We just have to work this out. There's likely only one way out and if we all make it, we'll be together again."

"Not sure if I like this new optimism from you."

Evren laughed a little. "Come on, we survived Serevadia together. A little maze is nothing."

"Fine. You goin' left or right?"

"Left."

"I'll go right then."

"Sounds like you."

Evren went left, keeping her knuckles on the wall and her eyes dead ahead. Nothing changed. It was like she was walking down the same corridor she left. When she looked back, nothing but mists gathered at the walls she left behind. She shivered.

"I don't think we have the option of going back," Evren said.

"I got that feelin', too. Makes this more terrifyin'."

It was like this for what felt like hours; a slow crawl forward and checking in with Arke every time there was a fork in the path. Time had lost all meaning, like it had in Serevadia. The vacuous corridors seemed to mimic the eternal and oppressive stillness meant only for the caverns deep beneath Eith's ground. How much time would they spend here? Could they even get the dagger in time? If they got lost, would they be doomed to forever wander the maze until they starved to death?

Evren found herself wishing for monsters. Monsters she could fight and kill. That was an easy challenge to overcome. The maze was just a constant, creeping fear that every step she made was leading her astray.

Her path turned a corner right, as it had the last three times. She hadn't had a left turn in a while and felt her frustration building. She could see up ahead the corridor turning again, this time left, and she picked up her pace while tapping her finger on the mirror.

When she rounded the corner, she was met with a dead end.

"Fuck."

"What's wrong?"

"Dead end," Evren looked over her shoulder to see the wall of mist cutting her off from her old path. "I'm stuck."

"Well . . . shit."

Shit about summed it up. Was this it? Cornered like a wild animal with nowhere to go? Could she risk the mist, hoping that it was an illusion?

Even shouldered her bow and used the mirror shard to cut the silk of her dress. She wanted just a piece of the sleeve, but the edge was duller than she expected, and she ended up tearing off the whole sleeve. She tore it off her arm and then tossed it into the mist.

The deep grey silk turned black immediately and started disintegrating. The smell of burnt hair filled her nostrils and she took a step back as the sleeve dissolved to ash and was swept away.

"Unless the mist has a vendetta against pretty dresses, I wouldn't risk going in it." Evren sighed. "I'm really stuck."

"Fuck that. There's gotta be a way. Can you climb the walls or—"

"Turn around, Evren." A new voice whispered through the mirror.

Arke trailed off into silence and Evren, at a loss for words, turned around.

The dead end was gone. Well, more accurately, it was changed. What had once been smooth, solid stone was now rippling like water. The grey was like the mist, soft and unassuming. Except the whole thing thrummed with magic and set the hairs on the back of her neck on end.

"What the hells?" she said.

"What?" Arke asked. "What is it?"

"I don't know. The wall's gone. It's magic, I think."

"It's the way forward." That voice again.

"Abraxas?" she asked, peering into the mirror, but she saw nothing but Arke trying to do the same thing. It sounded like Abraxas, but his tone was different. Far more reserved and cold.

After a moment's silence, his voice came back. "Yes."

Evren nearly melted in relief. "Great! Where are you? Are you all right?"

"As much as I can be. Listen, this maze is different. You want the dead ends. They'll lead you to portals like the one you have in front of you."

"Okay." Evren swallowed down her doubt. "How did you figure this out?"

"Sorin told me."

Arke's voice boomed over the mirror. "Sorin's with you?"

"No. We could talk to each other a few portals ago, but it's been a while since we've been in the same time."

"Time?"

"This maze is massive. If the Elder who controlled time truly built it, it's not too far off to say we're all in different eras of history, but in the same place. Going through those portals will shove you out into a different time. Survive that and you go to the next part of the maze. At least . . . that's my working theory."

Evren let out a heavy breath and stared at the portal. The air had changed the closer she was to it. Drier and warmer. A soft breeze cooled the sweat on the nape of her neck.

"If I go through here, I lose contact with you and Arke?"

"There is no 'if,' Evren. This is the only way through. Arke and I will find our way, just as sure as Anep will."

Fear curled like a cold snake in her belly. She tightened her grip on the mirror shard, as if that would physically drag her friends with her. If she failed, or they did, she wasn't just leaving them in the maze. She was leaving them in another time entirely.

And the only possible way of getting back to them would be the dagger. She hoped.

"See you both on the other side," she whispered into the mirror and stepped through the portal.

It was like stepping into a tornado. An unseen force jerked her through the grey, twisting and weaving to the point where Evren felt like a leaf in a storm. She barely kept a grip on her mirror and clutched it tight to her chest as the whirlwind turned into a free fall.

She shut her eyes.

She landed with a hard thud on something hot and moving. Sunlight blazed red behind her eyelids and the air felt like a heated knife down her throat. She held her hand up to block the sun and struggled to her knees. They sunk a little into the fine sand.

Sand.

She squinted her eyes against the glare as she looked up. A vast sea of crimson sand enveloped her vision. Dunes as tall as mountains and valleys deep enough to hold black shadows stretched as far as her eyes could see. There was no end to them.

The air smelled like blood and smoke. The scents of war.

A battle cry sounded behind her, shrill and desperate. Evren barely had time to duck out of the way before an armored figured hurled past her and stumbled into the sand.

In a swift move, Evren replaced the mirror shard with her dagger and held it in front of her.

"I'm not part of this. Leave me be," she cried on instinct.

The warrior stood back up, a wicked glaive dusted with sand and blood in their hands. Their armor was torn and ancient, patched more times than useful and stained black with blood. The helmet was broken like an eggshell, and Evren jumped back when it was torn off.

A half-elf stared back at her, but that was where the similarities ended. His head was shaved to the scalp and littered with dozens of scars. Dark brown skin glistened with sweat, and his lips curled into a snarl as he took his glaive in both hands.

"So many years in our land and you still can't bother to speak my language." The man hissed his accented Core at her like it was a threat. "The audacity."

Evren held her hands up in surrender. "I'm not here for you. I don't want to fight."

"Neither did we."

He charged like a wild beast, and Evren lunged out of the way. The long glaive swept up crimson sand where she'd been moments before, and the man whirled on her for another attack. She lost her footing on the soft sand and her fall was all that kept her from the blade.

He howled in frustration, bringing the weapon around for another blow, but Evren was already on her feet and lunging at him. She slid under his guard on her knees, and her dagger cut at the weathered armor, but didn't quite nick his skin.

He expertly darted out of the way, feet fast and sure on the shifting ground, but Evren knew that if she got out from under his guard, she was screwed. The glaive's reach would kill her in time if the sand didn't.

She lashed out at his leg and her dagger cut deeply into his thigh. The sand soaked up the blood greedily. He whipped around, glaive held high to smash down on her skull, but she slipped behind him just in the nick of time. Before either of them realized it, her blade was at his throat and her feet were steady on the sand.

"Please stand down," Evren begged in his ear. "I don't want to hurt you."

The laugh that came from him was desperate and mad. His glaive fell to the sand. "Your kind knows no mercy. End me so I might destroy you in the next life."

"I don't—"

His hand was around hers and the dagger in an instant, and he drew it across his throat. Evren stumbled away with the dagger in her hand, but it was too late. His life blood poured into the sand, and he fell to the ground, lifeless, his hand outstretched towards something on the horizon.

Evren gripped her dagger with bloody hands, and her heart thundered in her chest. That desperation and hatred was like what she'd seen in Anep, but somehow worse. She could feel it leaking into her own bones. At what point in time did people fight so much rage and grief?

The half-elf's hand pointed toward a dune like any other. Evren ignored the body and the heat. She ignored the heavy taste of copper in the air and the tears forming in her eyes and she climbed. The blood-soaked sand caked her fingers and filled her boots as she climbed. She climbed while the sun burned her skin like a hateful eye. The entire land seemed to hate her and want to destroy her.

Evren got to the top just as the sounds of fighting reached her. She stood at the crest of the dune and took in the sight before her with horrified eyes.

A city was bleeding.

Grand walls crumbled. Streets ran red with rivers of blood. The sky was black with smoke as parts of the city caught fire. She could hear the screams of the dying rattling in her skull and saw the same desperation in the fighters of the city. Their glaives broke under heavy maces. Their patched armor shattered against shields. Knights in silver armor turned red and black as they slaughtered all those who got in their way.

The flag of Etherak hung limply at the gates over a pile of bodies.

The fall of Vernes, or one of her cities, was where Evren had been spat out. When or where she'd been sent during the hundred-year occupation wasn't clear. Vernes had fought every day of those hundred years.

Evren felt sick. A hundred years of enduring this. How had Abraxas managed it? How had Vernes even survived long enough to banish his Divines?

A flash of grey caught her eye. There, just a few feet away, another portal opened.

Evren took one last look at the unnamed burning city of Vernes, trying to see if she could see the man she once called friend there. She saw nothing but armored murderers and ran towards the portal.

She didn't hesitate to throw herself in.

The same whirlwind snatched her from time and tossed her back into the maze. She stumbled into the corridor, shaking off sand and sweat. She put away her dagger, coated in the blood of a man decades dead, and pulled out the mirror.

"Is anyone there?" she asked and moved along the wall. She didn't hesitate to choose a random direction when the path suddenly split. Either she kept going or she found another dead end. "Sorin? Sol? Can you hear me?"

"Evren?"

She nearly wept in relief at the sound of Sol's voice. "It's good to hear you."

"You too. Abraxas said you might be headed this way."

Evren wiped the grit off her face and went to work, tearing off her remaining sleeve. "He's been getting around then. How many portals have you done?"

"Only two." She sounded like Abraxas. Quiet and reserved. Evren wondered what she saw.

"One for me. I wonder how many we need to do." Evren thought for a while before asking, "Have you heard from Gyda?"

"No, but Sorin did. He said she sounded all right."

"And him?"

"As he always is."

They talked very little as Evren walked through the maze this time. Sol found a portal before she did and left her in silence for hours. By the time Evren had found another, she was sick of hearing herself breathe.

She stepped through time with her eyes squeezed shut.

She managed to land on her feet this time, and her boots met cold, hard cobblestone. It was night, and the air held the tight chill of an approaching snowstorm and her breath fogged out in front of her. Cold, yes, but not the type she'd experienced in the Reino Terminan.

All around her were strange building covered in frost. Dark wood and stone, gated windows dark against the night. It was eerily silent. When she looked up, there were no stars, only a blood-red moon staring down at her.

Evren shivered and started walking. The streets were narrow and crisscrossed, not unlike a maze. A few iron-wrought lamp-posts flickered, but their flames were weak and dying.

This city, whatever it was, felt like a corpse. She'd seen Vernes dying, but this felt already dead. Like she was a maggot picking through the bones of a body.

"Where the fuck am I?" she whispered to herself.

Almost as if answering her, a scream pieced the still, cold air behind her.

It was so unnerving and unnatural that Evren immediately thought of Keres, but when she turned to find them she was met only with a deformed monster.

A pale beast standing upright on its legs, it almost looked like a man. But it's hunched back, two extra arms and swath of eyes staring at her through its gaping mouth told her if this had ever been a man, it was far from it now.

Evren knew monsters. This was something new, something different.

Something wrong.

Every instinct in her told her to run, and she did just that.

The monster screamed again and gave chase. Its steps thundered in the cobblestones behind her, getting faster with every passing second. Evren swung around a lamppost and down a smaller street. The monster slammed into a nearby building, but immediately got back up and continued the chase.

Evren was a hunter of beasts, but this was something else entirely. She knew deep down she wouldn't be enough to take down the monster alone.

She kept to twisting, sharp turns, hoping to throw the creature off. But those turns were all that kept her from being overwhelmed by it. It was supernaturally fast, and it wasn't running out of steam, unlike her.

Evren cut another corner, breathing hard. This street was wide and uncrowded by buildings. Instead, she could see a large chapel at the end, gated and strong. Also swarming with monsters and . . . people.

There were two more of the same monsters she was running from in the chapel courtyard. The people fighting them were varied and vicious. She watched as one, a human man dressed in a dusty purple coat, flicked a spell from his fingers and enveloped one creature in a ball of flame. There was no spellbook on him, and he yelped as the creature rushed after him.

Another human ran between him and the monster, bearing golden eyes and a wickedly sharp great axe covered in frost. He leapt into the air and impaled the monster right in its chest. The creature stumbled until two well placed arrows sunk into the cavernous mouth, inches from the human, and then it fell dead.

"Watch your aim!" the golden eyed man yelled.

The female elf did nothing but draw her bow on the next monster.

This one had two more heroes fighting it. One, a man with long black hair and a great sword wreathed in flames, and another, a half-elf woman with nothing but a glowing quarterstaff. While bloody and tired, they held their own just fine. The warrior pinned the monster's foot to the ground with his burning sword. Another arrow sunk deeply into the monster's gut and, without hesitation, the half-elf jumped up and used the arrow to nimbly climb the creature's body and come face to face with it. With a yell, she took her quarterstaff across its bulbous neck, slid to its back and jerked until there was a loud pop and the creature fell dead.

Evren was so enraptured she nearly forgot about the one chasing her until its long arm grazed her foot. She narrowly dodged and tried to run faster. If she could just get to them . . .

"Into the chapel!" The warrior with the flaming sword said. "All of you, now! There's more yet to come."

Into the chapel, yes! Those walls could stand against a monster. But the warrior wasn't talking to her. He didn't even look in her direction. He pulled the purple coated mage to his feet and started pushing everyone inside. They were so weary and terrified, that they didn't argue. And she was still too far away.

"No . . ." Evren panted, and her voice came out like a whimper. "Wait, please."

They didn't hear her. The last of them were pushed into the chapel and the warrior ran in to close the heavy wooden doors.

"Wait!" Evren cried, and the shout nearly killed her lungs. The ground under her feet quaked as the monster got closer.

The warrior met her eyes as the doors were closing. She watched the fear and hopelessness rage inside them, and then finally guilt before he shut the doors.

He made his choice, and Evren made hers.

She turned around and ducked.

The creature flew over her, its legs missing her by a hair's breadth. It stumbled to a stop, confused, before turning around. But Evren was already running back to where she'd come. Just a few feet away, a portal glimmered in the street where it hadn't seconds before. Evren leapt into it just as the monster let out another bone-chilling scream. Time snatched her out of the clutches of death, but it couldn't shake away the fear the dead city had left.

~

EVREN FELL THROUGH TIME REPEATEDLY. There was no keeping track because there wasn't any point. There wasn't a magical number of horrors to survive until she reached the end. All there was were the maze and the horrors of the past, present, and future.

Rarely did Evren actually know the difference. There were times she guessed she was far in the past only to see the impossible, like flying ships and a town growing out of the rubble of an ancient city. When she thought she was in the future, the past Eith came back to remind her how wild and ravenous it was. She saw giants stand with the rebel slaves of Gratey against their former masters. She saw Etherak, vicious and teeming with monsters until walls were built around the cities and magic was tamed enough to be used against the native beasts. She saw the first Vasa sail their ship under the sea and come back bearing the power of storms at their fingertips.

More often than not, Evren saw fear.

She saw a sky burning like fire, so hot it turned a sea of sand to glass. She watched a dark port city torn apart by the creature entombed under its streets. Where war turned the ground wet with blood, it carved a great canyon into the earth, its depth unending and its darkness impenetrable. A flying fortress fell to the earth like a falling star as two mages battled on its crumbling floors, heedless to the death they were courting by staying.

Evren saw Eith—chaotic, dark, and full of war.

Broken.

Evren fell into the maze again on her hands and knees, smoking and coughing up ash. What was left of her dress had been singed by dragon fire. Past or future, it didn't matter. She hadn't even been able to get anything more than a glimpse of the silhouette of wings before it had started destroying the mountain she was on. She'd been lucky to see the portal at all through the smoke and heat.

Groaning, Evren picked herself off the floor and prepared for another long walk to the next portal. But she wasn't in the maze anymore.

The room was vast and made from the same oppressive black walls as the ones she'd been walking through for ages. Soft mist curled at the edges but crept no further. Behind her, she felt the heat of the portal vanish and only the light scent of smoke lingered.

In the middle of the room, suspended in the grasp of mist, smoke, sand, and salt, was a gleaming ornate dagger. Its blade shone like liquid silver, the keen edge curved and shimmering with heat. The hilt was exactly how she remembered it in the mosaic, dipped in bronze and beautifully crafted, but . . . plain. Evren always expected artifacts of gods to be dripping with jewels and gold. This dagger had no need to show its importance.

It had shown Evren the whole time she'd raced to get it. And now she was here. Finally.

She took a step forward; the mist swallowing the echo of her boot hitting stone.

"It took you longer than I thought to reach me."

A figure cloaked in black emerged from behind the dagger. Evren froze, half expecting to see the Shadow Dancer since she was this far into an Elder's gauntlet. But she glimpsed scarred hands beneath the cloak, and a glowing gold eye peeking through the hood.

Her hand went to her bow. "Where the hells have you been?"

The figure shuddered. "Waiting for you," they rasped. There was a strange tone in their otherwise cold voice. Relief?

They took a step forward, and Evren shrank back to match.

They paused and then looked back at the dagger. Evren wished she could see their face so she could read them.

"I haven't seen you in months, ever since you warned me about the Long Night," Evren said. "I thought you'd come and give me more cryptic messages before I went to Orenlion."

The figure's shoulders shook, and a sound like hissing snakes coupled with crackled lightning came from the hood. Evren had her bow out and an arrow ready before she realized the figure was laughing.

She stared at them, stunned, until they calmed down.

"I am bound to that," they gestured to the dagger in disdain. "When I appear to you is up to my own strength and wherever it spits me out in time."

"So, you . . ." Evren swallowed. "You're not the Eternity Keeper, are you?"

"No. There is no control here. No power. Just a chance in the storm of chaos."

Again, Evren was struck by how . . . emotional the figure was. In the past, they'd always been cold and curt, maybe a little annoyed. Now she could see pain in the way they walked and kept their back hunched and low. She heard the cracking in their voice, as if their throat was still raw and bleeding. And more . . . it all looked so achingly familiar.

"Why me?" Evren asked. "If you have no control, why come to me?"

"Because you are my strongest connection to this time."

"So . . . I know you."

They paused, tearing away from the dagger to look at Evren. The weight of that one gold eye pressed down on her. She knew that gaze, didn't she? She stepped toward the figure slowly, her eyes locked with that eye. The closer she got, she could almost pick out the features of a face. The hint of cheekbones and a strong chin and raised scars everywhere. If she could just pull back the hood . . .

They were gone. The space in front of her was empty except

for the curling mist and salt around the dagger. She whirled around until she caught sight of them again on the other side of the dagger.

"Not anymore," they rasped, and the moment of familiarity was gone.

Suddenly, there was only the dagger. It reminded Evren why she was here. Outside the maze, people were dying for a war she promised to stop. Her friends were scattered through time because of this. Nerezza was somehow behind it all and would likely be waiting for her when she got back out.

If she got out . . .

"I need to take the dagger."

"You don't."

Evren blinked at them through the haze of salt. "Okay, then tell me how to fix this without taking it. I'm all ears."

"No." As Evren started to protest, they cut her off. "You don't need the dagger, but you will take it, anyway."

"Why? If it's safe here and I can fix things on my own, so be it. Give me another option."

"I cannot. Time is fluid and ever changing. Few things are set into the stone of the world, meant to happen. This is one. By taking the dagger, your actions will ripple across Eith for generations to come. Heroes and villains alike will rise and fall because of it."

Evren backed away. "No. No, the futures I saw—"

"—will happen."

"—are terrible!" she corrected them. "All I saw for a future in Eith is death. The earth splitting apart and swallowing an army, the Boreal Sea freezing solid, a red moon hanging over a dead city—"

"All fixed points."

"There was so much destruction! So much death and hopelessness . . ."

"Where do you think heroes come from?" the figure finally snapped. "Tragedy, war, blood and loss, *that* makes a hero."

Evren shook her head. "It shouldn't be like that."

"No," they agreed. "But everything you saw, every terrible moment in time, was fixed by people like you. The sea melted again. The scar in the earth was built over. The blood moon and the plague it brought were cured. That is the nature of this world. Gods or no, the world will break until someone is strong enough to put it back together."

Evren looked back at the dagger. She could feel the mist and smoke curling around her fingers, drawing her closer. She could taste the salt and ash on her tongue. A piece of an Elder, a being that called itself a god, was in her grasp, but all she did was hesitate. The maze had shown her nothing but darkness. What would the dagger do?

The figure spoke again, softer this time. "Someone takes the dagger out of here. It's needed later in the future. If not by you, then someone else."

"How do I fix this?" she asked. "The dagger . . . how do I use it to stop the war?"

"There are things in time that are not set in stone."

Evren looked up at them questioningly. She could swear she heard them grinning.

"So," they leaned forward as ash dusted their cloak, "move them."

A chill raced down Evren's spine and she closed her eyes. The darkness behind her lids was painted with the horrors she'd seen. The monsters, the blood, the death. But also, possibility. The flying ships, the new cities on top of the old, the heroes standing against all odds and reminding her of everyone she stood for.

"And my friends?"

"Right where they need to be, always."

When Evren opened her eyes again, the figure was gone. There was a strange loss tugging at her chest, but she ignored it. Her eyes were on the dagger again. She put away her bow and flexed her hands.

She could do this. She could control time. Maybe she could

stop the war from happening all together. She could keep Shelis alive and the Hisrachi from attacking, and then there'd be no war.

Then she'd deal with Nerezza.

The air in the room shifted as another portal opened. It carried the smell of crushed earth and a thousand sharpened swords, and out of it fell Anep.

He was in as bad of shape as she was, shaking and exhausted from all that he'd seen. He saw the dagger first, and she saw hope leap into his eyes. Then he saw her, and hate overcame it.

"I'm sorry," she said. "I'm going to fix this."

He raced towards the dagger, screaming, *"NO!"*

And Evren's hand wrapped around the hilt.

Evren was touching divinity.

Or rather, she was touching a sliver, a shard of divinity. There was sudden and certain clarity the moment her fingers touched the cool metal, and she was ripped from time itself. Anep's scream faded but echoed in the cage of her brain. The black disappeared and there was nothing but a blur of motion and color.

Evren was falling through time, clutching the very thing that could cut it into pieces and destroy it. How did she not realize how fragile it all was? The threads that bound the world were barely scraps of shimmering thread, almost begging to be cut. With one swipe, she could change the course of Eith forever. Vernes would never have to suffer for a hundred years, Heliodar never had to be born, Gail wouldn't have been stranded in the Reino Terminan.

She could change it all, and that terrified her.

Where was she falling? Would she ever stop? The figure said she could change moments in time to shape the future, but they didn't say how.

How does one, a mortal with half a heart, change the course of time without ripping it to shreds?

Evren reached out to the surrounding colors. Images, shapes, people in time. All threads on a tapestry she couldn't hope to see in full. It wasn't finished. Maybe it never would be.

She reached out with the dagger and nicked a random thread.

The scream that enveloped her shook her bones. Her vision was overcome with new images. A little boy running through the streets of a city built into the cliffs, his little sister trailing behind as she laughed. The same boy lighting two funeral pyres with tear-stained cheeks. The boy, older and taller, fixing the last button of his black and grey uniform. Him watching his sister saving every gold coin for an impossible dream to the south and giving her every ounce of gold the crown prince gave him.

Evren saw Chayne's life as she destroyed it. Not killed, because this was more than death. She'd erased him from existence.

Panic crawled up her throat. How would she get to the nest without Chayne? Who else could convince her friends to walk into a trap?

Mira.

Evren whispered her name, although no sound came out. She envisioned the human's tough way of standing, her hearty smile and the black of her bond tattoo around her bicep. She saw her learning from Evren all over again. What meant danger and what didn't, what to fight and what to run away from.

Evren picked her thread from the tapestry and tugged. It ripped free, loose in her hands, but still stuck in its origin. Evren could almost taste Mira's favorite ale on her tongue and the promise to come home to her husband. Her birth, her life in Etherak, everything that made her who she was and drove her to be at Barrion's side, Evren kept. But then she started to twist.

Mira escaped the Hisrachi first. She tried to save Barrion, only to realize there was no need. The plan to draw the Wandering Sols to the nest was similar, but Mira wouldn't act like she was afraid. She couldn't be something she wasn't. That quirk in her deception had gotten Evren and the Sols to the nest, and then . . .

Evren paused. How much could she change without changing herself? She didn't want to keep her old hatred of the Hisrachi, but as she tried to change the ambush, her escape, and Anep's fight, the threads wouldn't budge.

A fixed point.

Evren needed something from that fight, and perhaps Anep did too. She let Mira's thread fall back into place.

The tapestry was dizzying. Overwhelming. Where did she even start? What could she change?

She tried her father, thinking that if he'd lived, he could've gotten peace earlier, but his thread was firmly stuck. She tried Shelis and everything in hers was loose and malleable, except her death. Anep was stuck, his thread so intertwined with thousands of others that she couldn't find a spot to begin unraveling. Aster was next but there were many knots in his with so many other people. She couldn't find where his rumor started.

Evren sat back, frustrated. Who could she fix? No . . .

Who could she save?

Evren's finger plucked up a shining thread. It was tangled tightly with another, but veered off near the end. She felt the sensation of wind in her face, of heat in her throat and a bond so strong that it defied divinity's edge.

Evren took Saros's thread, and she tugged. The dagger flashed white and suddenly she wasn't falling anymore.

Her feet were firmly on the ground, which was littered with straw and warm cotton stuffing. The air smelled acidic and animal. As she stepped forward, something cracked under her boot. She pulled back and saw the remains of an eggshell.

In the corner of the nest was a young girl, no older than twelve. Her black hair was a mess, her full elf ears sticking out comically. She was asleep with a baby wyvern in her arms, and the wyvern was staring at Evren.

Saros, even as a hatchling, was sharp and watchful. He glared at Evren as she drew closer to young Mei and growled when she was a few feet away. She stopped as Mei shifted in her sleep and then settled back down.

Evren knelt, so she was eye level with the wyvern.

"Hello Saros," she whispered.

He cocked his head, knowing his given name already but confused why Evren knew it when the only two that should were him and Mei.

"I'm a friend of Mei's," she nodded to the girl. "She's going to love you with her whole heart, you know."

He chirped as if he did.

"I know this is a long shot," she said. "But one day, many years from now, I'm going to need your help. I know Mei is your priority, but her survival will depend on it. When you see me like this again, you'll know."

He sneezed, and Evren took that as a confirmation. The first hours of a hatchling's life were the most important. Imprints, trusts, and even orders could be given then and the wyvern would unconsciously follow them. It felt a little like cheating, but if it helped, she couldn't complain.

Baby Saros blinked at her and settled his head on Mei's shoulder. If the instructions stuck, Evren didn't know. Maybe this would keep Mei from being crippled by the Hisrachi and she wouldn't have to marry Barrion. Maybe nothing at Sterra's Tears had to happen at all. She could only hope as she smiled fondly at the wyvern.

"See you in a bit," she whispered, and then stepped back into the tapestry. The nest faded, as well as the young wyvern and rider, but Evren kept a hold of Saros's thread. She could already see some things had changed. Different knots in different places. The same sense of fierce loyalty, but also the underlying hint of anticipation. The constant question:

Where is she?

Evren found the perfect time farther down the end of the thread and tugged again. This time, when she landed in Orenlion, she felt how the passage of time changed the air. It was a little cooler with the night. She was standing on the edge of the Roost close to where she, Aster, and Barrion had talked before.

A rumbling growl sounded behind her, and she turned to see Saros fully grown and battle hardened, his bronze scales no longer the muddy brown they'd been as a hatchling. He lowered his head down to face her.

She grinned. "Happy to see me?"

His adult sneeze was nowhere near as cute as his baby one, and Evren shook off some of the wyvern snot.

"All right, we don't have a lot of time, so let's find us a Weaver."

Saros bared his teeth, and Evren shook her head. "Not to eat. To talk. It'll make sense later. May I?"

She gestured to his saddle. Mei had left in a hurry if she hadn't taken it off. She was still rushing towards the party then, and they didn't have a lot of time.

To Evren's complete surprise, Saros lowered his wing so she could climb on. She hesitated for a moment because it felt so wrong to take over Mei's saddle. No one else was supposed to ride Saros, but this brief betrayal could save her life.

Evren tucked the Keeper's dagger in her belt and climbed onto Saros's saddle. It was slow and awkward at first. She'd only trained on dummy wyverns before while she'd waited for a clutch of eggs, and climbing onto a living, breathing wyvern differed greatly from the wooden ones. But Saros was patient, and soon she'd settled into the worn saddle and grabbed the reins.

"I've never flown before, so please don't—"

Saros took off into the sky and it was all Evren could do to keep from screaming. She hung onto the saddle until her fingers felt like they were bleeding. Her thighs were locked so tight they ached up her spine and to her neck. Saros's whole body moved fluidly as he climbed into the air, and every rocking motion of his wings made Evren feel like she was going to fall off.

But once the fear fell away . . . she was flying!

Evren let out a strangled laugh that got drowned out by the wind rushing past her. Saros dipped underneath massive limbs and sailed smoothly around the monolithic trees. The air tasted of freedom, as wild and untamed as the wyvern who let her ride him. Every passing leaf, every star, was magical to her. The heat of Saros's powerful body under her legs, the cool, sweet breeze against her face. This was the life she almost had.

Evren took up the reins, flexing the leather in her fingers. Freedom was nice, but she had a spider to find.

Evren urged Saros to fly lower, completely under the canopy of the trees. The darkness wasn't quite so thick when she had an unrivaled view from above. They circled Orenlion once, and then twice, and then Evren saw him.

"Land there." Evren guided Saros to the tree she wanted. He did as she asked, and the frills along his neck stood up as he caught the scent of Hisrachi. Saros slammed into the tree and slid down a few feet with his claws digging into the bark. He hissed at the writhing mass of Hisrachi below, and they all hissed back. For a moment, Evren could see it all going wrong. The Hisrachi swarming her and Saros, Anep not listening and the whole city burning anyway.

She pulled out the dagger. "Anep! I have what you want."

The Hisrachi army froze, and then parted as a familiar black and yellow spider made his way to the base of the tree. He clicked his pinchers at her with open hostility.

"Firsst a traitor, then a thief! How?"

"It's a long story. I'll tell you in a few days."

He spat and started climbing the tree. Saros scrambled around so fast Evren nearly fell off his back, and she barely kept him from biting Anep's head off.

She kept the reins taunt, and with gritted teeth, talked quickly. "The attack on Orenlion is a mistake. Neri misunderstood what happened. The elf she overheard was trying to do many things, and convincing Barrion to give up the nest was one. But he didn't. He never went back on his word, and if you attack the city now then you'll doom him to side with Orenlion."

"Liesss!" he snapped. *"You want war. You hate usss."*

"I did. But I'm not the same person you met in the nest. The person that's in the city right now is a cold, heartless bitch who's drowning in her own blood."

"And what are you?"

"Everything she should've been. I'm sorry, okay? But we are both being manipulated to find this." She flashed the dagger again. "Whoever you're seeing, whoever is driving you towards this, doesn't care about you. She's pitting you and I and Orenlion against each other so she can take advantage of the chaos."

"Shelis wouldn't lie! She's saving us."

"It's not her! She wouldn't want this. In life—"

"She tried for peace and died for it. I will lay her spirit to rest with the war she now wants."

"Think for once!" Evren yelled. Below, the Hisrachi were getting nervous. She couldn't tell if what she was saying was working. "Shelis never wanted more blood spilled. She trusted Barrion, the same way she trusted my father."

"A missstake."

"Another Archdruid at your side is a mistake?" Evren asked and watched him balk. "Yes, I know. That's how I know you're seeing visions of someone you trust pushing you towards an object of power that's supposed to save your people. I saw it, one of the Sovereigns saw it, and now you. The woman behind this doesn't care about you. She's using your grief to use you. This dagger controls time, and I've seen what you've done to get to it. You sacrifice your own people, you destroy yourself, and you're losing."

The chittering of mandibles down below was overwhelming. Anep stared at her, unreadable.

"If I wanted you dead, I could do it without all of this,

believe me," Evren said. "All I need you to do is doubt, question, and stay away from the city."

A pause, and then, *"They'll hunt usss sstill. We have nowhere to go."*

"So, give them a reason to trust you. Instead of being the monsters they expect, be the heroes they need."

He tsked. *"Eassy for you to sssay."*

"It's not. But, just this once, believe me when I say that I don't want to be your enemy anymore. Maybe it's too late for you and I, but there's got to be a future for people like us where there's peace instead of hate."

"I hate you," Anep snarled. *"Everything you are, everything you ssstand for."*

Evren waited. "Please tell me there's a 'but' somewhere after this awkward pause."

"Give me a reassson to trust you, butcher."

Beneath her, Saros was quivering with rage and anticipation. Decades of carefully bred loathing was leashed by nothing but a firm grip on his reins. And Evren realized in that moment, watching the wyvern stare down the army of Hisrachi, that she would never be able to fix it all. She couldn't erase the bloodshed, the trauma, and the generations of torment on both sides. Even if this somehow worked perfectly, there would always be contempt.

There was no perfect happily ever after. At least, not one that she or Anep or Saros would ever see.

"I want the next eggs that hatch for your kind to breathe free air. I want them to grow up without fear of impending doom and war. You and I never stood a chance, you know. We were both raised to hate and kill. We both spent nights awake, shaking in fear and waiting for a nightmare to descend on us. I realize that I'm that monster for you, and I'll likely always be. But the ones that come after us don't need to live the same life."

Evren held her hand out, the dagger resting on her palm, to Anep.

"You want that future as much as I do," she said. "There are other ways to get it."

She couldn't read Anep. She couldn't fathom what was going on inside his mind. But she and every Hisrachi below held their breath in anticipation. Saros quivered in the night air; his eyes fixed on the dagger, too. The pure energy that radiated from it seemed to draw the attention of the whole forest, and it all waited on the whims of one spider.

Anep took careful steps forward, his legs reaching out for the dagger. *"I plan on dessstroying your people and you give me thissss freely?"*

Evren held still. "It's called faith, Anep. I don't believe in gods, but I believe that you'll do what's right, regardless of your personal feelings." She looked him square in the eyes as the gap between them closed to mere inches. "Because that's what Shelis would truly want, and you know it."

Saros didn't snap. Anep didn't attack. For a brief, shining moment, Evren was right.

And then the Deep Wood shuddered. Earth, roots, leaves and limbs, like the ground was heaving and spitting open. Anep and Saros jumped apart, both still clinging to the tree. It was all Evren could do to not lose her hold on the dagger as her blood ran cold.

The shaking stopped as a thunderous roar, ages old and holding the combined rage of mountains and firestorms, erupted in the air. The memory of a different time, where a mountain was burning and deafening thrum of powerful wings battered her hot skin. This was a different time, a different dragon, but the fear was the same.

And this time Evren couldn't run away.

"That's not possible," she whispered to herself. Saros let out a keening sound that only baby wyverns used to let their mother know they were scared. On the forest floor, the Hisrachi were scattering.

Evren met Anep's eyes again. "You have to go."

He stood firm, but the hairs on his legs were standing on end and he was shaking. *"Trickery! Thisss wasss your plan!"*

"Do I look like this was my bloody plan?" she asked.

The roar subsided, but the air held a rhythmic beat like a heart. Wings in the air, large enough to echo through the whole forest.

"Get your people out, Anep," she said. "It's the only chance we've got."

Evren gripped the dagger. She could get out now, she knew. She could escape this impossible horror, yank her friends out of the maze, and try to fix this new problem.

The wind tore through the trees now. Leaves flew in cyclones, twigs and small branches cut through the howling air.

Evren held the dagger out to Anep and let go.

Her chance to get her friends out slipped from her fingers. Her hope of getting back to the same night where Gyda looked at her like she was starlight taken form was gone. She wanted to break, to grasp for the dagger again. But what was faith if not blind trust in the unknown?

Anep took the dagger in his legs and vanished.

Steeling herself, Evren picked up Saros's reins. She could feel the fear shaking in his bones like her own. She'd survived one dragon by mere chance in the Eternity Keeper's maze. If the Storm of the Wood was somehow alive in this time, how did she have any hope of surviving her?

Evren didn't give herself time to doubt. She urged Saros off the tree and, without hesitation, he took off into the air.

If flying through the night air had been freedom, flying through the windstorm of an approaching dragon was like courting death. The wind buffeted them from all sides. The branches snagged on Saros's wings, and he shuddered with every tugging undercurrent of air trying to pull him to the ground. Evren lowered herself as close to his body as possible and held on for dear life.

As Evren steered him towards Orenlion, glowing like a

beacon in the hurricane, a shadow fell over them. She dared to look up.

Eclipsing the moon was a monolith of bones, sinew, and scaley flesh. Evren had just enough time to see the points of the dragon's vertebrae, the empty eye sockets glowing red in her skull, and the spiney wings glowing red where there wasn't any leather for reality to set in.

And then the Storm dove for Orenlion.

Saros let out a battle cry, all his fear gone. He folded his wings tight against his body and flew after the skeletal dragon.

But she was bigger and faster, even in undeath. Evren watched in horror as she landed on the city and crushed bridges and houses under her claws. The wind was screaming in Evren's ears, but she could hear the cries of the dying. The dragon's tail, almost as long as the city itself, whipped through the air and destroyed a wide swath of buildings. Their lights flickered and died, their walls fell on the bone and then to the ground. The bodies of the elves inside were so small she could barely make them out.

The Storm of the Wood, undead and brimming with wrath, stood in the middle of The Moving City like a cat who'd pinned down a bird, and roared.

A trembling rage overtook Evren. Her friends were down there. *She* was down there. Everything she'd bent time to save was turning to rubble under the dragon's claws.

Evren's battle cry joined the dragon's, and then Saros joined in. And they aimed right for the Storm's face.

Saros slammed into the Storm's skull with so much ferocity and speed that the impact nearly threw Evren off. He scratched his claws into the thick bone skull, trying to catch the eyeballs and finding nothing but glowing red light. He screeched in frustration, switching to the other one and spitting a wad of clinging acidic fire. The bone melted and shriveled under it, but the dent was minimal when compared to the sheer size of the dragon.

Evren tugged the reigns and jerked the wyvern to the side as one of the dragon's claws came up and nearly cut Saros in half. Another wad of burning acid cut through the air and melted some of her foreleg bone, but not enough.

A live dragon would have flesh, a beating heart, an eyeball to gouge out. How does one kill ancient bone?

Evren spent every ounce of her energy keeping Saros from being ripped apart as he tried to tear at the dragon. Her arrows were useless and clattered off the bone with every blow. Below them, Orenlion was dying. Even with the dragon's attention on them, with every turn of her head and movement of her body, more buildings turned to rubble.

Evren yanked on the reins again as the dragon tried to claw them off. Saros dodged nimbly and landed at the top of the dragon's skull. But before his claws could sink into the bone and tether him, she suddenly threw her head down and they were careening towards the forest floor.

Saros tumbled through the air, his wings not catching the wind as he flipped upside down. Fear crawled up Evren's throat as she slid out of the saddle. She griped the reins with numb fingers as her legs flew out from the stirrups. Through the haze of fear and rubble, she could see a fast-approaching bridge coming to meet them. A quick death.

Saros spun in the air wildly. Evren closed her eyes.

Then she heard the snapping of wings catching air. Her body slammed into Saros's warm scales once, and then again as they crashed into the bridge seconds later.

They rolled through their impact, bones aching, skin and scales smarting, until Saros stopped. Evren let go of the reigns and fell a few feet away from him, groaning.

The stone on her skin was blissfully cool. Through her hazy memory, she could pick out a moment like this. The Roost burning, Mei dying with Saros curled around her body, Evren choking on her own bloody spell against an army of furious Hisrachi.

The same night. Different destruction. And somehow, the same pain.

Evren pushed herself onto her back. The starry sky was bright and cold, as if the stars watching had no care for the people that prayed to them were dying. Then she saw shadows blot out the stars, the same way the Storm had blotted out the moon. One wyvern, then five, then dozens. All flying from the Roost towards the dragon, the same way Saros had tried to.

Evren gritted her teeth and pushed herself onto her feet. Beside her, Saros was watching the skies and getting ready to fly again. Too close for comfort, the dragon loomed over the city and dragged it down to its death with every beat of her wings and rake of her claws. The wyverns bounced off her bones uselessly. Arrows and spears were thrown like flashes of light in the night air, never to be seen again. Evren watched as the Storm took down three wyverns with one swipe of her claws. The spray of crimson blood in the air showed the surety of death.

Saros lowered his wing to her expectantly, but Evren hesitated.

"No," she shook her head. "Go get Mei."

Saros hissed in annoyance.

"She's your rider, not me." Evren pointed to the city. "Go!"

The wyvern looked at her with a strange expression in his eyes before opening his wings and taking off into the sky. Evren watched him skim the air around the dragon, dipping under battles and fellow fighters as he tried to reach Xun Manor. She prayed it was still standing.

"You're a lot stupider than I remember," a voice said from behind her. "And to think I almost admired your strength back in the White Cairn."

Evren turned and pulled an arrow from her quiver as she faced Nerezza.

The mage was much changed from how she'd left her in the glacier. Her alabaster skin glowed white in the moonlight, like the bones of the dragon. Her white hair was neatly braided back from her angular face, so no hair could shield Evren from her black gaze. Without the bulky furs Evren was used to seeing her wearing in the Reino Terminan, she was struck by how spindly she was. Nerezza had always been tall, but now she looked closer to a skeleton in her strange, ash-grey robes. One sleeve was gone, leaving her arm open and bare to the night air. The other was long and covered her missing hand.

"You've come a long way from walls of fire," Evren said, jerking her head back to the dragon.

"I've come to find there are no limits to power, so long as you ignore rules."

"And morality." Evren narrowed her eyes. "You got into my head."

"You made it easy."

"You pretended to be Viggo!"

Nerezza shrugged. "I have no idea who that is. Your mind made me who you'd listen to, and it was easy to answer your questions of the past vaguely enough that you'd believe me. You know, for a moment, I thought you actually saw me."

Nerezza's fingers curled in the air and wisps of red smoke like the dragon's eyes swirled in her fingers. It was laced with pitch-black shadows, eerily like Ainthe's. Evren brought her bow up, the string taunt as her jaw.

The mage tsked at the sight. "I should've known better than to rely on your so-called heartless nature to bring me the dagger. The boy wasn't nearly as useful as he claimed."

"That boy is named Gail," Evren gritted out.

"Not anymore."

Evren pushed aside the memories of the young Vasa crying out for her. "Call off your pet. Orenlion has done nothing to you."

"Except disappoint me," Nerezza snarled. "Wasanthi was less than useless. And no one else was foolish enough to tame. Besides, I thought you'd thank me."

"Nerezza, enough!" she cried over the screams of dying

wyverns and riders, of crumbling supports and burning buildings. "This isn't you. You're a hero, you've saved cities. You don't destroy them to get what you want."

"Do you even know what I want?" Nerezza asked, and the red magic at her fingers grew brighter. "Does your tiny mind have any inkling of what I'm doing beyond destruction?"

"You want the dagger to get more powerful. The soul of a god would—"

"Predictable," she spat. "As usual."

"Then what do you want with the dagger?"

Nerezza cocked her head to the side, her eyes flashing to the dragon and the burning city. A slow smile crept up her lips, and she looked back at Evren with a gleam in her eyes that made her shiver.

"I am potential made flesh, Evren. I want everything."

The only part of Nerezza's body that moved was the tips of her fingers. Suddenly, a wave of hot red light and pitch darkness was racing towards Evren. She shot her arrow wildly, knowing it would miss, and tried to dodge.

But the magic was faster and enveloped her. It was quiet, and that was the thing that struck her as the most odd. All magic she'd seen was primal and loud, like the crackling of fire or the rush of wind. This was silent.

And excruciating.

Evren felt like her blood was on fire. A wildfire tore through her body, scorching her bones and turning her marrow to ash. She felt her lungs blacken, and her teeth ached from the inside out. But her heart, Gyda's heart, remained cold and untouched.

She didn't remember getting an arrow out. Her muscles were so seized with pain she couldn't imagine moving them. But there was an arrow in her hand, and a gleaming arrowhead in the sea of red light. Before she even realized what she was doing, she dug the arrow into the soft flesh of her forearm and watched the boiling blood well up.

The blood coated the arrow. And, like a vacuous mouth, it

sucked all the red magic into it. The shadows snapped back. As fast as lightning, the pain was gone, and her arrow was burning with the same red light.

Nerezza stared at her with wide eyes, somewhere between impressed and terrified.

Evren was shaking. She gave herself one breath to ground her body, then fired the arrow at Nerezza.

The mage jumped back faster than should be possible. She was just a blur of grey and white until she came back into focus, the arrow landing mere inches from her foot. A wave of red fire leapt from the ground where the arrow landed, flaming fingers grasping for Nerezza even as she shrank back.

She lifted her hand, fingers curling harshly as she tried to call the magic back to her control. Her hand went stiff and fingers spasmed as an arrow punched clean through her. She clutched her bleeding hand to her chest, seething at Evren.

"Stupid idea, making a blood mage bleed," Nerezza hissed, and the flames in front of her calmed without so much as a twitch of her finger. The red shone in her eyes, and Evren was suddenly reminded of all the horrifying depictions of the devils waiting in the hells to steal souls.

"Probably," Evren said. "But it felt good."

She shot another arrow, this time at Nerezza's shoulder. The mage twitched out of the way, the arrow not even grazing her, and turned back with a sneer to see Evren launching herself towards her.

Nerezza didn't have time to react. Evren slammed the lower limb of her bow into her face and landed on her feet while the mage staggered to her knees. Without hesitation, Evren took her bow against Nerezza's frail throat.

And pulled.

She could feel Nerezza choking under the wood of her bow. Her long fingernails gouged welts in Evren's hands and arms. She bucked to try and get her off. With every futile gasp, she grew weaker. A burning flash of red magic and daggered shadows erupted from her, but Evren endured the pain. She didn't let go, even as she bit her tongue and screamed. Every pained choke sent Nerezza farther to her knees. It was almost over. All Evren had to do was hold on a few seconds longer.

Something like a sob fell from Nerezza's lips, and it brutally reminded Evren of how she made a similar sound when Vox died to keep her alive. She remembered the panic in her eyes as Evren and Vox brought her back in from the blizzard. The way she'd clung to Sahar after the battle of Direwall, as if she was the only thing left in the world worth living for.

And Sahar's voice when she'd left the Wandering Sols came back to her.

"I know her. She's brilliant and sharp, but she's not mad. She's my friend, and she's lost. If you see her before I do, don't hurt her. Just bring her back to me, I beg of you."

Before Evren even realized it, she was relaxing her grip. The pressure of her bow against Nerezza's throat slackened, and the mage gasped for air. Her magic fizzled away.

"I'm sorry," Evren stuttered. "I can get you to Sahar. We don't need—"

"Don't you fucking say her name like you know her!" Nerezza snapped, voice hoarse and broken.

Nerezza snatched the bow from Evren's numb fingers and tossed it aside. Evren couldn't even cry out as she watched it fall off the side of the bridge, because Nerezza was on her feet and out for blood.

Another wild wave of red magic nearly swarmed Evren, but she was close enough to dodge out of the path. It flickered and died until Nerezza summoned it again in her grasp. Her eyes were murderous, and her throat red.

Evren pulled out the wyvern dagger, still stained with the blood of a long-dead man, and faced off against her.

"There's got to be a joke about going against a mage with nothing but a dagger," she told herself, and then charged.

The fight was like dance. Evren and Nerezza weaved and

bobbed away from each other's blows, then twirled around to gain the upper hand. Magic the color of blood flashed in the night air, close enough to send Evren's skin prickling with needlelike pain all over. She swept her dagger in a low arc, barely skimming Nerezza's ankles before she was spinning away, and Evren matched her. Again and again, blow after barely dodged blow. Nerezza's magic honed to a fine, gleaming edge to kill, and Evren's dagger shaking with every near miss. She nearly caught Nerezza's red throat again and pulled back as if she could see Drystan's furious face staring through Nerezza's eyes.

Evren stumbled and bent backwards as a scythe of magic skimmed just over her nose where her head would've been. Her back ached when she stood up again.

She couldn't kill Nerezza, not without being forever haunted by Drystan, Vox, and Sahar. But her city was dying, and she'd die soon if she didn't do something.

She was out of choices, and she was running out of time.

Nerezza's next bolt of magic hit Evren square in the chest and knocked her on her back. It was quick and gone in a matter of seconds, but still left her body stiff and shaking, with tears streaming down her face.

Nerezza loomed over her, breathing hard. "I really wish you could understand, but you've stumbled into this plot, Evren. You're not the hero of this story, and I am not the villain. You and I are merely pawns in a greater game, set on opposite sides of the board. Our game has been lovely, but that's all it is, a game. The real work begins when the final pawn is taken off the board."

"Stop monologuing and get it over with," Evren hissed.

Nerezza raised her remaining hand, and all the red magic littered around the bridge gathered in her palm until her entire arm was covered in the writhing, glowing mass. It loosely resembled a sharp-edged gauntlet.

The light on the bridge dimmed. The death of Orenlion seemed far away now. All that ever mattered was her and

Nerezza. On a bridge, bleeding and dying, on the same night as before, Evren Hanali was going to die.

And she smiled.

Nerezza quirked an eyebrow down at her. "What are you so happy about?"

The air changed. Cooler, lighter, filled with the smell of sap and sunlight.

"Death by your hands is a lovely way to go," Evren said. "But that's not my fate."

All eight of Anep's legs wrapped around Nerezza's form. Her magic faded as her arms were pinned to her side. She screamed and writhed, somehow dodging every attempt Anep threw at her to tear out her throat.

"Don't kill her!" Evren cried.

Anep froze only for a moment, but that was more than enough. A wave of red magic poured out of her and Anep fell to the ground, spasming. Evren pulled her legs back, but the wave dissipated before it could reach her. Nerezza whirled around to face her again, furious.

"I see you can't even keep proper enemies," she said. "No matter, I can kill him, too."

She snapped her fingers, and a pulse of red light went to the dragon. She was still on her rampage, but her undead eyes fixed on Nerezza. And then she started lumbering towards them. It would take maybe five whole steps for her to reach the bridge. Every step crushed and splintered the city under her massive weight. Out of the dozens she saw attack, only a handful of wyverns remained.

Saros was not one of them.

Evren's heart lurched, but she couldn't focus on whether he and Mei lived through this night.

The dragon was looming over them now. Her foot pressed on the foot of the bridge, and Evren watched with sinking horror as a jagged crack spawned from her weight. The bridge was shuddering with every ounce of pressure.

Movement from Anep caught Evren's eye. He was uncurling his legs, shaking. He looked at her and if Hisrachi could grin; she swore he did. Then he flicked a leg out and something bright skimmed across the cracking bridge to her.

The Keeper's dagger.

Nerezza's eyes widened as she saw it too. She dove for it, just as Evren lunged from her spot towards it and the dragon snapped her jaws at all of them.

The bridge crumbled under Evren just as she grabbed the dagger. Before she fell into oblivion, she felt Nerezza's hand around hers, just a second from getting the dagger herself, and a mass of bones crushing them both.

28

The first fall through time had been a leisurely event that tried to show her the vast, unending tapestry of every life on Eith. Her mind couldn't comprehend it then, and now that her fall was that of a burning, falling star, she barely saw anything but the blur of brightly colored threads.

She was aware of Nerezza grasping for control of the dagger. She was aware of the dragon that had been pulled into the tapestry with them. But Evren shut them out. She tucked the dagger safely to her chest and plummeted.

She knew exactly what to do. The threads Anep had left her were as clear as day. She pulled gently on each one, tangling them in tight knots at the right spot. Five, each with their own part to play. The same timeline she'd created, but now not so alone. Five to her one to make six.

To bring them home.

Evren willed the dagger to go far away. She poured trust and faith through her fingers into the warm hilt. Then she let go and fell into the new present.

~

EVREN AND NEREZZA slammed into the forest floor just as a new day was breaking. They tumbled head over heels until their tangle of limbs were unlocked and Evren rolled to a stop at the base of a tree, blissfully alone. She wheezed for air, her lungs still coated with the ashes of Orenlion, and clutched the dagger close to her chest. She was barely sitting up by the time Nerezza was on her feet with her hand on her throat.

"What have you done?" The mage shook with fury, her thin fingers digging into Evren's neck. Evren didn't even fight her, she just let the pressure in her throat build.

With a frustrated growl, Nerezza slammed her back to the ground with surprising force. Her eyes went to Evren's chest and what she was hiding.

"Finally."

She pried Evren's fingers apart and snatched the dagger away. She held it up in the sunlight, triumphant, until her face fell. The dagger in her hands was exquisite, but made of burnished silver and bloody steel. The wyvern wrapped around the hilt almost seemed to mock her.

Evren started laughing.

Nerezza turned to her. "Where is it? What did you do?"

"I let go."

The mage backed away in horror. She turned, finally noticing that her dragon was missing as well. She clutched the wyvern blade with shaking fury and her voice was shrill when she shrieked again.

"*What did you do?* Where is the dagger? Where is the dragon?"

Evren looked at where they landed. How the sunlight was muddled by the thick coating of ash on the ground, and the burnt glimmer of armor littered the trees around them. She looked up and could see the smoldering remains of Orenlion in the distance. The destruction was that of the Storm, not Anep's attack. Still standing, but an army of dead at its feet.

Evren and Nerezza were among them.

"It's over Nerezza," Evren said. "Just stop."

"No."

"What's the point of all of this? You destroyed Orenlion, reignited a thousand-year-old war, and woke up a long-dead dragon all for a piece of time?"

"You wouldn't understand."

"Then make me!" Evren snapped.

Nerezza shook her head, still staring at the wyvern blade. "I was born with a purpose greater than this body. I was meant to bring light to the darkness, and I was snatched away before I could. And now I can't even return home. Not yet. Not until I make things right."

"Make what right, Nerezza? Tell me. Maybe I can help."

"You, help?" She snorted. "You'd sooner watch Serevadia burn. No, I have a plan that will bring my people from the dark and to the land they deserve. I will bring back the god they'll listen to, or," she shrugged nonchalantly, "I'll become a god they'll follow."

Evren's blood went cold, and she longed for her bow. "You plan on bring Serevadia to the surface."

"An army that Eith is unequipped to deal with."

"It doesn't have to be an army! We can do this peacefully."

"And where would Etherak let us live?" Nerezza asked coldly. "How about Terevas? Gratey? Vernes? Melkarth? Would any of them share their lands with a nation of people larger than they can fathom?"

No. The answer was easy. Most kingdoms couldn't bear to part with land to deal with friendly allies, let alone a lost race of elves from underground. She knew how they'd all react. War, death, destruction.

Everything she'd seen in the maze.

"This isn't the way, Nerezza," she begged.

The mage shook her head and took a step back. Evren suddenly realized that the corpses of elves and wyverns weren't on the ground anymore. They were all standing up and staring at Evren with red, burning eyes.

"This isn't the way your people survive, Evren," Nerezza said, and when Evren met her eyes again they were red again. "But it is the way for my people. We will not cower in the dark any longer while surfacers destroy the land they've taken. Eith will be better this way. It is almost a pity you won't see it."

Another voice came before Evren could argue further. This one was deeper, drizzled with a soft accent that made Evren's heart leap.

"I'd warn against making threats you cannot keep," Gyda said as she walked out of the trees.

She was a vision of death, covered in ash and blood. Her eyes were bright, though, and she spared Evren a soft smile before turning back to Nerezza.

"You and I haven't talked in a while," the warrior went on. "I'm disappointed in you."

Nerezza sneered at her. "Don't lecture me. You're the reason half my team is dead."

"I'd hate to tell Sahar I had to take another fourth out of the Ashen Bond."

"You couldn't even if you tried."

Gyda shrugged. "You're right. But I know who can."

The Deep Wood shook again, the trees trembling as if the skies themselves were coming down. A windstorm swirled the leaves at Evren's feet, and she looked up at Gyda with both fear and amazement as the roar of the Storm of the Wood shattered the air.

Nerezza's corpses closed ranks around her. "How?"

Gyda's fingers flicked into the air, and between them was the Keeper's dagger. "Trust transcends time."

Three things happened at once.

One.

The dragon passed overhead, living and as bright green as the leaves themselves. And seething with a rage that only came to something as powerful and intelligent and as dangerous as herself. Nerezza's reanimated skeleton was terrifying, but the living breathing Storm, snatched from her time, was something that shook Evren to her core. Seeing her wingspan blotting out the sunlight, seeing her chest glow brightly with the fire she was about to unleash and the muscles underneath her scales, was breathtaking.

Until she opened her jaw and spilled fire beneath her.

Dragonfire, as Evren learned first-hand, was not as light and fluid as normal fire. It was thick, heavy, and stuck to everything. No matter what it burned, the smoke was black as night. It was made to both destroy and incapacitate, and watching it eat away at the trees she called home was a warning.

Two.

Nerezza raised her hand, and the undead surged towards Gyda, broken jaws snapping and teeth bared. Evren, weaponless and daggerless, was all but forgotten. They clamored over each other with twisted limbs and still-oozing flesh to get to the warrior.

Gyda was unfazed. She swung her sword out swiftly and tossed the Keeper's dagger in the air. Evren, Nerezza, and the undead watched it careen in the air. It flipped, blade over hilt, then hilt over blade, into the open air quickly turning into an inferno.

Three.

And was snatched up by Sorin's nimble fingers.

The Vasa laughed as he flipped it over in his palm, letting the blade catch the light of the fire. "What? Didn't expect that, Nezza?"

She didn't answer, but the corpses did. They tried to break off and run around Gyda, but the large arc of her sword cut most of them off. The runes hummed in the air with specks of frost glittering along the blade. Evren watched the blade turn a ghostly green and tear through a wyvern's scales as if they weren't there at all. Her sword easily pierced the heart, and the wave of green from the rune overwhelmed the red. The wyvern writhed as if it was burning alive, but quickly calmed and threw itself at the nearest undead.

Still dead, still reanimated, but under Gyda's control. Gail's gift to pull souls hadn't been so ignored.

Gyda and her wyvern couldn't keep back all the undead swarming to get to Sorin. There were just too many and they slipped through the cracks.

Sorin tucked the dagger in his sleeve and pulled out his sword, and with a smile reminiscent of the Yawning Deep, he held his ground.

Evren had nothing. No bow, no dagger, no spellbook. She found herself back-to-back with Gyda, ducking under every swing of her sword, dodging undead claws and spears, flowing with the warrior's movements as if they were one body. Her heartbeat was ridiculously calm, even as sweat mingled with the smoke staining the air. She kept Gyda from being blindsided by calling out numbers of enemies and kicking those away that got too close.

If her world hadn't been on fire, Evren would've found herself smiling.

"You really do enjoy this," she panted, and pressed her back against Gyda's.

She felt the warrior laugh. "Now you can feel it."

And she did. She felt every blazing drop of adrenaline, every swing of her blade as if it was a song she'd finally understood the lyrics to.

But it wasn't enough.

Evren could see the forest catching fire, and quickly. The monolithic trees went up like the driest of tinder, and the blue sky was quickly turning black with smoke. The undead weren't thinning out, and she realized with growing horror that Nerezza was pulling the dead from the old tombs of the city as Gyda was destroying the new undead. Even Hisrachi corpses had joined the fray, their legs gangly and awkward as they skittered through the scorching battlefield. Sorin was pressed against the tree, a pile of bodies at his feet and his blade soaked with congealed blood.

Where was everyone else?

"Gyda, where—"

"They're coming." A massive swing of her sword shook the earth.

Evren was shaking. From fear? Uselessness? Overwhelming odds?

"It's just you and Sorin?" she cried and broke away quick enough to elbow an undead away. It tottered back and was cleaved in half by Gyda seconds later.

Evren felt her frustration rising as the dragon wheeled overhead, her fire dangerously close to an already ruined Orenlion. She snapped around to face Gyda.

"Why the hells did you bring the dragon back?" Evren demanded. Gyda didn't look at her, her concentration on the fight. Her sword cut inches from Evren's arm as she took down a charging corpse.

"Part of the plan," the warrior grunted.

"What bloody plan? The forest is burning! Nerezza is going to overwhelm us. We can't survive both her and the dragon!"

"We don't have to." Gyda skewered two undead along her sword and flung them at her dead wyvern. She finally faced Evren, chest heaving, and eyes lit up with anticipation and hope. "We just have to keep the dagger from her a little longer."

It came to Evren as suddenly as the dawn. "The Archdruids. You're trying to drag them into this."

Gyda shrugged. "They won't mess with mortal affairs unless the Wood is in danger." She pointed her blade to the dragon. "I made it their problem again."

Evren could see this disastrous plan. It felt like something she might've done before.

"But Sorin—"

"He's fine."

Evren didn't think he looked fine, backed up against a tree and facing wave after wave of undead. She thought he was crying, until she realized with a sudden jolt he was laughing.

Nerezza's rage could be felt through every body. With a vicious intensity she sent them all after Sorin. Even the ones still fighting Gyda and her wyvern broke away to deal with the human, who was nearly doubled over he was laughing so hard. Somehow his blade still found it's place and he dodged every blow thrown his way.

It was wrong. Sorin was exposed and vulnerable.

Evren turned back to Nerezza.

So was she.

The fire around Nerezza began to curl inward as if the air was sucking the flames together. If the mage noticed, she didn't care. All her focus was on Sorin. The fire left the trees blackened and smoldering, balling into a hovering sphere in the air behind her. Growing with every passing second. Heat and flame and light intensifying until Nerezza paused and started to turn.

The sphere exploded in a beam right towards her. White-hot flame suddenly engulfed her body and didn't let up. For a full minute it was nothing but fire, bright enough that Evren had to look away. Her skin was hot and tight from being too close. She heard undead screaming as the fire caught them as well.

And then it died down as suddenly as it arrived.

Evren looked up and her heart dropped.

The forest was black and grey where Nerezza stood, unscathed. She flicked her glowing shield away, her spine stiff as she turned her back on Sorin . . .

And faced Arke.

The goblin was hovering in the air where the sphere had been, his spellbook open and his teeth bared in a savage grin. A silent agreement went from mage to mage, and their magic suddenly burst into the air.

It made Evren's fight with Nerezza look like child's play. The careening of magic through the air, the smell of the elements fusing together and rioting against each other, the flare of reds and oranges and pure bright blues, it all dazzled like a deadly light show. And the mages themselves barely moved. Nerezza's fingers curled and spasmed. Arke's claws tore at pages. But their eyes remained unblinkingly fixed on each other and their bodies still.

Evren had never seen a duel between two mages. She couldn't tell who was winning and she didn't have the luxury of watching.

The sky turned blacker as a winged shape descended on Evren. For one panicked moment she thought the Storm had come for her. But the shadow was smaller. It flew through the smoke with a familiar twist of wings and tail and landed nimbly in front of her.

Saros.

She nearly wept in relief at the sight of the old wyvern. He looked a little worse for wear, but otherwise strong and ready to fight. He lowered his wing for her, the saddle empty and beckoning.

"We need you in the air," Gyda said.

Evren didn't need to be told twice. She leapt up on Saros's back, one leg easily slipping into the stirrup and the other falling right through. She frowned, looking down and seeing the leather was mangled and torn on the left side. The stirrup was practically gone and utterly useless.

Her heart sank as she imagined Mei's mangled leg. New timeline or not, the Khama wasn't in flying shape. Evren hoped that she was just crippled instead of dead. Saros whined lowly too, as if sensing her grief. But she pushed it aside and picked up his reins and took off into the skies.

It was nothing more than smoke and ash for a while. The higher Saros climbed, the more Evren struggled to breathe. Every beat of his wings burned her lungs and stung her eyes. She forced them open, her nails digging into the leather of the reins.

And then they broke through.

The smoke cleared, the canopy of the Wood was below them. The Deep Wood stretched like a blanket of green as far as Evren could see, climbing into the white mountains to the north and dipping into the hills of the west.

And it was nearly all burning.

From the ground the horror was manageable, easy to digest. But the sheer scope of the devouring destruction was enough to suck the breath out of her lungs. The green was being eaten away by burning gold and orange, barely seen through the pitch-black clouds of billowing smoke. Far above them, the Storm flew, raining her destruction that she promised centuries ago.

Evren wanted to fly after her. Maybe she and Saros could keep her from doing any more damage. But even as she started to urge Saros that way, she stopped herself. She and Saros had been a gnat to the dead version of the Storm, they had no chance against the living version of her alone. It would take an army to bring her down, or beings of the Wood themselves.

Reluctantly, Evren tore away from the Storm. She wasn't her problem.

"Fly home, Saros."

He needed no further prompting. With a large gulp of fresh air, he dove back into the smoke and straight to Orenlion. The trees and limbs glowing with hellish fire were easy to see in the haze of smoke, and Saros avoided running into them. But when the fire faded and left nothing but smoke, Evren's heart seized with worry. Could Saros see? Did he know where he was going?

A wall of white loomed from the smoke mere feet from them. Evren jerked the reins just in time and Saros flew up, avoiding the wall by mere inches.

When they leveled out, Orenlion waited for them, a citadel of ash and skeletons. The reflections of fire winked back at her a hundred times over and she squinted until she saw a hundred spears, swords, and bows. An army waiting at the base of Orenlion.

As Saros circled the city, five more wyverns trailed behind

him. Evren turned in the saddle, catching the eyes of the remaining Khama. Only five of the original fifty. Her heart ached. Their armor was dented and covered in ash, their wyverns tired and still healing. But there was a burning fight in all their eyes. One by one they saluted her.

An acknowledgment to follow her.

She turned back in her saddle as Saros landed in front of Orenlion's army.

The soldiers weren't much better off than the Khama, but Evren could see Etherakian uniforms dotted amidst the red and silver. At the front were Shao and Barrion.

"Took you long enough, Xun." Shao grinned sharply. Somehow, he looked like he belonged in the armor now. He hefted something up and then tossed it at her. She caught her bow easily. "You dropped this."

Evren relaxed a fraction with it in her grip. "And here I was thinking you'd keep it for yourself."

He shrugged. "The thought crossed my mind."

Barrion was different, but Evren couldn't tell how. Maybe it was the smoke and the horror setting in. Whatever it was, he shuddered like the rest of them as the Storm made another pass.

"Abraxas said you'd be here to tell us what to do," he said. "So, what's the plan?"

All eyes were on her. Khama, wyvern, Etherakian, and Orenlion. She found herself gripping the bow too tight and relaxed her hold.

"The Archdruids will take care of the dragon. We need to keep Nerezza from the dagger until then."

Shao beat his spear against the ground and a hundred spears followed. "The necromancer nearly destroyed our city. We'll gladly take her down."

Barrion nodded. "We'll deal with the undead and the mage. Evren, can you keep the dagger from her?"

"Not alone. But I suspect the rest of my party will have their own part in this." She took a deep breath. "It's the only chance we've got."

"Breathe until there's more smoke than air," Shao said.

"Fight until the Divines welcome us home," Barrion whispered.

"Make them pay for every drop of blood bled." Evren set her jaw. "Your lead, general."

Shao almost faltered, like her words were something out of a dream. Then the raised his fist and a hundred more joined.

"FOR THE WOOD!"

The Khama took to the skies. The soldiers charged. And the battle melted into a frenzy of blood, fire, and bone.

Evren watched from above when the elves met the dead. The flash of steel against bone echoed high in the ashen sky. She watched some falter when they saw friends they loved. She saw many fall. But she saw more fight with more vigor than she ever expected. Shao led the charge with Barrion at his side, the battle cries drowning out the unnatural screams of the dead. Mira kept a tight formation around Barrion and her orders were sharp and clear as her sword. The small army of a hundred quickly attracted the attention of the undead.

Before they could get overwhelmed, the Khama dove. Flurries of claws, teeth, and acid tore through swaths of undead before the wyverns took off to the skies again. Evren let Saros dive, attack, and fly three times to get used to the feeling. Then she let go of the reigns and kept her grip on the saddle with just her thighs.

"Aim for the hearts!" Evren yelled over the noise of battle as she nocked an arrow. The rest of the Khama did the same.

A rain of arrows and spears cut through the dead like a knife through fat. Dive, attack, rise, shoot, repeat. It was unnervingly natural how easy it was to fight like this. Maybe it was the knowledge that there was no choice, that the alternative was death. At least fighting meant a death well earned. And Evren saw many earn it.

But Nerezza's horde of undead grew with every felled soldier. Every sacrifice and last stand turned against Orenlion as the freshly dead rose to fight the people they'd just stood with. There was no denting Nerezza's army, and she'd lost sight of the mage herself, along with Gyda, Sorin, and Arke.

She was running out of arrows, and hope, as the fire and the horde grew. It would only be a matter of time before the city got caught in the blaze.

She couldn't even see Barrion and Shao anymore.

"Lady Xun." One of the Khama waved to get her attention, then pointed towards the forest floor. "Look!"

She did and, peering through the smoke and falling ash, she nearly gasped. The forest floor looked like it was moving. But the more smoke that cleared she realized it wasn't the forest.

"The Hisrachi." One of the other Khama let out a worried squeak. "They'll overwhelm us!"

"No." Evren shook her head. "Look who's leading them."

At the front of the charging mass of spiders, enough of an army to both give her hope and nightmares for months to come, were two beautiful sights. A dwarf with golden hair, and an elf bearing a blackened sword and shield.

They flanked the undead with fervor. Sol's daggers dancing among pinchers, Abraxas's sword cutting through hearts and making way for a thousand-legged army. The Hisrachi tore through the undead and Evren watched the army of corpses falter and start to break off into manageable chunks. The remaining Orenlion and Etherakian soldiers seemed to regain their hope and strength, and fought with renewed vigor.

Evren turned to the last of the Khama. "Work with the Hisrachi. Keep the dead separated and confused. Don't let them overwhelm us."

"Where are you going?"

"To finish this."

Evren urged Saros down into the battle. She skimmed a few feet above the fighting and let lose arrow after arrow into the hearts of the dead. Hisrachi swarmed the dead, Etherak pushed them back, Orenlion kept them cornered and confused, and the Khama rained death from above.

But Evren needed Nerezza. She needed her team together again.

All it took was finding Abraxas and Sol. They waded through the battle, the Hisrachi charge abandoned, with seemingly only one goal in mind. Evren followed where their path would lead and could easily see the bright dance of dueling magic.

She hadn't realized she'd traveled so far.

"Let's carve a path, shall we?" she asked Saros, and the wyvern's reply was instant.

He flew even lower, claws and wings outstretched to grab all the undead in his way. When his claws were full, he flew up and tossed them to the side. He did it twice more before Evren could hear Sol's laughter echoing in the battle.

"Thank you!"

Evren gave her a thumbs up and sped back to where she left Gyda and Sorin.

Arke and Nerezza were still locked in a vicious duel, the swath of Wood around them somehow all burned, frozen, and lifeless as stone at once. Saros had to sharply careen to the side to avoid a stray dagger of ice that impaled itself on a nearby tree, sizzling in the heat.

A little farther away, the undead were fighting each other. Nerezza's red-eyed ones outnumbered the handful Gyda had turned to her favor, and the warrior was struggling to both fight and keep control over her charges. She was fighting her way to Sorin, who'd managed to get away from the tree but was now surrounded. Gyda's wyvern was getting overwhelmed and acting more as a blockade than a weapon.

Saros needed no orders. His neck frills quivered and jaws unhinged as he dove towards the dead. He scooped enough away from Sorin that he could escape, and flung the rest at the fire. On the ground he spat sizzling acid and Evren shot her arrows with everything she had left. An arrow in the eye, acid through the heart. A corpse bitten in half and skewered with an arrow. Claws and teeth, iron and bone. Saros swept his tail and wings to keep them from being overwhelmed, and soon the ones around Sorin were blissfully dead.

"Neat trick, Evvie." Sorin winked at her, his hair grey with ash.

"You have the dagger?"

"Nope."

"Then who?"

"Gyda, of course. We're trading off." He flicked blood off his sword. "Keeps them confused."

Just then he caught sight of Sol and Abraxas running into the fray and whooped with joy. "Finally! Let's get Gyda and bury this."

Evren couldn't agree more. She urged Saros to leap up and then into a pile of dead. Bodies scattered, red-eyed and furious. Evren felt her blood singing with every draw of her bow.

The Wandering Sols fought like a storm taken form.

Abraxas used his shield to tear off heads and then plunge his sword into their hearts. Sol cut tendons, broke kneecaps, and hobbled all those in her path. Sorin finished them off with a laugh and a flourish. Whatever he didn't finish, Saros or Evren did. All the while, Arke was a blur of magic and elements, and the wind sparked with arcane energy.

"Time to pass the baton," Sol shouted, and nodded over to Gyda. "She's getting overwhelmed."

Evren nodded. "I'll get to her."

Saros responded to her before she could even give the order. It felt like they'd been flying for years. Evren barely touched the reins. As he landed between Gyda and a horde of undead, Evren finished off three in rapid succession and his tail sent the rest towards Abraxas's waiting sword.

Evren turned to Gyda, a little pleased that she was taller than her in the saddle. "Switch time."

The warrior nodded and passed her the dagger. The blade was warm and all too familiar in her hands. She had the urge to just . . . disappear. Maybe she could change this battle, so no one had to die. If she could just . . .

She shook her head. She'd dealt with time enough.

"Sol!"

The dwarf's head popped up over a pile of bodies and Evren tossed the dagger to her. Dead fingers, claws, and mandibles snapped for it, but it was Sol's expert hands that caught it. Immediately, all the dead on Sorin and Abraxas turned on her. She ran, ducking and weaving under every furious blow. The boys were quick to intercept and, before long, they were standing between Sol and the dead.

At her knee, Gyda was breathing hard. Her eyes were fixed on Arke and Nerezza's duel. The forest burned with the heat of all the hells combined, and the Storm flew unchallenged.

"I don't know how much longer we can keep this up," Gyda said.

"This is your plan."

The warrior laughed. "It feels more like what you would do."

"We'll make it, Gyda."

The warrior's gaze cut over to Sol, who'd gotten separated and was fighting off five undead at once. She cried out and threw the dagger at Abraxas, who barely managed to catch it with his shield hand. The undead all turned on him, like the worst game of cat and mouse she'd ever seen.

Saros was breathing heavily beneath her, his flanks shaking with exertion. It was hard to tell, but Evren could've sworn she could see Nerezza's red magic starting to overwhelm Arke. Evren's fingers went for another arrow only to find an empty quiver.

They were out of time.

The forest would kill them all. The blazing inferno was only getting hotter, and the ash was so thick it was all Evren could taste. Nerezza couldn't walk out of this anymore than they could.

The only survivor of this battle would be the Storm herself.

Faith withered in its home beneath her ribs. As it did, all she could see was the looming shadow of the Storm, as the dragon's attention was finally caught by the magic erupting below. All Evren could make out in the fire was one large green eye burning hungrily down at her.

Then, as if the sun was breaking through the clouds of a hurricane, the smoke started to clear. The fire crackled angrily but started to simmer away. Blackened husks of trees started to turn brown and regrow their bark. Green slowly started to creep up from the ground and into the trees.

The dragon hissed, and it sounded like a million serpents howling all at once. The sound shook Evren's chest. And the glowing eye, far more intelligent than it had a right to be, turned away from Evren. She saw fear there, as the dragon saw seven figures emerge from the smoldering forest.

The Archdruids were calm and still. All hooded and cloaked. Some had antlers on their heads, others were shrouded in living vines and flowers. Evren's eyes blurred with tears as a familiar figure covered in moss and mushrooms emerged. She saw him grin underneath the hood.

"The Storm must leave the Wood, for she will find no home in the forest she has ruined," The Archdruids said in unison. "All those bearing the Storm will be removed."

They lifted their hands and Evren felt the energy in the forest shift. The hairs on her arms stood on end. The ash started to float up around her. The dragon let out a howl of rage and with a thunderous beat of her wings, started to fly away.

And Evren knew what she had to do then.

She turned to Gyda, watching as the stunned look on her face turned to awe.

"You're everything to me," Evren said, and took her face in both hands and kissed her.

It was a hard and fierce kiss. She could taste the iron of blood on Gyda's lips, and the ash on her tongue. But it was wholly Gyda, and it felt so right. The way her lips melted against Evren's, the way she gasped a little when her lips parted. Evren couldn't believe she hadn't done this sooner.

She broke away just enough to breathe, her lips still brushing Gyda's. "I should've told you sooner, but I'll spend every day after this making it up to you, I swear."

Gyda's hand cupped her face before she could go. The blood on her fingers was warm, but it didn't disgust Evren. Her touch was so soft and gentle, and only for her. But Gyda's eyes were fierce and her voice strong when she spoke.

"Go," she whispered. "And come back to me."

Gyda kissed her again, desperate and quick, and then let her go.

Evren whirled Saros around and took him towards Abraxas. He saw her coming and threw down his sword and shield. He had nothing but the dagger as he ran up and took her offered hand. She hauled him up onto Saros's back and he sat down hard behind her.

"Hold on," she tossed over her shoulder, and Saros took to the sky.

Abraxas's arms wrapped around her middle as he clung to her. "You look like you've got a plan."

She laughed. "A bit. I thought you did too."

He shook his head and tightened his grip as Saros turned sharply to face Nerezza. "Just faith that you won't kill us both."

Despite the growing magic in the air, and the Keeper's dagger seeming to burn a hole in her back, Evren grinned. She flicked the reins and Saros barreled towards Arke and Nerezza.

They arrived not a moment too soon. The goblin's magic flickered out and the empty leather shell of his spellbook fluttered to the ground. Arke tumbled after it, hitting the ash-coated ground hard. He didn't move.

Nerezza gathered the rest of her red magic. The cloud turned into a blanket of daggerlike tendrils all pointed towards Arke.

She raised her hand, the spikes quivering, and just before she could release them, Saros grabbed her.

Nerezza screamed as his talons pierced her, and the magic dissipated. Then the wyvern started a desperate, fast climb, and it was all Evren and Abraxas could do to hold on. They broke the canopy, Nerezza still writhing in pain and the dragon in sight.

"You know," Evren said breathlessly as they leveled out and shot towards the Storm. "You could've given me the dagger and stayed behind."

Abraxas laughed. "And risk you getting all the glory again? I think not."

They laughed even as Nerezza cursed and the Archdruid's impending magic surged closer. Of course, they both knew they could escape. Just use the dagger and all would be well. But something kept both warrior and hunter from grabbing for that power. Some survival instinct in both that told them that playing with time as they already had was changing Eith. Anymore and they could break the world.

Saros was old for a wyvern, but he was fast. He was gaining on the Storm, who was taking her time trying to burn as much of the forest as possible before the Archdruids dealt with her. Evren wondered what they'd done to earn the dragon's wrath. She wondered if she'd ever get the chance to ask.

Nerezza had stopped screaming. Evren thought she was dead, or at least unconscious. But, as they got close enough to see the individual scales on the Storm, a flicker of red magic surged from beneath Saros and straight towards the dragon.

It sank deep into the scales, and Evren saw the dragon shudder, still . . .

And then turn to face them.

"Shit!"

She tugged on the reins, but Saros was already wheeling away as fast as he could. The dragon opened her mouth, her eyes burning red where they'd been green, and her throat burned a deep crimson.

Saros's wings flapped as hard as they could, but the Storm was no longer worried about the forest. Her new prey, no matter how fast, couldn't outrun her.

Evren jerked Saros to the side just as a wave of crimson fire flew past them. Saros screamed as his wing caught fire. He tried to roll to put it out, and nearly dumped Abraxas to the forest as a result. His grip on Evren, and Saros's quick recovery, was all that kept him from a quick death.

But the wing was still on fire, and it was creeping towards them. The smell of burnt flesh was all Evren could smell. Saros screamed in agony and started to fall. His one good wing flapped desperately, trying to keep them in the air, but the trees were approaching alarmingly fast.

"Let her go!" Abraxas shouted.

Whether Saros realized he could listen to him, or just knew that Nerezza was the reason behind his pain, he dropped the mage. She screamed as she fell, but she didn't fall for long.

Evren's stomach lurched as the trees beneath them turned to green scales. The Storm flew under them and grabbed Nerezza with a large claw. They were falling right into the dragon's open mouth.

Evren's eyes were blurring with tears. Every pained sound Saros made, every correction of flight that turned useless, made the tears well up more.

She didn't want to die. She'd made a promise to Gyda. Even more, she didn't want to take down Abraxas and Saros with her. She felt the same hopelessness that had burned in her for months climb up her throat. All she could see was the dragon's gaping maw.

The plan to throw the dagger and Nerezza at the dragon and have the Archdruids destroy them both would still work. But it would take them out too, and Evren felt her fingers losing their grip on the reins.

"I'm so sorry," she choked through her tears. "I didn't want this."

Abraxas's voice was calm, even over the howling wind. "Evren."

"It wasn't supposed to be like this, I swear."

"Evren, look at me."

She did. She looked back and saw her friend covered in ash and blood, smiling as his hair swept around him like a dark cloud. He was smiling, his eyes wet with tears, and he gripped her shoulders.

"Take care of them."

Horror struck her, and she grabbed his arms as he stood up, dagger in hand. "No!"

"Tell them I loved them." He tore out of her grip. "And love her with everything, Evren."

"Please don't," she sobbed. "Let me do this. It doesn't have to be you. I can't lose anyone else."

"My life is finished, my friend. If I go out saving the people I care about, then that's the best end." He stepped back, dagger flat against his chest, smiling as the tears cut through the soot. "Thank you for the adventure. Thank you for the light."

And then he fell.

Evren grabbed at the empty air where he had just been, fingers coming back empty. Saros careened to the side, spinning out of control. But Evren could clearly see Abraxas fall into the dragon's mouth. She saw Nerezza's focus, and the Storm's focus, leave her and Saros. She watched the mage dive after him.

Then the Deep Wood erupted in a ball of radiant light. Evren buried her head against Saros's neck and, when she looked up, dragon, mage, and warrior were gone.

29

Saros's fall was broken by a miracle. Shreds of Hisrachi silk slowed them as they tumbled like a fallen star through the trees. It snapped, and then another caught him. They still fell, in slow jerking motions, until finally they hit the forest floor.

Evren used the last of her dress to put out the fire on Saros's wing. She was heaving sobs as she did, and the wyvern whimpered with every flap of silk against flame. When it was out, her silk was nothing more than blackened scraps, and Saros's wing was mangled. The leather membrane that let him catch the wind had melted away. Pieces of white bone peaked through the burned skin.

Evren stumbled over to his head and sat down next to him. She was sobbing so hard she barely realized he'd laid his head down on her lap. Heavy, hot, scaley, and smelling of acid and death. She laid her hand on his frilled brow and wept.

"I'm sorry," she whispered again to the ashen sky.

WHEN SHE WOKE UP, Saros was gone. The forest was golden with sunlight. Grey ash glimmered as it fell like snow. The whole forest felt like a tomb.

Evren picked herself up. Saros's heavy tracks would no doubt lead to Orenlion, so she followed the same path through the ash. Her feet dragged with every step. She was numb until she remembered who she was walking towards, who'd she would have to tell about Abraxas's sacrifice. The thought tore at her new heart, and she was gasping for air to try and calm it down. Nothing worked. She was running out of tears. She hoped she'd be dry by the time she got to Orenlion.

It was midday before she saw the shell of the city. The silver gates were tarnished and coated with ash. Their Keepers were nowhere to be seen. Only one figure was there, waiting for her, and Evren was thankful then for the rage she felt spark in her chest. Rage was better than grief and tears.

Wasanthi was wandering up the path, coughing as the ash fell around him. He didn't notice Evren, not until she was marching towards him like death incarnate.

"You!" she growled.

He started to run, but his foot caught on the roots. He scrambled backwards, pressing himself against one of the massive trees. His white robes were stained black and brown with old blood. The cut on his cheek swelled like it was infected. And his eyes . . .

He was terrified of her.

Evren stopped at the base of the tree and knelt. "Do you know why I'm here?"

"Revenge," he rasped. "A foolish mortal quest. I did what was right."

"Which time? When you murdered my father? Or Shao's? Or perhaps when you let yourself be manipulated by the very woman who nearly destroyed your people, twice."

He shuddered. "I don't know."

"The answer is none," she bit out. "You were wrong. You

were weak. You were cruel." She curled her hands into fists so tight she could feel her nails digging into her palms. "You destroyed my family. You destroyed Orenlion. You nearly destroyed the Wood itself."

"I only did what I thought was right!" he sobbed. "Our Lady spoke through me. I followed her wisdom."

"A fraud's wisdom to a cruel old man too stupid to know the difference. That doesn't make you innocent, it just makes you complacent. And that's worse."

"What will you do?" he asked. "Kill me?"

"No."

He sagged in relief. "A trial then. The city will not be kind."

"The city doesn't decide your fate." Evren stood up; her jaw clenched so hard her teeth ached. "The Wood does."

Wasanthi stared at her, bewildered, until he started to sink. The roots wrapped around his limbs and throat. His eyes bulged and he let out a high-pitched squeak and tried to get free. He gasped, perhaps to plea for his life. His eyes bugged out of his head, his face turned red and then purple. Evren watched it all, unblinking and unfazed, until the tree swallowed him whole.

All that was left of Sovereign Wasanthi was a smudge of ash on the ground. The leaves fluttered until they covered it up.

Evren didn't feel better. She felt sick. But, as she turned back towards the city, she saw her father under the silver arch of Gate Xun. He held his hand out to her, face grim but eyes dancing with tears. She ran to him without hesitation and buried her face in his chest. He still smelled of earth and decay, but his arms were familiar as they wrapped around her. He held her tightly.

"My darling girl," he whispered into her hair. "My little Ren. I am so proud of you."

Evren thought she was done with tears, but she wept in her father's arms like she was a child again. Her fists balled his cloak up and she clung to him, a little girl one last time in a forest of light and falling ash.

~

"I MISSED OUR WALKS, you know. Almost feels like old times."

The setting sun caught Aster's hair like spun gold as he snorted. "You hate old times."

That was true, but the walk still felt good. Even if it was through ruins.

Evren and Aster walked a familiar path through Orenlion. In the month since the Storm's destruction, the city had changed drastically. It was painful to still see so much rubble. But the discomfort was like watching a healer set a bone. Behind the destroyed shops and burned homes were elves rebuilding. Vines still green and flexible were being coaxed into strong, brown maturity. The trees that had stood for thousands of years were growing again. The bridges weren't beautiful works of art, but patchworks of wooden planks so that everyone could get around. Lifts were working again, stronger and larger than ever. They carried supplies, fresh workers, and hope.

The forest was singing its sunset lullaby, a chorus of birds, insects, and a newly hatched clutch of wyvern eggs. Elves passed out drinks to workers from Etherak, who'd arrived a week ago at Barrion's request. Evren watched one of the humans take two mugs of water and offer the second one to a sawdust-covered Hisrachi.

She held her breath, watching the three strangers. The elf, young and terrified. The Hisrachi, older and cautious. The human, trying to heal when the world marked his legacy as a destroyer.

The Hisrachi sighed. *"I don't drink like that. Let me ssshow you."*

One by one, the three relaxed. Evren smiled a little as she and Aster passed.

"It'll take more than that to heal us of our shared wounds," Aster said.

"It's a start. A month ago, they would've torn each other apart."

"They still could. Nothing is set in stone."

Some things were, but Evren kept that to herself. They reached the middle of a new bridge, still rough and covered with dust as the sun turned Orenlion golden. She paused at the railing, taking in the sight.

Under the near blinding halo of the setting sun, Orenlion looked whole. She knew that was just a trick of the light, that beneath it all was a still-healing wound. But the infected bits were cut away. The bad blood was draining and leaving room for only the good. For the first time, Evren looked at her old home with a sense of pride.

Aster settled beside her, elbows on the railing. He hadn't been sleeping, and the past month had aged him beyond his years. The long cut down his face was still pink and tender and ruined the soft image she was used to.

"How's the face?"

He quirked one side of his mouth into a frown, still careful with the side that was hurt. "Well, I can eat without crying now. That's a win."

"Scars are sexy you know."

"Only for you."

She laughed a little, and while his tone was somber, she knew he'd be all right. There was a new fire in his eyes now that made up for his voice. A new passion.

"My mother gave up her seat this morning. Did I tell you?"

"No, but Shao did."

Aster shook his head in disbelief. "Generations of Sovereigns for the five seats, and in one day there were only two left. And now they've both stepped down. It's chaos."

"Who's going to lead?"

"The three smaller houses are discussing what's best for the city now. From what I hear, they're leaning away from hereditary leadership all together. Perhaps the people of Orenlion will have a chance to decide."

Evren worried her lip. That would take time. Undoubtedly, it would be an uncomfortable and awkward transition. But the idea of power going to someone other than the noble blooded was promising. Even if it turned out to be terrible, it was a way past the Sovereigns that had ruled them for so long.

"They're asking for you, you know." Aster bumped her shoulder with his. "The last of house Xun saved the Wood. The people would listen to you. The nobles would too. You could shape Orenlion to be what you wanted."

Evren did know. The heir of house Nailo had come to her personally, a small woman with goliath ideas. Evren told her the same thing she'd told everyone else that asked her to stay.

"I can't," she said. Below and above, Orenlion teemed with people. Elves and Hisrachi worked together for the first time in history. She'd found a strange peace here. Her father was alive, in a sense. She'd taken down those who'd hurt her and had healed most of the wounds she'd caused. But Orenlion wasn't her home.

"I'm not a politician, Aster. I have no idea where Orenlion should go next, or what's best for it."

"Well, I could help," he offered. "I could council you. Maybe have some good come from my choices."

Evren took his shoulder and squeezed gently. He shrank a little at her touch and bowed his head.

"You can do that without me," she told him. "You just have to trust yourself again."

"How can I do that when she won't even look at me?"

Evren winced and pulled her hand away. She'd seen little of Mei the past month, but what she had seen was hard. Mei's leg was still badly hurt from the fight with Nerezza's skeletal dragon. Even without Anep attacking the Roost, she still hurt herself too bad to ride. What was worse was Saros, who'd fallen into a depression from his own lack of flying. Mei spent every waking moment with him or yelling at the healers. The wyvern would live, but it was unlikely he'd fly again. Mei was bringing him with her to Etherak.

The more Evren talked to people, the more she learned about the tiny changes in this time. Mira's brash attitude had softened a little as her respect for Evren had grown, and she'd stopped Evren several days ago to apologize for the Hisrachi ambush. Anep's resolve to not attack Orenlion had bled over to into Neri managing to convince the rest of her people to help Orenlion against Nerezza. She was acting as an ambassador of sorts for the many nests in the Wood and, somewhere down the line, had forgiven Arke.

One thing remained the same, a strange knot that would never be untangled, was Barrion and Mei's marriage. In this time, Aster wasn't to blame for Mei's injured leg, but she still made the decision to marry Barrion to help her people. It was a decision that Barrion had, apparently, tentatively asked if she wanted to change now that the looming threat was gone. But the marriage had been sealed already. The rings couldn't be given back. It wouldn't be long before Mei would leave Orenlion for a bigger wedding in Etherak.

"Have you talked to either of them?" she asked.

He shook his head. "Not really. Barrion feels guilty. I know he did it to save us, and he tried to change it, but what's done is done. Their souls are bound and that can't be undone. You'd think it would hurt less knowing that it was just political; that it was just a gamble to save us. But it hurts more.

"Back when you and I were engaged, Mei tried to tell me that even if I didn't love you, it didn't make her feel better. I would still never be wholly hers. I never understood why she was so upset when she knew my true affections, but now . . ."

His shaky hand covered his mouth as he tried to breathe through the sudden wave of emotions rocking through him. "I get it now. Watching her with him . . . it feels like I have a dagger in my chest that I can't get out. Every time she smiles at something he says, it twists. Every time he laughs at one of her jokes, I feel like I'm bleeding all over the floor and no one can see. I know he's a good man. He'll take care of her and maybe she'll even find a better life in Etherak, one I can't offer her here. I just wish . . ."

Aster choked on his words, and Evren tried not to let her face show how much she pitied him. She knew he'd hate that. Still, when he looked at her and his eyes were brimming with tears, all she wanted to do was take that ache away.

"I just wish I wasn't going to miss her so much," Aster finally said.

What could Evren say to that? She had no words of comfort to offer him. No life lesson about losing the one she loved to another. She'd been lucky in love so far. She could even say she was happy. But she was no stranger to loss.

Evren took his hand, like they used to when they were kids. "She's not gone for good. You have centuries of life ahead of you. And with this new alliance between Orenlion and Etherak, who knows? Maybe somewhere down the line you see her again."

"It won't be the same."

"No," Evren admitted. "But she's here, Aster. That's more than some can say. She's breathing. She's smiling again. One day that smile will be for you."

He clutched her hand tightly. "You're both going away, and I'm staying here. You say I'll see her again, but what about you? You're family, too."

Evren smiled. "You'll see me again. Eith needs adventurers, but there's a lot of us out there. World-altering events can wait for you from time to time."

He laughed a little, his tears starting to disappear. "My best friend is a massive hero. The world needs her more than I do."

"The world is nothing without you in it. I'll find my way back to you, I swear."

∽

THE SUNSET WAS MORE orange than gold when Evren found herself back at Xun Manor. She took her boots off, sitting them in a row next to the other four. Then she walked into the place she called home.

The worg pup yapped happily and ran circles around her feet as she walked up the stairs. After tripping over him twice, she picked him up and carried him the rest of the way. She made her way down the hall, ignoring the quaint room with the neatly made bed and pile of armor in the corner, and walked into the one with two beds.

The room was full of people, friends and allies both. It had been made for twins at one point and was large and glowing with orange light. The windows were wide open, curtains fluttering in the light breeze. The small balcony outside was occupied, a large shadow catching the curtains.

Evren set the pup down. "How's the worst patient?"

Arke, from his bed piled high with pillows, was comically small. He gave her a very rude gesture though, and the color was back in his cheeks. "Ready to kick your ass the next time you call me that."

"Don't make it so true then."

Sitting on the bed next to Arke's were Sorin and Sol. They had a plate of desserts they'd stolen from Divines knew where, and the bedsheets were coated in old frosting and crumbs. The pup easily jumped on the bed and wiggled his way between them, licking crumbs as he went.

"No!" Sorin jerked his cake out of the way. "It's so bad for you, stop."

He didn't stop until Sol picked him up and put him on Arke's bed.

"I don't want him!" the goblin protested, but he didn't push him off. After some wiggling around, the worg settled down at the end of his bed, sniffing curiously at Neri's propped-up feet.

Her eyes twinkled at Evren. *"Arke's recovering really well, considering how badly duels like that usually end up for the losing party."*

"Didn't lose." The goblin grumbled.

"Of course not."

She patted his leg gently and a genuine smile brightened Arke's face. It warmed Evren to see their odd relationship blossoming, even if she didn't really understand it.

"The healers say he'll be able to travel by the end of the week," Sol said, dusting crumbs off her pants. "So long as he doesn't overdo himself, he'll be back to slinging fire and insults in no time."

"Hey, I can still do both. Just real slow for now."

Evren smiled at Neri. "Have you decided whether you're coming with us?"

The spider hesitated, her eyes darting back to Arke in a silent question. The easy smile on his face had vanished, but he nodded.

"I wish I could, but I need to stay," Neri said. *"There are still nests that don't agree with this new peace, and many more who don't believe it will last. If this is to last, someone needs to stay behind and make sure it does."*

It made sense, but Evren still found herself hating it. Neri was sweet, and it was good to have her around. The gaping hole Abraxas had left could almost be ignored when she was in the room.

Evren dug in her pocket and pulled out a glittering shard of glass. The mirror shard hadn't left her side, and she was enormously proud it had survived her many falls through time and air both. But she held it out to Neri.

The spider tittered anxiously. *"Oh! I couldn't possible take that."*

"I don't use mine nearly as much as the rest." Evren shrugged. "Besides, someone needs to keep the grouch from pouting once we leave. A talk every day or so should do the trick."

"You did help us figure out the mirror," Sorin pointed out. "It makes sense for you to have a piece. And, you know, Arke's not the only one that'll miss you."

Neri took the mirror piece with shaking legs. She hugged it close to her abdomen. *"Thank you. I-I'll talk every day."* She turned to Arke. *"Every day, I promise."*

He waved her off. "Bah, don't get worked up 'bout it. Still, good idea."

Neri was still admiring the mirror when a soft knock came from the hallway. Evren turned, not surprised to see Barrion standing there a little awkwardly. He'd been running himself ragged getting Orenlion back together, and it showed in his sunken cheeks and dark eyes. But he still held himself like a prince, and everyone in the room unconsciously straightened up.

"Might I have a word with you all?" he asked softly.

Sol nodded. "Of course. Cake?"

He shook his head and stepped inside. "No, thank you. Is everyone here? Where's Gyda?"

"On the balcony," Evren said immediately. "She can hear you, don't worry."

"Right, of course."

Barrion settled in the middle of the room, still and formal. He laced his hands behind his back and raised his chin. He was trying very hard to look princely, Evren realized. Her heart lurched when she realized why.

"I know Orenlion has talked endlessly about your heroism recently, but as Etherak's future King, I feel like I should as well."

"Whoa, buddy." Sorin held his sugary fingers up. "There's no need. We're good, promise."

"It is needed, though," Barrion insisted. "You've lost someone by partaking in my quest, and it's only right that I acknowledge that."

The tone in the room went from bittersweet to heavy, as if a fog had descended from the mountains to blanket them. Suddenly, they couldn't ignore the space where Abraxas would've lounged. The corner, draped in shadows, with a full view of everyone. The little smiles he would've tried to smother, the cake he would've stolen, the soft voice of reason amidst the chaos.

Evren missed him so much it was like the breath was stolen from her lungs. She closed her eyes and saw him all over again, smiling and content as he fell.

There had been no body to recover. No Abraxas, or Nerezza, or the dragon. Yuhan explained that the spell wouldn't leave a trace. No remains to burn didn't feel right, and it left nothing but a memory where a body should've been.

She opened her eyes when Barrion started to speak again.

"Abraxas was a citizen of Etherak," he said shakily. "No matter his past, he served loyally. Divines know he didn't need to. He had every right to spit in my face when I came to you for help. But he didn't. And now his bravery has given Etherak another chance, at the cost of his life. I know no amount of gold will make up for what happened. No apologies or condolences will heal you. But I have to do something."

Barrion pulled a crisp piece of parchment from his sleeve. "My uncle was forced to condemn all knights who fought in the occupations when he took the throne. It was the only way the other kingdoms would let us stay independent. Abraxas was one of those men, and as such he could never come home. I have written an amendment to that law that absolves him of all his crimes, for his service not only to the crown, but also to the world."

The paper shook in his hand, and he put it down at Sol's side.

"I know it's far too late for him," he said. "But it washes his name clean. And there are chances for other knights like himself to do the same. I know many are scattered throughout Eith as mercenaries, hermits, and adventurers. This could bring them home if my uncle allows it to pass. What is unconditional is the clearing of Abraxas Kain's name. He'll be remembered for the hero he was, not the horrors he committed under orders."

"His armor, sword, and shield, would normally be returned to the temple it was forged in, but I'm leaving it with you. This in no way makes up for what you've lost. But I hope it's a start."

A dark, pressing silence descended over the room. No one wanted to break it. Slowly, Sol picked up the paper. Her words were strong, but Evren caught the wobble at the edge.

"Did . . . did he have any family?"

Barrion sucked in a breath. "No. No living family members except . . ." he chuckled softly. "Except the lot of you."

Once again, they were quiet, and this time no one broke it. Barrion stood there for a while before Neri quietly left, then he started to follow her. Evren caught him as he turned to leave and laid her hand on his shoulder.

"You'll make a great King one day," she whispered.

His smile was tired, but hopeful. "So long as time and history are kind to me. I hope you're right."

He left them and closed the door softly behind him. Evren eyed the shadow on the balcony, silently willing Gyda to come in but knowing deep down that she wouldn't.

They passed the paper around, reading every carefully crafted word that Barrion had strung together to make Abraxas the hero he always fought to be. The ache in her chest would always be there, but it became somehow more manageable as she read it. If Barrion cared, then the world would too. It wouldn't just be Abraxas's sacrifice hanging over her every day, it would be his legacy.

Legacies were fickle things, but she found that this weight, like any good set of armor, was comforting.

"What do we do now?" Sol asked softly.

Sorin wrapped his lanky arm around her shoulders and let her melt into his embrace. His own lips were tight with a frown that kept back tears. On his bed, Arke rubbed his eyes furiously. The balcony was silent.

"Anything we want," Evren said. "But I think Sahar deserves to know what happened, and not through a letter."

Sorin rubbed Sol's arm. "We've been chasing Nerezza for so long without even realizing it. I mean, she kind of started everything. All our quests have led to her. And now she's gone. What do we do? Pick up another quest? Wait for the Collective to send us somewhere?"

Arke grunted and burrowed further in his pillows until only his ears showed. "Vacation would be nice. Terevas is all right this time of year."

Evren suddenly thought of Chayne, the boy erased from time itself, and the sister he left behind. No one remembered him, not even Mira or Barrion. None of her friends either. Chayne's memory was hers alone to carry, and the girl with the dream of moving south weighed on her like it did him.

"If everyone wants, that's where we'll go," she said. "But we don't need to decide now. Barrion and Mei won't leave for a few days yet, so we have a little time."

Evren wanted to sit on Arke's bed and make sure he wasn't smothering himself. She wanted to wiggle in on the other side of Sol and sandwich the dwarf in love and support. But there was someone else who needed her more.

Without a word, she walked across the room and ducked through the open window onto the balcony.

The Wood was pink and purple now, fresh shadows of night growing larger. Gyda sat slumped against the wall, staring at it all with a blank expression. She'd been like this since Evren had told her what happened. Evren had expected rage, furious and quick. This silent mourning was unnerving, but it was what she needed.

Evren sat down beside her, leaving enough room between them that they weren't touching but if Gyda wanted she could reach out.

"You heard Barrion?"

Gyda nodded once. "Yes,"

Evren chewed her lip. "It's good, but he's right. It's not enough."

"Nothing will be," Gyda grumbled. Her eyes shone wetly as she stared into the sunset. "I keep expecting him to be here. I practice alone in the mornings, and I swear he's there, commenting on my shitty footwork again. Sorin caught a lantern on fire last night trying to light it, and I half expected Abraxas to come into the room chiding him. He's everywhere, but he's not. I feel him, like I felt the ghosts of my clan."

Evren waited with bated breath. This was the most Gyda had spoken in the whole month. They'd been busy, and there had been small reassurances that the two of them were okay. A touch of fingers at breakfast, a soft goodnight in the evening. But whatever dam Gyda had built was breaking. Evren watched her crumble, brick by brick, until the warrior's head was in her lap.

The weight should've been awkward, but Evren sighed in relief. Her fingers reached out until they found Gyda's, callused and cool, and held them tight.

"I don't want him to fade, Evren," she muttered. "I'll lose him."

Evren blinked back her own tears, pulling her closer. Gyda's breath shuddered with barely checked sobs.

It broke Evren to see her like this. She was so strong and unbreakable. It was always Gyda who held her when she was fracturing—in the White Cairn, in the cavern with her father, and every small moment in between. Evren's chest was uncomfortably tight, but she wouldn't let go. She couldn't. Gyda needed her to hold her up when she couldn't stand herself, and she wasn't going to let her go.

"You won't lose him," she whispered. "We were his family, Gyda, the only people in Eith who gave him a second chance. We'll carry him with us to our deaths far in the future, and we'll see him again. I'm sure he's happier to be at his Divine's sides again."

"Fuck his gods."

Evren stifled a laugh, and Gyda breathed heavily on her thigh.

"They don't deserve him," the warrior said. "I'd take him back from them if I thought he would let me."

Evren brushed her finger along Gyda's knuckles, one by one. "I know. But he left us down here to take care of each other, so that's what we're going to do."

Gyda hummed noncommittally, still curled to the side so her taller form was comfortable against Evren. The sun disappeared below the trees and, one by one, the stars came out, bright and cold in their beauty. From the window, Evren heard the telltale notes of a sea shanty, and Sorin's voice floating along the evening wind.

"We're going to be all right," she breathed to the stars, to Abraxas. "I promise."

30

Abraxas

Abraxas Kain was not dead, although he very much wished he was.

He'd expected the afterlife to greet him once the dragon had swallowed him. He expected all the things he'd been taught as a boy. A kingdom of stained glass and clouds, unending light. Haphion waiting for him with open arms.

Didn't he deserve it? After all he'd done and sacrificed, after all he'd suffered, cut off from his Divine, he wanted nothing more than to feel that connection again. To let go of the aching pain that tormented his very bones.

And yet, he woke to the black of smoke and the stench of blood.

He wanted to cry out to the heavens, but he couldn't see them. He grasped for his sword, and found nothing. When he sat up, his clothes stuck to his body, wet with blood.

The air was cold, but he was steaming. There wasn't much light, but he could see the whisps curling from his arms. His whole, intact arms. He shook his head, trying to clear his thoughts. Was he in the Hells? Was the eternal darkness and blood to forever be his punishment?

If it was, did he not deserve it?

"You're no more dead than I, Abraxas."

His blood went cold at the sound of her voice. He shot to his feet, slipping on the ankle-deep puddle of blood, and barely recovering his balance. His hand met something hot, fleshy and smooth. In the low light, the massive ribcage glowed white, and he snatched his hand back.

"Where are you?" he growled. "Show yourself!"

She tsked, in that way he knew she did whenever she wasn't paying attention. She'd done it so many times when preparing Direwall for the undead siege, as if the whole city had been an inconvenience. And had it not? Their stand at the lighthouse had been worthless in the grand scheme of things.

"For a man without a weapon, you're very aggressive."

"Why am I alive? I should've . . . we should be dead."

There was the sound of ripping flesh somehow coming from all around him. Their voices echoed back and forth, both muffled and vast.

"You tried very hard; I'll give you that. Fate, it seems, has other plans for us."

Light and fresh air flooded the chamber as Nerezza ripped apart what was left of the dragon's chest. The ribs split, the skin unfurled, and blissfully cool air bathed them both.

Nerezza stood drenched in blood on a stack of bones, obviously built and fused herself. Abraxas had never studied dragons, but now he could see the anatomy of this one was all wrong. It was like she'd been torn apart inside and rebuilt to suit Nerezza's need.

She steamed like he did in the pale moonlight, her eyes dark and furious.

Abraxas's hand went for the Keeper's dagger.

"It's not here, fool." She rolled her eyes. "I tore this dragon apart from the inside out trying to find it. I'm half tempted to do the same to you, just for fun."

Abraxas took a step back. "And why haven't you?"

She cocked her head to the side, almost innocently, and smiled. "Because I need you, of course."

He tried to duck behind a rib, but her magic caught him first. It seized his muscles like hellfire, dragging him through the blood and sinew pooled at his feet. He tried to fight, teeth cracking with exertion, but it only burned more. Visions of Vernes, of hot blades digging under his skin, danced behind his eyes. He screamed without meaning to and fell to his knees. The daggers, the magic, made their way under his skin. Deeper still, into his muscles and marrow. They curled along his spine, at the very base of his neck, and jerked his head up.

He was at her feet, at the base of her bone stairs. She stared at him for a while before she flicked her hand and the pain ebbed away.

Abraxas fell to his hands, gasping and shuddering. He could still feel the precise blades of her magic under his skin, lying in wait for him to try and run. Or worse, kill her. Then they'd pull him back to obedience with pain so dazzling it put Vernes's torture to shame.

Her fingers were cold as she lifted his chin back up. Her nails dug into his skin, and her face was so close it was all he could see.

"You're mine," she gritted out. "We'll do this together, as the dagger intended. You can rage and scream all you want, but you can't break this spell."

"You can't keep it up forever," he hissed.

Her grip softened, and she brushed a blood-soaked strand of hair out of his eyes. "I can, and I will."

Nerezza pushed him away from her, flicking the blood off her hand and staring at the sky. "You don't realize this, but you didn't want to die, Abraxas. You moved us here and lost the dagger in the process. Wherever or whenever we are, you've severely fucked with my plans."

"I'm very broken up about it," he panted.

"I'm sure. But no matter, you'll have a chance to redeem yourself soon. Don't mope, the world is waiting."

She climbed out of the dragon's carcass with surprising ease, even with just one hand. Abraxas, stubbornly, stayed on his knees in the blood. Moments later, she looked over the edge and rolled her eyes.

"I said, come Abraxas. It wasn't a suggestion."

The blades surged to life again, and his vision went white. When he could see clearly again, he'd bitten his tongue and was standing next to her beside the dragon's corpse. A wide field of flowers and tall grass spread out before them, the stars wheeling coldly overhead. The moon hadn't risen yet. The air was still and quiet.

Without a word, Nerezza picked a direction and started waking. Her wet robes slapped against her legs with every step. Abraxas waited until she started to stiffen before following her. She relaxed when she heard his marching steps.

"Where are you going?" he asked. "You have no idea where we are."

"I'll figure it out," she said dismissively.

"And your plan? The one I ruined? Will you leave it be now that the dagger is lost?"

"Nonsense." She snorted and then turned to face him. He forced himself to stop instead of running into her, irritated that a woman so frail had more power over him than the dragon did.

"Where are you taking us?" he asked again, darker and full of unspoken threats he couldn't possibly enact.

Nerezza smiled, bloody and horrifying. "First to civilization. Then, we hunt."

"For what?"

"A relic, a soul, a following. We hunt for my divinity, Abraxas."

She turned her back on him and started walking again, her steps sure and graceful. "And then, I remake the world."

THE END

Thank you for reading WHERE THE HEART FESTERS.

The Blood of Eith series continues next with
WHERE THE LIGHT DIES.
available at
www.GillianGrant.com

~

Keep reading for a excerpt from
WHERE THE LIGHT DIES.

EXCERPT OF WHERE THE LIGHT DIES
THE BLOOD OF EITH, BOOK FOUR

Eith was blanketed in a dismal silence.

The soft, heavy kind in the grey of dawn. The kind that deafened even the blood rushing in his ears. There was no end in sight to the vast grey fog, nor the damp quiet it enraptured. Even the dark waters of the Boreal Sea were still and calm, barely lapping against the great wooden hull of the Crooked Wrath.

The Vasa ship was old. Her hull had been visibly patched with different colored woods, and the salt worn deck showed how vicious a mistress time could be to those who refused to die.

Like their ship, the Wrath's crew had fought like demons for every last breath. And in the end their fighting had been useless.

Abraxas gripped the railing of the ship with bloody hands. He was staining the wood with every desperate thrum of his finger. His eyes ached from staring into the unending grey in front of him. He hadn't known a fog this dense and enveloping so far out at sea. He'd never seen in all his many crossings the water so calm. The Boreal Sea was rage and chaos, the physical embodiment of the goddess who had once drawn her power from it.

Mituna. Young, prone to fits of violence and cruelty to get

her way. Daughter of Nomien and every bit as evil in nature. Whereas her father was calculating and patient in his evil acts, Mituna was anything but. Her actions were as unpredictable as the sea itself. The Vasa who made their home on her waters were at her mercy more than any other, but in all his years he'd never found one who willingly worshipped her.

The Boreal Sea hadn't been safer once she'd been banished with the rest. If anything, the frequent storms, monsters, and waves as high as mountains had gotten even worse without her there to control them.

But Abraxas had to remind himself when he was, just as much as where. It was still difficult for him to wrap his mind around, that in the moment that should've been his death he'd sent himself to a different time entirely. The first time he'd questioned someone, after they stopped gawking at his bloody form, they'd told him and he'd been too stunned to even attempt fighting the next three days.

He'd sent himself, with Nerezza as a passenger, one hundred years into the past.

His bloody nails dug into the smooth wood. The fog remained unchanging.

One hundred years. The gods were still in Eith. Etherak was fifty years into its hundred-year occupation of Vernes, Gratey and Terevas. The Wandering Sols, save for himself, had yet to be born.

Abraxas tried to breath through the weight that constricted his lungs each time the truth of what he'd done hit him. But the humid air did little to expand his lungs. No matter how hard he tried, he still felt like someone had their arms around his chest in a deadly squeeze he couldn't break free from. No amount of air was enough.

The hairs on the back of his neck prickled, and Abraxas fought the urge not to shiver as a dull scrapping sounded on the deck behind him. He knew what he'd see, but he couldn't help but turn around anyway.

The crew of the Crooked Wrath mired about the deck in a shambling but well-organized manner. No orders were shouted, and no shanties were sung. The deck was quiet except for the scraping of bones and the slapping of rope on wood. Several of the crew swabbed blood up from the deck, blood he'd spilled. More still climbed the rigging missing limbs. The navigator of the ship stood at the wheel, his jaw missing and his eyes glowing with blood red magic. The whole crew shared the same magic now, one that wouldn't let them rest beyond the death he'd brought upon them.

The grizzled woman who'd once been the captain shuffled past him, tripping over her broken leg with every other step. Her salt and pepper hair, shorn close to her weathered skin, was caked with dried blood. The wound where he'd caved in her skull with the pummel of her own sword had finally stopped bleeding. That same sword dangled from her belt where he'd carefully put it back after her death. She'd fought well, despite being clumsy and self-taught. He respected her drive to protect her crew, fruitless as it had been.

She was just like them all now. A corpse puppet, driving her home for her murderers.

Abraxas's fingers twitched for the sword as she walked past, reeking of salt and sea laden rot that had started to take hold of the whole crew. He could end it for them. Run her sword through her heart and every single one of her crew. He could lay them to rest the way Sorin had taught him back in Direwall, although he'd long forgotten the song he'd sung. It felt like a lifetime ago when he'd stood by the Vasa's side on an icy shore, sending a boy monster's body into the cold depths with a song and a prayer.

Divines, Abraxas missed him. He missed them all. In a future he imagined he succeeded in freeing the Vasa. He laid them and the ship to rest. He sunk himself and the witch behind it all with him. Whatever horror Mituna had waiting in her depths he'd gladly take and drag Nerezza there too.

The captain passed by him, once again tripping over her own ankle as she lugged an armful of rope. Abraxas reached his hand toward her belt, the sword's pummel still splattered with its owner's brain matter still waiting for him. His fingers brushed the metal, grim in their determination, until pain seized him.

His muscles spasmed and then locked up. His bones crackled under the weight of a familiar agony. But no matter how used to the feeling of boiling blood and quaking marrow he was now, it still brought him to his knees. His vision swam as the pain was leashed back like a rabid dog. He shook, still feeling it there waiting to be unleashed.

Abraxas never understood how Evren seemed to draw strength from pain. All it ever did was make him want to die.

Abraxas was still gasping for air when his vision started to clear. He saw the deck, crusted with salt and gore. He saw his own murderous hands keeping him from collapsing. And then a pair of boots stopped just shy of his fingertips. The ashen grey of the robes fluttered to a stop over his wrists and he jerked back. He drew as much venom and loathing as he could manage and lifted his chin.

Nerezza stood over him, as cold as she ever was. Her black eyes were voids he could discern nothing but contempt from. And she was staring down at him with an unhealthy dose of it now.

"I thought we were past such self-sacrificing ideas," she mused.

He sneered. "I don't know what you're talking about."

"Don't play the fool, Abraxas. You've never been good at it."

He shifted uncomfortably on his knees. She couldn't have known what he'd planned. He'd just thought about it after being at sea for over two weeks. He'd made sure to be as quiet and complacent as she expected him to be. When she ordered him to kill the crew a mere day ago and take the ship, he hadn't even protested. When she infected the dead with her necromancy, he'd bit his tongue and looked away. He'd thought he'd played the perfect, obedient attack dog. Unless she could control his mind as well as his blood . . .

Abraxas shuddered then and struggled to keep eye contact with her.

"You can't read minds," he said with more confidence than he felt. "You have nothing but your own paranoia."

"Oh?" She cocked her head to the side. "Is that so? Then enlighten me. What did you want our dear captain's sword for when you couldn't get it out of your hands quick enough yesterday?"

Abraxas opened his mouth and then shut it again. A lie would be useless. He didn't have Sol's talent for manipulation. He was an open book to Nerezza. She could read his motivations as if he'd written them in blood across his face.

No, lying would be useless and would likely just cause more pain. And Divines, he was so tired of hurting.

He bowed his head and heard Nerezza chuckle.

"That's what I thought. I'd hoped we were past this point, Abraxas. You learned weeks ago that fighting is useless."

He had. He'd fought Nerezza every step of the way out of the dragon's carcass, through the roads of Terevas and to the port city of Noxcairn. He'd almost gotten free there. The city was seated on the delta of the River Nox and had canals instead of streets. Abraxas knew them well enough from his time stationed there at the beginning of the war. He knew the bridges to take, the alleyways that had secret passages for smugglers, and which gambling dens would hide you for a time depending on how much you paid.

But the black waters of the canals didn't save him. The masks and parades didn't hide him. In the end, he'd stumbled into a small temple the occupying soldiers had built. Empty and damp, smelling of rotting fruit offerings and burnt incense. It wasn't built for Haphion. Instead for Eitrix, the shapeshifting god of wealth. It was the only god the people of Noxcairn readily accepted, from merchants and gamblers to politicians and thieves. Eitrix was a fickle god, and not his, but he prayed anyway. He was met with silence, but stubbornly stayed until Nerezza found him again.

The pain had been severe then. Enough to keep him in a daze for the next day. He hadn't even remembered her booking their passage on the Crooked Wrath, and he'd been too exhausted to ask why.

But now, after murdering an entire crew full of innocent people, he had regained his senses.

Abraxas looked her dead in her black eyes again. "I was going to take her sword and kill them all over again. I was going to wrench their dead hearts out of their chests and leave you with nothing. Then I was going to sink this whole ship and bring you down to death with me."

Nerezza blinked, her face unreadable as she took in all the hatred he was throwing at her. She seemed to relax a little, as if him saying it had confirmed something for her. And then she smiled.

"You're welcome to try. But, Abraxas, if you wanted a sword all you needed to do was ask."

She said it in a soft, crooning voice. Like he was a child who'd tried to steal a cookie instead of asking her for it. He bristled and pushed himself to his feet.

"I don't want a sword." He hissed, and his muscles were already tensing for another wave of pain.

But Nerezza smiled at him, amused. The fingers of her one remaining hand stayed loose and calm at her side, and he struggled not to watch them. One curl of her pinky would have him writhing at her feet again.

"You wanted one just a few moments ago," Nerezza said. She flicked her white braid over her shoulder and then snapped her fingers. Abraxas flinched, and she chuckled. But it wasn't for him. The captain tossed her rope down and lumbered back to

Nerezza like a bored but obedient pet. She stopped just shy of Nerezza's outstretched fingers.

In any other circumstances the differences between the two of them would've been laughable. Nerezza was thin and pale, like pieces of bone held together by gossamer grey robes. The captain, in life, had been a tall woman built with thick, corded muscle and more scars than Abraxas could count. She had been more pirate than sailor, which made sense as to why Nerezza picked her ship. No honest sailor would've taken them without the proper papers and authority during a time of war.

The captain of the Crooked Wrath could've snapped Nerezza in two in life. But in death she was nothing more than an extension of the mage's will.

"Your sword, captain." Nerezza said.

The corpse unsheathed it, uncaring to her own blood coating the blade, and handed it over. Nerezza regarded it closely, then held her hand out again. Without a word, the captain tore off part of her linen shirt and gave it willingly. Nerezza used it to wipe the blood and gore from the blade, and when she was done it still shone pink.

She held it out to him. "Here."

Abraxas didn't move. He eyed the sword, once a lifeline, like it was a waiting snake.

Nerezza rolled her eyes. "Oh please, it won't bite."

"You might."

"You don't want it? Fine." She shrugged and then hurled the sword over the side of the ship.

Before Abraxas even knew what he was doing, his hand shot out and grasped the hilt before it could fall into the dark sea. Nerezza laughed behind him as he stood frozen over the railing with the sword in his hand. He squeezed his eyes shut, trying to will his fingers to let go of the hilt and let the sword go. This was a trap. This was playing right into her games and would just end in more pain. He should let go.

The worst part was this was entirely him. Nerezza's compulsions came in waves of agony. His own reflexes had saved the sword, and it was so those ones that refused to let it go.

Eventually he brought himself away from the edge with the sword in hand and stood before her. Shame colored his cheeks, and he didn't know why. But he clutched the hilt tightly despite its power meaning nothing to him now.

"Why?" he croaked.

"My champion needs a weapon." Nerezza said.

He flinched again. "I'm not your champion. That service belongs to one."

"Ah yes, Haphion. How is he, by the way?"

Abraxas kept his mouth shut again. This time he knew the shame that burned well.

"Stop this, Nerezza." He said instead. "Please."

"You'll have to be more specific."

He gestured to the corpse crew. "Them. Me." He pointed furiously at himself. "All of it!"

She blinked, letting his voice echo across the foggy waters for what felt like ages. Then, she stepped closer. Just one step, but it was enough for him to recoil as if he'd been hit.

"Do you know how to sail a ship this size by yourself?" She asked.

He gritted his teeth. "No."

"Do you know how to navigate the Boreal Sea?"

"No."

"Then stop complaining," she snapped. "These weren't good people, so stop acting like I killed a bunch of orphans."

"They're still people, Nerezza." He argued. "This is wrong."

"This is practical." She corrected. "I need them to get me where I'm going. And if the captain hadn't threatened to slit my throat if I didn't pay her triple our agreed fee, then they'd all be alive. I'm not entirely malicious. My cruelty has purpose."

"And me?" he asked, already dreading the answer. "Why do you need me for this insane quest of yours? I'm more trouble than I'm worth."

"Oh, don't sell yourself so short. You're exactly what I need. A shield to keep me from harm. A sword to kill when I can't. And a guide for the journey ahead."

"If you wanted a guide, you could've had anybody."

"True," she smiled again, and this time it sent chills down his spine. "But only you know war torn Vernes well enough to guide me through."

Vernes.

No.

He couldn't go back. The mere thought of it sent panic and bile climbing up his throat. His sword shook in his hand, and he must've looked terrified because Nerezza's face softened. She let out a sympathetic noise and cupped his face with cold, thin fingers. He shuddered under her touch but couldn't find the strength to get away.

Nerezza brushed a damp strand of hair out of his face. "Vernes will not hurt you this time. If you believe anything, believe that. You are coming back stronger than your past self, more openminded. You will finally give that wretched place the reckoning it deserves."

Nerezza stepped away, and he found himself strangely still. But his mind was a storm, and he couldn't grasp a single thought. Long after night had fallen and he laid in his swaying cot, he clutched the sword as if his life depended on it. Until his fingers dug into the leather grip and he could feel it breaking.

Abraxas prayed to Haphion with fear coursing through his veins. He poured all his desperation and pain into every uttered word. He prayed like he did every night since Haphion had been banished. And, as with every other night, he was met with silence.

Thick, dismal, blanketing silence.

WHERE THE LIGHT DIES

**available at
www.GillianGrant.com**

ACKNOWLEDGMENTS

Where the Heart Festers became lovingly known by my whole team as the Problem Child, because nothing about this book was easy or straightforward. Despite all of that, you've got the final product in your hand, and there's a lot of people to thank for that.

• Stef, who accidentally made the cover way earlier due to some crazy miscommunication on my part, but also gave me the opportunity to gawk at it for months in advance.

• Laura, who took a sticky mess with time travel, spiders, daddy issues and lesbians and made it into something readable.

• Charity, who took the challenge of advertising Gyda and Evren's romance with a grin, despite the two foot height difference. And the multiple drafts of ARcs for Beta readers, the final ARC, and the shiny FINAL version of this book.

• To my fantastic ARC team doubling for Beta readers and picking apart all the plot points that didn't make sense, the words that I missed on my dozens of read throughs, and the honest reviews of this series.

• To my family, who endured my blank stares into the abyss while I wrote this during the holidays in stride and made sure I took care of myself.

• To my friends, who took my midnight rants like they were gifts and kept me going through the tough bits.

• And finally, to every reader who dove back into Eith for another adventure. I've got plenty more planned for us.

ABOUT THE AUTHOR

Gillian Grant was born in Texas and grew up enthralled with fantasy stories of all kinds. As she got older she often traveled with her family and imagined wild adventures while exploring the mountains of Colorado and the glens of Scotland. Back home in Texas she took her love of fantasy to the next level and sat a group of friends down to play Dungeons and Dragons. From there, they built the world her first novel, *Where The Shadows Beckon* was set in. When she's not writing Gillian is normally juggling too many D&D campaigns, grooming dogs, and imagining her next adventure. She still lives in Texas with her two cats.

www.GillianGrant.com

facebook.com/GillianGrantAuthor

instagram.com/gilliangrantauthor

amazon.com/Gillian-Grant/e/B09J94DBHP

www.ingramcontent.com/pod-product-compliance
Lightning Source LLC
Chambersburg PA
CBHW012011050726
47590CB00009B/3139